DOWNRIVER

Also by Peter Collier

The Rockefellers: An American Dynasty (coauthored)
When Shall They Rest?

DOWN

a novel by
PETER COLLIER

RIVER

HOLT, RINEHART and WINSTON   New York

Published simultaneously in Canada by Holt,
Rinehart and Winston of Canada, Limited.

Library of Congress Cataloging in Publication
Data

Collier, Peter.
Downriver.

I. Title.
PZ4.C6972Do   [PS3553.047465]   813'.5'4
78–2423
ISBN 0–03–043826–8

FIRST EDITION

Designer: Joy Chu

Printed in the United States of America
10   9   8   7   6   5   4   3   2   1

FOR MARYJO
with love

DOWNRIVER

Dear Papa Two:

In the dream, they're wolves and we're deer. Isn't that strange? I never thought that wolves were bad, but these are. They're wolves and they're all around us. They hold us inside their circle. They've got yellow eyes and cutting teeth. The better to eat you with. They block us no matter which way we turn. There's nothing we can do. She looks at them, Mama does. Her mouth moves, but the voice takes a long time to get to my ears. It comes from way off. Run, Joey! Run now! Get help quick! Run! Now!

I'll try, Mama! I can tell by her face she hears my thought. But there are wolves! The bad-smelling one has got me cornered. He's holding me in. I feel his hard spot in my back. But then, all of a sudden, I get away. Then I'm running, going fast, just skimming over the ground. The swift baby deer crashing through the underbrush, flying over rocks, bounding high in the air. Its dragging foot does not keep it down. Ah, running!

I'm almost there. I can see the top of the hill. A few more leaps and I'll be over. Then it will be easy, sliding downhill, bracing against the rockslide. You can get to the bottom without even trying if you get this far. Just slide. Almost at the top now, I can

1

already hear the water. I know you'll be down there on the other side of the hill, along the river. I know you're there without seeing you. Almost there! A few more leaps.

Every time I think I'll make it. But every time I start to slow down. When I'm almost to the top, my foot begins to drag, my legs get heavy. It's like I'm running through water. The wolf is behind me, gaining. I can smell him now. I tell my legs, Go faster! But they won't. They're hypnotized. They get heavier and heavier. Near the top of the hill, they stop.

The baby deer, the lame one, waits for the wolf to get him.

If only you knew what was happening. If you could only see what they're doing. I know you're down there. I can see you in my imagination, down at the bottom of the hill at the water's edge, downriver, dressed in buckskins like Jedediah. Your red hair poking out from under the leather hat. You're there by the river with the Tollowas, waiting for me and Mama. You don't know what's happening or you'd kill these wolves right quick. I can't get to you because of my feet and legs, heavy as rock now. My legs won't do what I tell them. They don't belong to me anymore. I know you're down at the bottom of the hill by the river with a chunk of red meat, bringing it up to your mouth every once in a while and then using it to point off into the distance, telling the Indians about your travels. I'm screaming, Papa Two! Come quick! Mama needs you! I'm screaming but no sound comes out.

The wolf comes up from behind and begins to eat the baby deer, the lame one.

That's the dream. It's with me in this white room every morning when I wake up. I have to hit things and talk out loud to make sure I'm really awake and not still dreaming.

This is a big house I live in now, lots bigger than yours or the one me and Mama were living in before it happened. It's up here on top of a mountain. Cold. These people never turn on the heat. They say it costs too much. Sometimes early in the morning it's so cold that I can pretend I'm smoking just by breathing out. Whoosh.

You know the window up there above this bed? If I stand

2

up on the mattress and look out in the mornings, I can fog it all up by my breath. That first day after the county people brought me here, I woke up and stood up there and drew on the window, making letters in the fog. I wrote our name: Joseph Hart. My finger squeegeed on the glass like a windshield wiper. The woman came in. She said, Stop that, it makes streaks, don't do it anymore!

So I just look now. No touching. The first thing I see is blackberry bushes. The last berries are drying up, just shrinking in the sun. Out beyond, there are pines and redwoods, lots of them. Millions. They roll down the hill to the bottom just like a green blanket. I can just barely see the river way down there. It's tiny, like water spilt out of a glass and running through the green.

When the toad man goes off in his car, I can watch him winding down the mountain. He'll be out of sight for a few minutes, then flash! his car shines in the sun, a little further down the hill every time I see it. Pretty soon after he goes, the woman brings me breakfast. She has to set the tray down and undo the chain lock. They put it on a few days ago. Know why? Because one day I snuck down the stairs when the woman had the radio turned up loud. I went right on out the back door. I was going to make a run for it and not get caught this time. I was going to look for Mama. I know she's out there, probably waiting for me downriver. Anyway, I was creeping along the side of the house looking back to make sure the woman hadn't seen me and followed and then bang! I ran right into the toad man. He grabbed my arm and slapped me. He said, Where in hell do you think you're going? Then he dragged me back inside. He was talking all the while. He said, You try this again, Mister Man, and we're going to have big trouble, believe you me! That was that.

In the morning, when I hear the woman coming up, I get down from the window and go down under the covers and pretend I'm asleep. She looks at me and then goes away. In the afternoons she comes up again. Her radio is on all day. She carries it everywhere. She brings a sandwich and milk and maybe cookies. Sometimes I eat the cookies. She sits down in a chair and does some sewing. Usually she begins by talking about things she thinks I'll like. She said she was going to get me a dog one of

3

these days, after I felt better, and maybe a bicycle. It would do me good to get exercise, she said, and help my foot.

While she talks, the spit comes to the edges of her mouth. I think to myself, Let me out of here! I never talk, but it wouldn't matter if I said anything or not. She'd just keep talking. Sometimes she holds my foot and looks at it. When she does that I just give it to her. While she's holding the foot, it's hers, not mine. After she's done, I take it back.

She sits in the chair talking. I hear what she says with part of my brain, but pretend I don't, and just keep looking out this window.

The first day I got here, the day the county people brought me, she looked me over and said to the man, Oh, he's so little! Later on she said I could call her Mother or Mrs. Bruce, whatever one I wanted. She was staring at me and I thought to myself, I'll never call you anything. She and the toad man smiled a lot while the county people were here, but just with their mouth, not their eyes. She said she'd had girls living here with her before, but no boys yet. I was her first boy. They have me because they get money. I heard them talk about it.

I hate the man worse. He comes flashing back up here in his car after work, winding up the mountain like a snake. After a while some doors slam, then he fools around downstairs. Sometimes he comes in here and sits on the bed and starts talking to me while the woman watches. His face is yucky. There's all kinds of warts. He looks like a toad. The first time he said, Now look here, your mother's gone, so just forget her, get used to living here now, this is your home. Like hell, I said. He got back at me for saying that by staying here on the edge of my bed talking about her, liking to do it, swallowing and blowing out every once in a while as if he was cleaning his nose out. That first time I put my fingers in my ears, but he got real mad and jerked them out. He said, you better listen to me, Mister Man, or you and me are going to have a big falling out!

Now I don't say anything and I look like I'm listening. But I plug my ears automatically. Without fingers. Know how? By starting music going inside my head, the loudest music I can make, marching music. The cymbals smash, the drums bang, flutes whistle, tubas go oompapah. After the music's going real good, I bring in the marchers. They've got shining boots. The heels snap and click on the pavement. I'm looking at the toad man, but inside my brain I see the march leader. He has a tall bearskin hat and a stick in his hand. His legs go up and down real high, knees almost to his chin as he marches along. His uniform is red, pure red, and there are glitters sprinkled all over it. I'm looking at the toad man, his mouth like a knife-cut in his face. But I see the marchers. Girls with yellow hair and red lips twirling batons through their legs so fast it makes the tassels on their boots go swish! It's like the Fourth of July going on inside my head. It gets louder and louder. After a while it almost starts to hurt my ears, and I have to say, Take it easy, you guys, please!

When the man and the woman get up to leave, the march slows down. The music gets quiet and the marchers stand along the sides of my brain, waiting for me to tell them whether to go or stay.

Yesterday as they were going back downstairs the woman said, He just can't seem to talk about it. Not can't, the man said. Won't is more like it. She said, Well maybe there's shock. He said, Shock, my ass, he's a crafty little bastard.

He's right, not her. I'm crafty, a cunning trickster, like Old Coyote. I'd never talk to them, never in a million years, not about it or anything else. But I remember. I remember everything that happened. I don't like to, but I can make myself. I'll remember so I can tell you when we get together. Mama always says, If there's ever any trouble, Joey, get ahold of Papa Two and tell him what's wrong. He'll help if he can.

Another time she said, Joey, one way to remember if you have somebody you want to tell something, is to write them a letter in your mind. That way you'll have it all memorized when you meet. I don't want to remember what happened, but I've got to. That's why I've been writing you in my mind.

I can remember it all.

It started off good. Mama and me, we had been working in the garden all morning. I had to hoe in between the rows of tomato plants and I had their tomato smell all over my hands. I held my fingers up to my nose and I smelled tomato. I was all sweaty and so was Mama. She was pink in the face and her hair laid down around her forehead because of sweat. She looked at me and said, You're all sweaty. I said, You too. She said, Well, have you had enough? I said, If you have. She said, Shall we make some sandwiches and go for a walk? I said, Downriver? She said, Sure.

We went down our road and over the highway. We hiked down to the riverbed and over the footbridge, like always, holding on to the cables and feeling it sway back and forth to our walk, the wind coming up cool and nice from the water underneath. I just had a bathing suit on. Mama had on blue jeans and a T-shirt. Neither of us had on any shoes and we just crunched right over rocks and everything. I like being barefooted. In shoes I feel clumpy.

After walking a little while, we got to a place where you can't hear the cars from the road anymore. There are huge trees. Redwoods. A hundred people holding hands couldn't make a circle around them. The Tollowas say that Earthmaker planted them thousands of years ago. Beneath the trees it's all soft and springy like a rug. You keep walking and you come to a trail. Follow that and you leave the trees and go downriver. You can walk and walk and not see anybody else. Mama says it's like walking backward in time.

Over in a clearing, I found some thimbleberries. They look like little hats. You can pick them and put them on your fingertips. I picked one for each finger and wore them for a while. Then I ate some and gave the rest to Mama. We kept on walking. She said, Well, just another couple of weeks and school starts, are you ready? I said, You bet. She said, I know you can hardly wait.

Sometimes I used to go out and watch the bus go by. Used to. At the other house, my home. I'd put my jacket on and get an apple and I'd go out and sit under a tree by the road. The first thing you see is the orange top, only about an inch high, as it comes up the hill. Then the whole thing, small but getting bigger. Then, whoosh! it's by you. When it's cold the children are hidden

6

inside foggy windows. When it's warm, they hang their arms out over the yellow side and try to touch the black letters. I know what words they say: Tollowa Union School District. Did you know I can read, Papa Two? I can already read a little. Once a fat boy stuck out his tongue at me as the bus whooshed by.

I was thinking about school while we walked. Mama picked some sap off the side of a tree. She smelled it and said, Ah! turpentine. She gave it to me and I carried it awhile, sticky in my fingers. I put it in my mouth to see if it would chew. It had a mothball taste and when I bit, it cracked into a million pieces.

Then I was walking up ahead. I saw a snake. It was black and red and yellow and lay there below a berry bramble, its eyes just staring up like black buttons and its tongue flickering out every once in a while. In and out. If the tongue touches you you die. I was afraid it would get me. I moved slow, got a rock and threw it. I think I might have hit it because when it wiggled back under the bushes you could still see the tip of its tail. Mama came up behind me. She said, Why did you do that? I said, Because I hate snakes. She said, That was a king snake. I said, So? She said, It's a good snake, you've got to learn the difference between good snakes and bad snakes, even the bad ones you don't kill unless you have to, just stay away. I said, To me all snakes are bad.

We walked some more. We got to these huge rocks and hopped from one to another. We're like mountain goats, Mama said. Then we came to the place where you can hear the river. You hear it even before you reach the top of the hill and see it. The sound is like a huge machine humming. On the other side of the hill there is a steep slide that goes right to the rocks beside the water. Out there in the middle the water is fast. That's where our bathtub is.

I think Mama was still mad about the snake, and so I came over and held her hand. We stood at the top of the hill and looked down at the river. She fluffed my hair and I knew she wasn't mad anymore. We found some sand and sat down and ate our sandwiches. I said, Let's go swimming. She said, No, we might get cramps, let's wait. She was reading a book about plants, and I was fooling around with a stick. Then after a while I said, Would we get cramps now? She said, I guess not, let's go. She pulled off her clothes and waded out holding my hand. I could see where she puffs out between her legs with hair that's darker red. We fooled around awhile swimming. I was doing a dog-paddle in the shallow part, and she was swimming and diving in the middle. She'd go way down under the river and I'd begin to worry, then she'd come up, way far away from where she started, blowing water and air like a seal. That's what she looked like, a seal, all sleek and curvy. I love to see her when she swims.

The water was cold so we didn't go out to the middle where our bathtub is. We got up on the rocks to dry out. It was hot and drowsy. We've done this a lot of times, always this way. After a while I started drawing on the skin of her back with my finger. She said, Ummm, I was almost asleep. I said, This place is best. She said, I think so too. I said, Why can't we live here? She said, Because then it wouldn't be as magic as it is now. We got dressed and started back.

I don't like to remember but I have to make myself. That's why I keep on writing you.

The water's roaring real loud on the way back over the bridge. The three of them stand on the edge, right where the cables you hold on to when you cross go down into the ground. One smelled bad, like stuff under toenails. The other was thin, with whiskers and a hat, the Cat. The third was the worst. I'd seen him in town before, once when he tried to talk to Mama and his hand hung down. He had a green army coat on then that said he was a captain, and I couldn't help from staring. Captain Hook, the leader of the gang.

They had guns, real hunting guns. They were propped up against a tree. I could see them. They were standing there near the bridge holding a bottle and laughing and slapping their legs. The Cat, he danced around real soft when he saw us coming, sort of rubbing against the others' bodies the way cats do. He took off his Cat hat and made a funny bow. Captain Hook looked up and smiled a mean white smile. I saw him. I thought to myself, What big teeth you have.

Mama stopped for a second. I thought maybe she'd turn around and go back downriver. We'd be safe there. But no. She took my hand and held it tight and walked right on. She wasn't a bit afraid. Papa Two. You'd be proud. She walked so fast I had to skip to keep up with her. She went right by those wolves, so close that I could smell the bad-smelling one's smell.

Captain Hook said, Well what have we here, our little town hippie girl, how you doing, red? Mama hates it when people call her red, and I do too. The Cat reached out and petted her arm and sort of purred, Hold on now, honey bunch. She looked down at his hand like it was a snail or something yucky. Then she looked up at Captain Hook. She said, Let's not play games, okay, why don't you and your friends here just finish your bottle and go shoot yourself a deer out of season and leave us alone. He snorted. I pulled on her hand. Come on Mama, I said, let's get going. She fluffed my hair and said, Don't worry, honey, it's okay. Captain Hook said, Is it now? The other two laughed like he'd told a funny joke.

I can see it just like it just happened five minutes ago.

The Cat came up from the side. Mama didn't see him because she was watching Captain Hook, just staring in his eyes and telling him with her look that she wasn't afraid. Suddenly the Cat was moving fast, springing on her, his arms surrounding her from behind. She let go of my hand and I felt like I was drifting away like a balloon. He held her tight and her feet went clear off the ground trying to get away. She came down kicking at his legs and stamping on his foot. He let go. Quick as a flash, she stooped down and got a rock. Captain Hook, he just stood and laughed with his real white teeth. He said to the Cat, Well, get it on, man, you're not afraid are you?

We were inside their circle now. Their eyes glowed and their teeth flashed. Mama looked from one face to another and sort of crouched. The Cat grabbed at her arm, and she brought the rock down over his face like a knife. The bleeding came down his nose in a line, dripping off the end like tears. It was like he couldn't believe what happened. He put his hand up to his nose and then held it way out in front of him, staring at it like it was the first time he ever saw blood. Nobody did anything for a minute.

Captain Hook moved and Mama turned his way. When she did, the Cat grabbed her around the middle again. She jumped up and threw her head around like a deer, jabbing at him with her hands and feet, rearing and jabbing. I tried to help her, but the bad-smelling one had me and was holding tight. He breathed like he had a cold and pressed himself against my back. He was hard there. He was laughing. I couldn't make my voice work.

The Cat was saying, Well come on, let's get busy, she's already damn near taken my nose off, the bitch. Hook raised up his hand, his good one, and slapped my mama's arm. She dropped the rock, and then he made a fist and hit her hard, real hard, right in the tummy. The sound went whump like a drum. Mama, she folded up. She just folded up and went flat down to the ground and lay there. Her eyes were closed and dust was on one side of her face like flour. She made an awful sound and opened her eyes big and looked at me. Veins like purple ropes were out on her neck. When she moved her mouth some green stuff came out. I couldn't move. I didn't have a voice.

My heart is beating like a bird. My face is wet, and I feel tiny like a doll. I'm thinking, Please, Earthmaker, make me big. They stand there looking down at her. She tries to get up. I get loose and run to grab Hook's leg. I hold on with all my strength. In my brain I see that hook coming down real slow to poke holes in my head, but I hold on with all my strength. Mama looks up. She isn't afraid, Papa Two, just trying to figure out what to do next. Hook reaches down with his hand, his real one, and takes me off his leg. He says, What the hell do you think you're doing? and throws me backward.

I get my voice back and I say, Don't you hook her, you!

He laughs with those sharp white teeth of his and says, Hook her? He looks up at the others and they laugh again. I'll hook her all right, just you watch.

He always wants you to watch that hook. That way he can paralyze you. I remember one day back when we first got here and we were living in town, I was watching him talk to Mama. He pulled out a cigarette with his good hand and then a book of matches. He tore out a match with his hook and held it for a minute. He knew we were watching. Then he struck it and lighted up his cigarette. I was staring at him and so was Mama. He just smiled.

Mama says, Run, Joey! Run now! Get help! Run! She's on her feet again, screaming loud and coming at the bad-smelling one who's got me, trying to rip his eyes out with her fingernails. Let go of him, you filthy pig, she screams. But before she gets three steps, Hook grabs her hair and whumps her down again.

Big boys don't cry, Mama says.

She's laying there without any wind. I can tell that. Hook gets down on her legs and starts undoing his belt, and the Cat gets down on her arms with his knees and rips her shirt. The two of them they look at each other and smile.

The wolves attack! I see Hook's fur under his belly and the whiteness between his legs, white like a white bone, and when he turns, his butt is white like dead fish, there are little red bumps sprinkled all over it. He's white as a ghost. Just before he lays down, Mama looks up over the Cat's knee, just peeks at me like in a game and says, Joey? Joey, don't look! I close my eyes.

My eyes pop open without me telling them to. The hook man is over my mama, covering her with his whiteness. The Cat is bleeding off his nose down onto her chest while he kneels. He's doing something on her face. Oh! The bad-smelling one is still behind me holding, but just with one hand. The other hand is doing something back there.

Suddenly, I get away. Just like that. And I'm running. I can do it, Mama. I'll stop all this. My foot doesn't drag me down. I'm flying over the rocks, going to get help. Skimming the top of rocks. I can hear the bad-smelling one coming after me, pounding the ground hard. But I'm flying, crashing over underbrush, springing high and free like a swift baby deer. I get to where I can see the highway, and then I'm running up to the road, looking for somebody to call you. I start slowing down. My side hurts like a knife. I say, Go faster, legs! But they won't. It's like they're hypnotized. They stop.

There was a car. I tried to tell the man and woman in it. I cried and cried. I tried to tell them, but I couldn't talk. I didn't have any breath. My voice wouldn't work. The bad-smelling one ran up and pulled out his wallet. He told them that my mother just had an accident down by the bridge. I could feel the words inside me. They were like bones in my throat, so big that they choked me and blocked my talk. You liar! Someday I'll kill you, bastard wolf! My Papa Two will get you! The man in the car let the bad-smelling one in the backseat and then they drove us down to Eureka. The ride in the car is the only thing I don't remember. How come is that?

At the county place, the bad-smelling one was walking all around, talking to people, shaking hands, showing them his wallet, whispering. He knows everyone and they all know him. I just yelled when I saw him. Wolves! Nobody paid any attention. A little later I started to tell the doctor who looked me over. At first I thought he was listening and I told him how it happened, how I had to get to you. But he had things in his ears and was just listening to my heart. He said, Your mother's had an accident, son, we'll take care of you. It wasn't no accident, I said. Yes, an accident, he said, calm down now. They gave me a shot. It hurt my arm. I went to sleep. When I woke up I was in a white room. I hate white.

Now I'm here. The toad man keeps saying things about Mama. The words don't hurt him to say but they hurt me to hear. Sometimes I wonder if it all happened. Maybe it was like they say. An accident. Maybe I just dreamed the part about the wolves. Which do you think is true?

Big boys don't cry.

You and me, we'll get those bastard wolves and find Mama. Are you all right, Papa Two?

ONE

1

The first and original Cabell Hart, the one who was not true, had been with him since the telephone call this morning. Silent, morose, reeking of his own and others' failure, the ghost had sat next to him in the airport bus, boarded the plane with him, and hovered close as he snapped his seatbelt. Over the past few weeks he had grown used to this figment, whose frequent nearness had something to do with the fact they were two guilty things with the same name, one living and the other summoned up, connected by genetic threads spindling down through history. But at one point in the flight, when the 707 entered a coddled mass of cloud and hung there like a flight simulator pretending movement but going nowhere, his ancestor's presence had become so real that it spooked him. He could almost see the gray frozen eyes; the grafted line where fresh-shaved scalp intersected sunburned neck; oily dirt at the collar of the black broadcloth suit. He had scrambled over the passenger next to him and escaped to the lavatory to stand looking in the mirror framed by harsh fluorescent light, staring at features that seemed more foreign the longer he looked. He had returned to his seat sweating, telling himself that it was just an anxiety attack, natural under the circumstances; but by the time the plane had rolled to a stop, he was elbowing his way to the front of the line, then pushing out the ramp and sprinting down the concourse.

It had taken almost an hour from the airport. He had been in a rush to get here and had nagged the cabdriver to hurry; but now he was stalling, desperate to organize that which he knew was out of his control. He looked around the lobby, almost snowblinding in its whiteness after time spent in the pastels of the afternoon smog outside. He tried to block that first Cabell Hart's return by other thoughts. *A sudden death is God's kiss on the soul.* He repeated that three times, a mantra of hope more for himself than for the one who awaited him six floors up. Then he closed his eyes, breathed deeply, and tried to concentrate on some image of regeneration. He thought of water—rain falling like mercy from heaven, rain that cleansed and renewed. But then two corpses began to float through his mind, buoyed by currents of time in which he too once swam. The first was waterlogged and crusty with marine growth, nibbled by sea things at the finger- and toetips, its black pigment bleached after a long cruise in the Bay. The second was schizophrenic on a coroner's gurney, one side clean and pink, the other torn purple like newly butchered lamb. There was a body yet to come. Had he become one of those disgusting creatures always seen lurking near carrion—a survivor? His great-grandfather seemed to pose the question merely by being in the vicinity.

The human Musak of the paging calls and the scent of antiseptic on filtered air caused him to slump further into the fiberglass chair. He watched as nurses' aides wheeled shrunken patients in and out. Their starched white jumpers rasped efficiently and their voices trilled with obliterating cheer. This hygienic assault was meant to make people believe this was a grand hotel and not a charnel house. *A sudden death is God's kiss on the soul.* Sweat tickled his upper lip.

Trying to buy a few minutes more, he fumbled the pack of Camels bought before takeoff, the first after a four-year abstinence. He struck the match, inhaled, then pulled the cigarette away in what seemed an amateur's mime. The smoke crouched in his lungs like mustard gas. When the cough finally came, he spasmed, bending over rolls of flab to knock head to knee. Vomit gathered in his throat and he tasted a putrescence of the Tums he had been chewing for days. He came out of it and looked around to see if his weakness had been observed, then stood and rearranged himself. An elevator was waiting, doors open. He stepped in and was encased in a gravity of dread. As he eyed the numbers lighting his ascent, it was no longer possible to deny why he was here. "My father is dying," he said aloud.

Barricaded inside their station, two nurses watched without being seen; one sheaved papers and the other stood behind her clacking charts.

"Excuse me, where's Six Twelve?"

"Patient's name?" The words mocked the remote etiquette demanding that one question not be answered with another.

"Joseph Hart."

"Are you family?" The question struck him as a fine issue for the philosopher. Was he? Was there a point at which you had committed so many petty treacheries that filial rights were forfeit?

"He must be the son." The other nurse stepped forward to take over diplomatic relations with him. "I'm Nancy Miles. I'm the one who called you this morning."

She smiled tightly as he thanked her. Her eyes were like pennies in a round of dough. They scanned his face, making no effort to hide the primary concern: Will this one give us trouble? Will he need sedation? Will he cling hysterically to the body? She glanced at the chart and staged an intake of breath to move into the deathbed manner.

"Your father is resting nicely, Mr. Hart. He was in considerable pain when he arrived. I'm afraid he waited too long before calling. Doctor was with him this morning and left instructions. There have been two injections for pain and another is due soon. You may find him less alert than usual, but it's probably a side effect of the drug."

"When will the doctor be here?"

"I really couldn't say. He has several patients, and it depends on his schedule." The prissy mouth made the point: there was a battle going on out there, and General Montrose was in the trenches; in times like these no one could question the necessity for triage.

"Well, when you see him say I'm here and that I want to see him, will you?"

She nodded and handed him a slip of paper with a telephone number on it as he started to go. "Your father asked me to call your sister too. I tried, but nobody answered. Maybe you'd like to take over now?"

His shoes hydroplaned the glassy floor. As he went down the long corridors he imagined himself in black hose and doublet, traversing the dank airs and fetid stone of the deathly castle. There was something rotten here. Coming to the room, he slowed to a sneak, approaching the doorway slowly. A shaft of late sunlight slanted through the gap in the louvered blinds, lighting up a colloidal storm of dust. Further on, in darkness, a bed jutted out from the wall. Atop it lay an untidy mound. There is a metamorphosis going on here, his sphincter signaled. He analyzed the components of the process: feces, dry hair, carbolic, some other element he didn't want to name. He had to force himself to tiptoe forward and look.

No! The word formed itself in his mind with such clarity that he thought for a moment he had shouted it. What he saw were legs raised to fetal curl and a death's-head that rested on clasped hands. Drool dripped onto the pillow below, forming a shadow at the edge of the mouth. The indented cheeks were sucking air; the eye sockets were drilled deep into the head. The russet hair that had once been the rooster's comb was dull and faded and stood up as if affrighted. As next of kin he felt he was owed an accounting. *Who is responsible for this awful cloning?*

The body sensed him and grew rigid, wary of intruders. Hazel eyes blinked, trying to fill the grid behind with focused image. After a minute, the face became more like the one he once had known.

"Ah, Cabe," the voice was laryngitic. "It's you. You snuck up on me. I'm not really asleep, just sort of daydreaming. You've changed. You're fat? No, you look fine." Dirty fingernails gnawed at the sheet. "Come on over and sit. Say, what time is it?"

"After three." Cabell squeezed the toes gently through the coverlet. "How you doing, Pop?"

His father rolled his eyes, mugging, glad to get a chance to say how bad it was without saying. "Just peachy. Peachy keen." Then he jacked himself up on rickety elbows and looked around. When he fell back, there was dampness at the hairline. "They're right about it all going through your mind. Like the old saying: death calls the tune, memory does the dance. I've been lying here remembering."

"Remembering what?"

"Everything. Just everything. Anyhow, you asked about my medical status. Here it is: the machinery stopped working last night. Couldn't swallow. Couldn't piss. I got out of bed to get some pills and goddamned if I didn't fall down. Ass over elbows. Couldn't get up, so I just pulled the blanket down and tried to sleep. This morning I got the phone down from the desk and told them to send the meatwagon."

An arm levitated from beneath the covers. Once thickly corded, the envy of his teenage years, the bicep had melted; flesh hung in a bolus from bone like an oriole's nest. Cabell watched helplessly as his resisting hand was seized by crone's fingers and guided under the sheet into a tropic of body heat. On the right side of the stomach it was forced to brush a hard lump poking out of the waxy skin.

"Feel that?" There was still pride in the body's excellence, if only in producing monstrosity. "A tumor as big as the Ritz."

His lips kept smiling although he was in a panic. He

wanted to snatch his hand away and run to the sink to scrub off the contagion, but knew that this was his penance for holding himself aloof during the time that the evil fruit had sprouted. He submitted, forcing his fingers to circumscribe and comprehend the growth; to appreciate it. A sob caught in his throat like a bone and he coughed quickly to disguise it. He knew what his face plainly said: *Pop! Help me! Please! I can't face this!* He could read the plea in the reply he saw: *I can't. Not now. I'm busy.* His father turned to look at the watercolor of a village on the wall, minutely inspecting the sundrenched plaza and adobe arch.

A nurse whisked in, whey-faced and officious, bearing a needle on a silver tray. "Better let my hand go, Pop. This lady here will think I'm taking advantage of your weakened condition." She ignored him, but his father turned his head and winked, grateful to be spared the crisis.

The covers were peeled and the gown hiked up as if the man was a nursing-school dummy. Turned quickly on his side, his father threw out an arm for support as if to stop the momentum from rolling his body over the edge of the bed. "Okay, Mr. Hart, don't worry, I've got you," she said. The shrunken buttocks and bony hams were from photographs of Auschwitz survivors. The nurse injected, righted him, smoothed the bed, and left the room, all in what seemed a single gesture.

Cabell could trace the morphine burning through the bloodstream like a fuse. The flare of nostril and slip of eyelid over glaring pupil told when it detonated the cortex.

"Cremated," his father said. "I want to be cremated. Things are all in order. Check the desk. No service, no big deal. Hear me?"

"You should rest now, Pop." He couldn't bring himself to acknowledge the request. "You'll feel better later on. I'll have them bring me a guest tray and we'll watch television. The impeachment hearings or something. Okay?"

"Hearings? Oh, right. Jesus, I hope they get that bastard. He's like a hyena: eat all you can and piss on the rest. They better get him soon or there won't be anything left. It's too late to do any good, but if they get him it will at least have the look of justice." The eyes engaged his; they were drugged-foxy. "Oops, I forgot. You're not still for Nixon, are you? This is a political matter we agree about, right?"

Cabell smiled and nodded. "Touché."

"Good. Back to solid ground then. Oh Cabe, this stuff makes you drift. You better get comfortable. You're the midwife here. Talk to Montrose if you see him and find out how much time we've got. Charley on the way?"

"Soon, Pop, she'll be here soon. Don't worry."

"Good, that's what I thought. Don't want her to miss an event like this. Only happens once in a lifetime. Make them let the kid in here too, if I'm up to it. They can bend the rules this once. Kick ass if you have to. Oh! It makes you drift. Makes you la-a-a-zy. Doesn't kill the pain, but puts it out there at the tip of you where you can watch it hurt."

Watching his father float away, he felt protective and wished there was someone to fight, some deed of derring-do that might prove his love at this late hour. *Do you love me, Pop?*

When the phone rang, Cabell tried to smother its brash sound. "Yes?"

"Joe? Joe, is that you? Who is this?" The throaty voice was agitated, suspicious. He'd recognize it anywhere.

"No, it's me, Cabe. How are you, Aggie?"

"Oh Cabe, God I'm glad you're there. I've been so worried. I called him this morning and there wasn't any answer. Then I got Wally to go over to the house at lunchtime and it was locked up. It finally dawned on me to call Montrose's office. They told me he was there. How is he?"

"Fine." He made his voice flat, coding it with implication.

"He's awake?" She got his meaning.

"More or less."

"I won't ask anything else. I know it's bad. I was over at the house last week and he could hardly move. I said, 'For Lord's sake, Joe, won't you please get Cabe and Charley down here! Please! Call Montrose and make him give you pain-killers!

Do something!' He said he figured he'd wait it out. So I just shut up about it. You know how he is when his mind's made up. I gave him a shower. He sat there on a stool while I washed his hair and soaped him. He was all little and shrunk up like a child. God, it made you want to cry."

"I know what you mean." It occurred to him that he had never seen her cry, not through all her troubles, not at her husband's funeral, never.

"Listen, honey, I won't keep you. I know you can't really talk now. Give him my love. Call me when you can. Should I come down?"

The offer was tentative, more than fulfilling the form but not insisting. It was a sister's place to be there, yet she knew that this was his deathwatch, his and Charley's, an opportunity for them to close the broken circle.

"No," he said, "not yet."

"Okay, honey, I understand. You call me back now."

"I will."

"Who was that?" His father's eyelids fluttered as the receiver went down.

"Aggie."

"What did she want?"

"To see how you were. She was worried. She said she loved you."

"I know. I love her too. Aggie's a good girl." He paused. The next words came as if from a great distance. "Know what I was thinking on the floor last night? I was thinking that we did pretty good, considering."

"We did very good, Pop." He held the hand until the fingers relaxed and the body became regular in its respiration. He watched the rise and fall of the covers, waiting for an intake of breath to recover each dying fall, calculating the remaining vital capacity. He remembered something that had happened long ago—what was he, nine? ten? Some sudden night fear had catapulted him out of bed and into his father's room. He recalled creeping into the doorway with the cold air all around him and the floor freezing to his feet, the breathing from within the quilt the only source of heat. It was after Edith had gone ("gone" was the word they used, as if she were on a journey), for his father had been sleeping on half the bed, lying on his side out of consideration for the invisible form next to him. The boy had been hypnotized by the sight of the open mouth as he grew near: the filament of breath delicate for such a large man, hardly enough to keep him going. The reason for his coming had been forgotten; he was aware only that he had stumbled undetected onto something forbidden, something he shouldn't have seen, wasn't ready for. Life was not the result of strength, competence, or virtue as he had thought, but of accident—the lucky gift from whatever arbitrary power worked the bellows of these begging lungs.

A deep exhale and the room had gone silent. The pause that followed had been magnified to a death in the boy's mind. He moved closer to look for vital signs—muscles twitching, the ribcase moving, anything. Seeing nothing, he had cried out and thrown himself onto the bed, burrowing into the body he thought dead. He even remembered his thought: *we're orphans now*. But then his father's magic prevailed. He had sat up, electrically alert, ready to protect the children from attack. The boy had improvised a quick lie concerning a dream of monsters, and until morning had been allowed to shelter in the unused space, hiding under the back that rose above him protectively like a stone wall.

Repressed for years, dormant in the deep space reserved for guilty witness of primal copulation and other dangerous magic, the insight returned to him and left. He was sitting there with the dying body across from him: diminishing, growing backward, composting down into itself, the molecular rearrangement occurring as if by reverse time-lapse; he could *see* it. In between that other time and now there had intervened an induction into mechanics, a burden of cause and effect, a death of his belief in magic, which prohibited him from flinging himself down next to the body once again for reassurance that what he was seeing was not true. He felt strongly the need for instruction about how he was to behave. He wanted to know what the moral was.

Sitting in front of the television set these past weeks in the company of the ghost of his dolorous ancestor, glutting himself on bulky foods before slipping into bed to be dream-tumbled like a dryerful of raggedy clothes, he had considered it all, trying to bring it together and make it *mean*, trying to assimilate the omnipotent sitcom father from his youth to this old man he knew would be frail and gruesome, silly in death. It had become his profession, this remembering. Digression had become his mode. He was lapped by it, awash in its tidal flow. Even now, as he sat in the naugahyde chair, kicked his shoes off, and hugged himself against the pitiless hospital air-conditioning, his mind groped for the past like a healing potion. *We did pretty good, considering.*

April 1 was the starting point. No benefits in going back further. What had gone before was part of a different life. April 1 was the beginning. The date had always possessed a quality of ceremony when seen on calendars or newspapers. It was like December 7 for his father: a month and number giving the hours it organized a special observance. April 1, 1949, spring of the fourth year of the Cold War, the day they had begun their second life.

It was something they had put off as long as possible, but sitting together there at the breakfast table, embarrassed by the sudden intimacy after all those months, they could avoid it no longer.

They were three: the perfect figure according to Pythagoras, but at that moment a clumsy geometry for living. The boy and girl had waited for something to help them get going, some sign from the father who was at that point not well known. Silverware had clanked portentously against ceramic. The brother read the offer on the cereal box regarding an atomic-energy ring; the sister floated a single Cheerio on her spoon like a life preserver in a sea of milk. The father sat there abstracted, slurping coffee and munching loudly on melba toast. Suddenly he bent under the table as if to retrieve a dropped object. Enough time elapsed to create suspense. Then he erupted with a violent jungle noise, majestic, terrifying, forcing the children to move closer to each other and touch arms as he rose into view, snuffling and snarling under a gorilla mask, crying out like a wounded Kong. The roar was heard several houses down. As they sat there, horror turning to blush, his eyes blinked foolishly under the painted rubber lashes and the ape spoke muffled through its stationary lips.

"April Fool!"

There was perhaps a real pain beneath the surface of the act, it later occurred to him, the pain of a breaking chrysalis, birth in a new form, a Rankian pain. It was six months since the funeral, and during that time their father had lived within a cerebral cocoon. The body had gone through mechanical illusions of movement, but actually it slept, spinning time and plotting the vast changes to come. The father had been just barely awake during the family councils that considered the semiorphans' problem. When a cousin suggested that they live with their Aunt Aggie, he roused himself long enough to note that she had twin babies of her own and was busy being witch-hunted. When someone else mentioned the dread words "boarding school," he glowered sleepily and the subject was dropped. It was determined that the grandmother would journey out from Sewanee to take charge.

All this took place just hours after the casket had been lowered into the ground at Forest Lawn. The historical mother was last seen looking waxy perfect, like plastic table fruit. After the sod had been rolled over her like a green rug, her trail went immediately cold, fouled and footprinted by the fantasies her sudden death inspired. When the girl later asked what the boy remembered about her for sure, he had said truthfully not much more than could be counted on the fingers of one hand.

One: she spoke with a drawl she worked to sound more Virginia than Tennessee, the distinction between aristocrat and white trash being an important one to her. Two: there had been bright lipsticks that bloodied the butts of Lucky Strikes and signed the cheek with perfect heart-shaped kiss-marks. Three: her strong word of censure had been "tacky," used for behavior as well as taste, and most often the failing of those called "Okies." Four: before arrival at some important destination there were hasty spit-baths with padded Kleenex that left the chin and forehead smelling vaguely nicotine. Five: there was a definite belief that taste and bearing would raise one out of caste and that such things as calling her Edith instead of mother would mark them as progressive.

The last event with which Edith could be connected was an outing to Los Angeles central depot, where she and the boy stood in line for hours to tour the Freedom Train. She had whispered about the Monroe Doctrine (accenting both words on the first syllable); afterward there were strawberry milk-shakes at the Pig 'n' Whistle and a discussion of world poli-tics quite different from his Aunt Aggie's version. *It* happened soon after. His information came from the girl Carlotta (the alliterative names were to mark them as thoroughbreds, a matched pair). Four years old at the time, she had total recall of the scene. Edith had gracefully fought her way to a sale table on the main floor of the Broadway and captured a beige blouse. She was holding it up to the light to study it for flaws and imagine it upon her shoulders, when she suddenly looked at the ceiling, put three fingertips to her temple, and said in a tone almost of scientific interest, "Lordy, now that hurts!" The eyes flipped white and down she slid, still holding her good bargain, falling slowly like a severed flower. The smell came up in a rush as the skirt turned fecal brown beneath her.

Not until they were teenagers did his sister reveal this last detail. "When that happened," she said with teeth black-ened by a slurry of Oreos and milk, "the people who'd stopped to help just turned their backs and walked. So much for Edith."

They had never seen their mother's mother before. She arrived wearing a crumpled hat that looked like something owned by Maggie of the comic strip. The satchel she carried peeled pebbled leather; she stood in the middle of the steam

and railway whistles, paralyzed by the swift comings and go-
ings of city life, until they claimed her like a piece of baggage and got her out the door. The girl had immediately
grabbed her by the leg and said, "Hi, grandma." The boy considered it tacky to give yourself so cheaply.

A bulky woman with steady eyes that recalled Cherokee
ancestors and a round, handsome face with wrinkles soft as
crushmarks on tissue, Mrs. Elizabeth Hooten was obviously a
primary reason why daughter had set out from Tennessee in
the middle of the Depression in a third-hand Ford roadster
purchased with money made working as an usherette in the
local movie house, driving alone from Sewanee to Los Angeles
to start anew in a world where caste didn't stick. An archetypal Okie, the old lady even looked like Jane Darwell's Ma
Joad. Stodgy shoes seemed to grow out of thick ankles, and
were run over on one side from the slew-footed walk. Ill-fitting
dentures clicked like wind-up teeth; she signed her old-age pen-
sion checks with an X, the boy having to countersign for her.
She came from a family whose women all seemed to have borne
at least one child by the age of sixteen, and whose men had
lost at least one finger by twenty-three. She had been married
four times and loved each husband's memory with fondness,
compensating for the fact that she had had only two children
of her own—Edith's little brother was four when he died of
diphtheria—by taking care of everyone else's. Somewhere
along the line her maternal manner got her the name of Mama
Bessie. She called everyone close to her, regardless of age and
sex, Sugar.

Mama Bessie's smell—a feminine yeast overlaid by lilac
powder and teaberry gum—enveloped them often during
those first weeks when she took over the house and left their
father to his business of change. While sweeping or mopping,
some memory of Edith would suddenly seize her and she would
gather the little boy and girl into the pungent folds of black
taffeta to knead and rock and finally keen them into a trance.
Listening to Stella Dallas—she had also lost a daughter—made
her weep. Yet beneath the sentiment was something tough,

something determined to survive even if her dying husbands and children didn't. Mama Bessie was the only woman he actually ever saw attack someone with an umbrella—a drunk who had pawed her granddaughter outside a Hollywood theater. On Christmas morning she cackled wickedly while modeling a pair of vast bloomers sent from some relative "down home." On Halloween she began to shake and rumble, then went into the bathroom and reemerged in blackface and wearing a bandana, doing an elaborate minstrel show for all the costumed children knocking at the door.

The last time he saw her, during a stopover in Nashville many years later when he was on the way to work with SNCC in Alabama, she was eighty-eight, gnarled and knobby with arthritis in a foul nursing home, yet sailing along beneath a defiant sign someone else had lettered for her: *Old Age Is Not for Sissies!* After smothering him in that well-remembered smell, she pushed him out to arm's length and squinted through milky cataracts. "Now dammit, Sugar, how come you down here to help all these niggers when you never been to see your old Mama Bessie once?"

She organized their lives and stood back from the mangle with hands on hips to say, "Oh Pewter!" or some other indication of disbelief at the strange stories they told of city life. She did housework and broke into snatches of songs he didn't hear again until he was in graduate school reading Child's *Ballads*. She allowed the father to keep to his silent, insulated world.

He had quit his job as insurance underwriter, supporting them with monthly deductions from the joint savings account that had once contained Edith's expansive dreams of vacations in Hawaii and Danish furniture. Although he still left each morning, carrying a sack lunch and saying goodbye at the back door, his job was staying home. He went no further than the workroom out behind the garage, remaining quiet within its walls, emerging only when one of them was sent to knock and tell him it was time for dinner. They learned a word to tell the people who called on the telephone. Unavailable: their father was unavailable just then.

Mama Bessie assumed that he would do what she had done in similar circumstances: remarry and try again to procreate. But he did not stray from the workshop. Seeing that his mourning had no term, she became testy and depressed. One night Cabell had paused on the way to the bathroom to peek inside her door. She sat in front of a mirror in her camisole, tears cutting down through the powder on her cheeks. The hair always worn in Scandinavian coils on top of her head was down almost to the waist: white at the ends; black at the roots. She whimpered softly with each brush stroke.

One night soon after that she had sat down at the dinner table after serving and dramatically raised the apron to daub her eyes, leaving little puffs of flour on the cheeks. Cabell saw it and so did his sister, but it took a loud sniffle to make his father look up.

"Mama Bessie! What's the matter?"

"Oh Joe," she said. "I don't know. It's just that things aren't a-changing here. You ain't never going to get yourself someone else, and I can't stay forever. I like being here and all, but I belong down home. I just don't know what to do."

A puzzled look had come over his father's face. It was as if he was considering the household's future for the first time. His chair scraped back as he rose and bent to hug her.

"God, I'm sorry. I should have seen. What would we ever have done without you?"

The next evening the satchel was packed again and the same dumpty hat sat rakish on her head. The boy had heard her summarize her impressions to his father in the front seat on the way to the station. "Little sister, now she's got grit. I think she'll make it. But I don't know about brother. He doesn't show it, but Edith's going to hurt him worst."

He had almost spoken up to disagree, "No, that's not right. I hardly remember her."

The next day was April 1, April Fool's Day, the day their father appeared in a gorilla mask. The chrysalis had split and produced a creature that looked the same as the one that went in, but was radically different. Within that quiet year long lull, the chemistry had paused and changed. He adapted functions, transcended role and gender, became man and woman too.

"Big fucking deal." Jill, a woman of a later time, had rolled her eyes and gushed out cigarette smoke in disgust when he tried to explain it years after. "I don't know why you go on and on like this. What you're describing is what a man should be as a matter of course. The only question is why he waited till your mother had worked herself to death and he had no choice?"

But at the time the androgyny had seemed a kind of miracle. The boy and girl had both appreciated it because they knew it came hard, was worked at, because there were alternatives that would have preserved his masculine state. But he had determined to be their mother and father both. He kept them home to watch MacArthur's farewell and McCarthy-Army, interpreting the issues at tedious length. He was the only male in their chapter of the PTA. He attended white sales at the Broadway. One night he banished Cabell from the kitchen and then sat his sister down to read her a handbook sent by the Kotex company, explaining menstruation in the pedantic tone of one interpreting a blueprint to another who'd never seen a house.

Each evening, as if by hormonal intervention, the square assertive body that came home looking Spencer Tracy–cocky softened its contours, entering an awkward communion with the lost Edith by slipping into one of the bright gingham aprons she had left behind; fixing dinner, doing dishes, supervising homework, achieving bedtime. At ten o'clock, his chores finished, he sipped a shotglass of cherry kijafa, listened to fifteen minutes of the Ink Spots on a scratchy record, and then went to sleep himself.

Within the reallocated responsibilities, the girl was her

brother's burden. He dressed and fed, protected and bullied. He possessed her as he couldn't the mother's unpredictable ghost. Other incarnations came later on; but a piece of them would always be fixed in his mind as urchins of descending size posed against the front porch. He in knee-pants holding her hand; she in velvet dress fringed by white lace one head lower down; one head lower still, the bedraggled doll Delilah grasped by a dislocated arm.

It was their father's vanity that no kids of his should have baby-sitters. For the first three years, until they were old enough to stay alone, the boy and the girl would leave school and walk two blocks to catch the bus that let them off on Hollywood Boulevard at the Hitching Post, a small theater across from the Pantages. They would straggle in with a bag of popcorn, sink into loge seats, and watch a different matinee every day. Wild Bill Elliot, Bob Steele, Lash La Rue, and other contract heroes of Republic Studios helped addict the boy to happy endings and full justice; the girl ignored them, sinking down deep in the seat and whispering to herself until the usher came to get them after six and take them to their father double-parked outside.

She was freckle-faced and feisty, the cropped reddish hair and swaggering walk causing people in markets and department stores to stop their father and say, "That's sure a cute little boy you've got there." She smiled covertly and fought with her brother for speaking up to say, "No, she's a girl." As a boy she would have more power and be a better accomplice —Tonto to his Lone Ranger, Robin to his Batman, eventually Watson to his Holmes.

She imprinted on him and trailed him everywhere. When he had a paper route, she got up early Sunday mornings to hallo down the empty streets, "*Examiner-Times* paperrrrr." When he was out for Little League, she shagged his flies and pitched batting practice. She tried to copy him by urinating standing out behind the garage and soaked her socks. When asked what she wanted to do when she grew up she said, "Marry Cabell." After they were older they went naked into a closet and groped each other. "Pee in me," she said, "and I'll have your baby." Part of her was his creation, and she willingly carried the name Charley, which he gave her during some game of fantasy with an all-male cast.

That April Fool's Day had set the tone for the years that followed. Life was cruel, but living didn't have to be. The only unit on which they could model theirs was the fifties television sitcom. The kids were calculating ingenues; the parent comically inept. "Father Knows Best": but the era's authoritarianism was subtly undercut from below. They created the burlesque character of "Pop," someone given to swift enthusiasms and odd fancies; someone capable of corny jokes and at times so childlike that they had to be his adults; yet someone granite in reliability. He seemed to understand that making him into such a figure was their way of handling their feelings for him, and he played the role he was given.

One day for no apparent reason he decided that he wanted to be rich. ("Rich" was what he said, not "wealthy," which would have been Edith's choice; he liked the nice vulgarity of the word and the way it conjured up spending instead of status.) He felt sure that a person with his background in mining could strike it rich in uranium. One good claim would be worth millions if the flaky ore became, as he forecast, the gasoline of the nuclear age. He bought a Geiger counter and an army-surplus jeep, and they spent weekends prowling the bleak Mojave in search of clicks. After a while he got gold fever. He paid fifty dollars to an old desert rat with the gummy laugh of Gabby Hayes for his secrets. They spent a day tracing out his hand-drawn treasure map and by sunset were parked at the edge of a vast hillside of feldspar glistening with mica like a field of diamonds. "Are we rich, Pop?" the girl had asked. "No," he answered, looking at their find. "But this is worth it."

Next it was chinchillas, the other archetypal fifties scheme. He built elaborate pens in the backyard and spent $150 on a pair of breeding stock. The man who sold them, a thin, nervous former GI who'd lost an arm at Iwo Jima and still wore his army decorations on his jacket lapel, assured him that he would soon have to move to the country to contain the beasts. "They go to it, they really do. Beat rats in heat any day. You'll have yourselves hundreds inside a year."

The first litter of three were scrawny, and the male finally ate them. Afterward the two animals retreated to opposite corners and sat glaring at each other, one of them making tiny snarling sounds if the other happened to stray over the invisible territorial line that bisected the cage. One day their father put on thick gloves and reached in to force their bodies into copulating position. Charley, who stood and watched, had tisked her lips and said, "Oh, Pop."

Eventually the animals' lustrous blue-gray fur became mangy and fell out in patches. He tossed the cage into the of the pickup, and then they drove up into the San Bernardino Mountains. He didn't speak until they reached a point below Lake Arrowhead where he stopped and tossed the animals out, yelling, "Be fruitful and multiply, you jerks," then got out and charged off in the opposite direction carrying a copy of Roger Tory Peterson and a pair of flapping binoculars around his neck.

He had come out of the cocoon saying that he wanted to be "his own man," and didn't want to go back to sitting at a desk. So he got a job selling insurance for a Beverly Hills company. He cut a strange figure, his son and daughter noted with embarrassment when they became teenagers, driving those gilt-edged streets in his pickup, boxes of melba toast crumbled into the crease of the seat along with bottles of minty mouthwash and compressed Fig Newtons. The clothes were pure Keaton: baggy suits, thick knit ties, droopy socks that he gratefully accepted each Christmas and then immediately remade by ripping the elastic tops, claiming that it cut off his circulation. There was always a book or two wherever he was. He read voraciously to try to get a systematic understanding of all fields, and purveyed misinformation with the same enthusiasm as fact. Seconds after giving a detailed explanation for why Wallace had as good a claim to originating

the theory of evolution as Darwin, he might be telling his children that they, the Harts, had less body hair than many other
people because they had descended further from the apes than
hairier people. Truth and fiction alternated in him like competing fields of energy.

Perhaps because he didn't seek it, he got the business of
some movie people. It began with George Pal, a producer
with whom he shared an interest in science fiction, and radiated outward to include others. He began bringing his kids
glossy pictures of Randolph Scott, Dennis Morgan, Paulette
Goddard and others, always with lengthy handwritten inscrip-
tions. The walls of their bedrooms looked like Sardi's.

One day Bobby Singer, the older boy next door, inspected
their collection of stars. "These signatures are all the same,"
he had decreed. "The handwriting's the same. The pen's even
the same. Anybody can buy these pictures. That's what your
dad did: bought them and signed them himself."

It didn't matter to the girl. But the boy was jolted by
such a piece of treachery. He moped for nearly a week. One
night when his father brought home a large manila envelope
containing Rod Cameron, he refused to accept it. When asked
what was wrong, he blurted it out. "This is all phony. You
don't know these people. You just buy their pictures and write
all that stuff yourself. I thought this was *real.*"

Two days later, his father had come to take him out of
school at midday. "I thought we'd go down to Hollywood for
lunch," he said. "Been a while since we spent time together.
I've been feeling bad about the other night." The boy had
wanted to tell him that it was all right, that he knew now
this was one of those pieces of deceit that made the adult
world turn. But he couldn't get the words out. His father had
hummed slightly and clanked the gears as he rattled in and
out of traffic, finally pulling into the lot of the Brown Derby
and allowing the scowling attendant a quarter for parking the
battered truck. Inside they ordered and sat silently. The boy
feared to see the man demean himself even further by a con-
fession. He was staring down at his plate when the burly figure

come toward them from the bar, shuffling and rolling in a bear's walk. He looked up when the wide boxer's face was beside him, smelling of booze and split in a smile. "Hey there, young fellow!" The huge paw swallowed his. "So you're the son of this good man here. He's a lucky guy to have a boy like you." Oblivious to the patrons eyeing them, the man took a chair and began to talk to his father about the size of oranges at his ranch and then of policy renewals. Victor McLaglen! He had thought to himself: *Oh, Pop!*

The three of them were the core of something—a family—whose outer rings comprised the world. There was Mama Bessie and the drawling relatives she sent to their house with presents when they came to California. There was also their Aunt Aggie and their grandfather, a tall and slender man with cropped white hair and hawkish features who lived in a rooming house in Pasadena, then in Aggie's spare room, and finally in a sanitorium in the Glendale hills. He wore cowboy boots and straight-legged jeans even in his late seventies. He always carried a pint of whiskey someplace on his person, and a sack of Bull Durham, which he might pull out while sitting before the television watching Roller Derby or wrestling, roll one of the wet-seamed cigarettes that browned the webbing of the fore- and middle finger, and get ready to stomp outside to smoke it in disgust when the unchecked evil of a Gorgeous George was allowed to defeat the trusting virtue of an Argentine Rocca.

His name was Laughlin Hart. In his time he had run cattle, prospected for silver, organized unions, played semipro baseball, and built buildings. But he always considered himself a farmer. "I never left the land," he always said in reference to the hard times when wind whipped the South Dakota topsoil with such velocity that it entered the house through cracks in the walls, coloring flour, sugar, and linen a silky gray. "It left me."

After leaving his homeland the final time—he never

mentioned the first time he'd left, when still a boy, driven out by the sort of tragedy that wrecked men's lives—he had wandered through the Rocky Mountain states prospecting and looking around. Once he turned up—or so he said in one of the stories told while sitting at the curb, spitting down into the gutter—at Joe Gans's training camp. A sign said that sparring partners would get twenty-five cents a round. He had earned a dollar and a half before both eyes swelled shut.

The man was a collection of atavisms that amazed the boy and girl. When stepping out the door he always mechanically checked the sky for the violence of seasonal weather he had left behind on the plains thirty years earlier. When there was menace in the clouds, he always smelled the air to see if cyclones were in the offing. He put spiderwebs over cuts to make the blood congeal instead of getting sutures; when his finger joints ached with arthritis, he plunged his hands into stinging nettles for relief. "Jesus, Dad," their father growled at these displays, "why don't you join the twentieth century? Can't you leave that goddamned prairie behind?" Laughlin had shrugged and said, "I guess not." To the end of his life he was always boarding buses to ride all over southern California to attend the South Dakota picnics he saw advertised in the paper, finding others there who were also immigrants and needed to remember the Old World to which they could never return.

Laughlin was often drunk. Their father scorned it as a weakness. Their Aunt Aggie apologized for it as understandable given the hand of cards life had dealt the man. But they, young as they were, saw it as an excess of something, rather than a lack. In one well-remembered incident, they were at Aggie's house, baby-sitting the twins Wally and Tay at lunchtime. Their grandfather came in through the back door, cowboy boots louder than usual and less precise in their thumps on the floor. He propped himself against the refrigerator door, leering at the contents. Then he picked out a can of catfood, took off its plastic cover, smelled deeply of the aroma, and dug in with a fork. "Tuna," he looked up bleary-eyed at them.

"I love tuna. Don't you kids just love tuna?" He thought it was his good mood and love for them that made them laugh. After finishing his snack, he'd joined them, laughing until he spasmed in a rheumy coughing fit that spotted his handkerchief with blood. After it had subsided, he sat down with them at the table and had a little drink.

Their father and grandfather were uncomfortable on holidays and other times when there was nothing concrete to accomplish. They would sit in overstuffed chairs and exchange sections of the newspaper with grunts and hand gestures. But they loved to work together. They collaborated on carpentry projects at Aggie's house, talking out the plans at great length and conferring while the work was going on. Every summer they would go up into the San Fernando hills to cut deadfall for winter firewood, taking the saber-toothed two-man saw that hung the rest of the year on a hook in the garage. Setting it to a log they worked with perfect timing, understanding each other completely, connecting through the five-foot blade in a way they rarely did at other times. Watching them work down rapidly through the wood without ever letting the saw buckle, Cabell had a vision of communication between the generations, a feeling of certainty that in the normal course of things he would live near his father when he grew older, and stand at the other end of this two-man saw.

On one of these expeditions, his grandfather had brought along the old pump-action Winchester .22 with the date 1896 in the blue hexagonal barrel. While the men worked, the children shot rusty cans left by day-campers. The boy had turned to watch the two men work, pulling and being pulled in return. Mesmerized by the synchronous movement, he almost missed the coil of muddy gray near his grandfather, trapped from exit by a square of logs and crawling toward the leg periodically exposed above the boot by the saw's motion. Afraid to speak or move, he raised the gun and sighted quickly. Both men ducked at the shot, pulling in their necks like turtles. His father had advanced on him with an angry look on his face. But his grandfather called out, "Hold it, Joe!" then held up the snake with bone showing near the ugly spade-shaped head. He came over and hugged Cabell to his hip, then deftly skinned the snake with his pocketknife. The rattles he placed carefully in the cuff of his jeans.

"Why are you putting them there?" his father asked with the beginnings of a smile.

"You know these rattles give off a dust that can make you blind," his grandfather answered from his bent-over position. "I'm not taking any chances."

"Oh, God," his father shook his head. "More witchcraft from the Great Plains!"

That birthday, his tenth, Laughlin gave a present wrapped in paper scavenged from a Safeway bag. Inside was a belt he'd made of the snakeskin, along with a small glass jar containing the rattles, with a silver dollar taped to the lid. The accompanying note read: "To Cabell, who saved his grand-dad's life with a good shot."

The children knew that part of the tension between the two men came from the fact that the older man symbolized something to their father; something that was old and valuable, but also out of date, stiff-necked in its refusal to yield to modern times. During Aggie's political troubles, there were frequent obscene calls despite changed and unlisted numbers. The postman once delivered a box filled with a stinking pile of chicken guts and human feces worked by maggots, all bedded in excelsior; the accompanying note told her to go back to Russia. Their father went to the city attorney's office but was treated like an illegal alien. The following Sunday, their grandfather rose early and, dressed in his rarely used ice-cream suit, he put on his good straw hat and took the walking stick made of willow with the legend "Black Hills S. D. 1913" carved into the shaft. By that time he was going blind, but wouldn't admit it. His only concession was to get a magnifying crystal for the pocket watch, which made the black numbers swim under glass like tadpoles. He felt his way out the front door.

Wally, the more adventuresome of the twins, followed

him as he set out, sneaking along behind from hedge to hedge. He later returned to tell the other children what had happened. Laughlin had waited outside the local church for services to let out. Then he picked out the two men he suspected were responsible for the package and, cornering them, began to thrash them methodically, bring hard blows down on their heads and shoulders as if he were cutting wood. When they escaped his range he had stood defiantly for a minute, then dropped the stick and motioned them to come and fight. Although together they had fewer years than he, both refused. Wagging a finger in warning, Laughlin said, "Don't you ever be doin' her that way again, you hear?" Then he picked up the stick, turned contemptuously, and walked home. Later that day he was arrested and spent three nights in jail before they could get him out. On the drive home their father lectured, "Goddamn it, Dad, frontier justice doesn't work here!"

Not long after that he was in the TB sanitorium, rail-thin in a hospital gown, his cowboy boots showing beneath, cruelly disallowed from touching them, but trying to amuse the girl from across the room by making animal sounds through the gauze mask. When the telephone call came about his death, their father had cried. He shook his head and said, "They just don't make them like that anymore."

One Friday afternoon their father had come home from work with weary tension in his voice. "We need to go someplace. How about Vegas?" They boarded the pickup and took off, speeding through the desert, swerving to miss the rabbits that jumped with eager shining eyes into the apocalypse of headlights. Outside of Barstow, with the girl singing "You Are My Sunshine" at the top of her voice, the pickup entered into a race with a locomotive on the tracks alongside them. At eighty-two miles an hour, the train began to pull away and their father accepted the engineer's taunting wave with a grim nod of the head.

He began gambling the moment they arrived. After

swimming and getting to know the bellhops and maids, they watched him from the casino fringe. Usually he played craps with the rhythm of a black in a back alley, cooing and talking to the dice, wanting to win but wanting even more the illusion of magic, the sense that his body was a lightning rod conveying a higher power to the bones. Usually he left the tables a modest winner, coming out whistling and making each of them cup their palms to receive a small cone of silver dollars as their share of the take. But this time he was feverish in the eyes, passing the dice to the next person down as if fearful of contaminating them, betting don't-pass like a misanthrope. He lost heavily.

On the drive back home he spoke over the pickup's whining engine. "Now if anything should happen to me, you know, Aggie's the one to go to. It doesn't really matter who's in charge, you've got to look after each other, hear? You belong to each other. You're all you've got."

That homiletic mode was not in keeping with their idea of themselves, and they had finished the trip in silence. A few days later they learned that on the morning before they left, he had undergone tests to see why he was passing blood in his urine. Ben White, their doctor, had not concealed his worry. But lab reports finally showed that it was just the rupture of some capillary. Their father had come through the door after learning of the test results, leaking actuarial tables and temporary binders, and called out in his Ted Lewis imitation, "Is everybody happy?" But a shiver had penetrated their triangle. There would come a time when they would be without each other. Then what?

When the boy was older, on the threshold of something, his sense of random, amoral change focused on his sister. Her transformation obsessed him: the breasts budding from darkened nipples; legs lengthening to make the chunky body supple; facial lines resolving the transsexual conflict. It was not something willed, but she seemed to feel almost guilty for allowing herself to be swept away from comradeship and willing subservience. Sometimes he caught a glimpse of her looking at him with sad traitor's eyes. But they were slaves of violent hormones, powerless to stop the process; they had allowed themselves to be segregated according to the iron laws of teenage sexuality, novitiates in their separate orders.

The problem washed over into relations with his father. A general wariness spread like ground fog through their dealings. The man denied his power, yet stood as a breakwater against his mortality. How to master without destroying him? The boy's calculating mood was contagious. They both became secretive, like primitive men hiding fingernail parings, pubic hair, and other private medicine to prevent each other from getting voodoo.

He sometimes stood unwatched and studied his father and sister together, noting that they were remarkably alike in coloring and composition, and also in a sense of spiritual gravity. He was more the copy of the lost prototype and therefore an unknown quantity. Rounder-faced and darker than they, he knew his sense of self was more dependent on what he could make appear in others' eyes. When he once tentatively mentioned how different he felt from them, how much less steady and dependable, his father had tousled his hair and said, "It's just a phase. Know that childhood fantasy in which you're sure that you're adopted? Well, this is the teenage equivalent." He had interpreted this statement as condescension, and it made him feel homicidal.

Unknown to anyone else, he spent that spring—it was his sixteenth year—being stalked by a gang of eighteen-year-olds, the borderline graduates and dropouts of previous years who still hung around high school. They had set up an elaborate extortion racket involving the lunch money of tenth-graders like himself. More from naïveté than principle, he had refused to honor it; the gang had decided to make him an object lesson for others.

Their attacks occurred after class, anywhere between the school and his house. Their hair was slicked back into ducktails; they wore silk jackets embroidered with dragons and tigers, which older GI brothers, themselves delinquents and failures of a previous graduating class, had brought back from Korea. Their car would pull up behind him, and doors would open and slam; then the familiar four or five faces would be floating around him like maggoty balloons, shoving, punching in the kidneys and under the ribs, hurting so covertly that passers-by could assume it was all good-natured teenage horseplay. He couldn't fight back and knew that it would be worse if he showed signs of weakness. He pretended that it was a game that he enjoyed as much as they did. When they finally tired and left, he found a sheltered spot to pull himself together and then continued home, repelling Charley's curious and concerned looks with some savage insult. The gang had embodied a world in which things worked by power, pressure, violence, a world of circumstances beyond one's control.

About this time, he began spending time at Aggie's house, traveling out to Canoga Park two or three times a week on the bus. Now that the twins were growing up and in school, the house had taken on a look of serious intent. Books and magazines, mostly relating to Transcendentalism, lay splayed out open on the floor; tabletops and other surfaces were lined with newspaper clippings margined with exclamation points in red and blue pencil. His aunt was always in the middle, unvarying in her uniform of jeans and sweatshirt, trying to engineer this benign chaos to some conclusion. He liked the way she looked: short and durable, the curly hair kept cropped, the angular face without a distinguishing mark requiring special attention. Although no sprite, she had a resemblance to Mary Martin; the impression she conveyed was of trimness almost nautical.

"Did you know Edith, Aggie?" He always had trouble beginning. Meant to be casual, the words always sounded blurted.

"That's a strange question, Cabe. Of course I knew her." She accepted the fact that the therapy would be nondirective and prepared for their sessions by sitting down in the chair under a lithograph of Ralph Waldo Emerson, the hero of the second, the post-Communist, part of her life. She lit a cigarette from one of the several packs of Chesterfields spread around the house.

"I mean really know."

"Ah, *really*. Such intensity. Let's say I knew her as well as you get to know somebody when they're your sister-in-law. It isn't necessarily the closest of relationships. To be honest, I'm not sure your mother really approved of me. In a certain way I wasn't what you'd call a *nice* person. I think I must not have seemed very ladylike to her. I was terribly concerned with facts, you know, and lacking in the social graces. Your mother was a person who believed in manners."

"I know."

He could remember his aunt's appearances during his childhood. They had always been intense and hurried, accompanied by a sense of crisis that was almost global. When Aggie had discussions with his father, his mother had somehow spatially isolated herself although not moving, as if by lowering an invisible oxygen tent around herself. In one repeated argument he remembered the ritual words "Potsdam" and "Yalta" occurring over and over again, the small, sturdy figure holding its own against his father's bulk until he finally reached over and hugged her, laughing, "You're a bear, Aggie, a bear. Uncle Joe would be proud. He'd make you a hero of the revolution."

She had been the indulgent maiden aunt bearing gifts in the glove compartment of the old DeSoto until after the war, when she married another teacher and party member named Robert Nathan. He was the first Jew to penetrate their Presbyterian endogamy—frail, with taut, transparent skin stretched across sensitive features. He was capable of violent political invective and obscene comedy, most often conveyed in phrases from a childhood spent in a vaudeville family on the borscht circuit. When he saw someone ignoring the obvious, for instance, Nathan might strike his forehead with the flat of a palm and say: "Took a bath, forgot to wash my ass." He told the neighborhood children riddles and they called him the Riddler, as if he were a character out of Batman. It was his sense of whimsy that coerced Aggie into naming their twin boys Wallace and Taylor, an homage to the candidates of the doomed Progressive party. It was his determination that led both of them not to admit that their God had failed when they were called to appear before HUAC, although they had both left the party by then.

After he and Aggie were fired by the Los Angeles County School Board, Nathan tried to finance the war of litigation he launched by starting a greeting-card business that would show-case his wry humor. It was barely established when he died one night in his sleep of a heart attack. At the funeral services at Mount Sinai, the Jewish section of Forest Lawn, FBI men had stood so close that the service seemed scored by the syncopated click and whirr of their cameras. Not crying, Aggie had looked defiant under her black veil. Cabell remembered his father throwing what could be interpreted as an accidental shoulder into one agent who came too close as their party left, hitting him with such force that the man's hat flew off and he sat down hard on the grass. Laughlin had smiled at that and patted his son on the back.

Aggie had made the business go, and when she sold it a few years later there was enough money to buy three tract houses in a row in the Canoga Park cul-de-sac. She and the twins lived in the center and rented the other two. The houses were filled with corners and closets: clean-cut right angles. It was understood that Wally and Tay would each be given a home beside her after growing up: a family compound to keep them safe.

"Was Edith pretty?"

"Mmm. A Southern belle, but dark and fiery."

"How did she and Pop meet?"

"I think it was in the parking lot of Bill's Ranch Market, as a matter of fact. Your mother tripped on something and fell. Joe helped her up. It went from there."

"Sounds like a movie."

"I know. Everything was like a movie in Hollywood in those days."

"What was Pop like when he was my age?"

"Well, first of all"—she smiled at his inability to make transitions—"he's over ten years older than me, and so I was hardly more than a baby when he was your age. But I'd say he was probably a lot like you—undecided."

"Undecided?"

"I mean he hadn't figured out what was important yet. He was just doing what there was to do. When he left the homestead and moved into Rapid City—that would be about 1919—our dad bought a poolhall, and Joe played for the house while he was a teenager. Pool and basketball: he was an athlete. Dad always claimed they made more off Joe's cue stick than off all the beer they sold."

"How did he get along with granddad?" He was probing for something, some humanizing failing that would bring his father close to him, and make it seem that he might become such a man someday.

"Pretty good, I guess. Joe didn't like living in South Dakota, though."

"How come?"

"Oh, I don't know. I guess he felt that the past was a burden on him. He didn't want to be what the past said he was *supposed* to be." She lit a cigarette off the butt of one she had just finished and became conspiratorial. "I probably shouldn't say this. It isn't really any of my business or yours either. But it might help answer your question. There was a time when he was about your age—no, I guess a few years older—when your dad got in some trouble. He was working part time at the Homestake mine and had a little money of his own. I guess he and some other young fellows got ahold of some liquor and got a snoutful one night. Anyway, at about midnight the police found him up at Deadwood cemetery. He had pulled down the first Cabell Hart's infamous gravestone and was whacking away at Gillette's marker with a shovel. First they charged him with graverobbing, then they modified it to vandalism and resisting arrest. The judge claimed that blood relationship didn't give Joe any proprietary rights over his grandfather's grave. He said it belonged to history, so to speak. Nothing really ever came of it. He lost his job at the mine, but that just gave him the excuse he'd been looking for to pack up and come out here. Don't you ever let on that I told you this. I don't think he's ashamed of it or anything, but I suppose if he had wanted you to know about it, he'd have told you himself."

"He never talks about living back there at all."

"I think he's got this feeling that it's not good to stir the past. When he came out here to California he figured that he was beginning all over from day one. That feeling got real strong after your mother died, but he was that way even before."

"Do you believe that?"

"What?"

"That a person can just go someplace new and start over like he was somebody different?"

"Not really. I think the past never buries its dead; you've got to do that yourself. But I can see how Joe would feel the way he does."

That had pleased him, the vision of his father drunk and disorderly, lurching around a deserted graveyard and brawling with the squadron of police sent to get him. It was a perfectly gratuitous act, inexplicable, literacy, irresponsible. He could see something of himself in that.

As issues came up during their séances that required authentication or research, Aggie would walk over to the bookcase where the scrapbooks were stored, stand on a chair to hand them down, and then help him spread them open on the dining-room table. The mummified pages cracked and dissolved on his fingers, becoming antique dust that caused his nose to run. They sat together, snuffling and sneezing their way through letters, clippings, and other memorabilia, some of it so fragile that they had to use tweezers to handle it. Although they were looking for clues for their own private questions, they collaborated. She was the guide; he willingly heard the same stories over and over, trying each time to view them from a different angle.

About a portrait of her aunt, Sophia Hart, beautiful and frail in a high-necked blouse, the hair a golden aureole in the backlighting of the old-time studio: "My Dad's older sister. I don't know too much about her except that for a while she was a 'dance-hall girl'—that's his term, and I think it's probably synonymous with 'fallen woman.' It was after their father left on a trip out west and got stranded that their mother died in childbirth. Sophia went to work doing whatever it was she did in that Deadwood saloon, because it was all there was for her to do, the only way she could take care of Laughlin. Dad once told me that some drunk got carried away during the act of love and bit her. It was on the breast. There was almost a severing and it didn't mend right. She got addicted to opium for the rest of her life. Maybe that's what gives her this dreamy look. This picture was taken about a year after the Gillette killing. She'd taken Dad back to Urbana where the rest of the Harts lived. She passed away three days after his tenth birth-day. She was twenty."

They always paused over pictures of Emma, Laughlin's wife, who had died in the flu epidemic of 1919 with four of her children, leaving only Joseph and Aggie, the first and last born. In one torn and peeling photo, Emma mugged at the camera in knee boots, wool pants, and an odd-looking tur-ban. "Dad met her at a square dance. He noticed her because she was the only one there willing to dance with a Negro farmhand somebody invited as a practical joke. 'That took grit,' he always said. This hat she has on here has a story at-tached to it. She and Dad were just married—he'd come back from Illinois to homestead a piece of land outside Rapid City —and they were living in a sod house. Prairie marble—that's what they called it. They were poor as churchmice. Came time for Easter and she didn't have money for a new bonnet, so she set out to make one. She killed three of the biggest rattle-snakes she could find, cured the skins, then wound them into this hat, which she decorated with a spray made up of the rattles."

The pictures of Laughlin as a younger man always intrigued him because he could compare them with the man he'd known and see the ravages of change. Taken against corrals, in front of clapboard buildings, or on prairies, these images reminded him of the bit players—vigilantes, rustlers, posse—in all those cowboy movies.

"Dad was a good old guy.". Aggie got a misty look when speaking of him. "That business with his father just simmered inside him all his life. After Sophy died, he just bummed around for a while. He got a job in the Pennsylvania coal mines and was at the Homestead strike when Frick brought in the Pinkertons. I think he got into some kind of trouble there. Maybe it was union work: I had to pry everything out of him, you know. I know he had to get out of Pennsylvania fast. He bummed around, one of those men who are on the road. He had this need to make things square. I guess that's why he went back to South Dakota. He got married and tried to start a family. But he never made a go of it. The land gave out, Mama and the other kids died when the flu hit. He went into Rapid City, and got the poolhall, and then later got into the construction business. I remember he built a block of houses there in town right at the beginning of the Depression. Shotgun houses, they called them, three rooms right in a row, straight as a bullet shot out of a gun. He got a couple of them rented, then things got bad. Nobody could afford to pay rent. The tenants in the ones he had rented began pulling the other ones down, just flat dismantling them for the wood. I went to him and said, 'Daddy, they're tearing down your houses.' He said, 'I know, honey, but what can I do? Those people got to cook for their children and keep them warm.' Then we decided to come on out here to be near Joe. Dad got involved with Upton Sinclair and his movement, the Ham 'n' Eggers, the Townsendites, and just about every other group on the side of the down-and-outers —I guess that's what got me started. But nothing really helped. That feeling that things weren't right and couldn't be straightened out by anything within his power stayed with him from his childhood. It ate at him. He drank to get free from the feeling."

She rummaged through some loose papers and handed Cabell what seemed a page from some sort of diary. The faded blue ink was in neat Spencerian script:

A wise man considers the periodic destructions and rebirths of the universe and reflects that our posterity will see nothing new and that our ancestors saw nothing more than we have seen. This from M. Aurelius. Take note!

"What does it mean?"

"It means what it means," she shrugged. "It was found tucked inside the Bible my granddad left behind. It was shipped to Sophia and my dad along with a few other things. Your great-grandfather was an educated man. He'd gone to a teacher's college back in Illinois before he moved to the Black Hills. He might have copied this out when he was a student and kept it. But I always thought that he maybe wrote it down after he got back to the house from killing Gillette and left it as a sort of last will and testament."

There was a picture of the first Cabell Hart as a young man surrounded by his family: his wife Eliza beside him holding the baby Laughlin, Sophia standing behind on one side, and the oldest son, Evan, on the other. Beneath the drooping mustache, the man's face was fine, almost feminine. Close together, the eyes were set midway between high forehead and smiling mouth, their look filled with satisfaction and certitude. In a few years, all but Laughlin would be dead, the family swept away in what seemed one continuous act of destruction.

There was another picture of Cabell Hart standing next to a horse. Alongside him was a square-jawed woman in a skirt of velour trade goods and a loose-fitting buckskin shirt. "Her name was Look," Aggie said. "She was a part-Indian who'd grown up with a band of Sioux living someplace out near the homestead. According to my dad, her people had died off of smallpox and she'd just shown up on their property one day. She became a sort of housekeeper. She tended Eliza during her sickness, and lived with Cabell Hart during his last months. A 'companion'—isn't that the polite word for it? A down-and-out white and a half-breed: quite a pair! They found her body in the cabin right next to his when the vigilantes went out to get him."

There were clippings about his great-grandfather's founding of the First Church of Deadwood, about the death of young Evan; there were huge banner headlines of the murder of Walker Gillette. But it was this picture that fascinated him. Although opposites, the Indian woman and the man seemed to belong together. She was exotic, impassive. He was changed from the other earlier picture. Thin, haunted-looking, his eyes almost white in the sepia print as if bleached or frozen by some cruel sight. Cabell asked to see this picture so often that Aggie finally gave it to him. He took it home and tucked it into the corner of the mirror on his dresser and looked at it every morning, wondering what it was he hoped to find out from it.

"Why did Pop name me after him?" In his paranoia he had wondered if his father had hoped to keep him down by cursing him with this mangled piece of history.

"I don't know, Cabe." Aggie shrugged. "Maybe he liked the sound of the name. Maybe he felt it didn't get a fair shake the first time around and deserved another chance."

"Well, he *was* a murderer, wasn't he?"

"Yes." The admission didn't cause her to yield.

"God, some family," he said, comparing it in his mind to friends' families, where people appeared in ordinary twos and fours, where genealogical trees were pruned and regular. He had seen their family portraits where the generations buttressed each other like pillars, a pyramid descending to the children down below the fathers and grandfathers. He wanted something regular and reliable like that: something you could study to see the terms of your descent, understand your potential in the incarnations of others. The Harts had no family picture. If they had one, it would be a motley group of half-breeds, killers, and missing spouses and children.

"It's what you've got." Aggie's face had a look on it that made him realize she was talking about herself as much as him. "It's your limits and your possibilities. Sometimes you'll get so far away from it you'll think you're outside its influence forever, then before you figure out what's happening, it will be right beside you, pulling the strings. Some people get crushed by their families. Others are saved by them. I think you ought to wait awhile before you say it's no good. See what life does to you and how you bear up."

By the end of that spring his interrogations of his aunt had become less pressing. He still went through the scrapbooks with itching eyes and running nose, watching collateral lines of Harts dwindle off into other parts of the nation, merge with other names and dispositions, become hybrids, and finally disappear, while the main branch came down into his own generation—to him and Charley and, to a lesser degree, Wally and Tay. But he was more aloof now. He saw it as an epic of space, time, and change and felt that he looked down on it from a vast height that allowed a view of the pulsation of surrounding events: settlers crossing the Appalachians and then edging out further; gold discovered in the Black Hills; Indians resisting and vanishing; movement further west; an angle of repose achieved just before the frayed brutality of the Depression and the coming of war. Encapsulated by this history, affected by it although trying to move independently, were the people who had produced him—children born and dying, some growing up to collide randomly with mates and produce offspring of their own, become old and sick, and die; families expanding and contracting according to laws outside their control, trying to preserve their symmetry. This process had a claim on him, he understood. When and how would payment be demanded?

The questions chased each other in his mind. He tried to extract some wisdom from it that would allow him to bear up under the gang's harassment. One afternoon near the end of the semester he was walking home from school and heard the familiar sound of their car pulling up behind him. The sounds were so well memorized that he knew them by heart, the movements rehearsed so often in the past months that they seemed choreographed. Steeling his body, he began to count, knowing that by the time he reached six, the faces would be bobbing around him and by nine the first punches would be thrown. He had made himself wise in preparation for the ordeal, bathing it all with his inner light: *I know it's going to happen; there's nothing to be done about it; I was born for this.*

They were in a circle containing him. Hair glistening with oil and combed up in pompadours making foreheads high, eyes cruel as minks'. He smiled at them: *my destiny*. There was a commotion behind and he assumed it was more of *them*. But they began to change: the heavy-lidded menace drained away, leaving them kids in clothes too large. The blur on his periphery was someone different.

He watched as Charley flew into the mass, lips pulled back over her teeth in a snarl, arms flailing and knees pumping, striking the first one with such force that he went down and then curled into a ball on the sidewalk to protect against her kicks.

He knew that his father would be there too. Inside a clarity that blocked out sound, he turned and saw him holding two of *them* against their car, bracing them with his body in the diagonal, holding their collars and threatening in a low growl. After his father had let them get loose and run away, Cabell saw his sister, still so excited that she moved in little chicken-hops. She came close to their father, whose nostrils still flared, and stood next to him on tiptoe with clenched fists, the body of a woman even then attempting to grow out of the body of a boy.

"You ever touch my brother again," she screamed at the departing backs, "and I'll kill you."

He was sitting on the pavement then, his books on his lap, laughing uncontrollably at the notion of his sister killing them, laughing until tears rolled down his face, until his father bent down to put an arm around his shoulder and say, "Come on, Cabe, it's okay now. Let's get going."

He stood up and went to the window, back in the sickroom world, massaging his eyelids with thumb and forefinger, punishing the swelling tear ducts with rubbing. He looked down into the dusk at the threads of people arriving for visiting hours. They moved against the stream of employees whose shift was over: ants weaving in and out and brushing each other in coded contact. The floor was cold against his stockinged feet; he shivered in the blast of air-conditioning.

There was a duty of self-criticism here. He accused himself of bourgeois sentimentality. He was airbrushing the inequities and petty tyrannies by which parents living and dying have their way and set their children's feet in concrete. He was like the lackey artists who kissed ass on history by making Stalin's sallow cheeks glow pink, capping the rodent's discolored teeth, hiding the withered left arm, and elevating the stunted size to a hero's stature. He was telling it like it wasn't so he wouldn't see how tawdry it had been.

Right?

Wrong.

He pulled down the extra blanket from the top of the closet and tucked it down around the fitful, shrinking body. No, it was right in essence, although a clumsy rendering.

He picked up his shoes and tiptoed off.

2

Annexed to the hospital, the coffee shop was self-abased in the presence of suffering. The waitress took his order in a hushed whisper. Swiveling in his chair and fingerpainting in a spot of moisture on the Formica, he imagined her in the cowl of a nurse in a field hospital at Ypres. A man four seats away knocked a spoon onto the floor and looked up in startled guilt as if suffering shell shock. Cabell took the steaming coffee inside the blind he'd made of the *Times* he had bought at the airport.

He stared at the paranoid, pear-shaped face on the front page. Wedged between two skyscrapers of transcript, eyes were preternaturally bright, incisors long and sharp. It was the devouring face of one grown used to dissembling the extent of his appetite: that was what gave those features strength as metaphor. *Throw that man into a pigpen and he'd get himself elected king of the hogs:* his father had said that. Cabell searched the face until it dissolved in printer's dots. It was impossible to conceive of this country without Nixon.

Focusing again, he began to read. The spectacle of Washington in chaos gave him pleasure. The war had finally come home after all these years, although too late and not by

54

their doing. No credit due. Turning the page, he was ambushed by a Reston column and immediately began arguing against it. *Fulfill our promise now? You must be joking. We fulfilled it already. In Vietnam. No, belief will be a forced thing now, divorced from purpose. We'll always be looking at ourselves out of the corner of our eye, wondering if we're going crazy again. Get down to the business of making this country better now? Bullshit! We'll become a nation of Swedes: above reproach only because of impotence; having too much sex and chocolate; fixated on death. Go back to Scotland and worry that dour country with your optimism!*

He looked up and saw the waitress standing in front of him with a look of disbelief and then realized that he was moving his lips. Shrugging apologetically, he dove deeper down into the paper, skipping the major Watergate take-outs in favor of the smaller stories, the ripples moving outward from the commotion in the pond, each with a little moral of its own.

Charles "Chuck" Colson was holding born-again meetings with congressmen, some on the Impeachment Committee. Alexander Haig was branding as nonsense rumors that the White House had asked certain National Guard units to stand at alert at positions around the capitol during the crisis. Reuters's roundup of response in the Communist world had Tass calling the president's enemies a small but vociferous minority; the New China News Agency indicated oblique support for the administration out of fear that Nixon's decline would signal a new isolationism leaving them to face the Russians alone. *Ah! The comrades.* The quarter tip he left quivering on the counter made a rotund sound that profaned the silence.

He stopped again in the hospital lobby, finding a bank of telephones and sliding into a booth. He gnawed open a new pack of Tums, shuddering at the metallic touch of tinfoil on filling, and bit down on two minty tablets. As the operator connected him with Halcyon, he scrabbled his fingernails on the pebbled walls. He let it ring seven times in accordance with the phone company's recommendation. Then seven more. It was nicely millennarian: the seventh ring would be answered by seven voices enfolding seven hellos.

He put the receiver back into its cradle and sat there limply, hating Charley for making him face all this alone. Outside the booth's accordion doors, he saw a man go by in the jake-legged walk of a recent vasectomy patient. It called up memories stored in the spongy tissue of his own crotch. *No time to squat along the side of the road and push out babies on this long march.* Jill had said it. *As soldiers of the revolution, we must deprive our bodies of procreation to make them sharper weapons in warfare.* At Oakland's Kaiser Hospital, he had watched the film and was counseled by a man whose head shone bald down to the ears, where hair suddenly began and continued in a fringe down to his shoulders. Their contract was sealed with his wink and an elbow in the ribs: "The girls find out you've been taken care of here, they'll really open their legs for you."

An aide had called him into the room. One step past black, purple-black, he flashed a stud in the ear; one front gold tooth had a star cut in the center to showcase white enamel. "Hey man, they done axe you to shave it good," he said, inspecting the honky pubis in disgust. "Now I got to do it again." The black had floated above him, razor in hand, disdainfully measuring his penis like an underripe banana. Then the tooth shone again in gums of mottled pink. "Shit man, you never catch me lettin' no white dude get *me* by the balls with no damn razor in his hands." The doctor came in looking at his watch and giving the big lie: there's no pain afterward. There was a slight snipping as he became a capon for the Left.

It was like his father said. *Death calls the tune, memory does the dance.*

As he passed the nurses' station, the Muzak voice was reminding stragglers for the last time that visiting hours were over. Miss Miles's replacement let him pass unchallenged. He went ahead, slipping along corridors that seemed out of a Resnais film: unending, bleak, an eternity of right angles, still except for the occasional cough of a patient not yet fully doped by the sleeping pills.

His father was on his side, head resting on clasped hands, eyes blinking slowly with the easy calm of a child accepting high fever. Although not seen, Cabell knew he was recognized the instant he went over the threshold, as if he had triggered a photoelectric cell.

"Oh. Cabe. It's you." The vocal chords had been ratcheted up a notch. "I was wondering where you were."

"Just getting some coffee, Pop."

"Good idea. Get ahold of Charley yet?"

"No, there's no answer. Maybe Aggie called her and she's already on her way down."

"Maybe."

"Want me to get the nurse to bring something? You hungry or anything?"

"She was just here. Gave me my fix."

"Oh."

There was a lull. Looking down, he realized his father was trying to fight back. Bodies were durable things, capable of taking punishment, ready to be tortured and not give up. Some part of him said: *Come on, let's get on with it, get it over, die already.* Another part had to fight the urge to begin chattering, singing, praying, reciting snatches of Hamlet—anything to keep the man from giving in.

"Montrose come while I was out?" he asked.

"No."

"That son of a bitch." He needed someone to hate. "That bastard. He's probably out somewhere working on his tax shelters."

"Doctors spend their lives trying to get away from moments like this, Cabe. It reminds them of their limits. They haven't never saved nobody yet."

He plotted vengeance. He would get a can of spray paint and inscribe huge letters on the white stucco of the Montrose

Medical Corporation: JOSEPH HART DIED TODAY. WHERE WERE YOU, MOTHERFUCKER? No, he would get a rock and stand in front of the building right at dawn, savoring the moment, then throw it into the top of the giant bay window of the waiting room and watch it heave and fall like a giant iceberg, winding up in shards of lacy glass on the street.

In his heart he knew he would do nothing. He never did.

"Listen, Cabe, I've got to tell you." His father's eyes were feral, glistening with a look he had seen on faces held incommunicado by acid truths. "I'm not sorry, you know, not sorry about anything. I want you guys to know that, you and Charley. Death is hardest on the ones left. I'm glad I was born American, before the Great War, on the prairie. Does that sound corny?"

"I'm with you, Pop."

"I don't mean patriotism. Screw that. I just mean I wouldn't want to have been another person in another time."

His father was silent a moment and then a hand raised jerkily, as if on a marionette's string. "When you're going, it's easy to think you're the last man. I don't want to be like that, but I look around and it seems to me that things have slid downhill a long ways since I was a boy. It's like somebody came along with a scythe and mowed everything in the world right down, got everything exactly the same height, no difference nowhere. In this kind of world a person could go a whole lifetime without ever having to discover what he was made of. This world needs some kind of renewal."

"Easier said than done. But what . . ." He wanted to steer the conversation so he could find out if "renewal" came from a deathbed return to religion, but his father didn't hear. The words were tumbling out of him, trying to survive, trampling each other to escape the gathering dark.

". . . For a while I had this notion that I had all this knowledge, sixty-seven years' worth, stored up inside me, and wasn't it a shame that I couldn't somehow get it to you kids in a way so you could use it—you know, survival knowledge. It gnawed on me these last few weeks. I've been spending hours at the desk making lists, drawing charts. But when it got down on paper it didn't seem so grand. Then I thought that my world, the world where it applied, was going down. What I knew probably wouldn't help you or Charley or the boy anyway. I cussed myself for a fool and threw the papers and charts away. But what kind of world does Joey get? Oh, Cabe, I could just talk your ear off. But I'm tired." The voice had slowed. "Did I tell you I wanted to be cremated?"

"You told me, Pop." The eyes dared him to deny that it would come to that; they were triumphant when he didn't.

"Okay, then. Did I tell you all the papers are on my desk at home?"

"Papers?"

"Deeds, records, stuff like that."

"No, you didn't tell me."

"They are."

Cabell thought he saw the body relax its hold and drift toward sleep, but last words squeezed out.

"Cabe? Cabe, you there?"

"I'm here, Pop."

"Oh. Good. Listen. I'm worried about you guys. Can't stop this bloody mothering. I'm worried about you most. Charley's had a bad time of it, but I think she's got a steady light. But you, you got to attach yourself someplace."

"I tried, Pop." He said it lightly as if his failure was a joke. "I'm all right."

"No you aren't," the voice was down to a whisper. "I don't mean to make any big last will and testament here. I don't have anything wise to tell you. Just get yourself a purchase someplace. Find something that's got some value so you can feel you're leaving a thumbprint on life somehow."

"You rest now, Pop." He realized that hospital clichés were meant to keep things under control.

"Righto." The whisper faded out.

"Pop?" Cabell was suddenly afraid of being alone.

"Mmmm."

"I have this weird daydream, like a vision. It's that other Cabell Hart, your grandfather. Sometimes I feel he's in the room with me. So real I can almost touch him. It spooks the hell out of me. Also, I dream almost constantly. What do you think it means?"

His father's answer was crushed in grinding teeth.

He sat down in the cold Naugahyde chair and put his coat on front to back, arms through the sleeves like a strait-jacket. Either because he heard his name, or because he was drawn by the smell of death, his great-grandfather was in the room now, somewhere across from him, on the other side of the bed. He tried to exorcise him by pulling out the sports page and reading about the Dodgers' surge. But the lines of print began to jump. He closed his eyes and leaned back.

The problem with their beginning, he thought, *was that it didn't fit the middle and prefigured no appropriate end. How can you live in a world without dramatic unity?*

He could remember the exact moment he had left their continuity, deserting the expectation that they would go through life in touch. He had been walking down from the library after an afternoon spent with Thomas Kyd and other lesser Elizabethans. He had passed students sunning themselves on lawns that seemed to stretch back into the fifties. There was a hallucination of music blowing up from the marching band's rehearsal for football Saturday. There were roving packs of dogs that audited classes with their long-haired mistresses and then came outside to hold disputes over abandoned bag lunches.

He could see himself as he had looked that afternoon—someone once known well, but now a stranger, the prior relationship creating distance instead of bond. The body was middling in height and much thinner then than now. The hair went thickly to one side in such a way as to have led to accusations (until the shots rang out from the book depository or the grassy knoll that previous November) that he tried to look like JFK. But as he now looked at that stranger in his mind's eye, he saw nothing like that Irish craft of one who knew his cravings. The septum was slightly deviated from an accidental fist-ing in a handball match but it didn't create distinction. There was justice in Jill's wounding description of the face later on: vanilla pudding.

Approaching Sproul Plaza, he had seen the jostling there. He paused at the edge, weighed down by books, to watch students swarm like sugar ants over the campus policeman's car. He had asked someone what was happening and found that the campus cops had tried to arrest a Young Socialist for forbidden advocacy and had been surrounded by protesters. Cabell had picketed HUAC and walked in the foggy vigil outside San Quentin on the last night of Caryl Chessman's life. But those acts were less of politics than of sensibility; part of the makeup of the professor-to-be, of a piece with admiring Italian films, Camus, Glenn Gould. He was ready to look long enough to be well informed, then go.

"Mr. Hart!" The fingers that reached out to grab his sleeve as he turned to leave had belonged to a girl named Melanie who had been in his 1A section the previous spring. "Listen, we need you," her voice was frenzied. "The jocks and fraternities are coming down to break up the demonstration. We need observers." That word, *observer*: it conjured fleshy stretcher-bearers and pale Quaker noncombatants. It reminded him that he was a graduate student, though still well under thirty, and he allowed her to pull him into the seething crowd. Once at the center, he stayed there, quickly discovering the narcotic of morality, of being near history and watching the processes that made it. He was still there, in the center of things, making history, when Mario Savio led the occupation of Sproul Hall a few weeks later. He had filed in with the happy few, joining Joan Baez in "We Shall Overcome" as if it were a Kyrie. Twelve hours later, when Alameda County sheriffs had entered the building like hungry crepuscular animals, he'd gone limp according to the wisdom of civil-rights veterans, and was dragged down two flights of stairs toward a makeshift booking station, noting the martyr's rhythm his spinal cord tapped out on the fourteen bumping steps along the way. As the Campanile had receded in the cross-barred windows of the prison bus, a sense of transition passed over him like a shudder.

"We should take it as a kind of failure if we live long enough to become middle-aged cop-outs," Jill later wrote him from Cuba. "We must be in opposition to all things of our criminal upbringing, but most of all to the notion of dead time." After that, his father and sister were living in dead time. He might be involved with the Free Speech Movement or civil rights, and they would sympathize—not because they were committed to the issue, but because they were committed to him. They made it plain that they did not believe in the history that had caught him up: it was a myth that existed outside their sense of time. He was moving and would have moved them if he could; but they were anchored in place. When the war grew hot, he tried to explain: if you're not part of the solution, you're part of the problem. But he couldn't make them understand, and after a while he gave up. Their unit was the landmark by which he came to measure how far he had traveled.

Berkeley was an idea beheld in the eye of the world, and he was now a resident, no longer just a tourist. There was a war going on, and he and Jill were part of the troops. When you stepped into history it was often necessary to forsake friends and family.

Visits home were for struggle. He knew it was absurd for someone his age to still be arguing with his father, but he found a kind of pleasure in it. He was preening his new self in the mirror his father had become. Because of this, they walked around each other, sniffing warily like stiff-legged dogs. His father said it was the wrong war in the wrong place at the wrong time. Cabell said that no war of this imperialism anywhere or anytime could be just. The national interest, after all, was a fraud perpetrated by Standard Oil and the Chase Bank. What was now at issue was the malfeasance of a prior generation, his father's generation, which had let these lies become the policy of the state.

Adept at the movement's jesuitism, he had no trouble in heading his father toward distinctions that would have dangerous consequences, blocking all routes of compromise and escape. With Charley looking on in horror, he got to the point where he could have the man speechless with rage in the space of minutes, have him sawing the air clumsily with his large hands in an attempt to make points for which there were feelings but no words. During these sessions he held part of himself back and watched his father, wondering if this was what it was to grow old: to get bad teeth, become hump-shouldered, and depend on pathetic threadbare myths. After making him seem ridiculous, Cabell was repelled by him.

Stopping in Los Angeles on the way back from Chicago, he had been in an ugly, apocalyptic mood. He had been tear-gassed by Daley's men and his mucous lining felt permanently damaged. Jill had been clubbed in the side of the head and remained in bed with friends in a Detroit commune. His father and sister listened to his stories with understanding; they had seen law and order turn to riot on television and were also appalled by it. But he didn't want it to be easy for them. At the dinner table he steered the talk toward the coming election, announcing casually that he hoped Nixon would win.

"You're fooling." His father looked up from the barbecued steak, taking the bait fatalistically. "Come on, Cabe."

"No, I mean it. Humphrey's been pimping for the war for four years now. He's tainted by it."

"Tainted! Elections have to do with politics, not theology. Anyway, what the hell do you think Nixon is? Talk about taint. Ever hear of the fifties, McCarthyism and all that? You ask Aggie who's tainted."

"Aggie? Oh, I'm sure she's for Humphrey too. All the tired old Reds are precinct workers for the Democrats now. That's what *that* scene came to. They've got such a deep desire to be legitimate that they keep forgetting things like the fact it was Humphrey who introduced a bill to outlaw their goddamned party! The liberals set up the witch-hunts then just like they've set up the war now. Humphrey's been sucking up to the vital-center gang since it began. Ask Aggie to think back to 1948 when she was out there collecting rotten eggs and ripe tomatoes for Henry Wallace. Humphrey wasn't taking second place to any Red-baiter then."

"Look, let's be reasonable." His father had pushed the half-eaten steak away in reluctant admission that the dinner was over. "Humphrey's got pressures on him to end the war. I'm talking in terms of his constituency. Nixon's got pressures to keep it going. If you're as political as you say you are, you'd be asking who's going to get this awful thing over with rather than worrying about taint and all that stuff."

"The lesser-of-two-evils business sucks, Pop. You still wind up supporting evil. Your generation gets self-righteous about voting every four years like it really makes a difference. You've been doing it since the New Deal, and look where it's gotten us. The ballot box is a bourgeois device used to discredit the people and sap their will to struggle."

"If you'd been alive during the Depression you'd know it made a hell of a big difference how an election came out. And let me tell you if it's a choice between getting controlled by the ballot box or the KGB, I know which one I'll take."

"We need to break clear of politics-as-usual. We need to dismantle the system so that something like this war never happens again." He had taken a perverse pleasure in the way both of them were deferring their respective orthodoxies.

"And how do we do that?" The look on his father's face was pathetic. "What new system do we put in its place? You seem to think there's such a thing as a pure choice in this life. But there isn't. That's the whole idea of choosing something— not to feel good, but to get something done. Sometimes you've got to make the best of a bad thing."

They were like two semideaf men dinning impotently in each other's ears. Cabell had felt the need to drive things to their logical end. "Well, I know you want to prolong the life of this corrupt government as long as possible, but I've gotten fond of Nixon. We should have our fascism up front instead of behind the liberal façade. We should get accustomed to seeing

64

the system for what it is. No more Band-Aids for cancer. Maximize the contradictions and move on to the next stage."

"Nixon brings the revolution, is that it?"

"He'll help."

"You're sadly mistaken if you think things work that way. Even if they did, what about the poor, the blind, the lame, the Negroes, and other groups? What happens to them if you help get this snake elected?"

"They're on the bottom. But they'd be there in any case. They stay at the bottom no matter who's in the White House. They're the waste product of capitalism. For them to rise, the system has to be destroyed, leveled; we've got to start all over again."

"Maybe the people on the bottom don't share your distaste for gradual change and betterment. Did you ever consider that? It might not seem like anything much to you, but a little more money in their jeans makes a difference to them. A little less makes a whole lot of difference."

"I don't think you care about them all that much. Anyway, you can't make an omelette without breaking eggs."

His last stony solipsism succeeded in its intent—to bring on to his father's face the befuddled look of someone who doesn't understand the seismic change that has altered a once-familiar landscape. Charley, silent for most of the discussion, stood up and shook her head in small negative jerks. The buttermilk skin was flushed at the cheeks. "Why do you even bother talking to him, Pop? Can't you see that he just wants to fight?"

They could not believe that it was really him. He knew they blamed Jill for what he had become. He insisted on bringing her home with him on the visits, rubbing their noses in her. His father was gracious, courtly, never realizing that she hated such demeanor. Charley didn't conceal her feelings. The two women were natural antagonists, even in appearance. His sister had the looks of an Irish farm girl, long and thewy, milkmaid skin, red-haired, still freckled. Next to her Jill seemed even darker and more veiled than usual, her small body a container for compressed violence. Their subliminal war was endless. Jill would light a cigarette and Charley would walk over to open the nearest window. Charley would suggest a movie, and Jill would note that the director had named names during the McCarthy period.

Sometimes he saw his sister make a special effort, a desperate gamble to make a breakthrough with her antagonist to win him back, a demonstration that she would accept even such a one as Jill rather than lose him. One evening he watched her assent to a discussion of feminism with Jill as a sign of her good faith. Drawing up her knees on the couch and allowing the shields to fall from her personality, she talked frankly of growing up without a mother, of wanting to do things to win status in a man's world but not wanting to lose her identity as a female in the process. Her vulnerability alarmed him. He wanted to cry out: "Watch it! She'll get you!" Drawing her out, Jill had begun to elevate her consciousness, working on her as if she were a cadre in a political-education session. Charley tried to keep to theoretical ground, but Jill bored in, using the particulars against her. When she referred to the tyranny of fathers, using their relentless sexual and psychological possessiveness as an example, the meaning was clear.

"Look Jill," his sister's cheeks were red, as if she had just finished running several laps. "Your father may be all the things you say, but mine's not. Get it? He's not. You can wallow in all this rotten Sylvia Plath stuff if you want, but leave me out of it. Some daddies are sons of bitches, some are decent men. Mine is in the second category. He gave me and Cabell a piece of his life, which is more than any of you radical fakers ever did for anybody." She had wheeled in the doorway on her way out of the room. "Another thing: don't ever patronize me again, you bitch. You may know more about Marx and Engels, but you don't know shit about human beings."

That night they slept as usual in his old bedroom, an out-of-wedlock arrangement he knew grated on his father. Jill provoked him to sex and began to keen prematurely in arpeggios of orgasm meant to carry through the thin walls to Charley's bedroom. After he was spent she bent down and sucked on him with noisy distaste, as if trying to draw snake venom out of a wound. Failing to arouse him, she went into the bathroom and returned with a plastic cylinder of shampoo.

"Here." She lay back and spread her legs. "Put this in me." It was dark, but he could almost see the adamantine eyes daring him not to pleasure her.

On the morning of Christmas Eve, 1968, they drove down to Los Angeles after cashing in the single air ticket his father had sent as a peace offering. All the way down Jill had talked about his ties to his family in a way he realized even at the time was meant to prepare him for the Götterdämmerung. They arrived and found Charley's boyfriend at the house. Marshall Johnson, at five-eight, was Charley's height, but broad and muscular. Although twenty-five, he had just graduated from UCLA after summer session, having dropped out once years earlier to return to Nebraska to help run the family farm because of his father's illness. Charley had been his teaching assistant in a biology lab.

The four of them stood in the center of the living room sipping cream sherry and eating from the card table of appetizers. His father bustled in the kitchen, happy that things seemed finally to be working out. Cabell noticed that Johnson avoided any topic leading toward the war with the insistence of one who had been briefed. When Charley went into the kitchen to help with the turkey, he moved to smoke him out, glancing periodically at Jill's fierce eyes to check for approval. He established that Johnson had taken a scholastic deferment on the off-chance that the war would be over by the time he graduated. But he had recently gotten an induction notice for January.

"Are you going to go?"

"Into the army?" The stall was desperate.

"To Vietnam."

"I may have no choice."

"You always have a choice."

67

"If they put me there, I'll go, but not in combat."

"You're shitting me!" He saw Charley out of the corner of his eye, frozen against the doorjamb with a ghastly look on her face.

"There isn't any alternative."

"You could go to jail, or you could get out of the country." He didn't try to make either avenue sound very attractive.

"Those aren't alternatives for me." Johnson's voice was barely audible.

"This stuff about not doing combat is a cop-out. If you're in the army you're waging war. What it comes down to is that you're going over there to help waste a bunch of people you've never seen for reasons you don't understand. Terrific. To my way of thinking that makes you a murderer and a dumb asshole to boot."

Charley moved between them with the cold fury he remembered from when they were younger. For a moment she seemed ready to hit him. Then tears splashed down her cheeks and her voice was filled with mucous. "What are you trying to do to us, Cabell? Don't you know that people have to *live*? You just love this fucking war!"

She took Johnson's arm and slammed out the front door. His father had come in the room to watch the scene end and now downed the sherry as if it were a shotglass of whiskey. For a moment he stared at the floor, reminding Cabell of the ominous silences that had preceded childhood punishments. At that moment the thought occurred to him that much of their energy, too much, was directed toward establishing their moral superiority over their elders, that they were a little crazy on that issue. *Kill your parents!* He saw Jill taking it all in from her seat in the corner, her head weaving slightly like a mongoose.

"That's a good question Charley asked," his father was stern. "Just what *are* you trying to do? Maybe you don't know. Maybe you've got us all mixed up with the people in the Pentagon. We're not dropping bombs. We're cannon fodder too." Fingers seized his bicep. "One thing, though. This is *my* house. I'll take almost anything from you, but not this god-damned calculating meanness, not to your own flesh and blood. I think it would be better if you and Jill stayed in Berkeley until you decide whether or not you like us."

That night they were on the way back north in her old Chevy station wagon. The road was deserted, the sky above black velvet. He was driving, and when they reached the top of the Grapevine he had looked over at Jill, watching the chin slowly descend to the neck, snap up suddenly, then sink again. He was mired in dark thoughts, wondering about the rough beast slouching toward Bethlehem. He gave a silent explanation of his sadness to the sleeping form: *We were not your normal two-and-a-quarter-child nuclear family; we were different; it was do or die for us.*

She didn't wake until they began dropping down from the Pleasanton Mountains onto the Nimitz Freeway. Then she was cheerful, glad *it* had finally happened. He was too old to still be under their thumb, she said. "The family is the beginning of it all, Cabell—racism, sexism, capitalism. On the one hand, the family is the root of the state; on the other hand, it is the root of all our neurotic bourgeois hang-ups. What you're feeling is birth pains. Your family is here." Her sweeping gesture included herself, the revolutionary commune of Berkeley, cadres plotting in small groups everywhere.

Five months later he got one of the terse notes that would be his only remaining communication with his sister:

> Marsh killed yesterday in Hue. He was working as a corpsman. Another Yankee aggressor down. Thought you'd want to know.

The words had deadly intent; he could see that. But who wasn't dying? In a vortex now, being drawn deeper down to some powerful core each day, feeling himself being separated from parts of himself he once thought were intrinsic, he had no time for such games. He and Jill were apocalypticians, stirring the dark entrails of the press for chips of bone, bright blood, dried screams; sifting auguries to divine the approaching breakdown. Household concerns would have to wait.

After that, news came as if through gauze. There were cards on birthdays and Christmases, sentimentalities he had to show to his comrades in the spirit of self-criticism. Hasty notes appended at the bottom told him the bare essentials. Charley was pregnant, by whom it wasn't said. After having the baby she lived at home, then stayed with Aggie for a time. The boy was named Joseph and had a congenital defect of the foot that caused them worry. Charley was sewing costumes for members of a rock band and occasionally traveling with them, leaving the child with their father to take care of, a task he had apparently gratefully accepted during these hard times.

Cabell didn't write back. What news could he give about *his* family? Well, Fred Hampton died of lead poisoning in his apartment the other day. As you may have heard, Eldridge is off on an extended trip to Algeria. James Rector had a terrible accident at People's Park and got a face filled with buckshot. Bobby Seale has to go to court. Jerry Rubin acts sillier every day.

Late in 1971, Charley appeared on the doorstep of Mad Dog. Buddy Wald called up to his room, "Cabell, your *sister's* here," as if it were amusing to have blood relatives. Her hair was frizzed into a permanent that stood up like red topiary; the white face was thin from unnecessary weight loss and looked like a waif's. She was holding hands with a tall man whose dark hair fell down onto the red and yellow of his Sergeant Pepper tunic. A Fu Manchu mustache bordered his smiling mouth, and he smelled like he had marinated his clothes in incense. Cabell noticed that they wore matching roach clips around their necks. He felt a vast disappointment and realized that he had counted on somebody somewhere—his father and sister had seemed most likely—to hold out against the history that was whirling the rest of them in its centrifuge.

"Hi, what are you doing here?" he brushed her cheek,

noting that the breasts were ripe and untrammeled beneath the sheer 1940s dress.

"Just passing through. This is Chick. He's the drummer with Dragon's Teeth. Heard them?"

"Can't say that I have." Cabell offered to shake hands. The drummer rearranged his fingers into a black-power grip.

"They're far out. A groove. I've been doing some costume design for them. Got a chance to go with them on a gig up to Portland and thought I'd stop by."

"Glad you did. Your kid with you?"

"No, Pop's got him. You should see them together. They go to ball games and chatter away like magpies. Joey calls Pop "Papa Two." It's his own pun, you know: Papa and grandpapa both. He's a cute little guy. I really miss him."

"I bet." The words sounded more heavily freighted with sarcasm than he intended. He looked down at his feet and rummaged his mind for something else to say. "So things are going good with you?"

She nodded. She began talking loudly and off-key, looking at the floor, at the walls, anywhere but at him. Twisting the kinks in her hair nervously, she spoke in rushed sentences filled with descriptions of pigs hassling them, breaking down doors, and busting their action. The lingo didn't fit her, and when she saw that Cabell had made that judgment she began to talk even more rapidly, trying to prove that they had something in common. By the time Jill had come downstairs to join them, she was in tears. "Sorry Cabe." She held tight to the smiling drummer's arm and backed him out the door. "It was dumb of me to come. I thought we could talk. I've got to get over these crazy hang-ups and lighten up. I don't know what I was thinking."

Walking them to their van, Cabell was passive, tongue-tied, unable to offer consolation. Jill draped herself on him in a mime of possession and gnawed at his ear. Her unflinching eyes watched them pull off and then she turned and walked back inside. "No shit!" There was triumph in her voice. "Charley's turned into a freak. Who ever would have thought?"

Eventually history had released its grip, discarding him and others, making them refugees of war, people who had fought for nearly a decade and lost more than they had won. His friend Jim Henry was dead, and Jill had whirled on without him, descending like a figure from myth into the terrorist underground. History, their history, was frothing at the mouth. Now he was working in a hardware store and spending as much time as he could washing his clothes, cleaning his apartment, and shopping and cooking—simple acts he hoped would orient him to life again and teach him how to exist. He sometimes thought that he would build a bridge backward and recover what had been. But the project seemed too ambitious. The rupture wasn't due only to his eccentricity. Their whole world had conspired in it. He knew it would take some extraordinary act to reestablish things. He didn't think himself up to it.

For a while he showed up compulsively at the Med and other Berkeley hangouts, hoping for someone who still believed enough in what they had been and done to provide an argument. But his fixation with cannibals and narcissists were tales nobody wanted to hear. He occupied himself by walking through Berkeley's war-torn streets, looking for some village drama, some piece of construction or demolition to occupy his mind, little children to talk to. He tabulated rainfall, keeping an accurate tally of what they got compared with season's normal. He waited for a sign.

It came on February 3, 1973 (another of those memorable dates)—an airmail letter from the northern California town of Halcyon, penciled notations indicating that anonymous handwriting had forwarded it from his previous address. He tore it open and read:

Dear Cabe.

Bad news. Pop is going into the hospital next Wednesday. It's cancer. Thought you'd want to know.

Love, Charley

Within seconds he was on the phone making an airplane reservation. Cancer: the sort of antagonist he'd been waiting for, the indisputable evil his life had lacked after the war-weary revolution had careened off into craziness and self-destruction, becoming locked in dreadful symbiosis with what it sought to change. His father was offering to save him yet again.

Joseph Hart's idea was that no carcinoma should have its growth fertilized by anxiety. He studiously ignored it, which Cabell found amazing, for his own reaction to even the vaguest symptom of erratic cell behavior was to give in, pronounce himself dead, surround the body with concern as if to immunize himself with fatalism. He had to piece together his father's medical history by himself. The cancerous mole—how could he help but see it as a vicious mole of nature?—had appeared in late fall, glimpsed accidentally in the mirror while toweling after a shower. The bizarre pigment was different each day from what it had been the day before, although in indefinable ways: darkened, perhaps enlarged, tingling with a manic energy all its own. His father had kept an eye on it, quizzical rather than afraid, possessed by the wonder of it, yet skeptical that it should gain dominion over him. A man who had scorned illness, grimly battled flus and colds to stalemate, he set his will against this thing that was of him, but not his.

Still it grew, crawling over the flesh like a poisonous hard-shelled insect, in an adult and larval stage at once, inexorably moving over the obstacles volition placed before it. On the day of the long-postponed examination, Ben White had inspected the area quickly, then took him to the window light and looked it over with a jeweler's glass, poking the thing angrily with an index finger as if to squash it. He cut it off and then stopped by the house with the results of the biopsy later in the day.

"I'm going to tell you the truth, Joe." His father repeated the speech verbatim to him later on because he thought it showed the quality of the man who'd been the family doctor for more than thirty years and brought both children into the world. "It's not something we doctors do very well or very often. But we're both old-timers and it's too late in the day to fool around with bedside manners now. Here it is: you're in great shape for a sixty-six-year-old man, as good as I've seen. You've got the heart and lungs of somebody fifteen or twenty years younger. You're going to need them because somebody —and you can bet your ass it won't be me—is going to cut on you, probably put chemicals into you, and shoot you with radiation. And in the long run, which probably won't be that long, it's not going to do any good. It's multiple melanoma and my guess is that it's in the lymph. It's the big leagues." Before Doctor Ben (as the three of them had always called him) left the house, he and Joseph Hart had hugged and cried.

Cabell was there for the operation, arriving within hours after getting his sister's note. His father required no explanation of his presence, although it was clear that their lost decade had changed each of them in ways that the other could never know.

The surgeon had dug down into the flesh where the mole had been and strip-mined four inches toward the side, uncovering such a rich lode of malignancy that he made an incision below the right arm, peeling out the nodes for delivery to the pathologist, who confirmed Doctor Ben's diagnosis.

Wheeled out on the gurney, his face gray and inert, his father was sucked and siphoned by tubes. Cabell walked alongside him and then went back to get the word.

"You just can't tell." A thin spray of blood seemed to have been squirt-gunned over the surgeon's green gown. "You can't even predict. Officially, melanoma has a twelve percent five-year recovery rate. But all those statistics are a lot of crap. Five percent is more like it. The question is how far it's metastasized. It might never show up again. It might sprout up all over his body in a few weeks. You'll just have to wait."

He haunted the library for copies of the *Journal of American Medical Society, Lancet, The New England Journal of Medicine*, and other periodicals the way he had once consumed the works of Bernard Fall, Burchette, Lacouture. Posing as a stringer for *Time*, he called leading Bay Area oncologists for interviews on experimental techniques and treatment centers. He poured his thwarted politics into the enterprise. Despite the billions of dollars and wide-eyed gullibility of *U.S. News & World Report* and other magazines regarding cancer society press releases, the five-year survival rate was about the same as it had been twenty years earlier. Society's technology was producing cancer at as fast a rate as its technology could cure it. The best that could be hoped for would be a continuation of this standoff on into a carcinogenic future: cancer and anticancer locked in a constantly escalating medical cold war. It was a disease of capitalism that successive administrations had covered up; a medical My Lai and Kennedy assassination all in one.

He called Charley in a high state of excitement to relay his findings.

"Poor Cabe," she said after listening to him for half an hour over the squawking connection. "You're like a squid. Always shooting your ink over anything that comes too close. Just covering it up with your essence and then getting away in the confusion. Where have you *been*? Don't you know that every time you turn on TV you see somebody dying of *cancer*? Every time you pick up a novel a character's got *it*. You think you're the first to discover that it's a symbol for our time? Anyway, who cares? I want to know what's in it for Pop. Are you going to overwhelm him with this jiveass attention now, the way you've been overwhelming him with indifference?"

"I don't expect you to understand my motives." He was annoyed that the self-pity and sisterly submission had disappeared since he last saw her.

"What are they?"

"To save his life if I can." He sounded like one of George Eliot's prissy vicars.

"Save yourself, Cabe," she said. "Get yourself a task you can handle."

"Is that what you're doing, then, surviving?"

"Sort of, but not in the way you mean."

"Like you say, what's in it for Pop?"

"Possibly nothing. But there's something in it for me, and maybe he's come to a point in his life where it's important to him to know that we'll manage to outlast him; that things will go on regardless of what happens to him."

"That's sort of the Woodstock approach to cancer therapy, I guess." He sneered into the phone.

There was silence and then she spoke again. He could hear weariness in her voice. "You're on some kind of weird trip, Cabe. You're getting off on this in a sick way. You're like one of those poets of the graveyard school."

"I get off on cancer, you get off on stoned-out drummers. Different strokes."

The conversation died. He hung up without bothering to patch things up. He was glad she was in Halcyon and hoped she'd stay there. He now had a routine and didn't want it interfered with. Every Friday afternoon, he went directly from the hardware store to the Oakland Greyhound station, arriving in Los Angeles by six the next morning and making it to the house in time for an early breakfast. Over coffee, the two of them planned the weekend. The doctor had said that exercise was important to reestablish the strength of the severed muscles on the back and side and to fight atrophy, so Cabell appointed himself trainer and playmate. He located a deserted basketball court in a nearby park and made the game a part of each Saturday.

They had played when he was a teenager. In those days he had been a hot-rod, trying to impress his father with his shooting eye and embarrass the old-fashioned two-handed set shot by long, looping jumpers and crisp hooks banked in with either hand. But he had never been as steady and even then lacked the claim his father's hands had on the ball, sending it up from the chest in a low trajectory that mentally avoided the phantom ceilings, light fixtures, and water pipes that had been part of the gymnasium impedimenta from his days barnstorming through South Dakota as a semipro. His own shots often tipped or bumped their way in: garbage. His father's had always slipped in just over the lip of the rim, cutting through the net with a smooth ripping sound.

Now Cabell stood under the basket, thirty-two years old, his career as a superstar ended. His job was to rebound and pass the ball back out, steady and dependable, the Wesley Unseld type of player sportswriters called "unselfish." He urged his father to shoot from different positions outside the peeling playground white that marked the key, to astound him with his prowess. Watching the old touch return, seeing muscles that at first could not boost the ball ten feet become precise at twenty-five, he had felt an almost paternal pride.

The legs were an old man's: his run was lock-kneed and shuffling. But his father's hands were still young and fully cooperative with the eye. The pleasure on his face at the *achieve-of*—the mastery of the physics that made the ball obey the will—was something Cabell had seen on the faces of the great black players. When people stared at the surprising sight they made—a young man throwing out passes between his legs and behind his back to the thin old fellow with rusty hair and pale skin who shot so well—he almost heard the strains of "Sweet Georgia Brown" and boogied in his mind.

One Saturday two high-school kids, one white and the other black, appeared at the far end of the court. They stood bouncing their ball desultorily and chewing gum, making slow-motion moves toward their basket. Cabell had studied them a moment and then hollered out: "You guys want to play a little game of two-on-two?"

"You nuts?" His father tried to restrain him. "Come on, Cabe, this is the geriatric league. We don't *run* here."

Ignoring him, Cabell vaunted to coax them into it. "Don't worry. We'll take it easy on you." They shuffled down smirking at each other as he set the rules. "Play half-court. Twenty-four's game. Winner's outs. Clear it past the free-throw line on defensive rebounds. Okay?"

The teenagers brought the ball in, moving with the assurance of good high-school players. The white moved under the basket and Cabell picked him up, hoping that he could muscle the growing body. More compact, the black moved outside, dribbling back and forth to get a rhythm for the game, then coming in on a give and go, taking the ball, double-pumping to avoid Cabell's desperate lunge, and laying it in.

He switched from one to the other, letting his father rove awkwardly, doing all the hard work himself, stopping their drives with hand and hip checks, often hacking at their forearms. Sweat poured off him and he sucked air like an asthmatic. His father did not strain to keep up and often patted the boys on the back and complimented them on their shots.

He magnified the game into a metaphor: goodness against the heavy certainty of odds; heart against machine; a wager with the gods. The score was 16–0 when the white kid hot-dogged a left-handed hook that spun off the rim into Cabell's hands. He shoveled it out to his father and yelled for him to shoot. He prepared to crash for the rebound, but the two-handed set lasered through. He grabbed the ball, inbounded it, and moved under the basket, again calling for the shot.

The teenagers decided to increase their glory by letting them make the score close. Sagging on defense, they had fallen behind, 20–16, when the black said, "All right, man, time to get it together. You stay on this guy. I'll get the old dude."

Cabell's heart was pounding wildly at the nearness of victory. Taking a pass from his father, he dribbled toward the basket, using his bulk to post the white kid, backing in inch by inch, spinning up and clearing him out with a hard elbow in one gesture, and then banking the ball in.

"Hey man, that's an offensive foul," the kid whined.

"Bullshit," Cabell said over his shoulder. "You never established position. It's twenty-two–sixteen, next basket wins."

Cabell managed to get the ball in, then ran forward and set a hard-moving pick on the black that momentarily freed his father for the shot. He knew from the way the ball went up that his father had tried to miss to punish him for his aggression. It hit the backboard first, then the front of the rim, which sent it up high, down onto the rim again. Cabell rose high in the air using the white kid's shoulder for balance, and tapped the ball in.

"All right!" he yelled, jumping up and down. He forced his father to slap palms as the kids stalked off and then hugged him. "We're winning, Pop, we're winning."

They looked forward to their weekends like a pair of aging bachelors whose only obligation was self-indulgence. Cabell was always keyed up after a week spent painstakingly choreographing the time they'd have together. After basketball they came home and showered, then went to lapidary exhibits, car and boat shows, garage sales. In the afternoon they went to the market and brought home loads of fresh produce and lean meats. Cabell cooked hearty meals bracketed with wine and dessert. They lingered over fresh-ground Costa Rican coffee, then built a fire and turned on the late-night television that called up the schlock they had enjoyed years earlier when they were a sitcom family: Sherlock Holmes movies, Creature Features, and when they were lucky, a western.

He watched for signs that his father was gaining weight, and gloried in the fact that he looked pink and healthy. He allowed himself to believe that the man's basic goodness, his lack of connection with the corrupt world of events, would pardon him. The restoration of moral order came to depend on it. Impure himself, he would nonetheless gain an absolution by helping in the miracle of the cure. As he watched his father get stronger, an almost fearful euphoria overtook him.

One Sunday evening early in May, as Cabell was ready to catch the bus back to Oakland, his father walked out the door with him. They usually stood for a few minutes like this at the end of the weekend, his father trumpeting small farts of contentment and scuffing the sidewalk with his house slippers, Cabell beginning to decompress. They talked of weather, or some upcoming feature of *The Wide World of Sports*. But this time his father had stalled, as if waiting for the right time to say something. Cabell was suddenly afraid that he would hear the announcement of some new symptom; his reconstructed world tilted from seismic doubt.

"You know, Cabe," his father said, "I've been thinking about taking a little vacation back to South Dakota."

"South Dakota? How come?"

"It's been over forty years, you know."

"I know. But I thought you'd cut all your ties."

"Well, I have. I mean, I'm sure that all the people I knew are probably gone. But I'm not going back for people. Can't really explain it. It's just an urge. An old elephant trekking on back to the burial grounds, maybe."

"Cut it out, Pop." He didn't like the gallows humor. "There's nothing weird about it. It's a good idea. It makes sense as a vacation even if there's nothing more to it than that. Listen, I could go with you. I've wanted to go back to the family stomping grounds. I used to talk a lot to Aggie about it."

He saw himself climbing all over the idea, inflating it, appropriating it as his own. "Listen, Pop. It would be good to get away. We could take our time and get in some side trips. No hurry. We could just mosey along. I'll get some maps and stuff this week and bring them down next Friday. We can start drawing up a master plan."

They established a route and made lists of things to get at the sporting-goods and war-surplus stores. They worked over the old Ford pickup, buying new tires and a camper unit for the bed. Cabell found a used 8-track and some earphones to shut out the engine's heavy drone. By mid-June, he was in a state of high excitement, feeling that the trip might become an apotheosis, some breakthrough for them both. His father brought up the question of Charley.

"I think we should ask her to come. I know you two are still on the outs. I think it's a goddamned shame and you ought to do something about it, but that's not why I want her with us. You guys can patch things up on your own time. I just feel that she should be in on this. It's a sort of family affair, the way I've got it visualized."

The idea of his sister coming between them, watching him and considering his motives, appalled him. He wanted his father to himself; he wanted full credit for the miracle under way. "I don't know, Pop. If she came, then the kid would have to come. It would get awfully crowded, don't you think?"

"Crowded." His father's look x-rayed him. "I hadn't really thought of that. Maybe you're right. Maybe there's not enough room."

"They'll be other trips, Pop." He didn't bother to try to exculpate himself.

"I suppose."

They left the first week in July, lazing along like easy riders. At Bend, Oregon, they detoured into the Three Sisters area and camped for three days in a huge forest of jack pines. As they walked through the turpentine scent, Cabell realized that his father's microscopic eye always searched the ground and saw things that he himself did not. Kicking around in the dirt the first afternoon they were there, he found a three-inch flat black stone with a small canal running down the center. "I'll be goddamned." He held it up triumphantly. "Know what this is? An arrow shaper. I'm almost sure of it. I found one once when I was a kid. The Indians used to put the arrows in this groove here right before they feathered them. They used it to work the shaft down so that it was straight and true."

In Pocatello, they saw a handbill and stopped for a day and a half to dig potatoes and made twenty-one dollars. Outside of Billings, they detoured up into the Big Horn Mountains, climbing up so high that they both got dizzy. His father pulled the truck over onto the side of the deserted road they were on.

"What's the trouble?" Cabell looked up from the maga-
zine he'd been reading.

"Just watch over there." His father pointed over to a
sloping hill just below the tree line.

They waited, the only sound around them the noise that
the wind made tunneling through the truck's cab. Then a line
of fowl came out of the trees and began walking in single file.
They were large-bottomed with skinny legs, parodies of a
chorus line. "Wild turkeys," his father whispered. Soon after, a
spot of beige detached itself from the trees, and then others, as
a buck antelope and two does cautiously picked their way
down to an outcropping of grass and began grazing. "Stay
here long enough and you'd see Noah's Ark," his father said.

After they had started up he brought up the subject of
Charley again, talking into the windshield and driving with
both hands.

"I don't want to intrude on her privacy, or tell tales out
of school, but I think you should know that it hasn't been easy
for her."

"So? Who has it been easy for?"

"Well it was especially hard on her," his father ignored
the brittle edge of Cabell's words. "She wasn't prepared for
things to fall out the way they did. The news about Marsh just
flattened her, of course. I think she went a little crazy.
Pretty soon she was going with anything that wore pants, and
not getting any joy out of it either. I saw it, I just couldn't do
much about it. It was like she was trying to get herself knocked
up so there'd be something solid in her life. After she finally did
manage to kill the rabbit, I asked her who the father was.
Typical old-fashioned parent's question. She got big fat tears
in her eyes and said, 'Pop, I just don't know.' I guess it didn't
matter. But then she got panicked. She realized what she'd got
herself into, and worried that she couldn't cope. She hung on
for a while and then went to Aggie—I found all this out later on
—and tried to get her to help her get an abortion. Aggie said
no dice, thank God, and pointed out that that thing in there
wasn't no wart or tumor, but at five months would come out

moving and bleeding and ready to breathe. She reconciled herself, and Doctor Ben got her through the birth pretty good. Afterward she picked up where she'd left off. She was out running around a lot during Joey's first couple years. I took care of him a lot. I was his nanny."

"Charley just handed him over to you?"

"Oh, sort of. But it was mainly my doing. I felt sorry for the little guy. He was so skinny and serious. I kept thinking to myself, This kid has been dealt a shit hand. I wanted to try to make it decent for him. He always seemed sickly, like he was trying to figure out if it was worth living. Damn kid had the worst colic of any infant ever born. The only thing that would calm him was going out for a ride in the truck. So there I was every morning at three A.M., driving the empty streets, barely able to keep my eyes open, him cooing in the seat beside me."

"Sounds like a drag." Cabell was suddenly jealous of the child.

"Don't you believe it. He gave me a second wind. I'd take him in a store and people would look at us. Both got this red hair, you know. And I could see them thinking, Now has that old guy fathered that little child? It was good for my ego. He became my sidekick. I took him to work with me. We used to go to the Dodger games. We'd get there early so he could watch the pitchers warm up. It fascinated him the way you'd see the ball hit the mitt and then hear the *thock* a split second later. Don Sutton finished warming up and threw us a ball once. Right to us. We had good times. I went so far as to go down to the Welfare Department to see if I could adopt him. That way he'd at least get my Social Security when I was gone. They found out I was sixty-five and a widower and damn near laughed me out of the office."

"I'm surprised that Charley freaked out." He tried to shift to a sibling rival he could defeat.

"Oh, she was into that music-and-dope scene and in with some desperate characters."

"What do you mean?" He could tell there was a reluctance to go into details.

"Oh, I don't know if I should stir that pot. The thing was that she got in over her head. I know you radicals thought you were liberating everybody and creating utopia and all, and believe it or not I was with you on a lot of issues. But one of the things that happened was that you turned some animals loose and told them it was okay to go on out there and start feeding. I didn't realize that until Charley started getting mixed up with some of the weirdos. Jesus, some of them gave me the willies. Some were just hyped-up zombies. But there were some big eaters too. One of the ones she got involved with was a Hawaiian drug dealer who was making big money running marijuana over here from growing grounds on the outer islands. Named Manoa. She got mixed up with him. One night she came home all beat up. It looked like she'd been in the ring: one eye shut, the other cut, mouth puffed up, nose busted. This nut had gotten upset at something she said and knocked her around until he got worn out, then picked up a wrench and laid it hard across the bridge of her nose. I got Aggie over to the house to take care of her and the kid, and went looking for him. I guess I'd be dead or doing life in prison if he hadn't been gone. I was mad."

"She sounded pretty together the last time I talked to her." Cabell was looking out the window, wondering where he had been when this happened.

"Yeah, I think you're right. I've got a good feeling about her now. It happened more or less overnight. I think the kid had a lot to do with it. When he started toddling it was clear that there was a problem with his foot. I took him to Ben and he said that the muscles were messed up and that he'd have to get some reconstructive surgery when he got a little older. When Charley found out, it really hit her. I thought, *Oh, Lord, more guilt to wallow in*. But it was just the opposite. I think she finally got the idea of what a miracle it was that the kid *existed*. I mean he was an inch away from being a blood clot in some doctor's stainless-steel sink. Sounds corny, but I think that she saw providence in that foot. Something like that. Anyway, she started taking charge of Joey and herself from then on. After a while she moved over to live with Aggie and got real independent from me. Then she went on up to Halcyon. I missed them like the dickens, especially the boy, but I was also sort of glad she was getting out from under my thumb. So that's it. I'm telling you this to fill you in, so you won't be so hard on her. I don't know what all's gone on with you these past few years. But I know for dead sure that she's gone through some times of the purest hell possible."

Cabell knew that there was an opportunity for him to accept some responsibility in this. Not that he had caused it, but that he might have helped mitigate it. He said, "What tangled webs we weave," and let it go at that.

They stopped at the Crow reservation and paced out the Custer battlefield. His father had it all in his mind from reading he had done. He pointed out where the warriors of Gall and Crazy Horse had whipped their ponies into a second wind and then risen up from the encampment; where Benteen's supply team was balked; where Reno was turned around with heavy losses. The wind was licking at the buffalo grass as they followed the trail of graves marking the troopers' chaotic, unbelieving flight, and saw the little cluster on the knoll where they were finally smothered.

"Some friends of my dad's knew Custer's brother," his father said. "According to stories they told, this whole goddamned massacre happened because Custer wanted to get real famous and run for president. Can you believe it? That jackal: he was the MacArthur of his day."

In Wyoming it was hot and dusty. Outside Sheridan, they saw a little place called the Dew Drop Inn and stopped for a beer. It was dark and humid inside. A rotating fan behind the counter made a feeble attempt to get air currents started. A bartender with a chaw of tobacco in one cheek served them two mugs of draft with listless heads that looked like styrofoam, then went back to work on a crossword puzzle. The Ray Coniff Singers were doing " 'S Wonderful" on the jukebox.

"Look at that." His father nudged him with an elbow, and Cabell followed his gaze up to the mirror. He saw three men in a horseshoe-shaped booth behind them, all wearing cowboy shirts and jeans and boots. They had a young woman sandwiched between them, and were pawing her and giggling. She was wispy blond, and her eyeliner had melted in vertical streaks like clown's makeup. She was trying to fend them off, half laughing and half crying like a painfully tickled child, but could only deal with two of the octopus hands at one time. One of the men was pinching her nipples, another trying to get his hand into the crevice that opened below the hem of her mini-skirt when she struggled. The third was force-feeding her beer with one hand and holding her head by the hair with the other. The beer spilled down over her chin and onto her blouse. She coughed and sputtered.

The man on the outside slid out of the leatherette seat and came up beside Cabell to order another schooner of beer. He was chunky and had the look of someone who weighed considerably more than it seemed at first glance. Having noticed Cabell watching them, he said out of the corner of the mouth, "That Judy, she's a pig for it. Can't get enough."

Cabell shrugged and smiled a smile that could be interpreted as disapproving or apathetic. His father spoke softly over the glass of beer.

"Looks to me like you're the one who's the pig."

"Eat shit." The man locked eyes with his father in the mirror then stood back and looked down at Cabell, blowing beery breath in his face. "You better shut the old fart up or he'll find himself shitting teeth for a week."

Cabell stood up, more to be even with the man than anything else, hoping to gain equal stature so he could mediate the issue peacefully. But the other saw menace in his rise and took one step back, aimed a punch at him that glanced off his shoulder, and then moved in. Feeling the pit of his stomach freeze as it always did when violence was in the offing, Cabell threw out his right leg in a clumsy kick to keep the charging opponent off. But he had not braced his left leg carefully, and it buckled. He was on a knee, hugging the stool with his arms and trying to escape the kicking boots when he saw his father get behind the man and put him in a half-nelson.

The man screamed, "I'll kill you, I'll kill you," and began thrashing around bumping into things like a Brahma Bull. His father rode him, keeping the pressure on the neck so that the man's head stayed down and the arms looped up helplessly. Cabell saw movement in the booth and went over and grabbed the heavy sugar shaker at the center of the table, holding it ready to throw if either of them rose.

The man continued stumbling around trying to brush his father off. On one revolution his father looked over and raised his bushy eyebrows as if to say: "Well, I've got the tiger by the tail now!" Cabell decided to smash the glass container over the man's head if he came close. The woman in the booth had begun to scream now, stage-screaming, high and piercing. He watched as his father maneuvered the man up to the next table, then brought a hard knee into his thigh and, taking advantage of the body's momentary sag, pushed the head down with all his force. Cabell heard the nose pop on the tabletop like the snap of a turkey wishbone. Then the man was on the floor with blood coming through the latticework of fingers over his face.

Cabell hooked his father's arm and they began backing out the door. He still held the sugar shaker above his head. Neither of the man's two friends moved out of the booth. The girl continued to scream. The bartender was on the phone, lazily dialing the police.

When they got out the door, he dropped the glass container and saw it burst on the sidewalk. They turned and sprinted for the pickup. Cabell got it going and peeled rubber taking off. He went through the gears in racing shifts, putting them out onto the highway at eighty miles an hour in seconds.

"Goddammit, Pop," he said, "don't be so nosey. That's a good way to get your ass kicked."

"All that is necessary for evil to triumph is for good to do nothing. Or something like that." His father was breathing heavily and rubbing his hands together. He smiled with vast satisfaction. "Old fart, indeed."

They reached Rapid City at midnight after a day's hard drive, the logic of their trip having told them it was time finally to reach a destination. They rented the first motel they came to and both fell into bed exhausted, sleeping with their clothes on. The next morning Cabell awoke to the pop and bubble of the percolator they carried with them. He watched through slitted eyes as his father came out of the bathroom and began prowling around the room, cracking his knuckles, glancing at Laughlin's old pocket watch, and whistling tunelessly to himself. This was the day they had set aside to go out to the family homestead.

The drive through the Dakota countryside seemed longer than it really was. Previously they had loafed through their days. Now, without anyone willing it, the trip had taken on a sense of portent. He could tell they were almost there; his father began talking in staccato bursts as if on speed, kept running calloused hands through his hair, and peered out his window at passing homes and faces as if checking for evidence that what was going through his mind had indeed taken place.

They negotiated a series of dirt roads, once stopping to ask directions, then parked under a stand of scrub oak, ducked some barbed wire, and walked through the knee-high grass where wind cut through like riptides. His father led the way, kicking the ground, stooping for a moment to prod and sift like an archaeologist on a dig, then walking on.

"Cabe! Over here! Look!" He was pointing down at the crumbled cinderblocks that had served as a foundation for the old farmhouse. He dug around with his heavy boots, uncovering a few old beams and joists mouldering in the loamy ground. Cabell bent to pick one up. It was white and spongy with dry rot and lighter than balsa. It had the rich smell of decay.

"Dad built this place with his own hands." His father was squatting down and pouring dirt from one hand to the other. "He cut the timber up there in the foothills and borrowed a couple of mules to haul it down here. Mother helped him rough-mill it, set the foundation, and raise the frame. They'd lived in a sod house over yonder someplace. For her this farmhouse here meant no more dirt, no more burrowing like animals. We were proper people. For Dad it meant that we were here to stay no matter what anybody said."

He stood up and swung off in a wide arc, looking back at the foundation as a reference point. Cabell dogtrotted behind him. We went about fifty yards down from the rise on which the house had stood and then came to a thin line of spindly cottonwoods in an almost petrified state along the bed of a dry creek.

"This was year-round when we were here." He scuffed the sand. "Once the well went dry, just bone-ass dry, and I had to haul water up to the house for damn near six months. There was this band of Sioux from Pine Ridge that used to cross our land about here every June on the way to their summer campgrounds. The head man was an old guy who had been related to that woman Look. He didn't wear any white man's clothes except for a gray fedora he'd gotten God knows where. Every summer he'd bring his people, twenty-five or thirty of them, right up to the creek here, then come up to the house very serious and ask Dad if they could camp here for a few days. Dad always said yes, then he'd go out to the pasture and butcher a hog and bring the meat down here. We'd all have a big feed. The ranchers around here couldn't believe that Laughlin Hart actually sat down at the same trough with a bunch of lying, thieving, blanket-headed, skunk-gutted Indians. It revived all the hard feelings about the first Cabell Hart. I think that by the time I was a boy they held it more against him that he had been a squaw man in the last months of his life than that he'd killed Gillette. At least that was the tone of the nasty talk that persisted. They gave my Dad a hard time about these Indians on his land. But he didn't give a damn.

He had a strange feeling about the thing with the Sioux. He used to tell us kids: 'We're standing on their bones, damn it; the least we can do is be decent to them.' "

Cabell started to say something, but his father had continued, almost talking to himself now.

"There was this one boy about my age. One year, I guess I was seven or eight, we fought like dogs. But then we got along okay afterward. He didn't savvy English, and of course you could count my words of Sioux on the fingers on one hand. But we'd play together in sign talk all the time during the week or so they were here. I remember once we were out there on the prairie and this Indian boy got the notion that we should catch a rabbit. He got me to understand I should walk around like a bush beater while he waited in the center. I did what he told me and pretty soon, up jumped a rabbit. It started to run and he ran after it. He chased that rabbit right down. I swear to God. He ran it down and caught it. Scrawny little kid. It was a wonderment. I've never seen its beat in my entire life."

He looked off and pointed up a rise. "That's where the barn and outhouse were. God, that outhouse. Used to freeze our asses off on those cold mornings. It snowed so bad of a winter out here that Dad used to run a rope between our front door and the entrance to the barn because you'd have to walk out there blind in the blizzard to feed the stock and he was afraid one of us would get lost and wind up a chunk of ice someplace."

Then he was off again, walking fast, and Cabell was panting behind him. There were some broken circles of stone. "This is where Mother and my brothers were buried after the flu took them. Somebody must have run off with the markers. Dad had them made special in Rapid City by a stone carver there. Must have cost him an arm and a leg. He made the caskets himself. I remember him working on them out there in the barn. He didn't have enough wood and had to take the siding off one of the bedroom walls. I can still remember the scream that crowbar made. Like a banshee. One big box and four little ones. There was a new death every couple of days. It seemed that he was out there in the barn for weeks. He'd come back inside and there'd be little curls of shavings on his boots and sawdust on his arms. I don't think he washed or changed clothes until it was done. My job was to take care of Aggie."

It was the longest sustained reminiscence Cabell had ever heard from his father; the first time he had heard him reach back into the past like this. The effort seemed to cost him something; standing in the wind he suddenly looked frail and vulnerable. Time was heavy on them as they stood slapping at stinging flies and listening to the wind in the long grass. His father was still sifting the dirt he had cupped from hand to hand. Finally he shrugged and said, "Oh, well." He let the dirt drop, and walked back to the pickup.

When he got up the next morning, his father was gone. A note was taped onto the bathroom mirror.

Hi,

Thought I'd go out and look around. See if I remember this old town. You can plan out your own day. Take the pickup if you want. See you later.

Pop

He arrived at the Rapid City library just as the cathedral doors were being unlatched top and bottom. Without being quite certain what he was looking for, he went to the reference desk and convinced a gray-haired woman in tweeds that he was a doctoral student and needed the first eight years of the *Black Hills Pioneer*. Sitting at the microfilm reader, he began with the first issue of the weekly, dated June 6, 1876. On the lower right hand corner of the one-page broadside was a small box in lopsided hairlines around the statement of J. W. Laughlin, proprietor:

We mark this occasion by saying that bringing the first newspaper to the Hills has been a long and arduous process. Importation of type and machinery from Denver, difficult though it was, took second place to the labors faced here.

We thank and commend the many who have helped in time of need, chief among them, John Alderson, Abel Martin, and the Rev. C. F. Hart, close friend and sage counsel.

As we approach the one hundredth anniversary of the nation's founding, we in the Territory are strong in resources, chief among them dependable citizens.

He continued to comb the paper for references to his ancestors. On December 18, 1877, with the paper grown into a six-page daily, he found a news story on the inaugural services of Deadwood's first church:

. . . and the congregation, which had met for over a year in tents, private homes, and the out of doors, had helped build this imposing edifice of stone and wood. At this first Sunday, there were thirty-two men, seven women and eleven youngsters. The Rev. Hart took his text from the book of Psalms 34:7. The Anger of the Lord encamps around Those who fear Him.

Services were briefly interrupted by a fight between two mongrel dogs attracted to the new building by the warmth of its stoves.

He began to see the story he had gotten in snatches from Aggie and his grandfather trying to emerge out of the brief, Victorian paragraphs. On March 3, 1878, there was an announcement in the first column of the back page:

The Rev. Wm. Petersen arrived in town this week with his wife Evelyn, and their children Tom and Maisie. He will take over the post at the First Church of Deadwood being temporarily vacated by the Rev. Hart, who recently asked for and received permission from church deacons to take a leave of absence of several months, during which time he and his son Evan plan to carry the Word up into the roaring camps of the Hills.

The Rev. Petersen is a graduate of Harvard Divinity School and was born in Springfield, Mass.

Two months later, on May 10, a black-bordered obituary for Evan Joseph Hart:

Word received in Deadwood yesterday of the tragic passing of Evan Hart, sixteen, son of the Rev. and Mrs. Cabell Hart.

Death occurred on May 2 as the result of an accident near the mining camp of Omega, when the lad fell down a steep incline and was fatally injured.

In addition to the mother and father, survivors include a sister, Sophia, 12, and an infant brother, Laughlin. "Farewell too little and too lately known."

During the next four years there was no mention of the man. It was as if he had dropped through a hole in the bottom of the prairie. But the *Pioneer*'s pages were filled with stories about Walker Gillette. Cabell skimmed them, watching his great-grandfather's future victim emerge as the town's first citizen, and soon the most powerful figure in the territory. In 1876 he had founded the National Exposition Company, and bought broad tracts of land in anticipation of the time when railroads would cut a line through the Hills. By 1880, four years after the Custer fight, this veteran of the Seventh Cavalry in its earlier days struck back by leading a group of armed citizens down on a band of Sioux thought to be responsible for the theft of a pair of oxen. The paper's headline read: PITCHED BATTLE AT INDIAN WELLS!

. . . and Black Hand's band offered brief resistance before seeking cover in the Hills. Thirteen of both sex were killed. One member of the party, Alfie Piersen, was seen flaying the skin off one of the Indian corpses to make, as he later said, a purse. He was stopped at gunpoint by Walker Gillette, who

93

said, "While red thieving is not to be tolerated, neither is white savagery."

One article contained an interview with Gillette after he had been to New York and met Cornelius Vanderbilt. "A fine figure of a man," Gillette had called him, "and one of those people who will help this country take its place as a leader among nations."

Cabell had spun the microfilm rolls quickly from one item to another, the trip through time conspiring with the physical motion to make him dizzy and a little nauseated. He saw the doom ahead for both the men. He approached the date of June 3, 1882, with a kind of dread. Coverage of the murder filled all of the first two pages and flowed into the middle of page three around an engraving of Gillette, lying on the saloon floor gripping his stomach and looking up beatifically into the halo of faces looking down. The headline seemed carved out of a tablet: TOWN LEADER COWARDLY MURDERED!!!

Not since the skulking Jack McCall perpetrated his black deed have the citizens of Deadwood been so shocked by an act of lawless violence as they were yesterday, when news of the brutal murder of Walker Gillette spread through town.

The assassin was Cabell Hart, one-time minister who had been living in seclusion outside town with his family for the last several years.

The killing took place in the New Era Saloon and Gaming House, where Gillette was with friends in a private celebration.

Hart, seen by witnesses standing outside for nearly an hour in the company of an Indian washerwoman, suddenly entered the New Era and leveled a pistol at the victim's chest. He cried, "You have done cheated me!", and then pulled the trigger. When the smoke cleared, Walker Gillette was on the floor mortally wounded and Hart was walking out the door. Those ministering to the victim heard his last words some fifteen minutes later, as spirit finally separated from flesh. "I'm killed, boys, done for by a crazy man!"

94

As word spread of Hart's deed, a group of citizens formed into a company. At first Sheriff Thompson tried to stop them, then joined in to ride to Indian Wells to bring the killer in. When he refused to come out of his house, they loosed a fusillade and then another. After several minutes without return of fire they went in and found Hart's body along with that of the Indian woman who had lived there with him for some time.

Mr. Gillette, a one-time member of the Seventh Cavalry, had been responsible for helping steer the town on its present course. He first came to the area as part of the Custer expedition of 1874. He had known James Butler (Wild Bill) Hickok, Martha Jane (Calamity Jane) Canary, and other of the colorful figures in Deadwood's past.

President of the National Exposition Company, and owner of several properties throughout the Hills, Gillette was known and respected by eastern financial leaders and had been widely regarded as a leading candidate for Governor of the new states soon to be carved from Dakota Territory. . . .

After finishing with the newspaper, Cabell went over to the history section to leaf through books on South Dakota. He found an old book bound in blue buckram, its title imprinted in flaking gold leaf: *New England Gentleman in the Black Hills* by James Cameron, a Connecticut geologist who came to the area in 1874 and eventually became chief of operations for the Homestake. Flipping pages, he came to the account of the murder.

The odd thing about it was that the murder seemed quite baseless, apparently springing from something like the motiveless malignancy Coleridge attributes to the villain Iago. The victim was popular with the townfolk, so much so that there was an attempt directly after his burial to change the town's name to Gillette. I knew the man well and found him a boon companion and also possessed of a shrewd eye for the future.

Hart I never really knew and think few did. He had kept strictly to himself in the years following his first son's death.

He seemed marked by fate, for during his trip to reconnoiter the Pacific Northwest as a possible homestead, his wife died and his daughter was driven to desperate straits to provide for herself and brother. To my knowledge he was neither friend nor enemy to Gillette. At most there was a business relationship. After his son Evan's death, when he moved out of town to his solitude, Hart sold three platted lots he owned behind the church to Gillette's National Exposition Company. It was said that of the original price only some thirty-six dollars was owing at the time of the killing, a sum withheld by Gillette's factor to cover repairs to the brick jacketing of a well. If this money was the cause of Hart's insensate wrath, then Dakota Territory was robbed of a leader for six dollars more than Judas Iscariot received for his treachery against our Lord. . . .

It was early afternoon when Cabell left the dark room and stepped into the sun. He found the pickup and headed for Deadwood, drawn there by what he had read. He drove quickly, passing cars along blind turns on the mountain road. As he got closer, he felt himself grow excited. He expected something that would look like a set for a cowboy town. Instead, he found himself in a halting line of tourist traffic dropping down into a modern city, which surrounded and choked the old town of high brick buildings with iron shutters. Authentic Deadwood bobbed in a small sea of neon-Hickok motels and Calamity Jane restaurants. Cabell got out and tried to visualize the town according to the plat map in his mind. He thought he had located where the New Era stood, but couldn't be sure exactly where the drama had been played out in what was now a city parking lot, and he had to work around phalanxes of cars.

After walking along the streets for half an hour he gave up, got back in the truck, and drove out to Boot Hill. Pushing past the crowd surrounding Hickok's grave, he followed the dirt path leading up a steep incline to the top of the cemetery. There he saw a cenotaph marking the grave of Walker Gillette. The inscription was in heavy Heidelberg lettering—The Good die Young that They may be saved; The Evil live on that They may Repent—time having nibbled at the chiseled characters. Up higher, six graves away, he spied his great-grandfather's marker.

He walked to it and knelt down, picking weeds from around the white-washed stone border and remembering that his father had once tried to pull it down. Gillette was the man riding the crest, buoyed by an ability to embody the common destiny. This man here was one of those who had tried the world and found it wanting, who inferred the general chaos from his own failure. The syndrome was familiar to him. There on his knees before the grave, his hands palm down in the dirt those old bones had fertilized, he felt himself the crossroads of the family destiny. The thought shivered him. The words on the plain marker seemed to point an accusing finger at him from reasons other than the coincidence of names:

Cabell Hart
1841–1882
WHY WAS HE NOT TRUE?

Tourists gawked at the young man who caused minor landslides of gravel in his haste to get down the hill and to the pickup parked below.

They drove out of Rapid City the next morning in silence. He could tell that his father was in a gray mood. He had already been asleep the previous night when Cabell returned to the motel, so he hadn't gotten a chance to quiz him on his day. He assumed it hadn't been good. Stopped in traffic, they saw a commotion in front of an official-looking building on one of the main streets. There were police cars and sawhorses cordoning off pickets from the crowd. A dozen or so young Indians were demonstrating in front of a field office of the Bureau of Indian Affairs, carrying placards reading, WOUNDED KNEE: GENOCIDE YESTERDAY AND TODAY, AIM-RED POWER! THE FIRST AMERI-CANS ARE LAST."

"Who are they?" His father craned his neck to see.

"I don't know. Part of the American Indian Movement, I guess. God, this is really Indian territory back here, isn't it?"

His father ignored the question. "The same ones as at Wounded Knee?"

"Right."

"Poor bastards."

"Yeah, they're rough on Indians here," Cabell misread him. "It's like the South for blacks."

"That's not what I meant," his father swatted at the orthodoxy with his hand. "Them trying to turn back the clock, that's what makes me feel sorry. It's hopeless."

"Oh, I don't know. They're raising the public's consciousness about their plight."

"*Plight!*" His father's lips pulled back in a soundless laugh. "God, if I was an Indian I'd kill that word. This public-consciousness stuff is bunkum. Every few years they discover the Indian and start raving about his problems and pass all kinds of bills and send money. But that's like pounding sand down a rathole. So they get the government to make Wounded Knee into the Tomb of the Unkown Indian or something like that. Then what? The only thing they get besides a worthless piece of ground is experience doubletalking with TV cameras and a bunch of snaky politicians. I admire their grit. But mainly it just makes me sad. They're the tail end of something that got started a long time ago and won't stop until it's putting people out from stamp-mills."

"Socialism, you mean?" Cabell tried to leaven the mood, but his father ignored him.

They had driven for nearly an hour when his father suddenly spoke again. "History is the nightmare I'm trying to wake up from. Who said that?"

"Stephen Dedalus."

"Who?"

"Actually, it was James Joyce." Cabell felt absurdly pedantic. "It was a character in *Ulysses*."

"Well, whoever the hell it was, I agree."

The pessimism held, settling in the cab of the truck like carbon-monoxide fumes. Later in the day, when they had climbed high into the Hills, skirting the crowds gathered at Mount Rushmore, his father spoke again, as in the middle of a continuing conversation. "Listen, I hope you're not romanticizing me."

"What?"

"I mean I don't want you to make me stand for something—old-fashioned virtue or anything like that. I play with my doing, do dumb things, and fuck up like everybody else. Believe me, I don't think the past was better; just clearer, that's all."

"Jesus, Pop, what's the matter with you, anyway?"

"Just a mood. It'll pass. I just get the idea sometimes that you want to go backward. I don't know why, but I know that sure as hell you'll come to grief if you don't accept reality and look to the future."

"Why are you holding your side?" Looking to change the subject, Cabell noticed that his father's hand was in his shirt below his heart.

"Oh this," he looked down to check. "Nothing. Just heartburn. Goddamn shitty restaurant food."

"The sign said it was homemade."

"Big deal," his father grimaced. "The question you've got to ask whenever you see that sign is, Whose home?"

By the time they had reached the summit and started dropping down, they were chatting easily again, his father having turned especially warm and solicitous as if apologizing for his lapse. When they pulled into the town of Hot Springs, things were back to normal.

"I've been here," his father looked around in the small town square. "Dad and I hunted rocks here back in the twenties. It was a health resort then because of the sulphur waters. There was a spur of the railroad that used to unload rich easterners right here by the carload every summer."

The mud baths had dried up, but the town continued

to have a medicinal identity in a large VA hospital perched up above main street. Sitting in the car, Cabell watched the men in bathrobes and on crutches, many of them younger than he was, walking up and down the long flight of stairs that connected the hospital to other people. Their pajamas and bathrobes seemed out of place in the late afternoon.

"I always think of people in VA hospitals being old World War I veterans," he said.

"Nope," his father shook his head. "Each generation gets its chance."

They took a room in the town's only hotel, the Peabody, a large, boxy structure adorned by scrollwork and gingerbread and trying to summon a hauteur in keeping with its name. Almost alone in its broad lobbies, they sat in overstuffed chairs on the porch after dinner, chatting and reading pulp fiction, then playing shuffleboard and drinking beer in the bar until after midnight. They slept late, had large breakfasts, and then prospected for fossils.

His father was like a rooster walking with red head cocked, now and then spying some rock and dipping down to peck at it, bringing it up to knock the surface off with the beak of the geologist's hammer he carried in the pickup. Once he found a large geode, struck it hard so that it split, revealing a miniature galaxy of crystal like one of those Easter eggs with a peephole looking into a completely formed world. Later on he dug into a bank of gravel and brought out long slate-colored rocks that looked like machine-gun bullets.

"Know what these are?" His father spit on them and rubbed the dirt on his pants.

"No."

"Petrified dinosaur claws. Dad and I used to find them by the lug. We used to find all sorts of stuff: petrified wood, palm root, even fishes. You could still see the structure of the scales. Mercy, sifting through that stuff used to give me an eerie feeling."

"How so?"

"It's just like you were seeing a stage of the process. It

made you aware of how long it has taken. I don't know how to explain it right. It was seeing God's time, not man's."

That night they sat on the porch surrounding the hotel like the gouty and arthritic valetudinarians of a prior age, sipping water still faintly sulphurous and listening to the muffled stridulations out in the dark beyond them. Cabell had a strong sense that time had slowed down and was somehow focused on them. His father didn't say much, but seemed at ease, exchanging sentences in the desultory way of someone who has eaten a good meal and is faintly sleepy.

They were looking up into the black night when they felt a faint electricity in the air, soon a heaviness and portent even his blunted California senses could interpret. His father scented deeply and looked up at the heavens where the moon rode swift tides of cloud. Then he tilted back in his chair and put his feet up on the railing.

"This kind of night always makes me think of Mama Bessie," he said. "When it was getting ready to split open like it is now, she'd start ducking for cover. She'd say, 'Gonna be rainin' pitchforks and nigger babies, shore enough.' That was a good woman. I hope she knew how much we appreciated what she did for us."

It began high in the mountains towering up above them. They could hear its fury before they saw it. Then the jagged streaks of light began to burst intermittently like the artillery barrage before some climactic battle. For a while it was far away. Then it swept down upon them, the sky suddenly illumined in stark blasts that turned the Hills white. Long explosions of thunder slammed down onto the porch roof. The rain gusted in off the street in thick squalls, soaking their pantslegs before retreating back again.

The few other guests who had been out there grabbed books and drinks and ran inside to watch from behind thick plate glass. Cabell rose to go, but his father motioned him down. "This is the kind of show you don't want to miss." They sat. The sounds and sights were symphonic. The rain felt like sweat in the humid night.

"There was this old Sioux, Amos One Feather," his father began talking in between the thunder rolls. "He must have been around seventy, because he said his son had been born the year of the Custer fight. We got to know him after Dad and Aggie and me moved off the homestead. Dad had watched the flu epidemic come and take Mom and the other kids and figured, well, he might as well try to make out as a city man. He got this poolhall, and Amos used to come around and ask for odd jobs. Dad would have given him the money but didn't want to insult him, so he let him earn it by chopping wood out in the backyard.

"Amos had this wonderful face, all lined and shrunk up like a dried apple. His nose had ridges and bumps and just looked like somebody made it by hand. When he worked, sweat would collect down at the end and drop off slow like a faucet that needs a washer. When he was drunk, which was most of the time, that nose flared up like a strawberry."

"What? I can barely hear you." Cabell tried to filter out the sounds of the storm, perplexed by his father's decision to be discursive at a time like this.

"I said old Amos drank a lot. He had gone to some Indian Affairs boarding school and learned to read and write." His father raised his voice higher. "And he fancied himself a sort of philosopher. One time he was out in the yard chopping kindling, and he was talking to me—not necessarily because I was me, understand, but just because I was there—and he wandered from one subject to another, grunting 'unhh' every time he swung the hatchet and making that sound a part of his story. Like he'd say, 'And then we broke camp, unhh, and went to Fort Abe Lincoln, unhh . . .' That sort of thing. Anyway, he got to talking about Crazy Horse and said he remembered when the soldiers rubbed him out—those were the words he used, 'rubbed out'—and how a couple of his uncles were in the bunch that went to get the body at the fort. They got it and took it up into the Hills. Amos said that they buried it there near this shelf of rock where Crazy Horse had gone ever since he was a young man named Curly to have these visions that he thought were the real world. In one of these dreams he saw himself riding a war pony that was just shaking with energy. It was after this vision that he knew he'd have powerful medicine as a warrior and took the name Crazy Horse."

"Speak up a little, Pop."

"Okay," the voice strained, and the words came quickly between bursts of thunder. "Anyway, all of a sudden Amos stopped telling this story and just looked off in the distance, sweat dripping down off that nose of his. He looked in my direction, and I got a sense that now he was really talking to *me*. 'We are a circle,' he said. 'All things are round—sun, moon, sky. The earth and the moon are round like a bowl. The tepee is a circle. The Oglala make camp in a round. The family is a circle around the fire. Everything in nature is round except the stone, which is for destruction. The white man uses his history like a stone to break our circle. The big train that cut across the buffalo land—that was your history. The miners who looked for yellow rock were your history. You won us. Now you say you know all the secrets. But remember, we still keep some locked up. I say this: someday the white will be alone, without his history to protect him, and will need to know these Indian secrets just to live. The Oglala will be gone by then, rubbed out, and you will have to learn them for yourself.' He went back to swinging the hatchet and grunting each time it hit. He sort of mumbled under his breath, 'If the white doesn't learn these secrets, he dies. If he does learn them, he is an Oglala. There will be two kinds of people—dead ones and Indians. There will be Indians again.' Then he started laughing to himself and kept that up for a minute or two, just cackling like a maniac. It was the damdest speech I ever heard. It scared hell out of me, I'll tell you. I can remember him saying those words like it was yesterday."

Cabell waited for the moral, which he assumed would have something to do with the ideas that had agitated his father the past few days: uncontrolled technology, the modern assault on the bonds that helped support individual existence. But there was no punchline, nothing further. For a moment, he thought he had missed something in the storm. When his father spoke again, the non sequitur was jarring.

"Did you ever hear Crazy Horse's last words?" he asked.

Cabell shook his head.

"Well, one of the soldiers that was going to kill him brought him out of his cell and stood with him looking off into the distance. He started taunting him: 'Where are your lands now?' Crazy Horse looked out there at the land around the fort where the settlement was built up and spoke in Sioux to one of the Indian guides with them. 'I have plenty lands,' he said. 'Wherever my people are buried is Indian land.' Old Amos told me that, too."

Cabell sat there, leaning back against the hotel's rough siding, tense and unbalanced by the incompletion in which the conversation dangled. Above him, the jagged electricity bounced from one mountain to another. He heard its sound, like the heavy buzz of a downed powerline. Suddenly he was afraid, and had a strong urge to move closer to his father, to protect and be protected.

The storm reached a frenzied pitch, a gust of rain rising through the porch and pinning them back in their chairs. His father had said something that the wind had snatched away. "What?" Cabell yelled and cupped an ear. Again the lips moved without sound. He couldn't read them and shook his head and shrugged. Then his father reached over to take his hand and guide it down inside his shirt, rubbing it in the dampness under the left arm. Cabell's fingers found a lump the size of a pea.

"*No!*" His voice rose above the storm. "Why didn't you tell me? Why didn't you go to the doctor?" He had stood up and was shrieking to be heard.

His father waited for a moment of calm to speak. "Because I wanted to make this trip, that's why."

Soon after, they went back to their room. Cabell asked if there were other signs. The answer had that nervy Hollywood jauntiness his father adopted when talking of his cancer.

"Metastasis is here." As he undressed for bed, he showed surface tumors the size of buckshot all over the body, between the toes, under the earlobes, on the hip—in all, over a dozen of them.

Cabell couldn't sleep. He lay in bed stiff and sweating, listening to his father's snores. His body itched all over, but he was afraid that scratching would sink the contagion down below his epidermis into the blood, and then he would have cancer too. The ceiling seemed close, and the room so stuffy that he felt he was suffocating. He turned as if on a spit. At some point in the night he felt another presence in the room. It was something, someone unfamiliar. He did not move for fear that it would spring on him. He almost rose to turn on the lights and look, but then he realized that whatever it was lacked corporeal menace. When the night was beginning to go gray and he was finally falling into fitful sleep, he realized who the visitor was: the first and original Cabell Hart, the one who was not true. Between sleep and waking he got the notion of a story that begins and ends in false and faithless men with the same name, bookends for oblivion. He tried to dismiss the ghost, but it stayed.

At five-thirty he rose and began packing up, then went downstairs and called the doctor's answering service to insist on an appointment in two days. He herded his father into the truck and set out into the grainy morning, driving like a madman.

"Slow down, Cabe, there's nothing to be gained by this," his father pleaded. But he ignored him, putting the accelerator to the floor and keeping it there, slowing only for gas, coffee, and urination.

At noon the next day they were speeding through Idaho when his father, who had endured a night of unquiet sleep slumped against his door, became adamant. "Listen, goddammit, I want to stop and I want to stop now. I'm not sweating it, and I don't know why you should. I'm tired of getting bounced around in this goddammed truck and seeing

you act like a maniac. This is my truck. I want to stop. Now!"
He took the map out of the glove compartment and found
the nearest town, putting a spatulate finger on the dot named
Carey.

"Some town," Cabell was seething as he pulled into the
narrow road leading through the town and then into the driveway of a pink motel his father pointed at.

"Didn't Hemingway have a place around here?" his father tried to conciliate by appealing to his literary sense.

"Hemingway was an asshole," Cabell said.

His father shrugged. After they had registered, he went
into their room and brought a chair out onto the porch. Ignoring Cabell, he put on his reading glasses, tilted back to the
stucco, and began writing postcards, looking up toward the
sawtoothed mountains above them every now and then as if
for inspiration. Cabell fidgeted with their gear and then stood in
the doorway, shifting his weight nervously.

"Don't you have anything to do?" His father looked up,
annoyed. "Go climb a mountain, take a walk, get some sleep.
Go fishing. This is one of the best areas there is for it. Just do
something. Here I am damned near three score and ten and
I've got this big baby mooning around me."

Cabell shook one of the flyrods out of its plastic carrying
case, and assembled it as he crunched off on the gravel road
cutting off behind the motel. After about a quarter of a mile
he climbed over a stile, walked through a field, and came to
the creek he'd seen as they drove into town. At this point the
channel was wide, draining off into sloughs filled with cat-
tails. He walked upstream until it narrowed and the water
rilled quickly. He waded out a few steps and felt his legs go
numb to the knee, hard rocks poking up through the soles of
his tennis shoes. He began flicking flies into the deep pools,
temples pounding, rage and fear boiling inside him as he imagined the metallic voices of his enemies taunting him for having
wagered and lost. He worked his way along, fearing that the
other Cabell Hart was nearby, fishing mechanically, only
vaguely aware of the rush and tumble of the water. In about an

hour he came to a brief trestle bridge without having had even a nibble.

"Any luck?" The voice above him belonged to a boy who was so short that Cabell hadn't seen him.

He shook his head. The boy proudly lifted an impressive string of trout off the bridge's planks. "They just planted two days ago. Got these on cheese. It reminds them of the stuff they feed them at the hatchery."

After the boy left, Cabell climbed up to where he had stood and stared down at the swirling pool below. He saw fish there, dozens of them, black shadows lazing in the middle and then kicking to the water's edge with one movement of the tail, weaving in and out of view there under the grass that waved like mermaid's hair from beneath the bank. He hated them. If he had had dynamite, he would have blown them out of the water.

He whipped his line out, often landing a fly within inches of the streamlined snout. Some fish rose and nosed it, but none struck. He changed flies three times without luck. Sweating and enraged, he put on a hook and weight and reached down for scraps of the greasy orange cheese the kid had left behind on the scarred wax paper. He scraped together enough to roll a ball that would cover the hook, then tossed it out.

Immediately the water seethed. He saw and felt the strike at the same instant and set the hook by reflex, moving back to horse the fish out of water and swing it flopping wildly onto the bridge, silvering the planking with scales. He dropped the rod and ran after it like a clumsy bear, getting splinters in his fingers as he tried to pick it up. The bait had been gutted. After trying for a moment to finesse it out he became impatient and jerked. The sound was of cloth tearing: hook and bait came out intact along with a small piece of gut; blood poured out of the gasping gills. He threw the fish down to die and rebaited the hook with the same ball of cheese.

The next time three fish struck together, fighting for the bait like chickens for a crust of bread: one trying to run with it and others trying to steal it from his mouth. Cabell pulled the rod in a high arc like a tuna fisherman. The trout flew off the hook at the apex, thudding down onto the bridge. It tried to flop back to the water, but he trapped it against an upright just before it managed to dive back down, picked it up by the lower part of the body with two hands and smashed its dorsal surface against the wood until the spasms stopped. The pounding in his head was getting worse, pressuring up from his spinal column to clang at the top of his skull. He held the fish up and looked into the eye's cold yellow celluloid with contempt.

He became selective, lowering the bait slowly until it was poised above the largest fish he saw, quickly jerking it back up if a smaller trout made a run for it. After a while he stopped chasing them on the bridge, allowing chance to have its way: either they bumped their way back to the edge and down to water or they drowned in air and the sun dried them in their death arch. He was the remote watchmaker God, and this was the way life worked.

After about an hour he stopped. Exhausted, pained, he looked around and counted twenty-six trout. He could see no more in the deep pool below; just his own face reflecting back in segments. Their slime had dried crackling hard on his hands. His pantslegs were covered with their ooze and sequined with their scales. Gouts of their dark blood clung to his shoelaces.

Suddenly self-conscious, he walked quickly to a Forest Service trashcan, rooted through it, and pulled out an old garbage-filled shopping bag. Emptying the campers' garbage, he took the bag back to the bridge and stuffed the fish into it. As he worked, a blackbird with red epaulets screeched accusingly from its perch on a swaying cattail. He was running now, through the water to hide his tracks and then up along the bank and out into a field, moisture squeaking in his tennis shoes and his wet pantslegs chaffing loudly. He slung the bag out into a marshy slough of still water. Before it hit, the fish began falling out like dead parachutists.

The sun was going down when he got back to the motel. A note on one of the beds read:

Out for a walk. Back soon. Relax, will you?

He stayed in the shower until the hot water went cold, scouring the deathly smell of fish off his body. Then he dressed and walked down the road to a restaurant and bar advertised in a sign on the motel wall.

On entering he sensed red leatherette, loud country music, the greasy sizzle of frying meats. The restaurant held a few families eating silently—men in straw cowboy hats with sweat stains leaking down the band; women in housedresses; children in T-shirts and worn jeans. Ignoring his rumbling stomach, he passed out of their world and headed for the bar in the back, passing through an equatorial door into cool darkness. He put a foot on the brass railing and looked at the fly-specked mirror. He downed the double bourbon with a shiver of distaste and asked the bartender for another. He took it with him to the jukebox in the corner of the room.

Mesmerized by the pulsing lights, he stood matching up the numbers of push-buttons with songs. The Beatles and Johnny Cash were the only gestures in the direction of modern music; most of the records had been on the machine for years. There were names from his growing-up: Les Paul and Mary Ford; Theresa Brewer, Rosemary Clooney. Each song brought back some episode. "Mister Sandman": in the background as he sat on a porch swing with Jan Clayton, the girl five doors down, feeling breasts for the first time, thinking that the proper motion was circular as if reaming oranges. "Earth Angel": on the radio as he drove down to Watts with friends in a fearsome rite of passage through Negroland to see the deejay Huggie Boy. "How Much Is That Doggie in the Window?": Charley in a new felt skirt appliquéd with a sequin-collared poodle.

He bought another drink and then returned to the old Wurlitzer, watching it shimmer gently in pastel colors as the arm shopped for a record, picked it up, and handed it on to the turntable. Moving on a trail of bourbon, he considered that current times were passion-spent. I must be getting old, he thought. I've got that old-man's feeling that life was better back then.

"Hi." The word blundered through his nostalgia and trespassed on his cheek. Feeling foggy, he turned and saw a woman standing next to him, the jukebox lighting the long curve of her neck.

"Hi."

"We been watching you and listening to all that good music you been playing and we thought you might like to join us." He inspected her as she talked: tight pants, cotton pull-over showing iced nipples, a tangle of bracelets on the fore-arm's downy hair.

"I'm Lois. Come on over and meet my friends." She seized his hand; his feckless body followed. At the booth there were others. "This is Joanna and Carl." He shook hands with slid in next to, the man looking like a sincere student at an them both, the woman across from him looking like the one he ag college. None of them could have been much more than twenty-two.

He exchanged names and vital statistics and bought a round of drinks, smiling dumbly as their talk picked up from where it had been before he came. "So anyway," Carl was saying, "his old lady said, 'Cool it, Slick, this ain't no peep show . . .'" and the girls laughed so hard that their hair came down on their faces.

Their talk was like battle; he watched it from an observation post high above. A burst rattled off from one side of the table with answering fire from the other. A heavy barrage and then light sniping, probing the perimeters. He followed the progress by its general movement, as if watching tracer bullets. The man and woman across from him declared a truce and got up to dance as "Moonglow," which he had programmed into the Wurlitzer's vast synthetic memory days, even weeks, earlier, finally came on. He watched the slow, boxy geometry of their feet, seeing their existence only from the ankle down. How to tell the dancer from the dance?

The girl next to him was fondling his hand. He turned and looked at her. The cheeks were stippled with acne, which grew up as far as the temples. His ruthless whiskey gaze saw how she had tried to putty the marks over with makeup.

"You Lois or Joanna? I forget."

"I'm Lois, silly." Her ingratiating manner was that of someone used to ignoring insults.

"Oh. Right."

"You said you lived out there in Berkeley?" She tried to deflect the punishing thoughts he vectored at her.

"Yeah. Used to. Don't live anywhere now."

"Where do you live now?"

"I'm on the road."

"Are you a salesman?"

"Sort of," he replied.

"What do you sell?"

"Eternal life."

She cocked her head dubiously.

"Haven't you ever heard of cryogenics?" His thick tongue had a mind of its own and curled around that word like a slug.

"No, what's that?"

"Well, when you die they freeze your body to preserve it from decay. When they figure out a cure for whatever killed you later on, some relative defrosts the body and then they operate and bring it back to life."

"Sounds like interesting work." She was speaking with a knowing smile in case he was putting her on.

"You bet," he said.

She came back at him after a pause, seeking a safer topic. "Used to hear a lot about Berkeley being a place of riots and all that."

"Right. I remember. *Pars magna fui.*"

"What?"

"They're all over now. That's all Dead Sea Scrolls stuff."

"Yeah, know what you mean. But people out here still think it's all communistic back there."

"No shit, really?"

"Really. People around here talk about fighting off the Communists."

"Tremendous. They could have another range war. Kill Communists instead of sheepherders."

"You ever get involved in any of those troubles?"

"Troubles?" he smiled at the word's savage Irish lilt. "I might have. I'm not sure. I've reached the stage in life where you can't tell what's real from what's imagined. Bad news."

He drained the glass and chewed the ice cubes, aware of the exact moment he passed the line from middling to very drunk. He craned his neck to watch the other couple dancing, feeling as he did that the movement of his head must look like one of those disjointed bouncing dolls in the rear window of a car. Then the music ended and Joanna was pushing Carl toward the door or Carl was pulling Joanna. They paused at the entrance and smiled over at them, then vanished like vaudevillians given the hook.

There was another drink in front of him and he drank it. He was alone at the table, and she was alone next to him. Then they were outside, walking in the chill mountain air on tipsy sidewalks. The girl guided and supported in the same gesture; his mind lumbered clumsily after some train of thought he tried to get to stop for him. It was Jill. He finally got her into focus, lying on the bed and holding her lover-prey with arms and legs and mouth, watching him watch her, the smell of sperm and female ooze heavy in the room like pancake batter. The image was not the thought; it was more complex than that, but he couldn't seize it.

He stopped and grasped the girl's shoulder. "God hath given you one face," he ranted, "and you make yourselves another: you jig, you amble, and you lisp and nickname God's

creatures, and make your wantonness your ignorance. Go to;
I'll no more on 't: it hath made me mad."

"Mad?" she asked, standing back from him.

"Don't worry," he smiled reassuringly. "He's just scape-
goating her. At this point he sees anything to do with animal
instinct, with sex or reproduction, as disgusting, revolting,
part of the criminal sickness spread over Denmark. In and of
herself, Ophelia's innocent."

By this time they were climbing the stairs of a large
house remade into apartments. He wanted to reassure her:
I'm no Jack the Ripper, lady, just a wild thespian and harmless
crank. But he could not believe enough in the gesture to make
it. He was on the turned-down sofa, watching her tentatively
undress to reveal a slender chest faintly tracked with acne.
She cupped the two small breasts imploringly in her hands and
looked at him with large eyes.

"Don't you like me?"

"Like you?" He picked up one of her hands and thought
to kiss it but instead banged his lips on empty space. "I love
you, Lois or Joanna. I love you." A fiery belch erupted in his
throat. "It's just that there has been a death in the family, and
it has undone me." Then he released and sank back onto the
pillow, the darkness of the room spinning all around him. He
thought she might have bent to feel his forehead but couldn't
tell for sure.

When he awoke the next morning, the first thing he
saw was vomit on the sheet. Its smell was acid; small particles
of it were trapped in his nose and throat, burning the mucous
lining. It caked his face and hair. The girl was gone, her side
of the sofa undented. He took two aspirin from a bottle on the
nightstand and went in to shower amidst the dead legs of
pantyhose. He let the hot water punish his neck for half an
hour. Then he dressed in yesterday's rank clothes, took the
fetid sheets and tied them in a ball. Before leaving he took
a twenty-dollar bill out of his wallet and stuck it on the bundle
with a safety pin.

When he got back to the motel, it was a little after nine and his father was out bustling around the pickup, loading things in the back and opening and shutting the door. His face was fresh-scraped and pink, and he whistled tunelessly under his breath as he worked. When he saw Cabell, he said, "Jesus, you look like two holes burned into a blanket. When the people up at the restaurant said they thought you were having a little party, I thought they meant fun. Lordy me, it's going to be a rough trip home. Well, come on, it's packed; let's kick it on out of here."

3 They were like a jaunty expeditionary force that had taken huge and unexpected casualties and returned home in disaster. The doctor who had operated the first time hospitalized his father again and removed the lymph nodes on the left side. Finding them contaminated, he sent him to radiology, where nuclear material was injected into the bloodstream so that the metastasis, product of the other kind of fission, could be traced.

"It's in the liver and lungs." The doctor spoke to Cabell with his father still unconscious in the recovery room. The voice was meant to convey no hope. "It won't do any good for me to keep on cutting." He handed Cabell a business card with the name James Montrose written on the back. "Here's a man working down at UCLA. He's an oncologist, and he's on a NIH grant to test a new drug. You might take your father down there after he gets out of the hospital. There's nothing to lose now."

On the way down to Westwood early the following week his father said, "I don't exactly agree with that verdict, you know."

"Which one are you referring to?" Cabell asked.

"The notion that there's nothing to lose. Right now I've got this mood of resignation. If I start trying to get a few days more, I'm liable to lose that. Then I'm up shit creek for sure. It used to be that people could face the idea of death without panic. They saw it in their daily lives. They were sandwiched in between what begot them and what they begot. When you start thinking that you're the product of a virgin birth and that when you leave all the lights go out, then you've got problems." Cabell quickly changed the subject.

Montrose was a dapper man with a vandyke beard and the hands of a Jergens commercial—long, slender fingers growing out of the palm like tubers. Although not much more than five feet tall, in describing the chemotherapy he was testing he talked with a kind of cosmic salesmanship that somehow made him seem larger than he was.

Montrose had ushered them to low-slung seats with a politeness that was almost Gallic. He then talked down at them from a nearby perch on the corner of his desk. "I guess you know as well as I do that I can't offer you much hope. We're not talking about years, but months. At present you don't have that. We're testing a new drug that retards the growth of carcinomic tissue. It's called 7-NU. If that sounds like a strong pesticide, don't be alarmed. We know that this drug kills cancer cells, but unfortunately, it kills other cells too. It will make you sick, but it will buy you some time. That's the bargain. You decide. And to be perfectly candid, it doesn't really matter whether you say yes or no, because there are many patients interested in the treatment. As a doctor I'm interested in your well-being, but as a researcher I'm interested in my sample. It may sound callous, but the primary reason I agreed to this interview is that I was short on melanoma patients."

Driving back to his father's house, Cabell enthused about the visit, insisting that they were lucky to have found such a man. Leaning weakly against the pickup door, his father interrupted. "No point in all this bother. Six weeks, six months: it don't make no nevermind. It's just another grain of sand. I'm not one of those who think you ought to give in. But I don't much fancy becoming a guinea pig living in a cage out there on the frontiers of science."

"No, you've got to do it, Pop." Cabell knew it was ridiculous that *he* should sound petulant and betrayed, but he went on. "In a few months they could easily develop something a little better."

"Come on, boy, don't shit me. I'm your daddy, I was here *before* you. I know what the score is. I'm not crazy about all those social engineers trying to convince us common folk to take a biological form of early retirement so they can free up more space. But I don't go for artificially prolonging life either, not when it's *my* life, at least. I've done the best I could with the tools I had. Be damned if I'm going to start weaseling around now to get a few hours more, especially if it's going to feel like hell to do it. You'll understand when the time comes."

"Pop, come on." He could feel himself teetering toward hysteria. "You owe it to me and Charley. You owe it to the kid. Please."

"I read about it. College classes in death. Counseling sessions in death. Experts in death. Making a big deal out of something you don't have a say in one way or another. The trouble with your generation is that you want to make everything into one big group-therapy scene. A lot of jabbering talk about what something means is the easiest way to make it not mean, don't you know that?" He was trying to keep it to a general level. But the look on his face showed that until then he hadn't realized the extent to which he had become Cabell's lifeline.

"Cabe, you need to get yourself something you can believe in," he added after a moment's pause, "something that doesn't require getting up every morning and checking to see who's still alive."

Later on that evening his father agreed to become Montrose's patient, bringing the subject up as if he had spontaneously changed his mind. Two days later he got his first shot. The needle seemed huge, veterinary; it was plunged into the vein of the arm by a technician and the contents were quickly expelled. His father turned pale and lay back for a time on the examining table. His head lolled to one side so that his face was even with Cabell's, who sat next to him. "This stuff is way out," he said. "I feel like I just got shot into outer space. Is this what you kids feel like when you take your LSD?" On the drive back home, Cabell had to pull the truck off the freeway so that his father could vomit.

The regimen of boarding the bus each Friday afternoon and returning on Sundays became an ordeal for him. There was no miracle to hope for anymore. Cabell knew he would find the man a little thinner and more wizened each week, a little more victimized by bizarre symptoms. He itched constantly and scratched in his sleep until his face and arms were covered by ringworm-sized sores and scabs. He was swiftly nauseated by the smell of food and forced Cabell to stuff a towel under the kitchen door when fixing dinner to keep the fumes from entering the living room and making him prematurely sick. He kept the house like a sauna because he shivered uncontrollably when the temperature fell below seventy-five degrees. He wore the thermal underwear Charley gave him when she came down for Christmas. On Superbowl weekend in January, Cabell arrived to find the furnace broken and the shrinking figure sitting in front of the oven of the kitchen stove wearing a mackinaw and heavy wool gloves.

His father tried to maintain his cocky superiority over the disease. Once Cabell arrived at the back door and found a note stuck to the refrigerator with a magnetic button:

"The occupant issues this health bulletin about the past week. He was visited by two villains called by the doctor Anorexia and Dysphagia. They took from him, respectively, his appetite and ability to swallow. They have since vanished, but might return if food is cook on these premises."

But without his fantasy of triumphing over huge odds, their weekends fell apart. They sat there waiting for the end that neither of them could now deny would come.

One Friday afternoon in late March, he called to say that he had been ordered to work at the store on Saturday for inventory and couldn't make the trip down. If his father sensed it was a lie he didn't let on. After that it became easier to defraud. His trips south became erratic. In April he managed to get there twice, in May only once. That was the last time he showed up. For a while he called Los Angeles twice a week, once to say he'd be there for sure and once to beg off. By June he had stopped calling at all.

He tried to will himself out of the spell, knowing that there would be dire consequences for misbehaving at so critical a point in his life. But he couldn't shake the voodoo that seemed to have possessed him. He had quit his job in April, no longer able to face the daily ordeal of civility. He went out of his apartment as seldom as possible. His great-grandfather was now his almost constant companion, hangdog and haggard. He took the sweaty, unexorcised presence as a sign that he was losing his hold.

One afternoon he was awakened by an authoritative knock. Still fully dressed from the previous night, he answered the door and found a policeman, one of Berkeley's new cops with a white afro and muttonchops. Cabell was immediately frightened.

"Are you Mister Hart?" The politeness was Police Science 1A.

"Yes."

"I'm sorry to bother you, sir, but I was hoping you might help us by coming with me down to the Alameda County Coroner's Office. I'm sorry to have to ask you to.do this, but there's a body. We believe it's Gillian McKeever, but we need a positive identification. We were told that you knew her better than anyone else in the area."

"Oh." Cabell felt a horror in his body like hemlock. "What happened?"

"That's not clear." The voice was still polite. "Apparently some explosive device malfunctioned."

"Christ." Cabell sensed that something was ending; it

was as though some bladder of fate was nearly empty. "Why are you asking me to do this? This is a family thing."

"Apparently the father has been contacted, but refused to come. We need somebody. It's a formality. We'd sure be grateful."

Failing to think of a way to say no, he got into the squad-car and rode through downtown Oakland. *I knew it would come to this,* he directed numb thoughts to the other Cabell Hart sitting invisible beside him. *I warned her, didn't I?*

The cop made small talk as they went. "Berkeley may be weird, "but it's not desperate. This city is a bummer. It's like one big Greyhound bus depot."

"A strange place," Cabell agreed mechanically, preparing himself.

"There is no there there." The cop pulled off the phrase with panache. "That's Gertrude Stein."

Standing in the center of the frigid room, he felt as though he was in a meat locker, and half expected to see the corpse come rolling by dangling from a hook on a track. The policemen guided him gently by the arm to a small area off the main room and motioned to an oriental woman in white duster to pull the drawer. She peeled back the winding cloth, and he was staring down at Jill's schizophrenia. One half of the body was pristine, carved from marble, that Burne-Jones beauty finally liberated after all those years. The other side was mangled, the tibia snapped and visible to the center of the marrow like a soupbone, the eye squished like a grape and gone opaque with all the vitrious essence leaked. She looked like Siamese twins joined at dead center, one of them demolished.

"Is that Mizz McKeever, sir?"

The "mizz" was a nice touch; she would have smiled at that. Cabell was looking directly at the cop, trying to say yes and be done with it. His lips did not pucker as in a stutter; they simply didn't move. He broke them apart with a wetness of tongue, but they sealed again straightaway. He was shaking his head vigorously up and down and grunting "uh-huh" low in his throat as if agreeing with something that had been said. The cop thanked him and led him by the arm out into the afternoon sunshine.

He spent his days sitting huddled on the Murphy bed watching television, beginning with the soaps in the afternoon, then the news, prime time, Johnny Carson, and the late night shows. The situations he saw became the real ones; his own was the exaggerated plot, the work of smarmy melodrama. His great-grandfather occupied one corner of the room. Cabell tried to get rid of him by cooing: "Rest, rest, perturbèd spirit!" Then he avoided that area when walking to the kitchen and bathroom; once he pissed there to mark it with his smell, to claim it against the ghost. He tried to think of insults against the apostate, using them like garlic on the windowsills of his mind to repel him. *I'm not of you!* But the ghost did not depart.

The two Cabell Harts watched all the medical shows: "Marcus Welby," of course; "Medical Center"; re-runs of "Ben Casey" on UHF; the odd serendipity of a dramatic hour, a made-for-television movie, or a film like *Doctor's Wives*. They saw Nixon stumble further and further into guilt with each sweating news conference. Cabell enjoyed the worm turning, but howled derisively at the fatuous self-congratulation of Sevareid and the others who had apologized for the war night after night in older times, his tender age of belief. Did they seriously propose that he should conceive a winter passion for this country now? He yelled insults at them so loud the lady who lived above him tapped on the floor with her cane.

He went to the hobby shop and bought model-airplane kits, then sat at a card table working at them furiously, trying by this act of creation to hold the first Cabell Hart at bay. He was addicted to their logic, the order they embodied: from plan, to skeleton of wood, to stretched and lacquered layerings of epidermal silk. Fokkers, Spads, triplanes, biplanes—the finished product was unimportant and discarded as soon as it was completed. It was the organic process that attracted him. Working with the thick glue and balsa wood, a plate of food beside him and the television flickering nearby, he felt he had a tendency to giggle at the wrong places in life. There was a jerkiness in his cervical movements, the constant hum of psychological white sound in his ear. He made models twelve hours a day and recited Hamlet's soliloquies.

Gnawing the dried airplane glue off his fingertips, he watched Watergate reports and coverage of the SLA. Cinque and Nixon converged, opposite ends of the same process, brothers in crime. He watched the Nixon gang melt in Washington and Cinque's gang fry in Los Angeles, the eternity of replays always ending in the same tacky apocalypse with cirrus clouds of teargas, gunfire that came through as the hammering of novice carpenters, and the unquenched fire that ate everything but teeth. He remembered Nancy Ling Perry from the days she had worked at the juice stand on the corner of Bancroft and Telegraph—serious, always half-frowning, intense, with a thing for blacks. Fitting wing to fuselage with an X-acto knife, he saw them as cannibals who ate their own fantasies; Nixon ate the larger dream. Seeing cops fire down on the ghetto house with ricocheting dumdum bullets and set the dry wood afire with canisters that looked like Nazi grenades, he cried unwanted tears, then made his heart flinty. *They said they wanted to die for the people. Fuck them.*

Although he ate constantly, he felt fevered and weak. One day it occurred to him with the force of an epiphany that he had leukemia. He went to see his doctor, an internist named Weiss widely known through Berkeley as a fellow-traveler who treated radicals at cut rate.

"The tests don't show anything," he said, bushy eyebrows hiding eyes that covertly probed at Cabell's face. "It's just a low-grade virus. Go home and get some rest."

"Couldn't it be leukemia?" Cabell asked, somehow wanting the answer to be yes. "I've got all the symptoms."

"No you haven't. You've got a low-grade virus. Relax."

"Cancer's a virus, isn't it?"

"Listen, Hart. You can't take on your father's cancer. And even if you could, it wouldn't be through some chickenshit version like leukemia. That's kid stuff. Melanoma is the big time, a real adult cancer, the worst there is. Leukemia is the sort of thing a little boy imitating his father might try to get. Go home and get some rest. Stop eating so much. I'm sorry to give you such a disappointing diagnosis, but you'll live."

He continued to stuff himself, regressively seeking certainty in the starchy foods of his childhood: peanut-butter and jelly sandwiches; bowls heaped with Shredded Wheat; spaghetti with melted butter. He started eating in the afternoon upon rising and continued late into the night, rushing to his refrigerator between commercials to see if, by parthenogenesis, something new to eat had appeared during his fifteen-minute absence. Between snacks, he sucked on Tums. His bowels churned and gulped in an effort to keep up. Each morning he studied the coil of feces in the toilet and wondered why so much less was extruded than had been consumed. He masturbated constantly, working his seedless seed into the fibers of the rug with a house-shoed toe.

After the national anthem was over, and the last channel had lapsed into static, he burrowed fully dressed beneath the rank covers and fell asleep immediately, guts heaving and bubbling as he tumbled from one dream to another. They were heavy and literal, the time for delicate lapidary dreamwork having passed.

Once he was sitting in an enormous classroom at his father's funeral, the service being conducted by a woman he remembered as his first-grade teacher. She sat at an old upright playing "Joy to the World" in soft honky-tonk as he sat in the first pew. Next to him was the first and original Cabell Hart, dressed in broadcloth preacher's suit, the caskets of his firstborn son and wife also in the room. When the older man tried to touch his shoulder to console and be consoled, Cabell had screamed: "Get this murderer out of here! He killed my father!"

Another time—it was after seeing *Fantastic Voyage* on the late, late show—he dreamed he was miniaturized, swimming through his father's bloodstream in an aqualung, carrying a laser gun to burn out the cancer, cutting his way through vast metastases collected on the liver like giant sponges, exiting through the tear duct of the eye after a successful operation.

He ate and slept. He dreamed. One night he was Hamlet, wandering through the menacing corridors of the castle, which was a hospital and in Los Angeles, not Denmark. Dressed somberly in the obligatory black tights and doublet, his father's breathing image engraved on the slate around his neck, he went from one ward to another. In the middle of the hospital was their house. His sister's room had the tools that had been Laughlin's, and then his father's. The saws were oiled and wrapped in cloth, the drill bits arranged in glasses of descending size. In his melancholy walk he came to his own room. An enactment was taking place there—a dream within the dream—in which he was forced to watch in impotent horror as a figure cloaked and hooded in a surgeon's gown stole up to his sleeping father and poured a vial of cancer-killing poison in his ear. As the murderer stole away, the sobbing prince caught sight of his guilty porcine eyes and purple jowls and shrieked, "Impeach Nixon!"

Finally the nurse had called, waking him this morning at nine o'clock. Mister Hart? This is Nancy Miles. I'm a nurse at Santa Monica General Hospital. Your father was brought in this morning. He asked me to get in touch with you. He says he'd like you to come down if it's convenient."

If it's convenient. He had put the receiver back down, humming loudly to himself. He caught sight of the face in the mirror—white as tripe and spongy from the recent gluttony; circles of ash under the eyes; hair receding in downy wisps from the forehead. Time, dread, mutability, death itself: they all worked within him like a convocation of maggots in a grapefruit rind. He cackled at what he saw in his soul: "I am but mad north-northwest."

He started up now, immediately alert, throwing off the blanket someone had draped him with during the night. He stepped outside to the hospital hall and looked at the clock above the nurses' station. It was almost eight. Breakfast trays were being clanked out of rooms. Back inside the room, he noticed an object on the nightstand that seemed a cross between jockstrap and kotex belt. Nausea enveloped him as he matched a purpose to the design: to diaper his father for the final moment. He took it out to the hallway and found a louvered window. It hit the pavement six floors down like a falling body.

He returned and saw that his father had one leg out of the bed and was struggling feebly to untangle the other from the sheet, his cheeks blowing like a fish out of water and his lower jaw drooping. He seemed almost singed, as if a great heat had encompassed him. He nodded toward the portable toilet in the corner of the room. Fighting the urge to vomit, Cabell lifted the feathery body out of bed and onto the cold ivory seat. His father clung to the handgrips, loose-fleshed calves quivering as he strained.

"If I can just get the plumbing going, I can hold on for Charley and the boy."

"You'll make it, Pop." Cabell heard a slight trickling sound. But his father was shaking his head and gesturing in disgust back toward the bed. As he got him up, Cabell looked at the bottom of the toilet and saw an ounce or two of urine red with blood.

His father ran a hand over his face, scratching at the gray stubble. "Didn't eat for the last few days. Didn't want to shit my pants at the end. Do I smell bad?"

Cabell shook his head.

"Oh. Good." He seemed to hold his breath, trying to rearrange the body without moving.

"It is bad now, Pop?"

The head moved slightly.

Cabell pressed the call button and met the nurse in the doorway. "He's got bad pain now. Can you give him a shot?"

"It's not due for another half hour. Doctor's orders."

Fuck Doctor! He wanted to scream the words that caromed off the sides of his mind. Instead he wheedled in a low voice: "Listen, it doesn't make any difference now. He needs it bad."

The nurse clicked her tongue and walked off, returning in a few minutes with the needle. His father took the shot in his haunch, the mouth moving convulsively.

"Cremated," Cabell made out the word and nodded his head.

His father was back asleep as if having fallen off a mountaintop. Cabell went out to try his sister's number again. The phone rang and rang; he tried to use some inner force to change it from a signal to a desperate summons. He cursed her in a chant as he banged his head against the pebbled walls. He felt suddenly claustrophobic, as if another body had wedged into the booth with him. "Not you," he said aloud, banging his knees to get away from his great-grandfather and the sense of failure, fermented in the musty storehouse of history that threatened to suffocate him. He finally managed to rip the accordion door open and bolted out.

A little after noon, his father opened his eyes. Cabell raised his head from his knees at the sound of lips smacking. He extended his neck like a communicant to receive the words.

"Did I die yet?" The foul breath scorched him.

"No, Pop, you didn't die."

"No, I didn't mean that. Did I die in my dream?"

"No, you didn't die there either."

"Oh. Good."

The body struggled weakly. Cabell intuited the purpose and pulled back the covers so he could put the bedpan on the mattress. He took his father's penis and tried to aim it. The organ rolled within the hooded foreskin at his touch. It strained and a few drops dribbled out and ran down onto the scrotum, staining the sheet Mercurochrome. He wiped his father with a tissue and took the bedpan away so that his father couldn't see it was empty.

Lips smacked again. Cabell braced the body in a sitting position and poured a glass of water from the pitcher on the nightstand. The mouth filled and tried to swallow, but peristalsis was gone and the throat had frozen in place. The water drooled out over the lips onto the chin. Cabel laid him down again and soaked a washcloth in the sink, then put it in his mouth. "Just chew on this, Pop, it'll keep your mouth moist."

His father lay sucking it like a baby. Cabell smoothed the dry red hair and rubbed the waxy forehead. He knew that the body had made a decision that it would work no more.

The eyes did the talking now. A look like a startled animal, a deer surprised at drinking, passed over them. "Pain?" Cabell asked. The eyes agreed. The same nurse answered the call; this time she brought the needle with her. The body jumped as if hit by a cattle prod. The mouth opened and moved but no sound emerged. Cabell bent closer, blasted by the mouth's stench. He though his father formed the word *Mother*.

After a half hour, with his father sunken in the bed, a new nurse came in. She was large, efficient-looking. Without asking Cabell's permission, she rolled the supple form to one side, hiked up the gown, and jabbed a thermometer into the rectum, taking the pulse while it calculated. She made notations on the chart, then sent a question in Cabell's direction. "Has he drunk any water?"

He shook his head. "Not to speak of."

"Excrete anything?"

"No."

"I'd like to give your father a little bath, Mr. Hart." She looked at him for the first time. "It will make him feel more comfortable. Would you mind leaving the room? I'll be just a few minutes."

He walked up and down the hall outside the door, counting the number of steps, his great-grandfather shadowing him in his sentry duty. Then the nurse beckoned him in as she left. "Mr. Hart, your father's kidneys have failed. He's in a coma now."

He went in and started to tuck the covers around the tiny body. He felt something under the gown and realized that the nurse had tricked him out of the room so that she could put the diaper on. I have failed you yet again, he thought.

The breath began to gutter, coming in gasps that sounded like a child's sobs. He put his head in his hands and thought for a moment that he might pray. But he ridiculed his hypocrisy even as he was trying. He had no power to provoke mercy.

When he looked up, his father's eyes had popped wide open and were staring straight ahead. The lungs were making a loud groaning noise, a noise to wake the dead. The noise was awful; it began to work the body up and down as if some invisible force was pounding the life out of him.

I should do something, he thought. I should end this, garrote him, smother him with a pillow, something. But he could not move.

Then he was keening. "Pop, Pop, I love you. Pop, you're doing good, so good. We're proud of you, me and Charley, so proud. Aren't we, Charley? We love you, Pop. You saved our lives. We love you for everything." His voice rose to carry over the noise. "You're almost there, Pop. We're with you. Come on, Pop, you can do it. We're here, we're with you. We're so proud, Pop."

He was still babbling after the sphincter had cackled and given up its tenuous hold, after the noise had stopped and the body was still. He opened his eyes and looked at his father. There was a slender gasp of air and then a sagging. The body stiffened as if trying to escape its confines of flesh. One last throaty sound like a growl and the rictus of a smile. The gorilla mask again? One final transfiguration?

He sat for a long time, holding the dead hand and looking down at the tears splashing the floor. He wiped his face with a forearm, snot leaving a snail-track of slime on his shirtsleeve. He stood up and tried to close the drooping mouth, but it fell back down, unhinged. He pulled the lids down over the bright varnished eyes, but as he let go, they crawled back up. He got up and walked through the doorway.

Miss Miles was back on duty at the nurses' desk. He stole up so that he was standing above her, then bent over and whispered into her frowning face, "Guess what? Six Twelve is dead."

In our old house, Mama's and mine, the place I lived before they brought me up here, I have all the pictures on my shelf. My family. There is one of you with your hair combed and a tie, like you're going to church. Another one with a monkey mask Mama said was taken a long time back, when she was still a girl. There's one of Mama and Aunt Aggie in their bathing suits. And a small one of Uncle Cabell. His face is blurry like he's trying to hide. It's hard to know what somebody moving fast like that really looks like. There's a picture of that soldier—my father? in his uniform. He smiles even though he's about to get killed. There are other pictures of people I never knew, old-time pictures. I look in their faces to see a part of me. Mama tells me about them all. My family.

In our house, Mama's and mine, when I couldn't sleep, when it was hot in the room or my face itched, sometimes when I just needed company, I used to bend these picture frames with my imagination, squeeze them hard on the sides and call for you all to come out. I'm huge, big as life, and you're all little, picture-sized. You do exactly what I say even though I'm just a child. All right, get a move on! Come on, get out! Uncle Cabell, walk along my finger! He does it, balancing like a tightrope man, hands out to keep from falling, blurry face looking down to the bedspread where he's about to fall. Okay, soldier man, march up here and fire your gun! He does it, and the bullet hits the palm of my hand and bounces down onto the bed. You can't hurt the giant. Your turn, Mama. Crawl underneath my shirt! Obey me! I feel her down there tickling all around me like a curious mouse. Okay now, Papa Two, you sit here on my shoulder and tell me the baseball scores! Gather round! Snap to it! Come here and sit out beyond my nose where I can see you. Now listen, folks, we've got ourselves some trouble. Big trouble. I'm trapped. They've got the giant chained up here in this foul castle. I need help. I mean it. There are things I've got to do. I need help. Isn't that what families are for?

I wish I had my pictures now. It would help to pass the time.

I suppose you're wondering, Papa Two, what I do all cooped up here. Not much. That's the answer. Nothing to do. Mainly, I just think. Most of the time, the man and woman don't bother me. He's off at work and she's downstairs where I can track her by where the radio's playing. If they start to come up here, I just bring on the marchers. They're really loud. Louder and louder. They can drown out anybody.

When the marchers aren't going on inside my head, I mainly think. I've got all the things Mama and me used to do completely memorized. Each time I think about something that happened, I try to remember another piece of it, some little extra piece to make it realer.

Here's something. This summer we went to the fair. It was down in Eureka. We went on the bus—the regular one, not the school bus. They give prizes to things like roosters and jelly. Mama said that next year we'd enter some of the tomatoes and other things we grew. We walked around awhile looking at cows and jars of food and stuff like that. I wanted to go where the rides were. Mama finally said, Okay. We walked underneath this big banner that separated the rides from the rest of the fair. I was looking at the people right in front of us. They were Indians. They didn't have any special kind of clothes, no feathers or anything like that, just regular shirts and pants and dresses. But I could tell. They had faces that were round and brown, and real black hair. A father and a mother and a big sister and a boy about my age.

This Indian family, they walked real close. They bumped into each other every so often like they were trying to make sure they were all still there. The Indian boy was on the shoulders of the father. He was smiling and every once in a while, he'd grab ahold of some of his father's black hair to make him turn one way or the other like a horse. Once the boy turned around and looked at my lame foot. I just looked right back at him. I'm lame and you're an Indian. We're both strange. That's what I made my look say.

When they got to the Ferris wheel, the Indian father got out a red bandana and wiped his forehead, and the boy watched the wheel go round and round, not moving his face but watching it with his eyes like it was a bee buzzing around his head. Just then Mama saw me and bent down. She said, Joey, don't stare! I said, Are they Indians? She said, Yes, Indians, Yuroks I think; they live all around here. I said, The same Indians that used to live near our house? She said, No, that was a littler tribe, like the Yuroks, but littler. I said, Bow-and-arrow Indians? She said, No, fishing. I said, What were they called? She said, Tollowas. I said, How come we never see any of those Tollowa Indians? She said, Well, they're gone. Gone? Yes, gone, died out. Every last one of them? Yes, hush now.

After we got home that night I asked her about the Tollowas again and she told me about them. She told me about the man who discovered them. He was Jed Smith. Jedediah. An old-time discoverer, a mountain man, the first man not an Indian to be around here. He came over the mountains. He had red hair like you, Papa Two. You know that river down there? Well, he named it. The Fortuna.

Jedediah discovered this land up here. Later on he got killed. Not here, but off someplace else, by one of the Indians in the mountains where he came from. A bow-and-arrow Indian did it, not a fishing Indian. Shot him in the neck with an arrow while he was sitting under a tree and that was the end of the famous discoverer.

When Jedediah got here, he was all tired out and almost starved. He had lost most of his supplies and his men had left him. The Tollowas, they were a little tribe, but they took care of him. They squatted down by the river and ate pieces of smoked salmon and talked sign language. They taught him to fish. You can live on fish.

I've always wondered, do you think there are Indians downriver?

A couple of days after the fair, Mama found out that some of the rangers were going to give a talk over at the park about the Tollowas. She took me over there. There was a campfire right down on the bank of the Fortuna. You could hear the river humming like a giant machine. It was nighttime, and the fire kept blowing smoke in everybody's face. One of the rangers told about the Tollowas' ideas and then he told some of the stories they used to tell when they were sitting around the campfire late at night. Mostly their stories were about Old Coyote. This was not just an ordinary animal, Papa Two. He was like part man and part animal. He was a friend of Earthmaker, the creator, the one who made the whole country up here, the sky and earth. Old Coyote was Earthmaker's friend and father to the Indians. He helped them whenever they got into trouble. He taught them how to do things and get along. If they hadn't listened to him they would have died out sooner than they did.

The Indians sat around the campfire at night and told about the tricks Old Coyote played. The ranger said that he was a Cunning Trickster. Like when he decided to get fire for the people. The only fire around in the early days was guarded by flies—not just regular flies, but real big and mean ones. They stood in a circle around the fire, making sure that nobody got any of it. Old Coyote came up to them and said, Excuse me, flies, but my friends the Tollowas need fire so they can cook their fish and keep warm when it's cold. Can I borrow some for them? The flies said, No, now get out of here. They stood real tight in their circle so Old Coyote couldn't get in. Know what he did? He thought for a moment, then turned around and flicked his tail so that it got inside the flies' circle and caught on fire. Then he went running off into the forest, stopping every once in a while to touch his burning tail to some leaves and make a fire for the people to use. He was laughing like mad.

Old Coyote did some weird things. The ranger said that Earthmaker made the world so that people wouldn't get old or die. When people felt they were getting old, they'd go to this lake Earthmaker made and dive in and get wet and be young again. Then here comes Old Coyote. He's walking around talking to the Tollowas and saying, Now listen, folks, don't you think this is kind of a dull life? There ought to be more going on. Maybe you ought to die. They all said, What's that? He said, Well, I don't know. But don't you think we ought to find out? Maybe if we knew what dying was we'd like living more. When Earthmaker heard all this talk he just shook his head up in the clouds and said, Oh, boy, are things ever going to go wrong now! Pretty soon weird things started happening. They were having a race and Old Coyote's grandson was out there, and he stepped on a rattlesnake and got bit. Old Coyote walked over and looked down where the boy was lying and said, Wake up, come on, jump up and start running. Then Earthmaker said, He can't. He's dead. You asked for it. Old Coyote said, Well, I changed my mind. Earthmaker said, No, it's too late. Old Coyote said, Well, we'll see about that. And he picked up his grandson's body and started breathing into the mouth. He carried the body around for years and years breathing into its mouth, and finally one day the grandson got up and started living again, and Old Coyote looked up to Earthmaker and said, See, I told you.

Sometimes he was totally silly. He was jealous of how pretty the leaves looked when they fell down from the trees and asked one of them how he did it. Easy, the leaf said, just climb up in the tree and fall. Old Coyote did this, but he didn't come down pretty like the leaves but fell down bang! right to the ground and killed himself. Then he laughed and got up to try again. All the time he was getting killed and jumping up to try again like the coyote in the Roadrunner cartoon.

But he kept these Indians going. Know what I mean? He taught them how to catch salmon. Besides their spears, they caugh fish in traps made of vines. And how to cook them. You know those holes in some of the big rocks down by the river? He showed them how to put water in these holes, then put in fish, then red-hot stones, and then a covering of moss. Then just leave it to cook. The ranger said he was a Cunning Trickster. The Indians sat around the campfire at night and told about the tricks Old Coyote played. He helped them against their enemies. Mama says he's out there still. The spirit of the place. I didn't hear the rest of what the ranger said because I got sleepy. I was dreaming about someone with a coyote head and a man body while he was still talking.

So that's what I mainly do: think about things. I try not to eat very much of the food they bring me because then I might owe them something. I don't talk. Like Mama says, Mum's the word. I stand here and look out the window, wondering about Mama. Sometimes I imagine that Old Coyote's out there. I can almost see him down there zipping from tree to tree like in the cartoon, coming up here to teach me a trick or two. I could use it.

I dream my dream in the morning, the dream of wolves and deer. During the days I sometimes almost forget what happened down there at the bridge, but then I tell myself, No, you've got to remember for Papa Two. He'll kill those bastard wolves for sure.

Hold it! Footsteps!

Quick, bring in the marchers!

TWO

4

He turned the machine off for a minute and rolled the window down to let the cold air sting his face and slap him awake. A truck went by in the incoming lane, blasting with a noise like a foghorn, its shock hitting the pickup long after it had roared by. Then there were no cars in sight for miles either way. He could tell by the smell of the night air that he was coming close to the ocean. He licked his lips and tasted a suspicion of salt. Shivering, he rolled the window back up and started the tape again.

". . . and by this time, of course, we were wiped out. I told Joey to get his sleepers on and then I came in to say goodnight. We went through The Ritual. I told you about that last time, didn't I? Weird. He's got pictures of everybody up there on his shelf—you, me, Cabe, Aggie, Laughlin, everybody, including Marshall, whose picture he found in my scrapbook. He's made a little arrangement up on his shelf. All it lacks are candles and tassels and he'd have himself a Shinto shrine where he could do ancestor worship. Sometimes I think to myself, Good

Lord, what is going on here? This is too totemic. But then I realize that it's probably my fault for dragging him up here where he doesn't have any real family and has to manufacture one. Anyway, every night we have a little conversation about the family. Sometimes we go back in history. He especially likes the idea that there's a desperado in the family, a gunslinger. But most of the time we concentrate on contemporaries. Since I told him about the operation, you've been on his mind. Do you have any pets now? Do you still have friends in the movies? Et cetera, et cetera. I say, Come on, Joey, you lived with Papa Two, you know what he's like. Yeah, I know, he says. Then the questions start up again. When you were a boy did you have a horse? Were there Indians back where you lived? Did you kill any? Same questions night after night.

"Tonight the questions had to do with Marsh. How did he die? Did blood come out of his mouth? Does it hurt to die? Is he with God now? What's God? Finally I couldn't take it anymore and I said, Okay, Joey, that's enough. Just cool it. Afterward it occurred to me that maybe he was asking about you—symbolically, I mean. About your illness. I felt bad about snapping at him. For him, everything is connected.

"I have to keep reminding myself of that. Every once in a while I get a glimpse into the way his mind works. A week or so ago I bought some magic tricks at the dime store and came home and practiced while he was outside playing. Then after dinner I dragged them out, put on an old black cape I'd gotten from Mrs. Downey, and made a big production of putting on a show. He was delighted to see me stand up in my mascara mustache and act extravagant and stagy, of course, but the tricks themselves didn't seem to turn him on. He just sort of sat there. You know: So what's new? My feelings were a little hurt. To tell you the truth, I really wasn't half bad. The Great Charley, I billed myself, since he didn't seem to appreciate *La Grande Charles*. I can pull quarters out of your ear and turn three red balls into four. Presto!

"Later on I was thinking about it and I decided that for him the supernatural is no big thing. I mean, for him magic isn't cheap tricks. It *is*. It's something you can *make* happen.

"The Ritual usually takes ten minutes or so, then he's off to sleep. When he first started this a few months back, I thought the question he was chewing on was Who Am I? But then I decided that this was too adult of me. It's more like Whose Am I? I've been vague about the Missing Father Problem. (The sniveling coward, her father says.) I let him believe that it might be Marsh, although never saying it was or wasn't. I keep hoping that he'll hang on and accept the non-explanation until he's old enough for the Big Talk.

"Anyway, he's asleep now, and I'm sitting here wiggling my toes in front of the fire with a cup of camomile tea. Yes, camomile!

"I guess you can tell from the clicks that mark my telltale starts and stops that this isn't all that easy for me. With letters at least you have the old formulas to fall back on. Dear Pop how are you I am fine tonight it's cold in the middle of summer. You know what I mean. This machine doesn't allow that. It's like being on the couch. Say the first thing that comes into your mind, dearie.

"Aarrgh.

"So. Where was I? I guess I was telling you about our day. It was like most of them—predictable, regular. That's the kind of person I'm becoming. Every morning, I have a three-minute egg. *Every* morning. I always read the paper while I eat, and take the sections in exactly the same order. Is that what getting old means?

"You might say that I live in a cerebral nunnery. I try to keep my mind tidied up. I'm not looking for objects to worship, but I'm not embarrassed to see the good with the bad the way I once was. I'm taking care of business. That means getting us in good shape. For myself, I've got that clear, pared-down feeling you get when you're on top of things. I stopped smoking, as I probably told you before. I can *feel* the lung tissue getting pink again, that tarry stuff disappearing. No dope, not even aspirin. When I look in the mirror I don't flinch. I tell you this not to flaunt my comparative youth and health, but because I know it will make you feel good. Your bone, your tissue, your flesh and blood are safe with us whatever happens, Pop."

"That was a long click. I had to replay what I just said. *Whatever happens:* I don't like the sound of that. But I'm trying to do what you said and face up to the possibilities.

"Joey says he sometimes thinks we live in an enchanted forest. I can see how he'd feel that. I can almost believe I'm Snow White and he's my dwarf. (I keep hoping that the forest creatures will come and do the housework while I nap.) But the days do have a special quality here. Nothing much ever happens, although you get the feeling that anything can.

"When I first got here, I met some people in town and hung out a little. One guy in particular. He'd been in the army. I guess he reminded me of Marsh in some way or another, although there's no real resemblance there. I saw him a couple of times and then I began to realize that he was just another casualty. Part of the walking wounded. In more ways than one, in his case. His wife had left him when he was in a hospital in Manila. Once he said to me, Well, we go together. You lost a husband in the war, I lost a wife. (I've let them believe I'm a Widow instead of an Unwed Mother. Another white lie I'll be embarrassed by one of these days, no doubt.) I thought to myself later on: Is that true? Are you forever mated to this man or someone like him? Are you going to be forced to live in Vietnam for all time? The answer was *no*. From then on, I decided to keep to myself, at least until I managed to create my own country, far away from that other one.

"Not that people are exactly beating the door down to be our friends. You hear all this stuff about small towns being open and neighborly. Not so. I guess you know that better than I do. After months of experience, my conclusion is that small towns have tiny hearts and long memories. I'm constantly struck by the way Halcyon's people look after their own. There are two types of people here. It's not black and white; everyone's white. It's not rich and poor; everyone's in the lower middle range someplace. It's Halcyoners and the rest; that's the division. They look over outsiders carefully. I'm sure there's a set of criteria you've got to meet to be accepted. I'm not sure what they are yet, but I suspect that we haven't gotten past square one. A Single Mother. What's her story? What does she want? Why is she here? (This is still the land where Men are Men and Women are Women, don't forget.) Maybe once they realize I'm not an undercover agent for the Sierra Club, or a prostitute on the lam, or something equally lurid, then things will be okay. I figure we'll get to know people in a natural sort of way when Joey starts school.

"In some ways I understand their suspicion. Part of it is because they've been victimized. Neocolonialism or something like that: Cabe would have the name for it. They've lived in a more or less depressed economy while the rest of the state has been civilized. Nobody paid any attention to Tollowa County. The hell with it—that was everybody's attitude. But now that everybody's starting to choke to death in the cities that are the result of this pride, they're starting to cast hungry glances up here at this fabulous piece of wilderness. An accident of neglect, really. Think of it. The only truly wild river in the state and the only pure water (everybody in town just siphons their household water right out of the Fortuna). The only part of this state that's virtually the way it was when the first white arrived.

"The point is that suddenly the people of Halcyon have got something valuable to sell, and they recognize it. They don't want to be screamed at regarding ecology and all that. For the first time they can remember, Halcyoners have got something the rest of us want—air, trees, water—and by God, they're not going to stand for any of this no-growth nonsense now. It's an attitude I don't like. But I understand it. As one of the natives said when I made a snide comment about his business, which is buying up beautiful old ranches with thousands of acres and carving them into tacky little parcels connected by gravel roads, which he sells like suburban tracts: Well, hell, it's the American way, isn't it? . . ."

He turned the machine off again. He wanted to ration this last tape so that there wouldn't be too long a period for him to be alone. He looked down at the speedometer and calculated that he had another forty miles to go. He decided to wait twenty miles before switching the machine back on. He ejected the tape, holding it up to catch a headlight glare from behind. The numbers were written in his father's spidery hand. 6/6/73: over a year ago. The tape fit into sequence. At that point she had been living in Halcyon for about nine months, having selected that small town on the Oregon border over all others because she and Marshall had once spent a pleasant afternoon there on the trip they took before he shipped out. About a month and a half earlier she had moved from the small apartment inside Halcyon proper, taking a cottage on two acres about a mile outside city limits. She was sewing for Vera Downey, a shopkeeper in town, and making about $150 a month to supplement the small GI insurance policy on which Marshall had named her beneficiary. In late April she and the boy had pruned the backyard orchard of arthritic apple trees and then scaled the bark to coax them back into production. In May they planted their garden. The Charley Tapes: he knew her through her secret words.

He was cramped and pained from hours of driving. Vibrations shimmying up through the pickup's floorboard had put his feet to sleep. The cold had been so bad, especially going over the Grapevine, that he had been forced to drive with one numb hand at a time, keeping the other inside his shirt thawing under an armpit for future use. Inert and sluggish, his body had gone past exhaustion. He could not have made it without her.

The voice was familiar but different. Listening to it was like witnessing the development of a character in a novel: each step made in continuity with the past, although it might not seem so at first; the whole enlightened by the steady expansion of sensibilities. She filled the dim space around him, a voice encouraging him to build handholds. Sometimes he reversed a passage and played it again, prolonging the guilty pleasure of his voyeurism.

It had been late afternoon—only yesterday? it didn't seem possible—when he got to the house. The sickly sun wasn't really setting, but just going out as if by power failure. The house was outlined in the anonymous bureaucratic shade of gray that settled over the entire city just before nightfall. He came up the street, realizing that he had approached this place from just about every angle over the years, spatially and psychologically, each time getting subtly different feelings. This time he felt it was not *his* house, though he'd been born there; and not his father's, for he was dead. It was *the* house. He no longer cared for it.

He had squeezed through the oleander hedge and gone around to the back. The screen door was secured only by a snaplock and gave easily when he pulled. He wrapped his coat around his fist and knocked sharply on the glass panel, breaking it, then reached in to unlock it from within.

The kitchen smelled of coffee grounds and Drain-O. He

walked into the living room and collapsed on the sofa. The room was dark and close, the feeling, that of an underground cavern. He told himself that he would sleep for a while and later consider what should be done. But when he closed his eyes, he continued seeing—first the orange backdrop of his lids with faint traceries of light and veins, and then, further back, growing up unbidden in the heavy undergrowth of the occipital region, a view of bright comatose eyes and an unhinged jaw.

He had risen quickly and begun bumping through the furniture like a blind man, shins barking on chairs, arms outstretched. He achieved the hall and then the bathroom, and turned on lights. Piss came out of him like a string. He watched it foam up in the toilet bowl. Shuddering, he shanked the last drops out and turned to the basin to wash. Snorting burning soap, he opened his eyes and looked up mechanically to check his bloated features. But there was no mirror. He realized that his father had pried it off to avoid having to watch the face die a little more each day. He cataloged the small pharmacy of amber vials on the glass shelves and found some codeine. Shaking out two tablets, he slurped a handful of water to slide them down, then put the rest in his pocket and sat back on the toilet seat to wait for the analgesic warmth to climb his spinal cord.

He got up and started his tour, pausing in each room to turn on lights and finger familiar and foreign items. In his old bedroom, model airplanes were still suspended by fishing leader from the ceiling; in Charley's room, the series of Hollywood dolls sat dusty and begrimed above the valances: pieces of childhood to be saved, to be passed on to children and children's children. *See, your daddy made this when he was a boy.*

Otherwise, the rooms were cleaned out, hollow to the step. A stack of boxes marked GOODWILL with black grease pencil stood in the hall. He stepped around them and went into his father's room, smelling the distinctive must that had always hung there like a bodyprint. Old coins, a flashlight, a diamond wedding ring, yellowed envelopes with three-cent stamps addressed in his mother's backhand script: he pawed the drawer like some Oedipal sneak thief, taking nothing, just searching for tactile impressions that would serve as pawns later on. At the foot of the bed was his grandfather's toolbox with everything neat inside, saws filmed with a blueness of oil, files wirebrushed clean of burrs. He picked it up to test his strength as he had when a boy.

His father's final days had been spent in the living room. He understood that after finishing his inspection of the back rooms of the house and returning there. The couch, the handmade bookcase of oak, the overstuffed chair, and the coffee table had all been drawn into a kind of square, narrowing the distance he must go for essentials, serving as a fort at which he had made his last stand.

He switched the desk lamp on. There was an envelope addressed to the Lion's Club. Beside it was a shaky note whose sentences drifted down out of the lines, a cashier's check for $1,734.58 stapled to the top right corner:

Okay you guys:

Drop the envelope in the mail to Lions. It's my vital statistics. Art Starkis down there called the other day hinting for such material. I said I'd get back to him and didn't. I decided to write it out myself. Why leave your reputation to chance? Also, I've arranged things with Frazier Bros. Mortuary. (Forgive me for being ghoulish here.) They are paid and instructed. Call Albert Frazier. His home number is 456-8724 if you need to get him after work.

The attached check cleans out the bank account. There's also the house, which I guess is worth thirty-five or forty thousand. I recommend you split the proceeds three ways. Cut Joey in as full partner. He's got a long way to go and might need a little nest egg one of these days. Also it will remind him that old Papa Two cared about him.

145

Well, look after each other. Maybe we'll get together again in the sweet bye and bye.

Love and kisses.

P.S. I think we did pretty good, considering.

Near the note pad was the jackknife with the mother-of-pearl handles that his grandfather had used for everything from sharpening flat carpenter's pencils to peeling apples. He opened it to test the blade, which had been whetted so often that it had taken on the shape of a Turkish hook. He still remembered the lecture he had received when he had been caught trying to stick it into a tree trunk from ten feet away: "Damn it, boy, this ain't no toy. This is a tool. You no more abuse a tool than a person. Not if you expect it to work for you." Sitting next to the knife was the pocket watch that had also been his grandfather's: chased silver case, the magnifying crystal, inserted after the old man's eyes started to go bad, covered with scratches now. It was wound down, but had kept perfect time for the last twenty years at least, dangling from a belt loop into his father's pocket by a suspension of brown shoestring.

He rummaged the desk drawers and found a manila envelope secured with a fat rubber band. Opening it, he found a jumble of different-sized photographs, some finished matt, some glossy. He saw his enigmatic mother wearing a wartime look of slacks and blouse with sleeves puffed at the shoulders; himself and Charley at birthday parties, looking up with new gaps in their teeth, in Halloween costumes. There were pictures of all the family except for his father: the man behind the camera who gave others image at peril to his own.

Below the envelope was a copy of his prospectus, "King of Infinite Space: Hamlet and His World." It had been written at a time when he still believed in orderly process: prospectus to dissertation to book; graduate student to assistant professor to tenure. It was an unclimbed ladder.

At the lowest stratum of the drawer were the tape ma-

146

chine and several casettes, each with Charley's name and the date received penciled onto the face. It had been his father's notion of painless communication, a twentieth-century epistolary form, and he had bought three recorders to keep them in touch. Cabell had never used his.

He picked a tape at random and put it on. The voice surprised and then comforted him. Listening to her, he felt that he had stumbled onto something well wrought, dependable, once a common household object but now, in a time of sullen craft, almost a piece of folk art. Hearing her, knowing that she was still there, gave him hope for himself. He listened to her while finishing his inventory. Occasionally some throwaway phrase would bring him up short and cause him to look into the infinity of wall at the other side of the room. In the first communication after the operation, for instance, she had begun: "Hi Pop. Say, that's great news about Cabe. He's been gone so long from us . . ." *Gone so long.*

He didn't finish until after ten. By then he had a second wind and had made his plan. There's nothing more here, he thought. I'd best be going. Putting the knife and watch in his pocket as mementoes, he scooped up the recorder and tapes and took one last look around. He put the letter in his pocket and made a mental note to mail it. He was about to go out the front door when he remembered to make the phone call. Dialing the number, he realized that if he hadn't found his sister's voice this would have seemed a tearful project. But now it seemed a silly piece of business.

"Umm." The sound was sleepy, warm, not getting there until the fifth ring.

"Mister Frazier? Albert Frazier?"

"Yes."

"Sorry to call you so late. I'm Cabell Hart. I think you had an arrangement worked out with my father, Joseph Hart."

"Oh, of course." The voice woke quickly and saluted with professional unction. "Is your father . . ."

"Yes, dead," he interrupted, not wanting another to say the word. "The body's at Santa Monica General."

"I'm deeply sorry, Mr. Hart. Your father was a fine man."

"Thank you," Cabell smiled at the reflex condolence. "You'll take care of things, won't you?"

"Of course. We'll make all the arrangements. Your father wished to be cremated, as you're probably aware. But he gave us no instructions regarding a ceremony."

"No ceremony."

"None at all?"

"Right. My father felt that life was for the living." He imagined the pajamaed mortician frowning.

"Of course, as you wish. You can rely on us. Your father game me his instructions, and as you probably know took care of payment in advance. Just one final detail, though. But perhaps you'd prefer to talk about it some other time?"

"No, I'm leaving tonight."

"Leaving?" There was a slight intake of breath.

"Yes."

"I see. Well, perhaps we could settle it now. Perhaps it was an excess of delicacy on my part, or maybe I just forgot, but in any case I didn't ask your father about the remains."

Remains. The image was of gray soot pyramided over tiny shards of bone. "Could I have them? Could they be sent to me up at my sister's home?" He had the idea of driving back to South Dakota with Charley and the boy to scatter the ashes at the windy homestead, a ritual to unite their future together.

"No, I'm afraid not. California law doesn't allow that. They could be placed in an urn in our mausoleum. That is the usual disposition. The alternative would be to scatter them at sea. The pilot is an ordained minister and the scattering involves a nondenominational service. It's up to you."

He smiled at the thought of this posthumous baptism. It didn't fit his father, a man who had lived on the edge of the Pacific for forty years, but remained spiritually landlocked in the Midwest. In all those years, he and Charley had badgered him into the water only once, during a vacation at Sequoia, when he had walked into a calm place in the river wearing bathing trunks, an undershirt, droopy socks, and wing-tipped shoes, paddled for a moment with head held high out of water, then got out, shook like a dog, and retreated far under a beach umbrella on the shore. He had feared water. But it was better that his dust should be broadcast for the communion of fish than walled up in one of their creepy buildings.

"Make it the sea-scattering, then."

After hanging up, Cabell took one quick look around and left.

That had been ten hours ago. He rolled the window down again and felt the air; salt on the lips, a sea air now for sure. He saw the moon reflecting off the water like a silver dollar. He could feel the melancholy tide come sweeping in and then withdraw. He watched until the road curved away from that eternal note of sadness and pointed inland again. The highway was suddenly darkened as huge redwoods rose on either side like pillars. He had to slow down as he collided with ground fog rising up from ferns and other supporting growth, penetrating the damp forest like smoke from a fire.

In the company of Charley, he had gone the length of California: over the central valley's inert plane, through the Bay Area, across the San Raphael Bridge and alongside San Quentin, up the coast highway. Two stops for gas. He pushed the pickup faster than he should have. He felt he had to get to her house before resting. He feared sleeping in a place without people who were his kin.

They had done their ration of unimaginable things, he and his sister, but they had been chastened by events. They had learned. Now they were out on the other side of all that death and self-abuse, ready to begin anew. He visualized their life together as that of contented brother and sister in a Victorian novel—in repose after the storm of history, drawing dignified pleasure from each other's company. Like Jos and Amelia Sedley, perhaps, after the wild events of Waterloo;

except they would be less silly and frivolous. He could see himself living in her small town, at least for a time. He would conceal his past from the people there, integrate himself into their community through a job: honest sweating work. He would take a lively interest in the boy. The three of them would build a hollow of calm arts. As he fantasized their life together, he smiled, half expecting the tape recorder's voice to reproach him for his precipitousness.

The twenty miles was almost eaten up. Cheating slightly on his rule, he switched the machine on again:

"Anyway, today we walked down the river. Joey calls it *downriver*, as if it was some spot of recognized geography. In a way it does have an identity all its own, for us anyway. It's downriver from Halcyon, back toward Eureka. Strangely, it's the wildest part of the Fortuna. Above the town is the Oregon line and all kinds of little villages. But below, in this area between the coast and Halcyon, there's virtually nothing. It's like they established this town as a kind of outpost, but were never quite able to civilize the ground in between. Bit off more than they could chew, I guess.

"We walk a couple of miles and we're absolutely alone. It's so secluded and hard to reach that none of the local yokels bother going down there. Tremendous walls of rock on either side of the river. You have to scramble over a lot of boulders, jumping from one to another like mountain goats. At one point there are some symbols scratched into the rock interfacing up above. Petroglyphs: isn't that what you call them? They're spidery things with lines squiggling out. I can't make head nor tail of them except for one: a fish. The solitude is so complete, I always half imagine that the blur I convince myself I just saw out of the corner of my eye is an Indian diving into the undergrowth to hide from us.

"It was warm enough to swim today. Usually June

is still winter up here. But today it was hot. We took off our clothes and waded through the shallows. Joey fooled around there for a bit and I swam until my body numbed. Then we headed to our bathtub, as Joey calls it. You approach it from above, after fording the river in a shallow place, like sneaking up on it. The Fortuna can be sudden and mean. Everytime it rains up here people start looking at it nervously, remembering all the times it has risen up suddenly to smash down their houses. It has the potential of taking you and banging you to pieces before you know what's happened. It scares me to death. I love it.

"This bathtub of ours is a rock formation where the water has come through and hollowed it out. It's big enough for our two bodies. You can sit there while the water circulates around you like a whirlpool bath, calm and relaxing, though raging like the very devil not three feet away. I can sit down. Joey floats like a buoy, water to his neck. Once he said, Mama, it's like sailing in a rock boat. And in a way it is. In it you have a sense of mastering the river, of sailing on this tremendous power.

"We sat there for a long time, numbed by the water, enjoying the sensation of navigating the river. I caught Joey looking at my breasts floating on the water. I felt guilty, and thought, Good God, I can't keep doing this to him. I'll maim him for life. But there wasn't any kind of weird fascination in his look, just a kind of nostalgia, like he was thinking about being full and warm and well taken care of. (I know what you're thinking, Pop. But I *was* an okay mother for the first couple of months or so, generously lactating and always there at meal-time.) Anyway, he reached over and touched me. With a sense of wonder more than anything else. I grabbed him and hugged him tight. He was all slippery and slick like a baby seal, and felt so good against me. I thought to myself, *Oh, God, how I love this child; without him*

I'm nothing. A few minutes later, we negotiated our way back to the shore and climbed on one of these mammoth rocks that overlook the river and lay there for a long time, getting warm both from the rock below and the sun above. He had goose bumps on his skin, the water sort of beading up on him. I looked him over. Perfect, except for the foot. And you can't see the defect when he's not walking. In a way I hate to think of the scar that will be on the ankle: the only mark on this perfect little body. But I'll be glad when he's old enough to get it taken care of. As it is now, I think he's starting to identify himself as a 'lame' person. I don't know where he picked up the word, but he uses it in moments of self-pity.

"He's a good boy, Pop, thoughtful and tough and funny all at once. I remember once when we were up here last fall during the salmon run. It was cold then, and we were sitting on these rocks watching them jumping the rapids, flinging themselves high in the air like sailfish, smacking down again, hitting rocks, water-logged trees, but getting the strength up to go at it again. I think Joey could sense the violence of the urge, the tremendous strength and tenacity of it, the need to get back there to the spawning grounds and duplicate their chromosomes. It frightened him a little. I explained the whole cycle as well as I could. (I often feel like I'm the head of the Woodcraft Rangers here, and barely manage to keep one step ahead of his questions, thanks to the good old Halcyon library). I think he got it pretty good, although he kept referring to the *milk* that the male puts on the female's *eggs*. Anyway, at one point there was this especially large fish that we'd been watching as it made his way up the current. It sidled over to a pool down below us to rest a minute and get its strength back up. It was big. You could see that dorsal fin cutting through the water as it swam. I watched Joey eye it, and sort of move backward when it came close to our rock. I could tell that his imagination was magnifying the fish to shark size. Almost in spite of himself he touched my arm and said, Mama, do salmon bite? I was thinking about that today, while he was lying there sunning himself like some water mammal, and it made me laugh out loud."

"That was another long click, Pop. I'm getting sleepy, and I think I've just about said it all. To summarize: things are okay here. Your daughter and grandson ride buses, study the insides of libraries and other public buildings, and take care of their garden. We're contented, I guess you'd say, and I hope that doesn't call up the image of a cow and her calf chewing on their cud. I never expected to be living here, and I'm not saying that I'll be here forever. But these last few years have given me a deep yen to make plans that can somehow survive the cataclysms of the outer world, if you know what I mean. What is it the Chinese say? Dig caves deep and store much rice? This seems the place to begin: outside the flow of events. It's entirely possible that I'll move down your way one of these days and become one of those nice bony ladies in elegant sundresses and floppy straw hats and spend her happy days breeding roses and looking after her dear Papa. *Très chic.*

"So. Well, okay, Pop, I have the feeling that I'm just filling up the airwaves here. You know how much we love you, and how hard we're pulling for you. I'll just close by including my love and Joey's. Bye for now.

"Oh, here's a P.S. Joey loves getting the week's summary of the Dodger scores you've been sending him. I'm not sure he understands what's going on, but it makes him feel like a big boy. He says that after his foot gets fixed, he's going to throw fastballs like Don Sutton. Who's Don Sutton?"

The tape was just ending as the official green quadrangle flashed by on his right, sandwiched in between a series of real estate advertisements:

HALCYON

Pop. 1095   Alt. 2350

He hauled out the pocket watch and saw that it was just before nine o'clock. Slowing the pickup to a cruise, he saw the character of the town in its main street. Overhead street lights; shops with awnings; old men in truckers' caps leaning against the eastern brick of buildings like lizards in the morning sun; a boy fixing the chain on his bicycle. It would be hard not to romanticize such a place and condescend to its charm.

Three days' beard itched demandingly along the perimeters of his cheeks. Exploring teeth with tongue, he felt a coated, grainy surface. The knotted, sour feeling in his guts was not so much from fear as from a failure to eat anything but stomach mints for forty-eight hours. Deciding that showing up at his sister's house in such wretched shape would prohibit him from dealing with her on equal terms, he worked the pickup into a diagonal parking space in front of a small restaurant. He got out automatically feeling in his pocket for small change, but after the dime was ready he realized that parking meters hadn't yet reached this crossroads.

Inside the smell was of maple syrup and bacon. He went directly to the tiny bathroom in the back, feeling a dozen pair of eyes x-raying his back as he closed the door. He washed his face, afterward studying it briefly for further signs of decay. Happy that little had changed since he last checked—no further erosion of hairline, no deeper wrinkles—he scoured his teeth with a paper towel coated with Boraxo, washed his mouth out, and then went out to take a seat at the counter.

He gave the elderly waitress his order and then looked around. It was as if he had intruded on a family breakfast. One man two seats down talked right across his front to the man at his left elbow in a debate on chain saws; he found himself leaning back to give them room. As new customers came in, the waitress automatically called out an order to the fry cook behind her, looking up for only the briefest moment to check in case the daily regimen had been changed. Putting down a dollar for his toast and coffee, he asked directions to Pioneer Street and was pointed back out of town the way he had come. Back in the morning chill, he fought off a huge yawn, then climbed into the pickup and ground the complaining starter until the engine caught.

The town ended as abruptly as it had begun and within seconds he was in open country, seeing the road he had just traveled from the opposite perspective. He turned onto a small country road as directed, then drove until he came to a silver mailbox with HART stenciled in black and a child's lopsided heart painted down at a corner. He parked and got out, closing the door quietly to preserve the surprise, then walked back along a narrow gravel path winding through thick stands of pine and scrub oak. He would knock on the door then hide beside it and grab her when she came out, yelling "guess who?"

Almost by accident he came upon the small house, knobby with dormers and gables, almost Tyrolean. It stood in a large clearing, flanked on one side by a vegetable garden and on the other by a child's playyard filled with little traffic jams of Tonka trucks. He saw the rehabilitated apple orchard further back on the property.

Little touches he recognized as coming from his sister's hand made him smile: an old bus bench advertising Bireley's Orange under a tree; bird feeders made out of milk cartons; a hand-cut tin whirligig in the shape of a biplane whose propeller was meant to frighten birds from the lone quince. But leaves had drifted onto the porch. Within the garden's careful calculus, the ground was parched and cracking. Unharvested fruit hung from the tomato vines like shrunken heads. The paradox was of something usable but unused.

Walking up to the front window, he remembered the unanswered phone. What if she had pulled up stakes for some reason? Shading his face on both sides, he peered inside, but was unable to reconstruct the whole from the slit of chair and linoleum. He knocked on the door and heard the echo from within. Panic rising in him, he grasped the knob and tried to force it. At that point a voice assaulted him from behind.

"What the hell are you doing?"

Snatching his hand away guiltily, he turned to see a short, plump, sixtyish man standing a few feet away. He wore a checked flannel shirt and wide brimmed planter's hat that hid the upper part of the face. Liver-spotted hands held a quivering garden rake with an air of vague menace.

Which dwarf are you, Grumpy? Cabell smiled as the question occurred to him and he smothered it.

"I said, What are you doing here?" The man took a step forward and shifted the balance of the rake to subtly change it from cudgel to lance.

"I'm looking for Carlotta Hart." He decided he didn't like the man and made his voice crackle with proprietary annoyance. "She's my sister and I'm her brother."

"Oh." The rake lowered until its tines rested impotently on the ground. The old man moved his jaws as if summoning spit to lubricate his speech. Cabell wanted him to leave before anything else was said.

"You don't know then?"

"Know? Know what?" The words had hit him like a blunt instrument. He didn't want to know.

"About the accident."

"Accident?"

"Down at the river." The old man took off his hat to reveal a gentle, almost hermaphroditic face.

"My sister?"

"She's gone."

"Gone?" He was powerless to break the antiphonal rhythm of the revelation. This old man was his Greek chorus.

"Dead."

The rough siding of the house bumped his spine as he slid down, driven to earth by that word. Then he was sitting, legs splayed out. He wanted to debate it, dispute the odds that it should happen so close upon the heels of that other death. *It can't be.* But he could feel the perverse rightness of it. There was a force in the universe in charge of punishment. In such coincidence was the hand of God.

"It happened a couple weeks ago." The old man had knelt to be at eye level with him. "Down at the river. She fell in, and it took her. They had search parties out to get the body but couldn't find it. The river's wild."

He looked up into Cabell's face, then bowed his head, allowing sun to glint off an angle of baldness. "Nobody knew how to get ahold of the family. We knew there were relatives down in southern California somewhere but not how to get in touch. None of us neighbors really knew her very good. We took up a collection for burial just in case they find her. Three hundred eighty-six dollars. It's in a special account, just in case."

The words came through cotton batting. He was obsessed with completing his cycle of shock, disbelief, and then resignation, with seeing that the transition from one emotion to the other was made efficiently. Existential lightning strikes twice: he could buy it. The double death would be a plausible wrench of fate within the framework of that Victorian novel he'd imagined them into during the trip from L.A. The author, Lord of his creation, would simply enter in and say: "But at that very moment, unbeknownst to him, his sister was struggling in the cold current of the river, going under for the third and final time into the black, beneath where she saw God's foot on the treadle of the loom."

He accepted it but wanted to stipulate that it wasn't fair. "Can you believe it?" he said.

The old man shook his bald head sadly in the negative, although Cabell had actually meant the question for the shade he knew was somewhere near, his ghostly great-grandfather, who would be gloating, waiting for him, last of the Harts, to die, so it would be all over.

There was a pressure building deep inside him. It offered

to expand and fill him, drive him to some kind of seizure, epilepsy or worse. He willed it to come, tried to push himself over the edge. But he remained himself. *In coincidence is the hand of God.* The proposition offered itself again. He wanted to cry, to lubricate this terrible pressure with tears. Tears, a sign of grace. They wouldn't come. He felt too much. He didn't feel at all. It was almost as if he had accepted it before it happened.

He was aware. The sun was on the other side of the house now. The mountain chill was coming up through the ground where it had gone to hide from the day. The slightest moisture, miniature rainfall, drizzled down from the silk oak above him. Ants and other insect populations were working the rich humus beneath the pine needles and oak leaves, endless industry that gave the ground a microscopic jump and crackle. He saw it all, but one detail nagged at him; there was something he should be remembering.

He heard the hyraulic snap of joints as the old man rose. He stood there edging the brim of his hat through ridged, yellow fingernails. His face was pathetic, downcast, like a saddened family retainer. The lips were moving; Cabell strained to catch the words. " . . . a doctor or somebody. I could just run over to the house and make a call."

"No," Cabell said. "I'm all right."

"Are you sure you can make it okay?" The old man looked doubtful.

"Yes, I'm okay." The detail kept escaping him, nimbler than he was. Then he stumbled into it by accident. "The boy too?"

"Joey?" The old face brightened, glad to have some good news. "Now Joey, he's just fine. No problem. Wasn't hurt at all, except for shock and the like, which is purely natural. He's up with the Bruces as his fosters until they could locate some kind of kin. The county decided. They had doctors look him over and all. I went to see him last week. Mrs. Bruce said he was napping just then and so maybe I should come another time, but that he was doing fine, just fine. If you want to see him, just drive on up the road a mile or so and then you'll come to the sign pointing up Battle Mountain. Take that, go a couple miles, till you come to a white house on your right. Only place up in there. You can't miss it."

The voice trailed off. The old man picked up the rake and was moving backward. Uneasiness fogged the growing space between them.

"Listen, how did it happen?" Cabell asked. "Tell me again. I didn't get it."

The old man had already turned and although the retreating flannel back seemed to flinch, he kept on going, seeking the trees and underbrush as if it were protective coloration.

"An accident," the words floated back.

Leaning against the rough wood siding, Cabell felt a premonition of fever squiggle up his spine. He felt immensely tired and thought that he would stay there and sleep. He curled on the ground, bringing his knees to his chest. But he was cold. He shivered. Steadying himself with one hand, he rose. He walked down to the pickup and started. Yawning time after time, yawning until tears came, he began to drive. Wondering where he was going, he came to a motel and accepted it as a fated meeting. He got a room. Taking one of his father's codeine pills, he sat on the edge of the bed and looked into the bathroom where a galaxy of flies and bugs swung in mindless orbit around a bare bulb. Then he fell back, feeling the row of tufted balls on the cotton spread against his back.

Once he awoke. He knew it was waking because he could still see the bugs swimming through the thick amber purged from the light. "Don't you ever sleep?" he croaked at his great-grandfather, who sat near his bed. Then he fell back into the dreams that had been waiting his return.

5

Swollen and aching from his twenty-hour sleep, he stood in front of the double door, listening to the small-town sounds of Halcyon and trying to overcome his aversion to going into the stucco office. He felt no suspense. He accepted it all. He just wanted to fulfill the forms and, after doing what was expected, leave.

Inside, the room was small, looking more like an insurance company's field office than a police department. His way was barred by a gray government desk commanded by a middle-aged woman in a red pant suit and blond bouffant hairdo. Unperturbed by his entry or the cackle of the CB set beside her, she read an Ellery Queen paperback.

"Excuse me," he said to rouse her.

"Yes, what is it?"

"I'd like to talk to somebody."

"You want to report something?"

"No," he said. "I want to talk to somebody. About my sister."

"What about her?"

"She died."

"When?" The woman was skeptical.

"I don't know," he shrugged. "Her name's Carlotta Hart."

"Oh." She set the book down and stood up quickly. "Hart. Yes, just a minute. Wait here." She disappeared through a door at the back of the room.

A minute or so later, a large shambling man in a khaki uniform emerged from the same door. He was balding and broad-featured, the nose pounded flat and scar tissue bulging the top of the eyes. He was rubbing his hands vigorously on a rag in an attempt to get oil off. The smell coming off him was of wet dog and solvent.

"You're Mister Hart?" Cabell nodded at the Grand Ole Opry voice. "Goddarn it. Finally. We been trying to find out about your sister's family for almost two weeks. I'm Vern Strapp, chief of the department."

The man gestured with a soiled right paw in apology for not shaking. "Lord in heaven," he continued. "This has been awful. We didn't know how to go about getting ahold of next of kin. We tried everything. I'm sure glad you're here."

The man put the rag on the desk and began inspecting his hands, picking at the oil that had gotten under the fingernails and into lines in the skin. Cabell watched him, acutely aware that he had no agenda.

"I was over at her house," he said. "An old man—I guess it was her neighbor—told me. I thought I ought to talk to somebody."

"I don't blame you," the chief looked up at him through eyes that were almost lost in the width of face.

"You looked for her?" The question seemed perfunctory.

"Lord, yes. We had near two dozen men out there on the river for a solid week. Up and down the bank, out in the middle in boats. There are some wild spots downriver. A body of water like that one doesn't always yield up what it gets. Maybe late next spring when it's snowed again and the river's filled with runoff. Something might float up then."

"I don't know quite what I'm doing here," Cabell said. "I mean I came up to visit her. And then this. I don't know. I was thinking that maybe I ought to see someone."

"Like I said, we've done everything we could. We ain't a big town and we don't have a lot of resources. But we gave it our best shot. You could check it out with the DA's office down in Eureka if you want."

"No"—the defensiveness in the voice made Cabell try to reassure him—"I don't mean that. It's just that I haven't really seen much of her in the last few years. I just thought maybe I ought to try to see somebody around here that might have known her. I don't know why, exactly. Just something I thought I should do."

"I can understand the feeling, Mister Hart. I can, believe me. Fact is, though, I don't think she had a whole lot of close friends. There's Vera Downey. She's got a little clothes shop over on Mill Street. I think your sister did some work for her. Also, there's Bill Hunter. I think he knew your sister. He might be someone to talk to. He's got a real estate office about a half mile north of town."

"Maybe I'll look him up," Cabell said. "What's the name of the company?"

"Jed Smith Realty." He picked up the rag again and gestured with it. "I'd run you over in the squad car, but something's wrong with the carburetor. One of my deputies is out sick today. The other's down in Eureka testifying on an accident case. I can't get a mechanic over here. We been hit by that law that says that everything that can possibly go wrong will go wrong. Tell you what, though. I'll call Mister Hunter and tell him you're on your way."

"Yes, sure. Thanks very much. I appreciate it."

"Nothing to it. I'm just awful sorry that you had to stumble into it like this. Must be a shocker."

If you only knew! Cabell felt on the verge of blurting it all out, seeking some kind of priestly guidance. He stopped himself by mumbling, "Yeah, it's tough."

"Well, if you want some more talk after going around town, just come by and see me, hear?" The hammy features seemed friendly. "We don't have your urban crime problem up here, and there's always time to sit and have a cup of coffee."

Cabell left thinking of the reaction of the Oakland Police when he had called them about Jim Henry. The contrast warmed him.

Jed Smith Realty stood in the shadow of a sign that read OWN A PIECE OF GOD'S COUNTRY! He smiled at the irreverence and pulled over the double line and parked on a quadrangle of freshly laid asphalt. He sat in the pickup looking at the signboard mural where a copy of Michelangelo's God reached an index finger out to touch a map of California, gray and sooty except for a verdant dab at the northern tip. The message below was in the form of an illuminated manuscript page:

> In the beginning there was land, air, water. In the beginning, but not now. Cities are groaning with people. Resources once considered unlimited are scarce. Crime spreads over the land like the plague. Yet not ten miles from where you now stand there is a little spot of land, an Eden, where deer browse in backyards and hawks soar majestically above rooftops. In streams that meander through stands of virgin timber, beavers build their dams. There are puma, coyote, and even an occasional black bear ambling through the surrounding forests. Life goes on the way it was meant to in God's Country. This 2000-acre development is like a natural preserve. To walk through it is to have a religious experience, to feel at one with yourself and with nature, to feel secure and safe. Jed Smith Realty is proud to present this unique offering assembled from ranches homesteaded over one hundred years ago, when Indians and settlers lived in harmony in this valley. One-acre lots begin at $12,500, electrical hookups and septic systems not included. This is your salvation.

A pencil point clicked on the window, and he saw a hand beckoning him into the office. He entered and saw a man in profile at the desk, phone cradled at his neck, hands in his lap, and feet propped on the windowsill. He nodded in Cabell's direction and continued to talk, looking out the window at the passing traffic. "Christ yes, we're willing to deal, but I'll be go to hell if I'm going to give it away . . ." The aubergine leisure suit and white patent-leather loafers fit the conversation. To keep from intruding, Cabell walked around the room looking at the frames crowding the wood-paneled walls. There were certificates specifying completion of real estate seminars; Rotary plaques; pictures of a pyramid of Little Leaguers wearing uniforms with Jed Smith Realty's logo; an Associate of Arts degree from Tollowa Junior College. Off by itself was a Purple Heart and other army medals clustered on a field of mauve velvet at whose center was the black horse guidon of the Eleventh Cavalry.

"I know what you're thinking." The words were out before he realized that the man had hung up the phone, brought his feet down, and swiveled to face him.

"What?"

"That all real estate agents are jerks."

"No." Cabell blushed at how easily his thoughts had been picked.

The other man laughed, flashing bright teeth as he stood. "I know. Just a little joke. Never fails to get people feeling guilty. Hits too close for comfort. Softens them up for the pitch." He was tall and well built, but extended his left hand in an effeminate, continental gesture. Cabell took it, embarrassed by the passive lack of grip.

"Mister Hart? Cabell, isn't it? I'm Bill Hunter. Chief Strapp told me you were coming." The pleasant face was drawn into a triangle at the chin by the spade of black beard. The smile dissolved into a serious look. "Awful sorry about the reason for the visit. I knew your sister. Not too well, but enough to know she was a fine person and to know how you must be feeling. It's bad news."

Motioned to the chair facing the desk, Cabell obeyed. As Hunter sat, silver flashed briefly at the empty right sleeve. It was like an eel glancing out and then retreating back into the dark.

"It really shook this town up some, that accident," he

164

continued. "I think everybody was grieved. It's like that poem says, a death like this diminishes us all."

Cabell shook his head in dumb agreement, lulled by the Rotary Club tone, wondering when the next revelation would come from the sleeve. Finally a chrome prosthesis with two hook-fingers ending in a cleft emerged slowly, as if trying to become accustomed to daylight. Hunter looked down at it and Cabell blushed, guilty at having been caught in the stare. *Forgive me*, he thought of saying, *I'm the sort of person who empathizes; I finish stutterers' sentences for them.*

The cold fingers extended to the desk and located a ball-point pen. They grasped it with a metallic snap, pushed the head down on the blotter so the retractable point appeared, then rearranged the pen and held it to begin doodling on a pad. Cabell felt a kind of magic had been demonstrated in this legerdemain.

"Grenade," Hunter smiled and nodded. "My platoon had been put down at Khe Sanh and pinned down in a firefight. This grenade comes rolling into our position like a bowling ball. I decided to do one of those dumb-ass John Wayne things and pick it up and heave it right back into Charlie's lap. Didn't quite get it off. Typical cockup. One of those days when everything goes wrong. A half hour earlier one of my own men stepped on one of our mines and went up like meat on a trampoline."

Charley. Cabell's brain lumbered to separate his sister from the Vietcong. The prosthetic rose to scratch at the bearded chin.

"Anyway, like I was saying, people are old-fashioned here. We don't make friends easily, but we know who's an asset to the community and who isn't. And people around here had your sister very definitely pegged in the first category. I guess you know that there was a collection to help with the burial if and when the body turns up."

"Three hundred eighty-six dollars."

"That's right. Not much, but it's the feeling that counts." Hunter lit a cigarette, held it away as if to evaluate it, then brought it to his mouth, sucking on it lovingly, and exhaled smoke that quickly wreathed him. A clock ticked loudly as John Denver finished "Country Roads" on the radio. Again Cabell didn't have anything to say.

"I guess you know about the boy." Hunter seemed anxious to help him out of his dilemma. "He's living up with Frank and Ella Bruce. Good folks. They've got a nice place up on Battle Mountain. Now there's a place that will be worth something someday. Smack in the middle of five hundred acres of Bureau of Land Management land. Complete isolation. They've been foster parents before. I suppose you'll be wanting to think about him and his future. The welfare people are in the county offices down in Eureka. They're the ones to contact. I don't know that I'd just bust in on the little guy without having a discussion with them first. He's had a pretty rough time of it, from what I hear."

"I guess so," Cabell agreed mechanically, mesmerized by the man's self-possession.

"I think I know how you feel, Cabell." Hunter put his left elbow on the desk and supported his chin with his hand, boring with his eyes. "You don't mind if I call you Cabell, do you? I had a lot of buddies get it over in Nam. This dinky little town sent five guys over. Can you believe it? Five guys. Four of them came back here in trash bags. I'm the one who made it. I'm a survivor. Like you. So I think I know what you're feeling."

"My father died yesterday," the words blurted out before he could stop them. Then hot tears gushed down onto his cheeks.

"Your father?" He heard skepticism in Hunter's voice.

"He died. Cancer. I was there." He felt he was pleading for absolution. "I sat there and watched him die, hating my sister for not being there to share the burden."

"God almighty." Hunter whistled softly. "What a mean bloody place this world can be." They both waited for the crying to stop.

"Coincidence," Cabell said irrelevantly, trying to clamp his eyelids shut and block them with his thumbs.

"Coincidence, chaos, whatever you want to call it," Hunter said. "It's life."

There was silence. Cabell felt the other man was waiting for him to gather himself together before proceeding.

"It's funny," Hunter began, his tone discursive, philosophical, "this dying business. When I was a kid living out in the country, there was a plague of ground squirrels up at my folks' place. I got my dad's twenty-gauge and took out after them. Every time I hit one I'd watch it roll over, kick its feet in the air real fast, then stop while it went glassy in the eye. I always thought to myself: Jesus H. Christ, this is awful. But I kept doing it. I kept shooting them and watching them die. Truth is, I was fascinated by it. I was willing to kill every one of them, wipe them out if necessary, but I was going to figure out what the hell death was all about. Jesus, I must have killed two or three hundred of them that summer. After a while I got to thinking: Well it's you, *you're* what death means. I wore white gym shorts and a white T-shirt. It occurred to me that the squirrels probably thought of me as the white death. The white death."

Cabell found himself listening closely, believing that he was being led toward some epiphany. Only something important would justify this sort of talk in the face of his grief.

"Same thing in Nam." Hunter reached over and brushed his arm with his good hand. "I had this one buddy of mine die on me. I held him in my arms and watched him die. He was gut-shot. He went, with me holding him. I could see it in his eyes. The exact moment. It was like somebody turning off the lights behind. Now you're here; now you're gone. Weird."

Cabell stifled his last sobs, agreeing in a thick voice, "Weird." He looked over toward the window, fiddling with his eyelid.

"Say, don't I remember your sister saying something about you living down in Berkeley?" Hunter changed the subject the way one diverts a fretful child.

"Right, I lived there. Used to. No more."

Hunter smiled again. "You know, some of the guys had

a thing about that town. Some of us were for the protesters;
I guess you know that. Others wanted to get out, but on our
terms, not theirs: you know? There were some guys who
talked about getting a leave and going home and kicking ass.
Kicking ass and getting some. Berkeley was the place, right?
I had this one man in my platoon, oh Jesus, he was a wild
man. Fearless: mean as hell. He was obsessed with hippie
and radical girls. You could have your centerfolds and Play-
mates, he'd take one of those hippie girls any day. I remember
once we were in this bunker up near Da Nang, and he had this
picture from *Time* of one of them with her arm cocked back
to throw a rock. She had a smoking-hot look on her face. You
could see that titty poking out of the T-shirt. Know what I
mean? That picture turned this guy on. He had it taped up on
one of the sandbags where we took turns on guard duty. One
guy on watch, the other smoking grass or catnapping. Sometimes when he thought I was asleep, he'd take his thing out
and start jigging it, standing there looking at this picture.
Pretty soon, I'd hear the sound. Splat, splat, splat as he got
it off against the sandbag. The picture was a sort of target.
This guy got wasted, too. Weird."

Hunter had taken a toothpick out of his shirt pocket and
was poking under his gums as he spoke, occasionally pausing
to look at some piece of decadence he had dug out, smelling it
before reinserting the toothpick into his mouth.

Cabell felt that he had to say something, had to prove
that those on the home front had suffered too, and been
equally hurt. "It was evil business, the war," he waffled.

"Evil?" Hunter's smile narrowed his eyes this time.
"Cabell, I'll tell you. You came back from a place like that not
wanting to use words like *good* and *evil* again. Those words
are out of date. Know what I mean? Being alive or dead, feeling fine or not: I can go with it. But *good* and *evil*? No way.
This is the twentieth century, man."

"The war killed off the future," Cabell said. He too felt
that good and evil were not distinct, but part of one gray
muddy mass of power, intrigue, and appetite. He too had seen

depravity, people's good intent consumed by their evil means. But he didn't want to share a vision with this man. That frightened him.

"Know what you mean." As Hunter spoke, Cabell thought he could see his own reflection iced in the dark eyes. "I came back not believing. In nothing, zilch. While I was lying there in the hospital at Manila getting healed and getting fitted for this thing, I got a Dear John. Didn't surprise me none. I knew we weren't going to come home and be hugged and kissed like conquering heroes. Not from that war. I had the same feeling you have: that I couldn't go backward because I'd seen and done too much, but still there wasn't much of anything up ahead either. That's a hard act to follow, believe me. I sort of wishy-washed around for a while, but then I said to myself: Hold it, Bud, this isn't the way. You've got something to believe in. *Yourself*. You *are*. That's all there is, but it's enough. After I got that through my head, I was okay. I realized that from there on out, I was taking care of Number One and that was it. I wasn't serving nobody else, nohow. I was going to keep my mind clear of intellectual garbage. So now when I see people standing around wringing their hands about My Lai, Watergate, and all that stuff, whimpering about *good* and *evil*, I feel like saying: 'Can it. When it comes right down to it you're like me—interested in what you had for breakfast and what you're going to have for dinner, and if you say different, you're a goddamned liar.' "

He should argue against this, he told himself. Instead he found himself shrugging.

"Well, Cabell"—Hunter was rising, the familiarity in his voice that of one who knows he has achieved a certain mastery —"we've gotten pretty far afield here. I didn't mean to intrude my petty little notions on you, especially at a time like this. I'm glad we got a chance to talk, although I'd give a million to have met you under different circumstances. If there's anything we can do—and I'm sure I speak for all of Halcyon in this—please don't hesitate. I know you've got some big decisions ahead. I'm sure Chief Strapp can help you get ahold of your sister's belongings and such. And the boy, well, like I said, he's in good hands till you get things settled with the county people down in Eureka. Might take a while. Damned bureaucracies, they're all like the military: forms in triplicate and go through channels and all that. If you have time when you come back through, drop in and we'll have another chit-chat. I'd like to get your ideas on things. Who knows, maybe I'll even be able to sell you a little piece of God's Country here."

The prosthetic hacked in the direction of the mountains and the dark handsome face smiled brightly. "The local real estate association argued against naming it that. Said it sounded a little sacrilegious. But I told them what was what in no uncertain terms: it's my fucking land. I knew it was just the thing for you city sinners."

Cabell pressed the soft left hand, mumbled a thanks, and got back into the pickup. He felt tranquilized. It was as if the steel hand was a lightning rod for some raw power. He saw Hunter in the rear-view mirror watching him drive off, arms at his side, the right sleeve with two inches of flap.

Gripping the steering wheel like an automaton, he headed south. He was not sure what he would do. But there was nothing for him to do here. Hunter's advice seemed realistic: he should drive to the county offices to clear things up. Then go back to Los Angeles and sell the house. He could put the money in a trust fund for the boy. But he could think of no plan that involved a future for himself. "I'm a burnt-out case," he mumbled to himself.

A small sign flashed by on his left marking the road to Battle Mountain. He went past it; the pickup seemed to hesitate for a moment like a guilty conscience. After about a quarter of a mile, he pulled over to the side of the road. He should see the boy, inform him of the plan. The detour would cost no more than an hour. For him, time was no longer of the essence. He made a U-turn and headed back, taking the turnoff and beginning the climb up into the mountain.

He drove over a Works Progress Administration overpass dated 1935 and slowed to look at the river down below. It seemed swollen even now, filled by high mountains where snows never fully melted. The muffled roar filled the cab of the pickup and sent vibrations through the tires. He shuddered that such a monstrous force should have violated his sister. He could imagine the cold water seizing her, smashing her against rocks and logs, pulling her down to the bottom, pinning her there and filling all her orifices. Checking the deserted road behind to make sure there were no cars approaching, he stopped. He got out and leaned over the stone railing to look down at the water. The Fortuna—medieval goddess of the wheel, many-armed, spinning with caprice, taking with one hand and giving with another. Feeling half mesmerized by the flow of water below, he tore himself away from the guardrail and ran back to the truck.

The road narrowed and went from paved gray to black asphalt, winding into the timberline. Climbing higher, he now and then caught sight of the water below, smaller in the distance each time the trees let him see it, less malign, making quicksilver changes from deep azure to a green the color of copper ore. How could something that beautiful be capable of such an act, especially to someone who loved it? The water diminished to a glassy thread as he made his way higher, the road so steep in places that he had to shift down to second to make the hairpins. He smelled the menthol of pine needle.

Two miles up, as the old man had said, there was some cross-fencing, a patch of white, and the momentary signal between the trees of sun on windowglass. A small sign studded with reflectors spelled out BRUCE. He pulled over and got out, walking tentatively down the gravel drive to discover a house built into a hill like the keep of a Norman castle. A pencil line of white smoke rose out of the chimney like steam. Otherwise the place seemed deserted. The porch needed jacking up at one end; the clapboard siding was not white, as it had seemed from the road, but gray and flaked. He listened for a moment at the door, hearing voices deep within. It seemed incongruous: happy conversation within this grim place. Then he realized it was a radio playing.

He knocked and waited. Hurried noises came from inside like a scurrying of rats. Some rearrangement seemed to be taking place for his benefit. He knocked again. The curtain flashed on his right. Finally the door opened a foot. A thin weary face was bisected in the doorway. The woman wore an ancient housedress. Her hair was pulled straight off her forehead and trailed down her back. There was a worn Dorothea Lange look about her.

"Yes?" The word slipped by narrow lips.

"Is this the Bruce residence?"

"That's right." The door closed a couple of inches as a result of his salesman's salutation.

"You're Mrs. Bruce?"

"What is it you want?"

"Well, my name is Cabell Hart." He paused, expecting the words to elicit some sign of recognition. But there was nothing. He felt like a door-to-door salesman hurried into his pitch. "I'm Carlotta Hart's brother, Joey's uncle. I understand you've been taking care of him."

"They told me you might be coming. Yes, we're his fosters."

"Well, I'm in town and I thought I'd see him."

"Not now, he's napping." The door moved to shut. Cabell barely managed to stop it with his hand. He felt the woman's weight on the other side. Pushing hard with flat palms, he slid her back on the waxed entryway.

"Listen. Maybe you didn't understand. I'm the boy's uncle. His mother's brother. I've come a long way. I want to see him." He was standing with one foot in the house. The woman let go of the door and moved to block his way with her body, trying to make him guilty of assault as well as breaking and entering. They were stalemated. There was motion at the top of the stairs. He looked up to see the boy, coming down slowly, one step at a time, stabilizing himself with the banister. The pajamas were absurdly small even for his slight form and gave him an Ichabod Crane look. The facial structure and russet hair were so like his father's that the sight of him caught Cabell's breath.

"You go on back upstairs now," the woman said over her shoulder. The boy looked down at her and shook his head defiantly.

"Joey?" Cabell called. "I'm Cabell, your Uncle Cabell."

The boy cocked his head slightly as if considering a question. Cabell recognized it as one of Charley's gestures. Then the thin form moved, rushing down onto the landing with surprising speed, evading the woman's hands and climbing up Cabell's leg and into his arms like a monkey.

He grew angry at the protrusion of ribs. "What the hell's going on here? You been starving the kid or what?"

"No," the woman became defensive. "We feed him good. We try to. He won't eat. It's not our fault. There's good food here."

She stepped forward and grabbed the boy's hand, trying to peel his grip off Cabell's shoulder. "He stays here. We're certified. We're in charge of him. You stay here with Mother Bruce, Joey."

Cabell realized that until that moment, until the boy began to shake his head and cinch his legs tightly around him, he had thought only to say hello, perhaps take a brief walk in the woods, and then leave. Now, he realized, he was committed. He stripped the woman's fingers off the boy with his free hand and swung his hip around to put him out of her reach.

"You want to stay here, Joey?" When the thick red hair shook a vehement negative, Cabell backed out the door, keeping his body between the boy and the woman.

"Don't matter what he says," she followed them onto the porch, growing increasingly tentative as each step took her into a more neutral territory. "We're in charge. The county put us in charge. The people down there wanted it that way. He's ours now."

"*Yours?*" The claim of ownership struck him as obscene.

"Like hell he is." He turned and hurried back to the pickup, feeling the thin legs riding his midsection. As he put the boy in and walked around to the driver's side, the woman's witchy voice followed him.

"You can't do this," she shouted. "I'll call my husband. I'll call downtown."

The boy huddled against him as they sped down the hill. Concentrating on negotiating the curves, Cabell could only steal quick looks at the pale face. He noticed the purple rings under the eyes, and the stubborn seal of lips. He saw that the right foot hung down over the seat at a strange angle, as if its hinges were sprung.

"Don't worry, Joey," he said in what he hoped was a reassuring voice. "Things are going to be okay." He had the feeling now that this area was no good, that it was the dominion of bad powers. They must fly, break out of its malign gravity. By the time they passed across the overpass and heard the rushing river, sweat was trickling down the inside of his arms.

A mile or so down the highway he said, "My idea is that we should get the hell out of this area and not come back. How do you see it?" There was a suggestion of a shrug as the boy kept looking back over his shoulder as if he'd forgotten something.

"You've been to Eureka before, right?" He wondered to himself: *How do you talk to a child?* The red head bobbed up and down.

"Listen," he tried to cover his rising irritation with a jocular tone. "I might be crazy, but I haven't gotten to the point where I talk to myself in public yet. What's with you? You take the vow of silence or something?"

The boy was studying the dashboard. He rotated his head slowly and looked up, still frowning slightly. "We never met before," he said solemnly. "I really don't know you very well."

"I'm your flesh and blood, what do you want?" Cabell bit down on his annoyance, and concentrated on driving. After several minutes he saw a lunch stand molded in the shape of a giant hamburger. Remembering how malnourished and bony the little body had felt, he asked the boy if he'd like to eat. The head nodded enthusiastically. As he pulled into the parking lot, the child quickly slid out the door and walked toward the entrance. Cabell thought his odd gait was due to the heat of the parking lot on bare soles until he remembered how the right foot hung loose. The boy glanced up and saw him studying the deformity; Cabell quickly looked away and walked ahead to push open the swinging door.

The waitress looked curiously at the boy's pajamas while Cabell ordered him a hamburger, french fries, and a large glass of milk. He sipped coffee while the boy bolted the food, washing it down with gulping sounds that moved his adam's apple. After finishing, he dabbed at a spot of mayonnaise with the last morsel of bread.

"Want some dessert or something?" The question brought the first hint of a smile to the corners of the small mouth. He got the waitress to recite her litany of pies, and ordered apple a la mode.

Afterward, they sat there, almost alone in the circular room, air from the old-fashioned four-bladed fan circulating around them. The boy was building a pyramid of a pile of salt he'd collected on the countertop, smiling shyly at secret thoughts. Cabell was beginning to wonder what he had gotten himself into when he decided to seize this mute child without any inkling of what he wanted or needed. He began to feel walled in, resentful.

"Where's Papa Two?" The boy's words were sudden.

"Papa Two?" he stalled. "Well, Papa Two couldn't make it this trip. He sent me instead." Cabell blushed under the child's close scrutiny. "No, that's not right. You knew he was sick, didn't you? Well, he didn't get better."

"Dead." The word was a declaration rather than a query.

"That's right."

"Oh." The head shook knowingly. "I was afraid of that. Like my Mama?"

"Yes."

"I thought so. The toad kept telling me she was dead. At first I didn't believe him, but then I did."

"The toad?"

"The man who lives up there on the mountain where they put me." The boy's voice was impatient, as if he were annoyed at such obtuseness.

"Oh, I see." Cabell was thinking to himself that he should probably take the child directly to the county offices, tell them that the foster home was not right, and ask them to take charge of the situation, at least for the time being while he got his act together. He was about to suggest that they go when the boy spoke again.

"They were like wolves and we were like deer."

"Pardon?" He felt himself mentally locating the exits in the situation.

"Wolves, the ones that got Mama. I was going to tell Papa Two so he could kill them."

"I see. Well, look, we ought to be thinking of moving along," Cabell fished among wadded dollars so he could pay the bill. The last thing he needed was to be conscripted into a battered child's fantasy world.

"You don't believe me," the small voice accused him.

"It's not that," Cabell replied, stopped in his rise off the stool. "It's just that I've gotten accustomed to living in the real world the last thirty-two years."

"What?"

"Forget it. Come on, let's get going."

"They did it on purpose," the boy was trying again. "She tried to fight them off, but they got her. She said, 'Run, Joey, get help. Go fast.' But I couldn't. After a while my legs wouldn't move. They got her. Three of them."

"Come on, finish your milk. We've got to move it." Cabell felt bad about being so harsh and tried to soften his tone. "Look, Joey, it was an accident. They told me how it happened in town. I spoke to two different people. Your Mama fell off the bridge. The water took her, knocked her around,

176

dragged her under. She drowned in the river. That's what happened. I know it's been bad for you. You'll be taken care of better now. I'll see to it."

"Wolves lie."

"Sure." Cabell was annoyed by the persistence. "And pigs have wings."

"Aren't you going to get them?"

"Who?"

"The wolves. Aren't you going to kill those bastard wolves?"

"Not today." He slid off the stool, embarrassed when the shrill voice drew curious looks. He beckoned for the boy to follow. "Come on."

The boy's head lolled against the pickup's window. He had the autistic look Cabell had seen on the faces of teenagers walking down the street listening to music on portable earphones. There was even a tuneless hum he thought was from Sousa. He had been wrong in heisting the kid. He was not the type to be able to recreate that sitcom world and play bachelor father.

"Listen, I hear you're a baseball fan," he said, trying desperately to fill their vacuum with some topic there would be no arguing was real. "Let's get off the subject of toads and wolves and deer for a while and talk about baseball. Okay?"

The little head moved slightly to one side, although the eyes kept staring straight ahead. Cabell took it as a sign that he might continue. He ransacked his mind for some anecdote, a story from his boyhood reading of Grantland Rice, any gently nostalgic tale by which older men mediate between the past and present. He began to sweat.

"I hear you like Don Sutton. I've seen him. One of those good, steady pitchers. Sandy Koufax was the great one when the Dodgers first came to L.A. Ever hear of him?"

The head didn't move.

"He was before your time. Actually, when I was a boy, there weren't any Dodgers in L.A. Can you believe that? A time when there were no Dodgers. They were in another town.

We had a team called the Angels. Not the California Angels of today, a different team in a different league, the Pacific Coast League. Confusing, isn't it? Life is confusing. They called it a minor league, this Pacific Coast League, but it was a major league to us. Papa Two and me and your mama used to go to the games down there in old Wrigley Field. Doubleheaders. The enemy team was the Hollywood Stars. We hated them. They used to have big fights when they played the Angels. We had this guy on our team, a great big guy. In his time he was more famous around town than Don Sutton. His name was Steve Bilko. One year he hit more homers than Babe Ruth. We also had this pitcher named Cal McLish, Calvin Coolidge McLish. The Cubs called him up just as he was getting good. He was an Indian from Oklahoma. He was able to throw with either hand. You know how they take pitchers out in the middle of the game when they get tired? When I was your age I used to have this idea that when McLish got tired, the manager should just come out and tell him to start throwing from the other side."

He felt idiotic and jerked the pickup to a stop at the side of the road, causing a sandstorm of rocks and dust. "Look, Joey, I've never been around kids much. I don't really know how to talk to them. Know what I mean? Maybe I don't know how to understand them either. But death is a serious thing. Papa Two just died. Your Mama just died. I don't understand how you can be talking about wolves and deer. You were there, dammit."

The boy was tracing the pattern of the pajamas with a forefinger. "Want me to show you where it happened?" he asked.

"Sure, why not?" Cabell pinched the bridge of his nose with thumb and forefinger, wondering how child therapists worked.

"First, you've got to turn around and go back," the boy said without looking up.

They turned around and drove back toward Halcyon for perhaps fifteen minutes, passing the cutoff to Battle Mountain and nearing the city limits, when the boy spoke again. "When you get to where our house was," he said, "our old house where me and Mama lived, you stop."

When he reached the county road where he had pulled off to drive up to his sister's house the previous day, Cabell pulled over. "Okay," he said. "We're here. Now what?"

"Follow me."

By the time he had turned off the engine, the boy was already out, shuffling back down the road in his lopsided walk, and then disappearing when he came to a place where foot traffic had chewed an indentation out of the embankment. Cabell saw him below, holding his arms out of the pajamas like an aerialist, trying to keep his balance as he slid down twenty feet to a dry wash below. He followed, tobogganing down the crumbling dirt on his butt until there was solid footing below and then running down the rest of the way, taking tiny steps to brake himself when he reached a plane of brush and rock. By this time the boy was far ahead, working his way through boulders the river had thrown out of its way eons ago, climbing like a gnomish creature native to the area. Cabell yelled for him to wait, but the wind coming off the river threw his voice back into his face. He tried to speed up, but his ankles creaked and wobbled and excess fat made him feel gravid. His lungs grew hot at their base.

He made his way through a glacial field of granite, mounted another boulder, and jumped four feet down to sand, where river rock was white and polished like dinosaur eggs. The breeze now brought a spray of moisture, and he saw the Fortuna spread out in a broad channel, the green top moving swiftly, a harsh tumbling swirl colored deeper blue slower down below. The boy stood on a footbridge, swaying slightly in the water's updraft, a spot of color against the heavy redwood forest on the other side. He worried for the thin, forlorn figure riding the undulations of the span, barely three feet above the river's snarling whitecaps. He wasn't even holding the rusty cable handrail above his shoulder. In his mind's eye he saw his sister suddenly tipped up by the trampolining motion of the bridge, backed into one of those cables, which somehow slipped below a buttock and broke her foothold; over she had gone, gulping bright surface water and then finding herself pulled into the purple down below it, shooting downward in a sudden jetting motion like a squid. That was the way it must have been.

"Joey!" he screamed. "Joey! Be careful! Hold on till I get there!"

The boy frowned to try to get his message, but kept walking toward the other side, turning like a dog and coming back a step every few moments to urge him to follow. Cabell felt the bridge sway beneath him and was hit by vertigo. He grasped a handrail with each hand and shuffled across, concentrating on the little spit of land where the boy waited, hopping with excitement.

"This is where." When Cabell drew close the boy began shouting over the rushing sound of water and pointing his face up so that his lips could be read. He was gesturing down at the flat area a few yards beyond the bridge, where the cables were spiked down into the ground.

"Where what?" Cabell's heart was racing from the exertion.

"Where they got us."

"The wolves?" He barbed the word.

"Yes," the auburn head bobbed solemnly. "Three of them, three bad men."

"Men?" Cabell felt disgusted by the new element.

"There were three of them," the boy continued, speaking in a singsong that was almost bardic. "The bad-smelling one held me tight. I felt his hard spot in my back. He laughed all the time. And the Cat got down over her head, kneeled there and did something on her face. Captain Hook hurt her the most."

"Captain Hook?" The child's invention caused Cabell to smile in spite of himself.

"He was the worst. He's the one that hurt my mama bad. He hit her so that she just folded up on the ground."

Suddenly the serious, big-eyed face had terror on it.

Cabell turned to see what the child was staring at. Back where they had come from, the Bruce woman was climbing down over the rocks, wind currents billowing her dress to show heavily veined legs and a fish-belly whiteness of thigh as she approached the footbridge. She was followed by a short man in a windbreaker and porkpie hat. As he looked up Cabell saw a rash of warts on the side of his face. Coming down the wash from a different angle, the police chief had on a leather jacket and a cap with a star on it. The three of them stood, their gestures a dumbshow from melodrama. The woman shakes her head and glances: *He's the one all right.* The husband looks over impatiently: *Well, aren't you going to do something?* The policeman shrugs and waves imperiously: *Okay, come on over here, young fellow.*

"Quick," the boy grabbed his hand and began to pull. "Let's make a run for it. We can go downriver. They can't get us there. Quick. I know the way. We can live there."

Cabell shook his head. "We can't." He began pulling the boy across the bridge, calmer now, glad to be back in an adult world, even if it was an angry one, confident of his ability to negotiate the difficulties it presented. The child cringed against him, grasping at his pantsleg, trying to free his clasped wrist with his free hand.

"It's okay, Joey," he tried to soothe, "we'll get things squared away. Nobody's going to hurt you." He let the river take the boy's desperate jabber.

When they reached the other side, Strapp advanced to meet them, catching the boy's tiny arm in his thick grip.

"Listen, this is crazy," Cabell began, feeling like a Judas goat as the boy was separated from him, kicking and squirming. "The boy's mother was my sister. . . ."

But they paid no attention to him. The struggling child was handed to the woman. She yelped as he bit her arm to break the grip. Her husband reached over and slapped him on the jaw, a short vicious blow that torqued the small face several degrees. Cabell moved forward to protest, but the cop tripped him and then landed heavily on his back with a knee that snatched his breath away. One arm was wedged up into a hammerlock, handcuffed, and then the other arm brought up to meet it. He was spitting sand as a hand pulled him up by the back of his collar and pushed him up the hill. "Uncle Cabell!" he heard the boy call behind him. "Watch out for wolves!"

Sitting in the back of the patrol car, still cracking grit in his molars, Cabell was unbelieving. He looked up into the rear-view mirror trying to catch a piece of the police chief's face, but all he saw was the impermeable silver of one-way shades resting on a flat-septumed nose. He assumed that his own fear and anger contributed to the fetid animal odor that hung there in the heat. Then they pulled onto the road and air flowed through the open windows.

"Where are we going?" he shouted into the grillwork separating front and back seats.

"Back to the station." The reply was bored.

"Are you arresting me?"

"Right."

"What the hell for?"

"You took the kid."

"Come on, Strapp, that's bullshit."

"*Chief* Strapp," the Nashville voice corrected.

"Listen, what's the problem? I'm the nearest living relative, practically the only living relative. Why make a big deal out of it?"

"You might be an imposter." The man sounded as though he was amused by the discussion. "Even if you aren't, you didn't select what could be called a very good way to assert your claim, did you?" They slowed for a boulevard stop and the smell came again. Cabell knew it was not his. Paranoia prickled along his spine. He was missing something here.

"Listen, what the hell's going on? What happened to my sister, anyway? Why is that boy saying three men attacked her?"

"Men?" The creased neck thickened with a chuckle. "I thought the kid was raving about wolves or something. No matter. I already told you what happened. An accident. She slipped on the bridge, fell into the water, and had a death." The twangy voice made it seem part of a slapstick act. "The matter at hand involves your kidnapping."

The police car slid through traffic like a barracuda, pulling into a reserved spot in front of the squat stucco building Cabell had visited that morning. Strapp got out and came around to pull Cabell from the backseat. A few pedestrians stared as they went up to the door in lockstep, the cop holding him by an elbow with his left hand while his right hovered in the vicinity of his holster.

"That's right." Cabell looked at him and said, "You'd better watch me close. I might snap these handcuffs and go on a mad-dog rampage through your dipshit town." *Mad dog!*

"Never can tell." The voice was laconic. "You look pampered but maybe you're dangerous."

The gray desk inside the door was now occupied by a buck-toothed young man whose combed-back black hair was parted precisely in the middle. As they entered, his feet came down hard onto the floor.

"Hey Vern, what we got here?" he asked.

"What we got here is a young fellow decided to take the Hart kid away from Ella Bruce," Strapp said.

"No shit!" The deputy shook his head in wonderment. "Kidnapping."

"Listen." Cabell tried to dispel their badinage with authority. "I'm entitled to a phone call, or don't you observe that rule here in your hick jail?"

"Well la-de-dah! *Pardon* us," the deputy rolled his eyes, causing Strapp's generous gut to jiggle over his belt.

"We got a three-person force here," the chief said. "Sometimes we go a whole year without getting to a police-science brush-up course. We forget the right procedures. We don't exactly have your urban crime problem here."

"Yeah, you already said that," Cabell replied. "The point

is that I'm entitled to a phone call and I want it now. I'm going to call someone in L.A., but I'll reverse the charges. I'm going to get a lawyer up here to see what the hell is going on."

"No rush." Strapp pushed Cabell in the small of the back, propelling him forward into a doorway at the back of the office. "We take our time up in these parts. Live longer that way."

The room they entered was gloomy. As his eyes adjusted, Cabell saw two cells. Strapp braced him against the bars with a heavy hip while unlocking the door, then pushed him in and clanged it shut behind him.

"Yep, we take our time," the chief continued. "We find it's healthier."

"Jesus, I love the way you talk," Cabell turned to face him through the bars. "You ought to be doing Dodge commercials."

"Don't get testy now." Strapp seemed to take no offense. "Back up there and I'll take these cuffs off."

As he felt the circlets being taken from his wrists, Cabell was assaulted by the foul smell. "Listen," he said. "This place is putrid."

"Sure, I know, a regular tiger cage. You be sure and mention it to the ACLU when you get that telephone call."

Strapp turned and fumbled on a shelf, then handed in a small box of Target tobacco with a folder of cigarette papers. "You know what you remind me of?" he said. "A little dog I had once. Name of Louie. Cute little devil, but he used to scrape on the screen door at this place where we lived. Just shredded that screening right up with his little claws. I got sick of repairing it. So I got me a 'lectric cord, bared one end of it, connected the wires to that screen, and plugged it in. Pretty soon, here comes that little dog again. He puts a paw up to the door and blam! there's a puff of smoke. That Louie took his paw down right quick, I'm here to tell you, and sat there with a blank look on his face like he'd been hit up alongside the head with a hammer. Sat there for near an hour before he moved. Never did touch that door again."

"Is that supposed to be a parable?"

"If you want. Take the wheat and let the chaff be." The chief pulled what looked like a business card out of his breast pocket, and handed it through the bars. "Here, this will set your mind at ease."

Cabell read it as the man left the room and closed the door behind him chuckling. It was a Miranda card advising him of his rights.

He turned to take stock. For the first time he noticed that there was a young man in the cell's other bunk. He had lank yellow hair, and a blue eagle was tattooed onto the arm just below the sleeve of white T-shirt. He was curled up and sleeping heavily. Cabell cleared his throat loudly to wake him, but the sound didn't penetrate the aura of deep breathing. He sat down on his own bunk. The blue-striped pillow was greasy with hair oil. The blanket folded up under it was moth-eaten army surplus. The mattress smelled of urine, stale sperm, and vomit fermented by cheap wine. He looked up toward the concrete ceiling and saw a narrow ventilation slit. It was covered by chicken wire; a No-Pest Strip dangled from one of the hexagons.

The wall over the bunk was frescoed with graffiti. A woman's wide-opened legs connected in a triangle covered with tight hair curlicuing into a script message: *If you want good pussy call Darlene in Eureka.* Another hand had written below in angry capitals: *WHAT'S THE PHONE NUMBER, ASSHOLE?* Down in a corner were small urgent letters like timid spiders: *If you read or hear about anything happening to Alan Davis, he was here 8/14/71. They hate gays here.* Above, curved buttocks extruded droplets of shit onto kinky hair that topped a face with large lips, flat nose, and wild eyes. The letters wandering through this drawing were fourth-grade cursive: *I hate Fucking Niggers because they teare down the System so kill all Jungle Bunnies and Boogies fast.*

This modern cave art would survive them all and be available to be uncovered by some future generation who would be amazed to have such an accurate account of man's fears and desire in the downhill half of the twentieth century. He sat on the corner of the bunk as if on the edge of some new Dark Ages, revulsed by it but almost glad he was there. Jail absolved him of further responsibility.

There had been another jail, once. But it had not been filthy and fouled with this sense of human limitation. Being there had been proof of superiority, not defeat. They had been out to gentle the world's savagery then, not realizing that in a scant ten years they would have caught its diseases.

The memory came without being asked, releasing him. They were piling off the prison buses at Santa Rita like new arrivals at summer camp. Singing civil-rights and folk songs, they allowed themselves to be segregated from the general inmate population, word from on high indicating that petty larcenists, burglars, and bunko artists should not be allowed to contaminate the college kids. He wandered by himself at dusk through that exercise yard almost twenty-four hours after entering Sproul Hall, sleeplessness intensifying the portent of the step he'd taken. On the other side of a cyclone fence that enforced their apartheid, a black about his age was cupping hands to mouth against the wind to get a cigarette going. He summoned his gall.

"Excuse me, I was wondering if I could borrow a smoke."

"Borrow?" The voice had a memory of the Indies in it. "This ain't no banking situation."

"Can I *have* a cigarette?"

"Yep." Dark fingers pink on the inside handed it through the fence. "What you in here for anyway?"

Grand Theft, Auto, Murder One: he had wished for some serious offense that would place him on the side of society's refuse. "Trespassing," he said. "A mass arrest at the university. The Free Speech Movement, FSM. Trying to get the administration off our backs."

As he described the struggle, emphasizing its macho aspects, the black stood impassively picking small shreds of tobacco off his tongue, examining them closely, and then brushing them on his pantsleg. "Yeah, I been reading about it," he said after waiting for Cabell to have done. "Trespassing, disturbing the peace: the Man's catchall."

The face was fine-boned and delicate around the flare of nostril, the skin grainy cordovan. The eyes were round and vigilant (in one of her moods, Jill later called them the eyes of a capuchin monkey). Cabell listened to his story of being hauled off to jail during a Student Nonviolent Coordinating Committee demonstration against hiring discrimination at Jack London Square, arrested for insulting William Knowland, after the one-time senator had rammed his way through the picket line.

"The motherfucker called me a jungle bunny."

"What did you say to him?"

"I said that my folks had been here since 1619 when one of them cracker pilgrims brought them to Jamestown, and as far as I was concerned he could get his white ass back to Formosa where he came from."

Their laugh was two-piece harmony with Cabell taking the tenor. Then an index finger poked through one of the diamond-shaped gaps in the fence. "My name is James Henry Jackson, Jim Henry."

Cabell looked down and then understood, winding his own finger around the other in a miniature handshake. "Cabell Hart."

After a few more minutes of desultory talk, they slid down and sat, back to back. Cabell doodled with a stick in the space between his shoes. Jim Henry picked crumbs of asphalt off his pants and tossed them at a trash container, his shoulder motion making little jangling waves in the fence. They spoke without turning their heads. A novice in civil disobedience. Cabell didn't have much to say. He encouraged the black to talk.

"I grew up thinking that white folks were all liberals." The words were an odd hybrid of street corner and grad school. "You know, people who gave money to the NAACP and had integrated cocktail hours to which they invited black professionals like my daddy. My daddy the dentist. I didn't have to change my way of thinking none when I got to Stanford. I was one of fifteen bloods on campus. The other fourteen on the football team, but we got treated okay. My family had as much money as most of the other Stanford families. Lots of bread in ghetto dentistry: all them gold teeth, you know. That's how come we could afford to live in a nice house over in Pacific Heights and have all these enlightened folks around.

"Couple of years ago, Daddy decided to take us all back home to Mobile to revisit the place of his humble origins. Here we are, outside Montgomery, moving along real fine in our new white Lincoln—*white*, how's that for cheek?—when there's a red light back of us. 'Oh, Lord,' I heard my mama say. A couple of cracker cops with Dixie flags on their shoulders pulled us over. 'What seems to be the trouble, officer?' Daddy says, rolling down the window. You could see them look at each other and get all piggy-eyed because his diction doesn't shuffle. One of them says to the other in this big fat Kingfish voice, 'Say, whatcha got dere, Andy? Do mah ears deceive me or do Ah hear de voice of an eddicated specimen of de colored peoples?' Something like that. They took Daddy's license and see that his name is Hannibal. 'Well, saints declare, we got us a Hannibal here. Hannibal, now why don't you just get off your big white nigger elephant here and let us take a look at you?'

"They put him on the hood and ripped through his pockets. By the time he got back into the car, he was damned near crying. Couldn't believe they'd do that to a man who's had Ralph Bunche in his house and read Virgil in Latin. Been living with his head in other people's mouths too long, I guess. It didn't shock me and my brother near as much. After that, the soul had done gone right out of the trip for him. We went on down to Mobile and had a big get-together. Daddy's got thirteen brothers and sisters and Mama's got ten, so I met one hundred eighteen cousins at this barbecue. I ain't shittin you, man: one hundred eighteen! That was fun. But Daddy kept on sort of looking over his shoulder, like he was afraid he'd get it in the back from a Ku Kluxer or something. Came time to leave and he packed us into the car about midnight and took off so's we be over the Alabama line by sunup."

They were silent for awhile. Cabell asked him what his bail was.

"Two fifty."

"Will your father make it for you?"

"Probably would if I told them I was here. But since I been working with SNCC, my folks is uptight. Daddy especially. He worry I'll become what his generation called a Race Man. That someone who draw attention to the Problem. You know?"

Later on, Cabell asked about joining one of the voter-registration projects Jim Henry worked on in Alabama.

"Man, you high on all this now, all this *involvement*." The word was gently ironic. "You check out your feelings in a month or two when you're back on solid earth. Thing is, there ain't no TV cameras following you around down there ceptin when Big Daddy King and his bunch come through. When people get put out with you they don't use words like *disciplinary action* and *in loco parentis*: it's more like *shoot that nigger-lover's damn head off*. This ain't something to be solved overnight. Black folks going to haunt this country in body the way Indians haunt it in spirit: history not going to get rid of these two bad scenes."

They sat silently for a time. Jim Henry lit the last cigarette after crushing the package and letting it fall to the ground. He passed it through the fence without a word, and Cabell smoked it until he heard the voice say, "Give it on over now." And then, "Come on, man, you done nigger-lipped it."

Soon afterward, Cabell's name came over the PA system and he found he had been bailed by the FSM defense committee. He went home and slept for twelve hours. The next afternoon, withdrew $250 from his bank account and dropped it by SNCC headquarters in downtown Oakland, specifying it was for Jim Henry's bail. Two weeks later the money was returned via a cashier's check with no covering letter.

He tried to return to his work, feeling that he must get a handhold on the crumbling ground he had once occupied before it was too late. He spent January and February at his desk circling around his Hamlet thesis without any notable success. "What you're going through," his advisor Barton McLaine had said, "is the archetypal dilemma of Western culture—the contrary pulls of the world of action and the world of contemplation." After sitting hunched at his desk listening to the latest in a series of increasingly unlikely theories Cabell had propounded—in this case, that the key to the play is in the action that takes place off stage, during the interlude with the pirates when Hamlet undergoes a sea-change—McLaine said, "Look, Hart, the best minds in literature have agitated the question of this play. Every year there are three hundred new dissertations on Shakespeare, about one every working day. Many are about *Hamlet*. I was dubious about your project from the beginning. Now that your concentration seems to have deserted you, I'm even more so. Why don't you find yourself a nice little piece of unworked ground: Jacobean drama, or the pre-Elizabethans if you *must* do that period. I know it sounds vulgar, but take my advice: be a big duck in a small pond."

"I think I'll stick it out a bit longer," he said, uncomfortable under the owlish glance. He knew McLaine would be placated if he'd simply agree to restrict his concern to some small aspect of the play—say, textual quibbles between the folio and quarto editions. But he couldn't. He was obsessed with sophomoric issues to an extent he wouldn't have admitted: the *mystery* of the play; what Eliot called disproportionate grief and how that searing nihilistic vision could suddenly turn around and affirm the value of man and God. No matter how he tried to narrow his scope, his mind kept returning to these questions, a tongue compulsively flicking a cavity.

One night early in the spring when he had been walking around in his kitchen, reading portions out loud and trying to find answers in the rhythms, there had been a knock at his apartment door. He opened it to find Jim Henry framed in his doorway. He was holding up a bottle with the familiar terriers on the label. "Black and white together," he said, gesturing with the scotch. "Never got to thank you for springing me from jail."

Cabell cleared off the kitchen table and was making polite conversation when his guest looked up slyly. "What's the matter with you, man, ain't you never had no black folks in your house before?"

He blushed, less at the accusation than at the word "black." He had grown up assuming that you called somebody a "Jew" if you meant to insult him, "Jewish" if you meant to be polite. He assumed that the same held true for "Negro" and "black."

"No, can't say that I have."

"Lordy, boy, this is the age of take-a-nigger-home-to-lunch. Where you been?" The smile had the effect of pearls on Spanish leather. "Okay, okay, never mind now. You got all the liberal's usual reactions. You pass the test."

"What test?"

"The recruitment test."

"For what?"

"For to go down South, that's what. You forgot?"

"No." Cabell remembered their jailhouse conversation. "I just figured you thought I wasn't combat-tested."

"You'll get there in time."

"Okay, then, I'm ready."

"For what?"

Jim Henry deflated him. "Got to go in with the right attitude, though. Think of it as being like the Peace Corps: don't do a whole lot for the natives, but the volunteers have fun."

His air fare provided by the Southern Regional Council, Cabell arrived in Birmingham early one morning in May after stopping over in Nashville to see Mama Bessie. Visions of Goodman, Chaney, and Schwerner were on his mind as he walked through the terminal to pick up his bag. Moving through knots of good ol' boys lounging by the baggage-claim area to check incoming flights for carpetbaggers and agitators, he was feverish with paranoia, imagining toothless, grizzled hillbillies in long johns and baseball caps standing over a campfire drinking moonshine and passing his white naked testicles around.

For the first few weeks, he lived with the certainty of violence. He accepted it, even in a sense hoped for it: a sign of purity vouchsafed to the very few. He was caught up in the vast rhythms of suffering embodied in the swooping Negroid Christ in stained glass commemorating the spot where the four little girls had been blown up at Sunday School the previous year. He would take the death to get the transfiguration. Expecting the sniper's bullet, he walked the bald streets of Bessemer and the dusty backroads of the chigger-infested countryside, handing out leaflets with Jim Henry or some other partner, drinking rusty water from old wells, and eating oily shreds of possum meat to sign people on to the voting rolls. The Klan was always near, sharks in pickups cruising around the registration project. There were whiskey bottles lobbed like hand grenades from speeding vehicles, but no shotgun blast. He felt that he was in a battle zone, but always somewhere behind or beyond the engagement. News of the war seemed to come from afar.

Cabell felt he couldn't do enough. He began an evening class in composition for a dozen or so graduates of the area's black high schools. Most of them still struggled with basics, but there was one student, a young woman named Hazel Neal, who wrote so well it stunned him. Large-eyed and spindly-legged, skin the color of mocha and hair in tufts like coal-dusted cotton candy, she was too shy to carry on a conversation. Contact with a white made her foot-scuffing nervous and drove her voice into a high register that made her sound like Butterfly McQueen. But she could write.

One week it was a lyrical evocation of the spiritual endurance of black women, the next it was a cold dissection of the homicidal intent of white history. Her essays were the height of the week for him. He felt like Alan Lomax discovering a native folk genius. In his mind's eye she became a metaphor: hope attenuated, sensibilities atrophied from disuse; the Negro embodied. He sent off letters to professors and friends in Berkeley, describing the girl and urging them to arrange some kind of scholarship fund. One Sunday afternoon he decided to drive out to her home to tell her parents of the plan.

It was the deepest he had yet gone into rural Alabama, forcing the rickety station wagon over rutted clay roads, past tiny truck farms and sharecroppers' shacks half-hidden by scraggly pine. The girl hadn't known he was coming. When he pulled up, she was sitting alone on the front porch looking dully out onto a yard littered with old toilets and washbasins, rusty streaks bleeding down onto the white porcelain. As he got out of the car, she stared at him. Neither of them moved for a moment. The only sound came from a loose piece of tarpaper flapping against the side of the house. Then, with startling speed, she rose and bolted around the corner.

Looking through a torn spot in the screendoor, he saw a giant black woman sitting on a sofa beneath a painting of John F. Kennedy on purple satin. Sipping a Coke amidst a monsoon of flies, she looked back impassively as he knocked and blurted out who he was. He asked if she was Mrs. Neal. She nodded and asked him in. He sank into a horsehair seat and began stammering out his concern for her daughter's wasted potential. The mother nodded in gracious agreement throughout his speech; when she smiled the tongue poked through the gap where lower front teeth had been. He knew that he was being Mister-Charleyed, and sensed that unseen eyes watched him from behind.

"So would you let her go if I could arrange it?" He tried to cinch the deal.

"Well," she smiled, "we jes wait and see what happen. They a lot of peoples involved in this."

It was a week or so after this visit, while skimming through some out-of-print anthologies of black writing from the Harlem Renaissance, that he came across a section from an essay by James Weldon Johnson that struck him. He knew he had seen it before, and for a day and a half it nagged at him. Then he could not forestall the realization any longer. It was the core of one of Hazel's essays, and no more than a perfunctory effort had been made to hide the plagiarism. He spent a whole evening with the book and uncovered in bits and pieces the bases for all the other work she had submitted. He sat up until sunrise wondering what to do.

The next morning he stopped Jim Henry in the hall outside the kitchen and told him about it, watching the smile begin to bloom on the shining face midway through the story. By the end, he was bent over, laughing and pounding a thigh. "Cabell," the words came out in jerks, "I thought you a smart-assed white boy. But here you been spendin the whole summer whackin away on de tar baby and don't even know it. Look down there at those hands, Jack. Don't you see that black sticky stuff? Man, you just got that epiphany you come down here for and you done let it whiz right by you."

For the remainder of the summer she turned in cribbed essays and he annotated them and handed them back. He never mentioned Berkeley again; she never asked.

Back in the Bay Area one night early in October after stopping in Los Angeles for an uneasy visit with his father and sister, Cabell had found Jim Henry at SNCC headquarters working to get a duplicating machine going. He joined in, getting giddy on the formaldehyde fumes of the fluid. They worked until two in the morning, and it established a regimen they were to follow for months: getting together at the North Oakland office late in the afternoon, hanging around with the neighborhood's black teenagers for an hour or so, going out to dinner, and then working on some project until after midnight. Jim Henry's world was the real one; all the others were make-believe. Clutched by history, Cabell had felt that he was discovering America with a black guide. Jim Henry indulged him. Once they entered a party together and he lassoed two white girls with his articulate Stanford charm, then began to jive. When one of the girls asked who they were, he adopted his rich darky voice as he danced around her, "Why honey, don't you know? Dish here Huck Finn and I be Nigger Jim."

"I-i-i-i-eeeeeeee!" The shriek was accompanied by a loud thumping and Cabell jumped out of the bunk with his body hair bristling. "I-i-i-i-eeee!" It came again, he couldn't think from where. Then he saw motion in the other bunk. There was wild thrashing, then the yellow-haired man fell to the concrete, convulsing, eyes embedded in fat edema, the face a dark bubonic color. The lips blew bubbles; the hands conducted spastic music. The thumping was his head knocking on the floor with the ripe full sound of a watermelon. The man seemed to be choking to death.

"Help!" Cabell shrieked. "Help! Help!" He had the premonition of yet another death. "Help me! Oh, God, help, please!" The man had shaken his way closer to his side of the cell. Cabell moved up on the bunk as if the body was a rabid animal. "Help!" He put his two baby fingers in his lips and blasted a piercing whistle.

"What in Christ's name is going on here?" The deputy burst through the door carrying a truncheon.

Cabell pointed down at the writhing body. "He's having some kind of seizure or something. You'd better get help quick."

The deputy unlocked the cell and bent over the man, darting periodic looks at Cabell, his right hand menacing with the club. "You try something," he warned, "and you'll be a sorry jerk." Then he tried to pull the yellow-haired man up by his collar.

"Don't do that," Cabell yelled. "You could cause him to strangle to death."

"Shut the fuck up." The truncheon pointed at Cabell's face. "I want a medical opinion from you, and I'll ask for it." Then he called over his shoulder. "Vern! Vern! Better get in here, Tull's having a fit."

Strapp filled the doorway. "Don't mess with him, Leon."

He looked amused. "It's the emperor's disease. He'll get over it. Reach your fingers into his mouth and grab his tongue so he don't gobble it down and choke hisself."

"You out of your mind?" the deputy recoiled. "I'm not getting anywhere near that mother's mouth. That's all I need: to get bit by this sick dog." He took two steps back from the shaking body.

"Well, let's have Florence Nightingale here take care of it." The flat face nodded in Cabell's direction.

"Reach in there and save the man's life," the deputy ordered.

"Fuck you," Cabell said.

The truncheon cracked him in the elbow, sending an electric charge up to his neck and down to his ankles. "Move it, asshole."

Bent over from the excruciating pain in his arm, Cabell felt the club point down on his spine, pushing him the rest of the way to the floor. The purple face revolted him. The mouth slavered, leaking drool down the chin and neck. The crotch was dark and wet, and brackish piss pooled beneath the shaking body. He felt a bruising jab in his ribs. And with infinite loathing, he pried the clenched teeth apart and grabbed the swollen tongue. He held on until the body had stopped writhing, then released the tongue.

"Now that was a humane gesture," Strapp said. "Looks like this feller's in your debt. Why don't you just help him back up into his bunk so it won't hurt so bad in case he decides to start whomping his head around some more."

Cabell picked up the dead weight under the arms, cringing as the damp underarm saturated his skin. He put the torso on the mattress and then got the feet. He saw an eyelid flicker over white, and when he finished the man was back in the same heavy sleep as before.

"These goddamned alkies always having something wrong with them," the deputy was saying rapidly as they left the room and closed the door. "Booze fucks their whaddyacallit."

"Metabolism," Strapp said as they went into the other room.

Cabell lay back on his bunk, trying to wipe the viscous saliva off his hand onto the blanket, but only spread it over a wider surface of his skin. Nauseated, he tried to gain control of himself, seeking some mantra that would deliver him. He concentrated on recovering his train of thought, ignoring the squalor of the cell, desperately seizing another memory of that voice rich like melting chocolate.

"So, how fares the Melancholy Prince?" There had been a riff of scotch in the words on the phone one night when Cabell was staying home from the SNCC office as part of a last attempt to make progress as a student.

"Not bad," he replied. "Tonight we are drinking hot blood. The fool Laertes is about to get his fat ass kicked."

"Ooo-wee! Gettin' heavy now. Who said that man doan take care of business? I doan care what you honky intellectuals say about him being undecided. Take him awhile to get goin, but when he do, that man is bad. B-a-a-ad! He get right on down and *do it*. Doan fuck wid him."

"What's happening, Jim?"

"I just sittin down here talking to Reggie and thought you might like to join us. There somebody here you might like to meet."

Regina, owner and operator of their restaurant hangout, must have weighed 250 pounds. Her round face never strayed far from the grill where she did business. Grease and sweat gave it the look of freshly oiled ebony. As he entered, she was shaking her head dramatically, gesturing with a spatula, and muttering at Jim Henry, who sat at the counter with a white woman and held out a button reading NO VIETCONG EVER CALLED ME NIGGER. Winking at Cabell, he continued his exaggerated plea.

"Come on, Reggie. Listen, woman, this goan be good for business. Believe me. Dig: Cassius Marcellus Clay wearin this button. You put one on and all the brothers and sister goan know you on the right side. They be linin up to get in to get some *enlightened* food."

"No sir, you ain't agonna get me to put on that word," she spoke through a splattering of home fries. "I done spent a whole damn life getting way from that word. I gone from a Nigger to a Colored Person to a Negro to a Black and I too old to be goin backward now."

Jim shrugged, put the button on his own coat, and made a face at Cabell. "Mean work, raising consciousness of the masses. Cabell, this here is Jill McKeever. Jill, Cabell Hart."

His first impression—of someone who spent considerable time struggling against her nature—would never be altered in all the time he knew her. He could see immediately how she had worked to change and remold her appearance. Dark hair that would have curled naturally was cropped close to the head. Baggy clothing tried to bulk out the petite shape. The face might have been pre-Raphaelite, but sober lines effaced that gypsy beauty. The only things not meddled with were the eyes—gray and of indeterminate depth: old stone under water. There was no mistaking their message: *I dare.*

After entertaining them for a few minutes, Jim Henry rose and stretched. "Well, time to move it."

"Where we going?" Cabell stood too.

"Whatchou mean *we*, white man? I'm goan where you can't come." The breath was Johnnie Walker Red.

"Where's that?"

"If you really want to know, to a meeting to figure out how to get whitey out of SNCC." Jim Henry forked the last bite of sweet-potato pie ceremoniously into Cabell's mouth. "And now, my son, *ego te absolvo.* Go thou and sin no more. And gain the peace which passes understanding." He went out chuckling as if he had just said something outrageously witty.

Cabell tried to make conversation. The woman answered him briefly, holding the coffee cup in both hands, looking down into its depths, submitting to the small talk with the coiled stoicism of a zoo animal receiving petting. Smoking rapidly,

198

biting the inside of her mouth with incisors, excavating gnawed fingernails with the cover of a matchbook, she threw off a kinetic energy that made him feel uncomfortably warm.

When he asked what she did, the stony eyes struck him as if to say, You don't really want to know. She began to recite details in an ironic tone as if ridiculing some third party's *curriculum vitae*. The name was Jill McKeever, once Gillian but changed under court petition to free her from the pretentiousness that had been her father's idea. "Part of his attempt to boost himself out of the merchant class. He was a poor boy from Newark who had put in twenty years with Dillon, Read, and then got called to a middle-level government post by McNamara. You'd think the chariot had been sent to carry him over Jordan."

"Must be an interesting man." Cabell realized that he had sounded the wrong note as soon as the words were out.

"An asshole," she answered. "A shanty Irish who's on his third marriage, each of them enough of a step upward so that my most recent half-sister was going to deb parties with Rockefellers and Mellons this past summer. She's ticketed for Bryn Mawr. In my day it was necessary and prudent to settle for Columbia. He loves the Defense Department. It's the capstone of his career."

She told of choosing Berkeley for grad school in anthropology because of news of the FSM. For the past several months she had been working with a group called the Peace Action Committee.

"I suppose you want to know about my personal life, too." Her look was that of a cat eyeing a distasteful meal.

"Not especially."

"Come on," she said. "You want all the relevant data, don't you? I had my first sexual encounter when I was twelve. A middle-aged man in a car with a bag of cookies. He had a mustache. I've hated mustaches and cookies ever since. Until a few weeks ago I was living with a guy named Stanley who teaches political science at San Francisco State. An assistant professor. For the last year he's been sweating it about tenure. Sometimes I'd wake up in the middle of the night and find him on his hands and knees beside me sucking his thumb and crooning in his sleep. I could take that. I couldn't take his faith in the strategic-hamlet program."

She downed the rest of her coffee and slapped the cup down on the Formica. "Now you."

"Me what?" he asked.

"Who are you? What do you believe?"

"What do I believe? Nobody's asked me a question like that since I was ten years old standing out behind the church worrying about whether or not there was a God."

"Well, you believe in racial equality, right?"

"Right, I believe in it. But not like you mean; not like I used to believe in the Easter Bunny."

"Either you believe in something, or you're some kind of parasite." The gray eyes struck him. "I know what I believe in."

"What's that?"

"Self-determination for oppressed peoples."

"Far out," he said, staring down petulantly.

"I've just got one question," she said, bending over so close that he could smell her sweet coffee breath.

"Yeah, what's that?"

"Are you in a fraternity? You have a certain fraternity-boy quality about you."

"What is this, *épater la bourgeois* night?" Sick of the schizophrenic catechism, he rotated off the stool, leaving money for the check, and walked out into the chill wind slicing up off the Bay. She followed, her narrow shoulders drowning in the army field coat.

"Aren't you even going to walk me home?" she clutched at his elbow.

"You don't need to worry," he said without turning. "Anybody get near you and you just start talking. They'll know you're crazy and leave you alone."

"Sorry. I'm not as insulting as I appear. The words don't mean what they seem to. I figure talk is like making a bid in bridge: a way of seeing what other people have got."

'exposes her genitalia to the male in a gesture accompanied by a fixed look over the shoulder."

Lying there still trying to comprehend it all, he suddenly deciphered Jim Henry's pun as he left the restaurant. He had to disguise his chuckle as a cough. The piece which passes understanding.

Later, when they'd coupled a second time, she began laughing into her pillow.

"What's so funny?" he said.

"I'm thinking of Stanley," she surfaced. "He needed a text to do it by. You could always tell exactly what he'd been reading by what he wanted to do. Weird gymnastics? That meant the collection of erotic Japanese woodcuts. Drape me over the armchair and go up the dirt trail? That meant he'd been at his collection of Victorian smut. Pinching and biting? That meant Harriet Daimler, his favorite. Finally, toward the end, I just said to him, 'Stanley, goddammit, you're so predictable. You're like the guy whose dinner you can figure out by looking at the spots on his tie."

"So why did Jim Henry put us together?" he asked the next morning, smelling cuntish fingers as he brought the plastic coffee cup to his lips. "He's never worried about the quality of my erotic life before."

The gray eyes had seemed suddenly cobra, lidless. "It was a changing of the guard."

"How so?"

"You don't get it? He's going black. You're a political responsibility he can't handle anymore." Cabell realized that his look was blank when she pursed her lips in exasperation. "He's got things to do and figures you should, too. He was helping you make the transition from civil rights to Vietnam. Dig it."

Not only Vietnam, but all of Southeast Asia was an equal partner in their relationship from the beginning. The Peace Action Committee was a small group whose membership changed according to Jill's whim and whose work was financed by a grant she had gotten from a local foundation by using her father's connections. They had a room in an old Berkeley office building where they turned out pamphlets on the war for schools, churches, public-service groups. Jill said, "This is just the first step. Make the moral-legal point, then move on to the political case." She started him reading Burchette and Lacouture, *Le Monde* and the *New Statesman*. He found himself picking up her mannerisms, referring to "the Vietnamese" as if they were a poor but worthy family down the block, and to "Mao" and "Fidel" as if they were old friends. They spent several months picketing troop trains and leafleting draftees at the Oakland Army Induction Center.

"We don't have a relationship," he said once when hit by jealousy. "This is a *ménage à trois* with you, me, and Uncle Ho." It had been meant to force a denial, but she had just shrugged as if to admit its truth. Gradually he accepted her terms, and the war became their constant companion, present not only when they worked, but when they ate, read, and loved. In this last regard, the war was not only voyeur, but aphrodisiac as well. They usually lay on the bed just before dinner, reading and listening to the Pacifica news. Often she would slip off her clothes with that same workmanlike seriousness as on the first night, and come on top of him, smiling grimly as reports of troop pentrations and body counts became puns, and news from the front acted as a metronome for her movements. Their feral troth was pledged in the Mekong Delta and the DMZ. "This is our Spain," she said, lying quietly beside him after a tight-lipped orgasm.

The war was a system, a cosmology, a sacred fire that would purify them. They resisted all efforts to alter its hold on them. In the Summer of Love, when Jerry Rubin wandered around town issuing vatic pronouncements on the new lumpen he had discovered in Hashbury, Cabell and Jill collaborated on the PAC position paper denouncing his lack of seriousness. They became part of the core of people who could be counted on to form a steering committee for demonstrations, gather organizations into popular fronts, get a speaker, or put out a leaflet. The word used to describe such activists had an irony that wasn't lost on them: the troops.

Vietnam was a moral template that made the world comprehensible. In 1968, when Hanoi agreed to negotiate and the Progressive Labor leader fumed, "Here we struggle, struggle, struggle, and then they sell us out," Cabell and Jill used the statement as an example of dangerous ultra-leftism, but secretly they too wondered what would happen if peace should break out.

"It's not going to happen," Jill said one day. "Nixon will never end it, and marches will never do shit. We've got to get ready for action."

By then the original Peace Action Committee had melted away, leaving a nucleus of Cabell and Jill with the name, the bank account, and the South Berkeley headquarters. Jill saw it as a vanguard situation and looked to build a cadre. They would study Marxist-Leninist thought; they would be internationalist.

Soon they were seven. The five others included Nora Wilton, a blond former high-school pompom girl whose good looks had made her so clearly the reigning queen of the Bay Area Left that there had actually been talk of putting her on a float during an antiwar demonstration in the days before the Left became sensitized to sexism. Michael Wertheim, a onetime academic with wild wispy hair and smudged glasses that magnified his eyes, had been in the economics department at the university until refused tenure because his book, a study of monopoly capital published by a small leftist press, was seen as unforgivably socialist. Miles Keogh, tall and thin, with black eyes glinting out of a moonscape of pock, was a former leader of SDS who had come to Berkeley after involvement in the Watts uprising and the Columbia demonstrations. Suzanne Ardzinty, niece of a Czech immigrant who had been a delegate to the Comintern, had made a reputation by denouncing the Old Left as cowardly and reactionary. Mike Gonzalez was their third-world member. A spokesman for the Chicanos during the

Third World Liberation Strike, he had a chubby face and pencil mustache and resembled the Frito Bandito; they called him Frito. Finally there was Buddy Wald, a member of a Madison research collective, which had first exposed the CIA's involvement in assassinations of NLF cadres under the Phoenix program. Bearded, astute, manic, he had been a rising New Left journalist until deciding that he must prove himself by getting involved in action. He had compromsied his reputation by getting stoned one night and, finding an isolated Xerox machine, stretching his penis over it and making copies, which he autographed and mailed to women he knew. Held on probation by the women's movement since then, he had tried to recoup by becoming a vigorous spokesman for feminism.

"Well, we've got a representative crew here," Cabell had joked after the core was built. "A Czech, an Irish, a Jew, some WASPs, even a Latin. Just like the B-29 in World War II movies, except that we need a black."

"That would be incorrect." Jill had taken him seriously. "Blacks have got to get their own thing going. We've got to do the same. It's time for coalition, not cooptation." Still, she spent considerable time at Panther headquarters, saying that they were exactly the sort of revolutionary class Fanon had written about.

One night they sat around the living room trying to decide on what to call themselves. Keogh suggested the Berkeley Liberation Front. Nora, whom he had already romanced away from Wald, smiled sweetly and agreed. Suzanne shook her head. "Too fucking pretentious," she said. "We haven't done shit yet by way of liberation. We haven't even liberated ourselves from our bourgeois hang-ups." Wald sat at the back of the room where he could see the dialectical flow of the discussion before committing himself. "Mad Dog," he said. "Mad Dog, after the Bogart character in *High Sierra*, Mad Dog Earle." He was on his feet now, working into his pitch. "The medium is the message here. Mad Dog. Because our mission is to bite this country in the ass and give it rabies. Bring the war home, right?"

Mad Dog it was. Their house became a main stop on the underground railroad shuttling deserters to British Columbia and a munitions dump for the Panthers during their war against the pigs, a war Mad Dog supported as the first signs of the coming revolt. When they went to demonstrations, they wore motorcycle helmets and carried concealed blackjacks made of buckshot poured into specially designed leather cylinders shaped like condoms. After Bernardine Dohrn called the Tate-LaBianca murders a metaphor for the class struggle, Jill pasted a picture of Charlie Manson on their bedroom door.

They went to Berkeley parties and took acid. Pleasure was not the motive, but rather breaking down the boundaries that contained them. "You'll get to a level," said Nora, the hedonist among them, "where you'll see that all the things that have hung you up, all the things you've feared, are really paper tigers." He made his first trip at a get-together held by some people from the East attempting to break through the old-boy politics of Berkeley and get a Weatherman collective established.

There was a rock band playing. A teenager was haranguing some middle-aged women on the need for a children's-liberation plank in the platform of a slate of radical candidates attempting to take over the city council. "We've got to do away with X ratings on movies and lower the drinking age to twelve," the girl was saying. "This is the worst kind of ageism. Discrimination is discrimination."

Giggling as the drug moved him into a different time warp, Cabell bent over and whispered to Jill, "She's putting us on, right?" Jill shushed him. "These kids are stripping things down," she said. "They're the rock on which we're going to build our church."

Sliding along the conduits of time that marked his passage through the stages of acid, he careened through the house, from room to room. At some point he found himself in the bathroom looking at his face, his lovely growing face. He stood there appreciating it in the mirror, cooing to the face, seeing the fine craft that had built it, aware that he was a plant and depended on photosynthesis. As he stood there, the face began to seam and crack. Frightened, he had tried to reassemble it, catching the pieces of muscle and tissue that dropped off like plaster. He was staring at the mirror, but there was no image there, nothing. There was no silver backing; the medicine chest was a black hole in space. "Who am I?" he asked. "What is it I've become?" He left the room to go and find another, anyone, to take his hand and lead him back to himself. In the hallway he was suddenly paralyzed, unable to walk the spreading corridor of fear. He heard a rattle behind and turned to see a paper tiger, huge and sharp, its striped essence all around him. He fell against the wall and then buried his face in the floor. "Don't tell me," he begged the animal. "I don't want to know."

Wald had a way of hooking on to whoever happened to be hot. One night he brought Cleaver to Mad Dog. They smoked grass, ate Szechwan food, and then sat in front of the fire talking. At one point Suzanne used the term "Stalinist" as a pejorative. Soft-voiced, deliberative, Cleaver turned his green sloe-eyes on her.

"Time we get away from all this bourgeois claptrap, ain't it, sister? Time to figure out who's who and what's what. You people got to get on down and start dealing with reality. You got this thing for Trotsky. Way I see it, he's just another jiveass intellectual parasite. Living off the people. Way I see it, Stalin a brother off the block." Suzanne struggled to insert something about the purge trials but he interrupted. "Don't tell me about no purges. Those damn traitors enemies of the people. Dig? Enemies of the people, enemies of the revolution got to die. Otherwise you're back where you started. You all don't like Stalin because you're afraid of violence. Your split-off intellectual, the one with no roots in the people, he's the one put Stalin down. Shit, more people killed from being trampled to death to get a look at that brother's casket than ever got killed in purges. Don't tell me about no purge trials." Somebody changed the topic, and Suzanne was left staring in the fire, jaws working and a faint blush on her forehead.

Wald went to Cuba to solidify their internationalist connections. While there he arranged a trip to North Korea for a hand-picked party including Jill but not Cabell. They were gone six weeks and came back wearing Korean down jackets and Mao caps. They made the rounds of Berkeley's collectives, giving slide shows and talks on what they had seen in Pyongyang. Within the next few weeks boxes of literature began arriving from North Korea, books with soft spines, uncut pages, and detailed errata sheets. The collection of Kim Il Sung's press conferences was several volumes. Cabell picked up the first volume and read the first question: "Mr. Chairman, tell us please how will the just and glorious People's Republic repel the imperialist agressors and their lackeys in the South?" Then he saw that the answer took up forty-eight pages.

He saw Jim Henry at a Free Huey rally standing on the fringes of the crowd wearing a red-and-brown batiked dashiki with his thick hair molded into the topiary of an afro. They had seen each other over the years, but a barrier of embarrassment stood between them. Each tended to stare at a point just over the other's right shoulder in their conversations.

"Free Huey, brother," Jim held out a palm to be slapped.

"Right on," Cabell said, then parroted Cleaver's latest aphorism. "Baddest black man that ever stepped inside of history."

"Huey? Black?" Jim elevated his eyebrows and voice to make it clear that his salutation had been ironic. "He not black. Man, he *beige.*"

Cabell stood there silently, looking up at the speaker's platform and pretending to listen to the words that came out of the PA system oblong and distorted. He didn't want to risk another put-down.

"See in the papers that your friends been traveling in the third world," Jim's voice was remote now, and his eyes hid behind the roseate tint of his glasses.

"You mean Wald?" Cabell said, still feeling defensive.

"My man. And Jill too."

"Yeah, first group from the Left since the war, I guess."

"All expenses paid, too. Outasight. Shows what happens

when you keep the faith. Hang in there, boy. Who knows? You might get to be part of the first bunch to get into Albania." Then he had moved off with a handsome black woman, her hair plaited into elaborate corn rows.

One day Keogh came in at dinnertime with a bandage above the temple. Under questioning he admitted having gotten the worst of it in a fight with a member of Progressive Labor. His humiliation provoked a session of self-criticism about Mad Dog's lack of a fighting edge. Jill and Wald made a deal with a squat, bushy-haired Maoist named James Wu from Chinatown's Red Guard to be their *karate-ka*. Like all others, this decision had involved a struggle session. Wald had argued that they would study *tae-kwon-do*, the hard, punishing style from Korea. Cabell had proposed the Chinese *kenpo* because it was more fluid and esthetic. For once he had won out, although he had to use the ideological superiority of the Chinese to gain his point.

Wu drilled them hard, his own stubby arms moving like pistons and making the canvas *ghi* snap like gunshots. Rising at six in the morning for the Tai Chi exercises that preceded the long lesson, Cabell's naked skin goose-bumped against the coarse cloth. He moved through the *kata* smoothly, exulting in the strength of movement, the poetic control over murderous capacity. His form was the best in the group, yet in sparring matches he hung back, content to block and parry and occasionally throw a perfunctory pulled punch to keep the opponent off balance. The thrill was in the art; as action it felt absurd. He couldn't imagine ever *doing* it to someone. Once Wu took him aside and thumped on his breastbone with a thick finger that felt like it could penetrate brick. "You make me wonder. I say, would he even defend hisself when somebody attack? It make me think there problem here. How come you do this?"

There were also weapons classes. Drills in the house, and trips by van to the Sierra foothills for practice at a ranch owned by Nora's parents. They were taught to shoot by a shy, slightly built young man with a startling resemblance to Wally Cox.

Going by the *nom de guerre* of Wendell, he had deserted from Camp Pendleton late in 1970 when assigned to a second tour in Vietnam, and since then had gone through the movement, earning room and board by teaching demolitions and weapons.

There was a life-size plywood target with a cop's blue uniform and a pink pig face. When each of them had taken a turn with the M-16, Wendell took the weapon, then came to stand in front of them, bawling out like a drill instructor, "Goddamn it, you're holding it soft like it's going to hurt you. The point is to make it hurt somebody else, you morons." He took the gun, planted himself, and fired off a clip, then inserted another and emptied it rapidly. A jagged circle from heart to pancreas flew out of the target. Looking at the spit at the corner of the mouth, and the hypnotic eyes smiling at the damage, Cabell had known that in the grottoes of his mind, Wendell was still wasting slants.

Once, chasing down Shattuck Avenue at the head of a crowd trashing windows, Cabell caught a glimpse of Jill beside him, pacing herself like a quarter-miler, the breath coming in ragged gasps. Above and behind them, quadrangled of glass collapsed from great height, heaving up for a moment in slow motion and then sinking down like icebergs into a sea of crystal. Her face was luminous, enraptured. *We are all, all mad dogs.* The thought had formed calmly, almost pleasantly at the top of his mind. Off to the right, Wald squealed in fright as a cop collared him from behind. As Cabell moved to free him with a rolling cross-body block, the soft give of the adipose body within the blue serge uniform proposed itself as a metaphor for America.

Their world was suddenly filled with fear of agents and informers. FBI agents had interviewed them. Once Suzanne picked up the phone and heard a conversation from the previous week played back for several seconds before the interrupting squeak. People took their pictures; mail delivery was erratic. Under surveillance, Mad Dog developed safe houses, mail drops, false-identity kits, escape routes out of the country through Baja and British Columbia. But they were never used. The revolution remained *in utero,* a giant fetus conceived by an act of imagination, which no amount of labor could cause to be born. They took out their sense of frustration on each other, rigorously scrutinizing and scouring, anxious to do away with impurity or individual quirk. They were all demoralized except for Wald, who saw that it was possible to rise in the updrafts of dissension, and Jill, who set about incubating an even more ferocious nihilism. For Cabell the vasectomy was proof that he was a dedicated soldier in the increasingly military atmosphere that enveloped Mad Dog.

Their sturggle sessions were interminable. Once they sat up all night arguing about whether or not it was bourgeois to take showers with the bathroom door closed. Monogamy was also an issue. Nora rose to report on contact she had made with a Detroit Weatherman collective. "They've abolished possessive sex altogether," she said. "At first they found that privileged relationships kept cropping up even after the group made up its mind to ban them. They had to appoint someone to post a nightly fucking list. That seems to have worked. Now they have a democratic rotation."

Pressure was put on Keogh and Nora, primarily by Wald. Stroking his well-trimmed beard and seeming to be addressing history itself, he perched on a desk so that he was slightly higher than Keogh as he spoke. "If you're fucking one person and one person only, then you're obviously loyal to that person above all others. That sort of exclusive loyalty is bourgeois, like valuing yourself above the collectivity. Its dangerous."

Soon Keogh grew disgusted and left for Southern California to become guru to Hollywood liberals. Cabell and Jill were the next targets of the smash-monogamy campaign. In meetings when the subject was raised, Jill stubbornly let it be known that she would not submit this part of her life to the group's dictation. "I'm a revolutionary," she once screamed at Wald when he began badgering her. "Sex plays a miner part in my life and I want to keep it that way."

"Don't think I was being sentimental," she told Cabell later that night when they were alone. "At Columbia I worked with this professor named Devlin on those famous experiments with rat sexuality. We used to let them start fucking and then pull the male off to see what effect interrupted copulation had. We found it speeded things up: they went apeshit to get it done, became obsessed by it. I don't want the same thing to happen to me. Get it? It's sex or violence: you've got to choose. For me it's violence." After that he had become canny in intercourse, worrying that he was the male spider for whom ejaculation was a prelude to a beheading.

He learned to have some statement proving redeeming ideological merit in case he was caught reading a new novel. When he played handball or pickup basketball games, he always took Wertheim along with him as protective coloration. Born into a family whose God had never failed, Wertheim had joined a chapter of the John Reed club when he was twelve, and had been a true Communist ever since. A genius in dialectics, he was a child in daily life. He was oblique, naïve, his behavior showing the cost of skipping adolescence. Soon after he came into Mad Dog, Cabell had found him reading Germaine Greer and asked why. "Because I want to learn the difference between men and women," had been the reply. "Look between your legs; that's as good a place as any to begin," Cabell had said in what he thought was a joke. Wertheim actually looked.

Long arms flailing, making enthusiastic charges into teammates and opponents alike, kicking shins and crushing toes with his clumsiness, Wertheim was a menace on the court. At first Cabell had taken him along because he knew that if he did nobody would dare accuse him of ideological dereliction. But their relationship grew on the basis of a shared respect for Earl Monroe and hand-eye coordination. Sports became a release for them both: the moment when people ceased being bogged down in their own specific gravity and broke free into pure, unfettered space. Whenever the Bullets came to town, they snuck off to the Cow Palace guiltily standing for the national anthem with everyone else and then concentrating on Earl Monroe's every move. They cheered when he came off the bench and booed when he was taken out. After some move defying the laws of motion, Wertheim would hug Cabell and pound him on the back, eyes shining through thick glasses. "Oh God! Oh my! The Pearl! The true and perfect revolutionary!"

There weren't enough games. There were agents everywhere, forcing them inward. They began to feast on their own scabs. The agents were the best revolutionaries, professing most strongly, gut-checking the recalcitrant, proponents of the-heavier-the-better. Life at Mad Dog and elsewhere became a long dance down a hall of mirrors.

One night when they thought the others were out at a meeting, Cabell and Wertheim sat in the darkened living room watching Alcindor take UCLA into the NCAA finals. There was a rustle behind them and then a torso came across to black out the screen.

"This is an emergency meeting." It was Wald, his voice sunk into an octave of conspiracy. "I'm convening it. Nobody else is here. The three of us got to decide."

"Decide what?" Cabell was impatient.

"Frito's an agent," Wald continued. "I just found out. Bastard's been snitching to the pigs all along. They planted him in Berkeley after he got busted on a pot charge in L.A. He's been feeding them stuff on us for over a year. We got to off him. The question is who's going to do it."

"The question is"—Wertheim tried to crane his long neck around to see the action—"why the fuck you don't get out of the way."

"Didn't you hear me?" Wald's voice rose and he moved a hip to block the slice of screen from which they tried to infer the whole. "He's an agent. He's here, inside this house, fingering us to the pigs. He did time down in L.A. He's been feeding stuff to the pigs ever since he got here. I got it from the Panthers."

"I don't give a shit if you got it from W. E. B. DuBois."

Wertheim was up flapping his long arms like an angry stork. "If you think somebody's going to start blowing people away just because you say you've *got information,* you're fucking crazy. That's not what we're here for. Now get the hell out of the way."

The next morning Gonzalez was gone, leaving a note behind addressed to Wald: "You and your friends got a Tackwood complex. Like we always used to say about guys always accusing people of farting: the fox always smells his own hole first. Dig it, people of Mad Dog. Goodbye to your fucking gringo Stalinism."

There was a paring-down taking place, even within the organization. Jill, Nora, and Wald appointed themselves a kind of presidium. They started bringing in the intestines of clocks, black powder, heavy tape. A small storage room downstairs was suddenly padlocked and the words ULTRA ROOM were painted on it in black. Cabell asked Jill what was happening.

"We've got security problems," she said. "Information should be passed out on a need-to-know basis."

"I need to know," he said.

"No you don't. You're under discipline. This whole collective is under discipline. Either you believe in democratic centralism or you don't."

One night she woke him up. She was dressed in a black turtleneck and navy watch cap, as were Wald and Nora, standing behind her.

"Get up, Cabell," she whispered. "We got things to do."

He rose and dressed and then came downstairs. She handed him some keys and hustled him out the door. There was a rented car parked in the driveway. Cabell noticed that mud had been splashed with apparent casualness over the license plate.

"You drive," she said, as the three of them squeezed into the back seat with some stuff in a paper sack. She told him to cross the bridge and head for Golden Gate Park.

He became exasperated after passing over the toll booth. "Look, Jill, I know you guys are into playing commando, but I don't like the idea of all this cloak-and-dagger stuff, especially when I don't know what's happening."

She leaned forward so that her lips were close to his neck. "Come on, Cabe," she whispered. "Just do what I ask. I'll explain it later on."

They told him to stop in a secluded spot along the park's edge, then got out with their packages and ran bunched across the lawn into the darkness. He sat there waiting, playing the radio. In about a half hour they returned and he drove them home. In bed he asked Jill to explain. She brushed him lightly on the lips and then rolled over. "Not now," she mumbled. "I'm dead tired."

The next morning he read of the explosion at the police department station that had shattered windows for blocks around and put a large hole in the occipital lobe of one desk sergeant, a twenty-year veteran with four teenage kids.

He caught her in the hallway and dragged her into the room, shoving the paper in her face. "What's this, goddamn it? What in Christ's name are we doing?"

"You don't have any responsibility," she sneered at him. "You were the driver. The wheelman."

"Listen," he pleaded. "Here's some old fart who isn't doing anything but shuffling papers. How does offing him make the revolution?"

She shrugged. "For one thing, the pigs, all pigs, are an occupying army in the ghetto. Anything we do to them shows our black comrades we mean business. But they're not just symbols of authority. They *are* authority. Like Buddy said, we're supposed to be biting this country in the ass, giving it fits. You begin with the authority that keeps the lid on. Make chaos!"

"This guy is a victim too," Cabell argued. "He comes home and takes off the uniform and he's a father, brother, son. His kids go into the army and get wasted. It's not like you've just done in Kissinger or Westmoreland."

"Okay, Cabell, enough of this." She pulled away disgustedly. "Next you'll be reminding me that Goebbels liked animals and dangled small children on his knee. Nixon had a cold father. Et cetera, et cetera. You're the perfect casuist. If there's some argument for inaction, you'll master it."

"It wasn't so bad when we created the slogans. But now we're acting on the slogans we created."

"Next time I'll leave you out altogether," she said on her way out of the room. "That will keep you pure."

A week or so later, Wertheim stopped in front of the doorway to Cabell's room. He had a duffel bag slung over his shoulder and looked even more harrassed than usual, the greasy lenses of his glasses heavily fingerprinted, his hair standing out in electrified strands.

"So where you off to?" Cabell had known it was coming.

"Europe. Florence maybe. Borrowed fifteen hundred from my brother. Got to get off someplace and sort all this out. Things are going a little too fast for me right now."

"I can relate to it. This is the moment of elemental mitosis."

"What about you?" Wertheim asked.

"I don't know. I guess I'll hang in there for a while and see what develops."

"Don't put all your eggs in one basket." Wertheim was blushing.

"You talking about Jill?"

"Yeah."

"You, who have to *read* about the difference between men and women?" Cabell made him laugh. "Don't worry. Things will get ironed out."

"If not, take an Italian vacation. They got good basketball over there. Each team in their league is allowed two American players."

"I might take you up on it."

It was not long after Wertheim left that Cabell ran into Jim Henry at the Med. He was sitting at a table stirring sugar into an herbal tea, breathing up the steamy aroma with closed eyes as if taking a sinus treatment. It was several seconds before he realized that Cabell was standing near. As he looked up, something like fear darted rapidly across his face and hid.

They had learned to measure each other during brief encounters by changes in their outward styles. Jim Henry's hair was trimmed close; the dashiki had been replaced by a suit of faded denim that accented the lithe narrow body. The round, wide eyes were sicklied over with yellow. There was a looseness of gray-brown skin around them, but the overall impression was of tautness. His fingers drummed compulsively against the table's marble top, and every few seconds he slightly rotated his neck as if relieving pressure from below. Cabell knew he was working as head of a drug-abuse project in West Oakland and had run afoul of the Panthers. Movement gossip said that one of the field marshals, a huge black known only as Cherokee, had stood up in a meeting to denounce Jim Henry as a cultural nationalist: "One of them dudes who say that ghetto schools ought to serve their vanilla ice cream with black food coloring so it won't be *white*." A number of ipso-factos had flowed from this accusation: to be a cultural nationalist was to be in solidarity with Ron Karenga and US; to be in solidarity with US was to be a police informer; to be an informer was to be an Enemy of the People; and this was to be in jeopardy.

"How you doing, man?" Cabell felt his words bounce off their past relationship. "Long time no see."

"I'm sneaking along. How 'bout yourself?"

"I'm okay. I hear about you every so often." He had wanted to say: Jim, I'm sick of myself and these other foolish honkies. When I come to earth again I want to be a black basketball player—singer, Earl the Pearl and Otis Redding.

"Indeed so, I'm sure you do."

"Some weird rumors going down."

"I have no doubt of it, not the slightest." The smile was teeth bared in warning. "People *will* talk."

"Mind if I sit down?"

"It's a free country." Jim Henry gestured at the chair across the table.

"Listen, Jim . . ." Cabell was going to say that he didn't believe in any of the gossip, but that there was danger. But he was interrupted.

"I sure do hope you ain't fixin to run some of your revolutionary bullshit by me, Cabell, cause I've done had it with all that stuff. Dig?"

"No, I was just going to say that there's this talk going down about informers . . ."

"What's the matter with you? Don't you see where I'm comin from? I said I don't want to hear it. I'm sick of it. You all responsible for what's coming down. You white radicals for blacks the way you for football teams. You for the ones that act the baddest. If they wave guns around and get their black asses shot off by the pigs, so much the better. Y'all stroke them by saying *right on*; they stroke you by dying or killing."

"The Panthers aren't into guns anymore, they're into community organizing." He felt he had to defend himself. "They're into electoral politics, that sort of stuff."

The wooly head shook in disgust. "Trouble with people like you is that you see what you want to see. Breakfast for children goes on during the daytime, all kinds other shit go on at night. Hear what I'm saying? Cocaine and hookers come out at night. Cocaine need pushin, hookers need pimps. Niggers that own bars down in the ghet-toe, they been payin protection to the Black Panther party. Dig? And a political machine is just a legit way of having a gang. Hear it? You rub one of them suckers the wrong way and he just take you on down right in the street!"

There was disgust in the voice, and the eyes seemed deep and lifeless, as if implanted by taxidermy. "It's like Malcolm said: if you see some dude winning all the time, he ain't gamblin, he cheatin. You folks so naïve, it's a waste of time tellin you bout it. Y'all done turned your Frankenstein loose and now you got your head up your ass. Up there in the dark lookin around and sayin to yourself, ain't nobody here but us chickens, boss! But there are people who know what's happenin. Hear me? People who *know*."

"What do you mean?"

"Hell, I'm tired of talkin bout it. Y'll just hear what you want to hear. You just doin what people tell you to do, supportin what people tell you to support."

Cabell sat on for a few minutes trying to make conversation, trying to draw him out, but Jim Henry just sat there silently, inhaling the tea. Finally, desperate to unburden himself, he said, "Jim, did you hear about that bombing of the Golden Gate station?"

"Yeah, but don't be telling me no more," he hissed. "I ain't your guilty conscience."

That evening Cabell mentioned him to Jill. She shrugged "Remember a year or so ago when he got busted—when they raided Lumumba House? Word is the pigs turned him around when he was in jail. They kept him in there on high bail until he agreed to feed stuff back to them. That's the word."

"The *word!* What are we talking about, the New Testament? Where does the *word* come from, our trusty comrade Wald?"

"How do you think Jim's been getting all that federal money down there for his drug project—by being a *revolutionary?* Use your head, Cabell. I also heard that he's into smack and has been running errands for some big dealers. He's got himself a scam."

He had wanted to argue, but she waved him off impatiently. "Who the fuck cares, anyway? It's no big deal."

The ante was being upped every day. Cabell was frozen in the grip of time, unable to affect his own course, yet feeling that some peristaltic action was on the verge of extruding him into a limbo where he would belong to no one. He found himself secretly hoping at times that Nixon would be successful in his Nazification. That would justify their efforts, make the play-acting real, justify their murderous fantasies. He found himself looking forward to the earthquake predicted by hippie soothsayers running for high ground in their caravans. Any disaster would do: anything that would clarify things.

Late in 1971, a spokesman for the PLO was making the

rounds of the movement drumming up support for the guerrillas. Cabell attended a meeting with two dozen radicals comprising the center of what remained of the Berkeley Left. They listened as the young Arab denounced Israeli aggression and the corrupt foreign policy of the U.S. and its Jewish lobby. The proposal seemed reasonable: a binational state. Then when the questions came, someone asked how the Israelis could be made to accept membership as a minority in it.

"They will have no choice." The answer was Delphic.

"It's no solution," Cabell heard himself speaking up. "It's anti-Leninist. Lenin said that no group should be forced to become a national minority against its wishes."

"There is no reason to be ossified in dogma." The words were unhurried, mechanical. "We must adapt ideology to current exigencies."

"How can we rationalize supporting a plan we know would lead to disaster?" Cabell felt Jill move a milli-inch from his side, enough to indicate that there was no necessary connection between them.

"They must be made to do it." The Arab was patient. "It will be good for them. Really, it is the humane solution. The Zionists are like a man with a mouthful of rotten teeth who won't go to the dentist. It is your duty as a fellow human being to knock all those teeth out."

After the meeting broke up and they were going back to the car, Jill said to Wald, "I think Cabell's going through some sort of crisis."

"Right," Wald replied. "I think he needs a little political reeducation. Too bad we don't have sugar cane he can go cut for a few months and give that tired brain a rest."

He flew to Southern California for what he promised himself would be a peace meeting with his father and Charley. Instead he hitchhiked directly from the airport to Aggie's house. Wally and Tay now lived in the two houses beside hers, making the cul-de-sac into something like the family compound she had visualized when buying the property. Cabell was surprised to see the tricycles and other toys on the driveways. He realized with a start that his cousins were married and had children. Where was his own flesh and blood?

Aggie was in the living room, glasses down on her nose, working her way through what looked like the same vast piles of reading material that had been there when he was a teenager. The hair was frosty with gray, and wrinkles had begun to melt the smooth cheeks, but she still looked trim.

"Jesus, Cabe, you look awful," she shook her head and scowled at him after he sat down. "What in God's name is going on with you? I ask your Dad when I see him, but he says you've fallen out of touch."

"I'm okay. I'm just getting my head together right now."

"Getting your head together. I love that phrase. Makes me think of someone with their mind out in the palm of their hand fooling around with it like it was a disassembled toy or something: looking at it, examining it, fiddling around with this part and then that one." She mimed the actions with spidery fingers in her palm as she spoke.

"I agree. But this isn't an examination of life. It's tinkering. The old idea of self-examination, Emerson's for instance, was to lead a person to live effectively and morally. Nowadays this process is to lead to more ecstasy, more influence, more sex."

"God, you don't waste any time hopping on me, Aggie."

"Well, dammit, nobody sees you down here for months on end. I read about all that craziness up there and I think, Jesus, I hope Cabe's not mixed up in that."

"Craziness?"

"You know what I mean."

"Yeah, I guess so."

He drank the lemonade she brought him and began to pour out a diatribe about the narrowing base of action, the increasing solipsism and paranoia, and his sense of isolation in it. He wanted her to be uncritically sympathetic, the member of one low, dishonest decade commiserating with another. But her questions were hard and brittle, inquiring into the nature of Mad Dog. He had to fend her off, at one point saying that there were things he couldn't go into.

"Why not?" she asked brusquely.

"I'm under discipline." It was true, but he had meant it as a little irony to throw her off the track.

"*Discipline?*" Her laugh was like a hacksaw. "*Discipline. Democratic centralism.* God I haven't heard all that stuff in years. History *is* condemned to repeat itself. Lord saves us, the lingo is even the same. Know what it reminds me of, Cabe? God, I haven't thought of this in years. It reminds me of an afternoon back in June, 1940. I was with some other good red ladies picketing a meeting of the Fight for Freedom Committee in New York. That was Dorothy Parker and a bunch of others who were trying to get us into the war against Germany. Naturally we were opposed. It was the time of the Pact. The friend of my friend is *my* friend, and all that. So when those *warmongers* went into the hall around three in the afternoon, we had signs saying 'Down with the Wall Street–British Imperialist Alliance' and all kinds of stuff like that. By the time they came out around dinnertime, we were handing out pamphlets urging the U.S. to get into the war immediately and even criticizing it for foot-dragging. 'Fight Fascism Now!' Why? Because of news that Hitler had invaded Mother Russia. Our marching orders had changed. How could I act like a goddamned zombie? Because I was *under discipline*. Ugh! It's embarrassing."

She misinhaled and got lost for a moment in a storm of coughing. Returning, she clasped her hands under her chin like a little girl about to play a guessing game. "Oh, Cabe, forgive me. I know what you're looking for, but I just can't give it. I'm not the person to look to for sympathy. Call it the generation gap or whatever you want, but I've been where you are now, and when I look back, I don't see much that can give anyone comfort. It was like having cancer of the mind."

"Nobody *made* you stay," he felt himself put on the defensive, forced by her assault to guard values he had come to condemn. "You could have left with Trotsky, during the Purges, at the time of the Pact, or dozens of times after."

"Don't you think I know it? And for that matter, you could leave the game you're playing this instant. But you probably won't. The problem was—and God knows you must feel it too—that there weren't any alternatives. That's what makes you shut your eyes and bite your tongue. Right? What else is there? Don't you ask yourself that question? Membership in some pathetic little sect? Becoming a *Democrat* and working for the election of pimply-faced law students you know are crooks? What? In my days, there wasn't any other vision, no other movement with the potential the party had. It was that or nothing. Don't think we didn't see what happened to the ones who *did* leave, what sorry, isolated wretches they turned out to be. To answer your question, then, it took me so long because I believed in the necessity for radical change. I wanted to be *effective*. I was afraid of impotence. I know you probably think of us as a bunch of Stalinist graybeards, but we did have a mass movement for social change, the only one there's ever really been in this country. What you have are these little head games."

He escaped by saying that he was on a tight schedule and had to leave to see his father. The look on her face said, Well it's about time. Outside, he smelled the stench of nerves rising from his body. He felt dangerously vulnerable away from Berkeley. He hitchhiked directly back to the airport and waited for a flight to the Bay Area, feeling like an illegal alien.

Four days after Christmas, he picked up a late edition of the *Examiner* and carried it to the Med for coffee. He looked through the sports section first, having to search through the agate type of the box scores to find that the Pearl had poured through thirty-seven points against the Lakers the night before. After that he had glanced through the first section for war news. On page eight, under the small headline

BAY AREA MAN IDENTIFIED, there was a brief item that froze him in his chair:

> The San Francisco Coroner's Office revealed today that the body found yesterday near the entrance to the Golden Gate has been identified as James Henry Jackson, 31, an Oakland resident and son of Dr. and Mrs. Hannibal Jackson of San Francisco. The body had been in the Bay at least twenty-four hours, according to Coroner's Office spokesmen. Preliminary results of the examinations have determined that death resulted from massive head injuries. The victim's hands were still bound behind his back when found. Police say their investigation is continuing. . . .

He had run all the way back to the house, carrying the paper under his arm, tears whipping back along the sides of his face. It was the evidence he had been looking for, the proof he needed to blow the smug look off Jill's face and catapult them out of this swinish time that held them so tight, this movement that had gone mad and was now like a sow snuffling up its farrow.

His heart was beating savagely as he took the stairs two at a time and threw open their bedroom door. He hit a wall of incense and marijuana smoke that stopped him in his tracks. When he pierced the veil, he saw a man he recognized as a low-level Panther functionary standing naked above the bed, looking on, a thick joint smoking in his mouth. Jill and Wald were in the middle of the mattress, yin and yang, she holding him like a crab, arms and legs wrapped close, immobilizing, draining his juices as they sucked on each other with the perfect synchronicity of two ends of one tube. She peeked up through the trellis of thigh and calf, moving the limp organ in her mouth like someone shifting a cud to be able to speak. His eyes locked hers there on the far edge of time where it was dark, quiet, the motion so fast as to be imperceptible. She seemed to say: Have you finally had enough? He projected the reply: Yes. When their stare broke, it was with the deliberate calm of rocket stages uncoupling in deep space. He moved back down the stairs knowing that this was the exact moment when time moved on without him.

Jim's death had festered for two weeks. Then Cabell made up his mind to call the Oakland police department. He used a false name and talked to Lieutenant Trauscht, who was heading the investigation. They fenced for several minutes, each trying to get more information than he gave.

"We just don't know," Trauscht said. "Some of the leads go in the direction of drugs, some go in the direction of politics."

"Maybe it's both," Cabell said, trying to steer without being a quisling.

"The Left's supporting itself by dealing?"

"It's worth investigating."

"Listen," the voice grew familiar. "Maybe we should arrange to get together. It's important to us to develop reliable sources of information. We're able to offer certain incentives."

Cabell had suddenly flashed on it: he was being tape-recorded; they didn't want to act on what he knew but to contain it; they were all in it together—Panthers, police, the mob.

"Fuck you," he said and hung up.

He dreamed of Jim Henry for weeks, had visions of him shooting up with hideous needles, swimming in the Bay in an old-fashioned bathing suit, screwing Jill. He dreamed of Jill too, without Jim Henry, but those dreams were not remembered.

Once, months later, she came into the hardware store where he was working. He knew of her evolution by gossip. She had gone into a lesbian group for a month or two and then joined the New Era collective, a guerrilla unit comprised of the hardcore Left after everyone else had quit. It was rumored that New Era had been responsible for knocking over a National Guard armory in Monterey and was using the stockpile of arms for anonymous military action against targets of opportunity.

His heart stirred as he thought for a moment that she had come to see him. But her look told him it was coincidence. He waited on her as if she were any other customer. She asked about pipe.

"Doing some plumbing?"

"Plumbing?" She looked at him blankly as if being interrogated by the FBI. "Yes, that's right."

"Where are you working?"

"Everywhere." The eyes shone beatifically.

"Jesus, you never give up, do you? Always the last dog in. Haven't you gotten the picture yet? It's over. Mao and Nixon are comrades. You're left holding the bag. Don't you get it? It's over."

"It won't ever be over, not in our lifetime. Not in mine, at least."

"Don't you get a little lonely out there leading when nobody's following? Who in God's name ever voted you into office as exterminating angel, anyway?"

"The people."

"You're fucking crazy." He had followed her to the door, a small crowd collecting to hear him rant like a cheated shopkeeper. "You're going to wind up like the rest of the underground—working for Kelly Girls under a false name, and sitting home watching the soaps and eating Quaaludes."

"What about you?" she snarled. "What are you going to do—become one of those *Commentary* reactionaries who makes a career out of moaning about his youthful errors?"

"You've got a bony soul," he yelled as her back merged with a weave of pedestrians.

"That's Wells on Beatrice Webb." She turned ferociously. "Jesus, Cabell, don't you think anyone else has ever read a book?"

For a while he spent time at the Med, looking for arguments about the decadence of the Left, about its cannibalism and narcissism, its myrmidonism and custerism. He sought out true believers and chivvied them with current events. He was filled with theories. He wanted to tell people about the lunacy

227

of this country: how it had fabricated the notion of a Russian threat to justify the Cold War but now, after its truculence had made the Soviets into the monstrous, devouring state it hadn't been in 1945, Kissinger declared a peace with them; how the trouble with Hoover was not his omnipresence but the fact that he directed Keystone Cops who would never catch Jill and the other truly dangerous people. But the metaphysical lurch of the seventies sent the faithful into ashrams and body movements, law school and drugs. He had to search for people to rail at.

Once he ran into Wald in a Safeway. The uniform of workshirt and levis had been discarded in favor of a sheer shirt open to the breastbone; the beard and hair were styled.

"Looks like you changed your image, Buddy," Cabell said, moving his shopping cart into a position to block Wald from moving off.

"Cabell," the smile had come only from the mouth, not the eyes. "What's happening?"

"Still at the hardware store, still talking to all the old lefties. How about you?"

"Oh, I'm doing a little Fisher-Hoffman, getting my head together, starting to write again." Wald fondled an avocado with a lasciviousness that enraged Cabell. "Seen Jill?"

"She was in the store a while back."

"Her group is into some heavy-duty stuff."

"They're crazies," Cabell heard his voice become shrill— "doing their little military actions. Terrorism might be okay in a dictatorship where it voices the general frustration of the people. But here it's just the tyranny of a self-annointed bunch of elitists."

"Dictatorship?" Wald's eyes slitted. "You join the American Legion or something?" He pushed the carts to open a path of egress.

"You people are moral imbeciles." Cabell knew he was on automatic pilot now and could almost see the words glance harmlessly off Wald's retreating back. "You go to places like North Korea where they're wasting dissenters and come back here praising the lack of smog and garbage on their streets. That's like praising a man without a hand for not having dirty fingernails."

More and more he walked Berkeley alone, oppressed by its bombed-out quality, the sense it conveyed of having been struck by some secret weapon and then stealthily rebuilt by architects using new materials that didn't quite match the old. It was a city of hasty mendings, and had that massy, bricked-in look associated with fear of thrown rocks and the sudden savage swell of mob movement. Heroin addicts, thin and toothless, huddled like Bombay beggars in the doorways and storefronts of the avenue. There were black bikers up from the ghetto looking for fresh meat, crazed freaks wandering up and down the street making bubbles from a jar and wand and reciting free verse about their orgasms, carloads of tourists gawking as if on a Gray Line tour. Rising above it all, like mealy smoke from gas chambers, was the stench of dead politics; the lie of progress; of history that was not, as he had tried to believe, the inevitable march from one amelioration to another, but a dark field worked by the blind burrowings of worms. It had taken cancer to rescue him from that vision.

6 The yellow-haired man made a thick, bubbling sound that might have been a cough, and jingled the springs on the bunk frame. Cabell got up and covered him with the blanket that had fallen to the floor, then sat back down on his own bunk. He looked up at the wall above him, tracing the despairing messages on its pocked surface with his finger. If he had had a pencil he would have added his name to it. *Cabell Hart did time here, no better than the rest of you.* He turned on his side and embraced the smelly pillow, no longer holding himself aloof from a comradeship with it. Who was he to pretend superiority to the miscreant's pissy smell? The image of a police uniform with a bloody stump at the neck floated before him, the offering to nameless abstract violence. He acknowledged that he had victims as surely as any cut purse or hit-and-run driver who ever did time here in Halcyon. He knew his great-grandfather was nearby, sad and pathetic, boundless in his guilt. He sent the ghost a thought and rolled to his side to offer him half the bunk. *Rest, perturbèd spirit. Oh, rest.*

A tremendous exhaustion overtook him. He felt himself drifting away. Perchance to dream.

The Campanile had struck and he was late, late and unprepared, running for the small classroom hidden deep in Dwinelle Hall, always one more corridor away. He prepared his excuses as he jogged but knew that no Berkeley student, not even a freshman, would ever swallow them. He conned a quick rap on Shakespeare as he ran and computed ways to avoid questions regarding ungraded papers. Anxiety was all around him, an environment almost aqueous in its density, not so much breathed as gilled. Finally he found the door. Sullen faces looked up from wristwatches. Oh Christ, he's here.

"In this play"—he quickly began his spiel—"what we have is the complete shattering of order, the irreparable chaos brought by death and disillusion, the destruction of the family, that perfect form, that triangle from which Hamlet had inferred all decency and justice in the world. He'd given up his philosophical studies and returned to his family. When that form is broken by faithlessness and death, order is itself destroyed —you can see that, can't you?—and the universe goes dark. All things are colored by that cataclysm. Clearly so. Appetite becomes bestial, ambition evil, altruism a sham. He sees the terrible task: to take upon himself the work of recreating what has been destroyed. It's not just mindlessly striking back. Laertes has lost a father and sister and wants to get even in a rash and superficial sense, and there's nothing sympathetic in that callow youth. What Hamlet does—and you may not see this for a few years because the play is for a person on the verge of middle age, someone like me or Hamlet himself: remember he's over thirty and his mother says he's fat and scant of breath—what Hamlet does, I say, is try to build belief when there's no reason for believing. He learns to see beyond his pain, affirm that there's a divinity that shapes our ends. Because he's seen that, when he does purchase justice at the cost of his own life, it has a kind of force that simple reflex vengeance would surely lack. Am I coming through on this? Let's be clear on this matter of his death. Certainly none of you can feature Hamlet living on and marrying, can you? Having children and settling down to practice petty statecraft? No way. That sickness, that cancer, has touched them all. The killing we have in the grand finale of the last act is not the petty vendetta of a Sicilian caught in some small-time feud whose origins don't matter. Don't think that. It is the recognition on the hero's part that the universe cannot be sound again until all connected with this primal crime, including most obviously himself, are gone. . . ."

He knows without looking down at them that they are snickering at the banality of it, squirming and whispering, looking at their watches again, not listening. They are nudging each other truculently and looking at the ceiling in such a way as to make it clear that they consider it so much pap, another Cliff Notes lecture. They blame him for his lack of preparation and for his ineffectiveness as a person, his chronic incompletion. He stops, wiping sweat at his hairline.

"Boy, I had a run to get here," he says, smiling to lighten the mood. Suddenly he recalls a trick he has seen his professors play—getting good dramatic value, eliciting support and sympathy by claiming sickness in the middle of a class. He feigns the feeling so well that he actually feels sick, feels a fever creeping into his bones, rising within him like mercury in a thermometer. "I'm feeling sick right now," he said, "but I'll be back, with your papers, I swear to God, tomorrow." Picking up the books he is out the door before they can traduce him with criticism or comment.

Outside in bright grass shade-mottled by spreading Chestnut trees, he runs into a picnic. Then he realizes: these are his people! His father is in charge, whole again, wearing a chef's apron and making extravagantly epicene, Gallic gestures as he cooks. His sister stands nearby, laying out the food on a redwood table, the one they laboriously painted green when they were children. Tomatoes, onions, and lettuce are arranged artistically on a paper plate; she puts a little parasol of cheesecloth over it and the potato salad so the flies can't lay their larval poison there. Smart girl! But he means to tell her, Don't stay in the sun too long yourself, you know about conception!

He walks up behind them, wanting to eat but not wanting to draw notice until the proper moment. He overhears his sister tell his father, "Cabell has been gone so long from us." He will fool her soon. They turn and see him stealing off with food and, instead of blaming, rush to pamper him with hugs, looking at each other now and then as if to say, Can you believe it? It's really him. After all these years. He cries out joyfully, "You're not dead then?" They laugh and roll their eyes: another one of Cabell's silly notions.

He notices that his mother is off to the side, the lost Edith, exempt from them but interested, wearing the same knee-length blue-and-white print silk dress she wore to see the Freedom Train convey the ark of the American covenant to Southern California. With sinuous southern grace she bends from the waist to smell gardenias, taking the odor in without touching the flower or allowing herself to be polluted by its dusty pollen. "So where's the little fellow, then?" she asks in a soft drawl, not looking up. Charley rises in alarm and begins to look around. "Joey!" she calls, "Joey! Joooeeey!" His father whips the apron over his head and moves off quickly in those finely controlled movements that are the athlete's response to danger. He returns. They turn to look at Cabell, all of them, staring in disbelief. He runs.

He awoke in the dark, glad to be delivered, but sad to be without them, even if only as the object of their censure for losing the boy. He lay there for a moment awaiting the interchange from dreaming to waking to be completed. When the cell had established itself as reality, he sat up on the edge of the bunk. Some part of this world was missing. He looked over and saw that the yellow-haired man in the next bunk was gone. Dead? It seemed natural to wonder.

There were sounds, voices, on the other side of the partition. The dream sweat was like ice water on his forehead and chest as he listened. But it was impossible to make words of the muffled sounds. So he rose and walked to the door of the cell. He pulled out his grandfather's watch and managed to angle a glint of moon or streetlight onto the face from the meshed slit at the top of the cell. It was nearly four in the morning. He had slept for hours. Now he was ready to live again, hungry and thirsty. He wished for a tin cup or some other implement to xylophone the bars as in prison movies. He began to yell.

The voices stopped. In a few moments footsteps approached and the door was flung open. A squat shadow attenuated the greasy yellow light. Cabell felt confident that he would win his release. He wrinkled his nose. A sudden waft of wet dog and toe jam was not part of the acceptable human misery of his cell.

"Okay, slow down now, stop that hollerin'. You like to wake the dead with that caterwaulin' of yours." Strapp's voice did not appear to hold grudges for anything that had passed earlier in the day. As Cabell's eyes adjusted to the light he saw that the uniform had been exchanged for street clothes. Strapp bent over to unlock the door.

"What now?" Cabell asked, as he was led into the office, surprised to find no one else there.

"Nothing now," Strapp was genial. "You can go."

"Just like that?" Cabell felt angry, but also like giggling. "Lock me up for no reason and then tell me I can go for no reason. This place is fucked."

"It's like that movie said: what we had here was a failure of communication. You can go. But you can't be bothering the Bruces until you get an okay from the county people down in Eureka. Hear?"

"It took you twelve hours to decide to tell me this?" Cabell shook his head in disbelief.

"Out here in the boonies the wheels of justice turn slow. Pace of life is different. You know."

"Yeah, we been through that before." Blinking in the overhead light of the office, Cabell was beginning to feel a kind of affection for the unflappable police chief and thought that under other circumstances he might learn to like him. As he went out the door, he couldn't resist one last lame piece of melodrama.

"Listen, we'll meet again."

"Don't forget the story I told you about that little dog of mine." The hammy face was looking at him with amusement as he slammed the door.

Neon lights flickered weakly at the tops of store windows, making the town's main street seem like it was in REM sleep. As he walked down the high sidewalks, traffic signals blinked yellow caution, the on-and-off light splashing down onto the pavement. An occasional car passed. One of them, a late model Buick, he thought contained the police chief. He looked after the finny taillights and saw an ironic wave of the hand. "You motherfucker," he said to himself as he held his middle finger up high, "the least you could have done was give me a lift."

He moved along quickly, hands hunched down into the pants pockets as the cold penetrated his thin summer shirt. There was no doubt of it: he was getting sick. Soon the side- walk was interrupted by stretches of vacant lot; then it gave way altogether. He was walking on the shoulder of the high- way, half-jogging, colder as he moved away from the radiated heat of buildings and into the forest. The only thing on his mind was getting back to the pickup as soon as possible to get on a jacket and stop the chills puckering his flesh.

A small foreign car pulled up alongside, crunching gravel. The driver leaned over to roll down the window on the passenger side, his face obscured by the bill of a cap.

"Need a lift?"

"Yeah, I do." He assumed the man was a lonesome gay gone randy late at night. If it hadn't been so cold he would have refused the offer as an unneeded human complication, but his skin was crawling in such a way as to make him shiver every few seconds. He got in. "It's freezing out there."

It was not a baseball hat as he thought, but a jaunty

trucker's cap, the logo on the front for caterpillar tractors. The bill wagged in agreement with him, "Colder than a witch's titties."

Cabell shivered again and moved his feet to catch the air coming through the floorboard heater. "I appreciate the lift. I'm the green Ford pickup. A mile or so down the road."

The driver nodded and concentrated on going through the gears. After attaining a cruising speed, he looked over, showing a thin, almost Frenchified face in the green dashboard light, slit-eyes, a mustache in horizontal feline wisps that twitched as he smiled. There was a pink scar on the nose.

"You're the Hart girl's brother, aren't you?"

"That's right." Cabell's defenses had been mobilized against homosexual proposition; this took him by surprise. "How did you know?"

"I heard about them bringing you in today. What was that all about, anyway?"

"I don't know. They didn't like me taking my sister's kid, I guess."

"Weird." The man shrugged and then reached out a hand. "Oh, by the way, I'm Melvin Davis. Mel. I'm in lumber."

"Glad to know you." Cabell released the hand as they pulled over onto the side of the road and the headlights materialized the back of the pickup. "Listen, thanks for the help."

"Just a minute," the driver turned off the motor and pulled a bottle out from under the seat. He took a pull, whooshed out his breath and shuddered, and offered the bottle. Cabell shook his head.

"Listen, Mr. Hart. I didn't just happen by accidentally. I'd been waiting for them to let you go. I knew your sister."

"Yes?" Cabell listened out of duty. He just wanted to forget everything, to get in the pickup and drive to Eureka, find a luxury motel, and prepare for whatever lay ahead by sleeping and getting warm again.

"Well, I have reason to believe that what happened to her wasn't an accident."

236

"What do you mean 'reason to believe'?" Cabell was vaguely amused by the conspiratorial tone and Perry Mason language.

"Well, I was down by the bridge not long after she was supposed to have drowned. It was before the chief got there to investigate. I was out looking for rocks with my son. Anyway, I found a certain article of clothing."

"Article of clothing?" Cabell was beginning to feel that the circumlocution was purposeful, intended to hook him, to make him keep seeking qualification. "What are you talking about?"

"Panties."

He tensed at the prurience of the word.

"They were torn at the seams and they'd been scuffed off into some bushes," the man continued.

"Why do you think they were hers?"

"There were some other things. Evidence."

"Evidence? Have you said anything to anybody about this? Have you gone to the police?"

"No sir, I haven't."

"How come?"

"Well, you were just at the police department, weren't you?"

Cabell nodded.

"Was it what you'd call a comforting feeling?"

"Not especially."

"Well, that pretty much answers the question. Word gets around in a small town. One person sneezes, everybody catches cold, if you get my meaning. I'm a family man, Mr. Hart. I know it might not sound good, but up here you learn to watch yourself and not get singled out."

"Are you saying that there's been some sort of cover-up?" The Watergate word came naturally.

"I'm not saying there hasn't been. Let's leave it at that. If you want to walk down to the bridge with me, I'll show you what I'm talking about and then you can make up your own mind. But remember, I want anonymity."

Cabell shrugged. He would just as soon have said no. But it would have made him seem callous. "Let's go."

The man drew a flashlight the length of a billy club from the jumpseat and then took off, trailing the shaft of light into the darkness. Cabell followed after him, remembering the path from the afternoon. They passed over creeks that he knew were capillaries to the Fortuna; he heard frogs gargling at their edge and occasionally a hatch of mosquitoes rose to tickle his face as they climbed down over that field of rocks the river had heaved out of its way in some other age. The whirring sound of bat wings fanned his ear, and Cabell suddenly feared dark and slimy things, the offspring of evil living by night. He moved closer to the man in front of him, the light-bearer and his protector; he almost touched his back, deciding that it was better to trust him than the menacing nightworld all around him. He heard the roar of the river ahead. The light shone steadfastly on the ground, a piece of humanity in this dark Miltonic chaos. He followed it with confidence. Soon rocks grew smaller and they were on a sandy path, then on the bridge itself. The water passed below with such velocity that it sent up air currents that billowed his shirt. Their footsteps made competing undulations. He steadied himself by reaching out to touch his companion's shoulder.

"Up there ahead," the man shouted over the water, casting the beam at the end of the bridge. Cabell now led, not knowing what he was looking for, but ready for any clue that would illumine the darkness in which he had moved since arriving at the hospital two days earlier. Following the flashlight's trail, he felt close to something. The first faint druidic gray was beginning to blotter up the night. They were off the bridge and on solid ground. Ahead he made out a stand of trees yearning out almost in the horizontal toward the water. He stopped, the man behind bumped into him, starting him up again. There was movement out of the trees up ahead; the flashlight beam crossed with another one then broke apart and crossed again.

"Hey Mel, over here." Two darker forms detached themselves from the general gray. The flashlight revealed boots stomping to keep up circulation and for a moment a pair of hands jammed into pants pockets against the cold. The man behind herded him gently ahead. There were two other pair of shoes and they semicircled around him. The deflected glow of flashlight illumined protrusions of nose and lips, prognathous jaws. The eyes were dark; steam escaped from open mouths. He saw it through other eyes. *Wolves!* The light shifted and caught the sleeve of an army field jacket terminating in a glint, silver fingers not of bone and sinew. *Captain Hook!*

"He was right," he said out loud.

"Who was right?" Strapp's casual hillbilly voice intruded as the face, frypan flat, loomed up next to him in the company of the nauseating odor. *The bad-smelling one!* That left the other with the logo on his hat and the wispy whiskers. *The Cat!*

"Joey."

"About what?" Strapp interrogated.

"My sister."

"So what?" Davis was near him.

"What Melvin means," said Hunter, whose bearded face swam into the light, "is that there's something to be said for learning to go with the flow. Look out for number one. Don't sweat it. However you want to put it, she should have understood that we were just out for a little fun. You don't make a moral issue out of everything. She could have relaxed and had some fun, too. It's not like we're riffraff. We're the town's gentry."

"You raped her." Cabell's voice drowned the appreciative chuckles of the other two.

"I'm not real crazy about that word *rape*," Hunter said, moving his body so that it closed the circle around Cabell. "It's got the feel of prosecution about it. She struggled. It incited us. Let's just leave it at this: we knew her carnally, me and Mel. The good police chief here had recourse to Mrs. Fist and her Five Lovely Daughters. But me and Mel here managed to give

239

a good account of ourselves. We got our jism into every available opening, didn't we Mel?"

"That we did." When Davis spoke, he now seemed to Cabell to be purring.

"Yes indeed, every opening."

Cabell knew that they were trying to bait him into the first move, that they needed their quarry to take flight or strike out to establish the perverse morality that would justify their attack. He stook stock still, trying to think of some bargain he could strike. *Look, the boy doesn't mean that much to me* —he tried the speech out quickly in his mind—*he'll do all right up there with those people. I don't know what happened here that day. I don't want to know. A confusion of intent. Just let me go . . .*

"Look," he held his hands out, showing the palms as if stopping traffic. "The boy doesn't mean that much . . ." The betrayal choked him and he couldn't finish.

"You bastards!" He bowled the Cat to the side with a shoulder and broke through their circle, taking them by surprise. He was one step onto the bridge and sensing freedom, plotting out what he would do with it, when they recovered. Out of the corner of his eye he saw Hunter's lunge, the hook shooting out of the sleeve. He felt its icy touch on his shoulder, shearing away flesh, and catching on the seam of his shirt, throwing him off balance for a moment, just long enough for other legs to tangle his, arms to begin encircling his chest. He turned, ready to plead again, but their momentum carried him off his feet and into the handrail of the bridge. The hook hit him in the forehead, pulling away with a sensation of extraction that was almost dental. He was bending backward, blood rolling down into his eye. He went over backward and grabbed at the bad-smelling one's meaty arm to keep himself from falling. They cooperated, trying to retrieve him. "Goddamn it, Strapp, haul him up here," was Hunter's shout.

The railing slipped lower, below his buttocks, jackknifing him backward. His weight carried him down. He left them with shredded fabric in their hands.

His head hit first, the rushing water filling his nose and taking him down, tumbling him over in a looping somersault. His fingers dragged the sandy bottom, dredging filaments of moss and slime in the search for some slight hold. His body was supple in the current, sailing smoothly past logs and rocks. He tried to strike for the surface, but couldn't find a leverage to arch himself out of the water's contour. His mind had time for one large thought at a time. *No air* came first. Slowly it gave way to *poor Joey*. He saw the surface far above him, dawnshine coming down as if through a pane of frosted glass. He reached up trying to break through with his hand, wishing only to grasp a piece of the sweet gray. *I'm drowning.* Face downward in a glide, he thought he saw a mermaid pinned between submerged logs, hair waving like sea logs, arms held up by the water. He tried to touch her as he passed. *Charley?* The back of his head hit something hard, and as he opened his mouth to cry out in pain and pity the water entered him. Down at the very bottom of his panic there was a small clarification. *We all owe God a death.*

The thing about the marchers that I don't like is that sometimes they won't go. They won't leave when I want them to. They're good because they keep me from having to listen to the toad's words. They're bad because their music keeps getting louder every time they come. It hurts my ears. I can't think about anything else. What I'm saying is that they stay too long. Their music starts up sometimes when I don't expect it. Suddenly here they come, marching right down through the center of my brain. I say, Go away, Leave now, I'm trying to write a letter in my mind to Papa Two! But the man with the bearskin hat just keeps on smiling and stepping high. The girls laugh with their red lips. The sun shines so bright off their clothes that it hurts the back of my eyes. Leave now! I shout it loud to make them hear. I keep on shouting and finally they stop and move over to the side for a while. Every so often a little sound comes from one of the marching band's instruments, like they're practicing. They give me dirty looks like they don't like me telling them what to do. But I can think again.

Did the killing frost come last night, I wonder? All I see from here are berry bushes, and they don't show it. But it feels like last night may have been the night. I look at things outside and it looks like something has come to get them. A killing frost? Mama says that all the vegetables have to be in before it comes or they won't make it. What about our tomatoes? The last time I saw them they were hanging there like Christmas ornaments. By now the killing frost has probably come and got them all.

Uncle Cabell says you're gone, Papa Two. Like Mama. Gone. I just can't believe it. I can't believe you'd die without giving me a chance to see you. You must have been sicker than I thought. I can't believe it.

When I was a littler boy and lived with you we did everything. We went to the games. Remember? We always got there early so we could see the guys practice their throwing. You said that was the best part of the game. Remember the time Sutton threw a ball up to the bleachers and you got right in there with the kids and got it, then brought it back to me?

Once I was talking to Mama and I was saying that I bet you wouldn't remember me, it had been so long since I saw you. I meant that I had gotten bigger. She thought I meant something else. She said, No, Joey, don't say that because Papa Two won't ever forget you, never, you can count on that. I said, I know, I do. Well, I won't forget you either. You'll never be gone to me, not ever. I'll keep on writing you this letter in my mind. That way I can stay in touch with you. That way I'll always remember. Who else is there?

I don't know if Uncle Cabell liked me or not. I couldn't tell. Sometimes I thought he did. Other times, he didn't. He looked sort of sick. Fatter than in that blurry picture, with bulges under his eyes and thinned-out hair. He kept jangling his keys and tapping his foot while we were eating like he had someplace to go. He chews his fingernails and is always looking around like somebody might be following. He told me a weird story about an Indian who can pitch with both hands.

He didn't believe me when I told him about the wolves. I wasn't sure I was right until the bad-smelling one came down to the river to get us. Then I knew. Uncle Cabell still didn't believe me. He gave me back to them. How come?

The toad man came in tonight and said that Uncle Cabell

won't be coming back. He said, He's fish food now, Mister Man, so you might just as well forget about that. I'm theirs now, he said, so I ought to get used to it.

I didn't say anything, but I knew he was right. They've won. I won't get away now. I'm going to have to start eating what they give me and talking to them. I'm just going to have to act regular, like nothing happened. I'll take their bike and dog and go to school. I'll act like a regular boy. I'll grow bigger and get stronger. Get my foot fixed. I'll grow up. I'll do what they tell me. But I won't forget, not ever. That's what they want, but I won't do it. They want me to believe that I should be whoever's boy they say. They want me to believe that when you see somebody on the street you know is a wolf you should just act like he's a regular person. I'll pretend those things are true, but I won't believe them. I swear to God.

You can't do anything now. I know that. Nobody can. These wolves are too smart and mean. But I'll keep this letter going. I need to remember what I know. When I get bigger, I'll kill them all. I'll remember who they were and what they did and I'll cut their heads off. I'll slice off each bastard penis. I'll lay the heads and penises out in the sun to dry. The yellow jackets will come and suck the eyes until they're holes going down to gooey brain. They'll eat the penises down to white bone. I'll just stand there and laugh.

The only way to fight a wolf is to be a wolf yourself. What did my mama and me ever do to them? What did my father ever do? We didn't hurt them any. We were just trying to get along.

It's like the Tollowas. They got killed off—women and children—because they weren't as mean as the settlers. Mama told me once that the settlers used to get their guns on Sundays after church and go out and kill some Tollowas, just for fun. For fun! Can you believe it? If I had been an Indian boy then I would have hidden and waited until I got bigger and got my power up and then killed every bastard settler I'd seen hurting the women and children. It wouldn't bring them back, but it would help make things equal.

After they took me away from Uncle Cabell and brought me

245

back up here, the toad man got in his car and went back down the hill to finish working at his job downtown. A little while later, the Cat came up the drive. I could see him out the window, and just the look of him made the skin on my back cold. The place where Mama got him on the nose is a scar now. I hope he remembers what he did to her every time he sees that scar in the mirror. I opened my door and listened. The woman treated him like a regular person. They sat there drinking coffee downstairs. It sounded like a big meeting of people because of her radio. They left it on when they came up here. I heard them tiptoeing up the stairs so they wouldn't creak. They must think I'm stupid or something. They went into the bedroom next door. The Cat was grunting every once in a while. Unh. He went like that. Unh. Like somebody chopping wood. Unh. The woman started humming. At first it was soft, then she hummed real loud for a minute and stopped. Did he do that thing to her he did to Mama?

Nobody realizes it, not even that woman. To a wolf, you're not a human being. You're just a piece of meat, something to bite and chew. Nobody cares how bad these wolves are. They treat them like regular people. When I get big I'll cut off their heads and penises. I'll rip open their bellies and spill them on the floor. I'll jump rope with their guts. I'll put gasoline on their bodies and light them with matches. I'll take a hammer and pound that man's hook into a spear and then drive it through his heart. I'll burn this town down. When the wolves are howling, begging for me to stop, I'll just laugh. I promise you I'll do it, Papa Two, I promise. That's my reason for deciding to go ahead and grow up.

That was what the Tollowas did wrong. They should have killed Jedediah, killed him dead as a doornail. They should have killed every person that came near them, just killed them automatically without asking questions. That's the only way to be safe.

Don't trust people.

They might be wolves.

After I've killed every wolf and burned this bastard town, I'll go downriver. I'll live there. We'll all be there together. You, me, Mama, maybe Uncle Cabe. We'll be a family again just like we were at your house. That soldier will be there. His wounds will be all healed and he'll be fine. He'll take me on his shoulders and ride me around. Old Coyote will be there too, showing us how to live and play tricks on all our enemies so they never get us. Mama says he's still out there someplace, the spirit of this country. We'll sit around the campfire at night and tell stories about the things we've done. Old Coyote will be there with us. I'll tell the one about how I killed the wolves. You'll say, Good boy, Joey.

I hope I can get rid of these marchers. They come when I don't want them. Too loud!

THREE

7 Separating suddenly from the branch whose twig it was, the insect animates. Stepping down onto the soiled white curve, it picks its way along through dirt and debris, moving on stilts, extraterrestrial, fallen from space into this bubbling Jurassic world of stagnation and steam where heat cracks mud into long fault lines leading away from tidal lap and flow. The mandibles work like knives sharpening against each other. A jacketing of bronze armor glints. The eyes are shields and sensors welded onto three planes, alert for enemies. It rears, waving its antennae to vector in on the pain glowing up above, to understand why it hurts so in that volcanic cone.

The crusty surface on which it rides suddenly tenses in a seismic shift. The creature moves back slowly, wisely covering its retreat, sensing something unpredictable here. Backing down the too, too sullied flesh, it reaches a spear of coarse grass, swings down to a patch of sand, and rushes back into habitat.

He sees all—there is a *he*—but feels nothing. He is eyes, nothing more. As the mantis (preying; praying?) explored the arm, he didn't feel but watched. He knew the wound in the·

space above the brow not through his own damaged nerves, but as if by seeing, watching the insect's empathy with his pain. He did not will the muscle twitch, that rippling of distaste that sent it stilting away.

Eyes are quite enough. Leave it at that. Yet eyes alone are vulnerable. The orb can be popped or pecked; the vitreous fluid, sucked. To succeed, eyes must be embedded in bulk. He makes an effort to move them back into that form lying there battered, dangling mud and moss like some old carapace kicked up by the mad current. He backs in cautiously, like a hermit crab checking potential shelter. Seeing that the body is unoccupied; he floods it with his essence and seeks to control the perimeters. A finger moves; he accepts the disagreeable sensation of grit under nail. A calf flexes; he is reminded that there is buoyancy behind. The mooring is tentative. Too quick a gesture takes this waterlogged thing backward, allows the river to reclaim it. He lies there unmoving, no longer aquatic, yet not fully earthborne. In between states, he is a creature of the alluvial ooze.

A good time to explore his new shape. The lower part is smooth and streamlined, sinuous in water. The part above is beached and wears a contracting coat of mud; a scaly thing and ugly. He hears its rasp, liquid still heavy in the air spaces, excremental particles embedded in the mucuous lining. It is all part of the traumatic semipassage onto land. There is pain at the temple. By tracing the course of the blood that curdles in the sand below the arm on which the chin rests, he gets a mental picture of the wound.

The pulling from behind is as urgent as memory. He has been saved by some diving reflex, a remainder of the amphibian past that allowed him to spend long periods underwater while blood still coursed to the vital tissue. But now it is time to separate forever from that world of effortless float and make this cumbersome form responsible for its own weight and motion. *Move!* The command goes out like a random signal probing deep space. It is at first refused, then accepted with mutinous slowness. Claws reach for land; finny feet brush a slope of shore and then kick forward. Eons are compressed in the decision that takes him out of the water's lick and tickle.

Gasping there on shore, he suddenly realizes the true nature of the dilemma: *he lives.*

When his eyes open again, the sun is straight above him, beating down. He is on his back, staring up at cirrus sailing swiftly north. A shriek bounces off the water. He raises his head and looks down between the splayed feet to glimpse a large osprey, blue-white and dancing in the sky. It courses the center of the river, a deep hunter. Too far away to prove the detail, he knows by some instinct the beak's turkish curve and the deadly barb of talon. The bird's eye is golden resin and it picks up an incipient flash just before it glints like tinfoil on the foamy wave. The wings fold in, and the bird crumples, exploding in a savage strike on the water, missing the surfacing fish and then rising again in the updraft, hanging in the sky once more like a killer kite. It shrieks.

What he has seen makes him fearful of his unprotected underside. He struggles to attain all fours. The effort is depleting. In time he recovers and begins to crawl, head down, hands and knees in no more than tentative sync. There is no way out. He makes a path through mud, splashing over stagnant pools cut off from the main flow. This brings hatches of mosquitoes up into his face like raw wool. Eyes shut, he moves ahead on faith, crossing the swamp to solid ground. Eyes open again, he pauses to watch insects that work between land and water, building and carrying, nomads of the interstice. He inadvertently breaks a tiny dam and floods their valley. Ants form a double line of bearers passing the white eggs out, holding them high, drowning as they go. No screams for help or fear of cowardice. Their bravery is insured by the detailed instructions written in the cells below the cuticle. Do everything you can to save future generations; sacrifice individuals to save genes: evolution's law.

Crawling, he passes into a Gobi of sand and wallows like a heavy tank. Then he finds firm ground again—the river's high-water mark from a prior era—a pavement of sharp stones whose points bruise him. One knee is trapped high on a log the other avoids. Unable to bring the competing motions into harmony, he falls onto a side, rights himself, then plows ahead. Finally fingers scrabble red siltation. Good dirt, friable and fresh.

Up a steep incline he labors, leaving the rushing sound of water. He has taken too long. The sun is going. The rocks can only hold the heat so long. The thought of cold nights makes him sluggish. He would stop except that these horny vertebrae of his are exposed to paralyzing rip of tooth and claw. He tries to camouflage as he goes, to blend with the undergrowth that thickens as he rises higher.

He is in a field of granite, black flecks on gray. There are crevices and furrows for handholds. He snakes his way upward on his belly. Above is a ledge of rock his fingers tell him is smoothly tabled. He is almost exhausted, but manages to pull his eyes up level to look. There is a floor, and what looks like three walls and a roof. Shielded from above by an overhang and on sides by a landslide of boulders at their angle of repose, it is like a little room.

It is dark when he finds the strength to pull himself up. He sits cross-legged in the middle of the floor and his head does not touch the ceiling. He explores further back, finding a shallow indentation at the back. He pokes his head in and smells the must of afterbirth and fur. There are shards of bone in padded dirt. He forces his inelastic form to fit the place and tries to make his heat warm the rock. He feels safe from night hunters. In his dream chrome-toed wolves snarl and rip at fresh meat and bay at a frozen moon.

He wakes at first light, thinking: and rosy-fingered Dawn had risen from her couch. He sees his den for the first time, marveling at the porch of rock extending out from where he slept. It is smooth as if cut by a saw. He pulls himself forward to the front of the ledge where the sun angles down fiercely. It penetrates his battered muscles like hot oil. He looks out of one slitted eye at the forest surrounding him, then down to the river below. He is surprised to have come so great a distance.

Somewhere in the vast carpeting of green a bird raps out a staccato burst on wood. The breeze makes tiny whirlwinds that pick bits of dust off the granite.

I have been a fool too long, he thinks, as the sun kneads him.

He reaches into the pockets of stiff-dried pants and spreads the contents before him: a five-dollar bill and some change, a pocketknife, and a watch. He feels for the wallet but it is gone: an offering to the wine-dark seas of his dim odyssey. No credit cards, no license. All those years he had thought himself an everyman, he comes to this: without official identity, a no-man. He throws the money over the side: metal falls fast; paper glides.

I am alone. At this thought his tear ducts itch and swell. It is not because he lacks people that he feels this sadness, but because he lacks connection with the mechanical world —the rise and fall of despots, conquest and enrichment, unending gossip: the *news* of modern life. Is Nixon gone? Has the spell hanging over that wretched world been lifted yet? He wonders only for a moment.

He decides to rise. His legs are wobbly and he braces them as if against the quarterdeck's pitch and roll. The morning is engorged with sun. An aura shimmers where the scissored green of the redwood forest joins the blue of sky. The colors are so pure they hurt his eyes. He finds that he is shaking, skin tightly beaded with bumps that make him cold from marrow out. He measures the fever within him, watches it ripple the surface of his skin like twitches on a horse's flank. Do you want to live? he asks himself. I think so, he answers. Okay, you're going to get a chance to see how much; get ready.

He takes off his soggy shoes and walks to the wall on his right. *I'll climb to the top and see what I can see,* he thinks. Then he wedges himself into the crevice between boulders, going up by bracing with his low back and hands on one interface, and walking his feet up the other. He is like a crab. He feels as though he goes straight up. He gets to the top and pulls himself up to a plateau of rock. Standing, he judges himself twenty feet above his floor. He walks out to the edge of this dome, his roof, putting his feet on the lip as if it were a diving platform. He wobbles there as if ready to take wing. His eyes rove through the forest looking for blanks in the green, dead sockets where trees have fallen. Then he looks down. There is a vertiginous surge, and he almost falls. It is sixty feet straight down to the rocks below. After recovering his balance, he calculates that a body falling from such height would go limply like a doll, falling in a double gainer and tearing into the jaggedness below to burst its sawdust guts. Could such a thing happen to him? He has to force himself to back away from the fascination of it.

He stands on the dome trying to understand what makes him resonate with the danger of this place. Then his toes release their grip and he goes back down, the human fly creeping down the wind space between two rocks. When he reaches the floor of his den, he pukes. He waits for a moment, then goes back down the rock slope, retracing the trail he traveled yesterday on hands and knees. He passes over an outcropping of rock before he comes to loose dirt. His simian body crouches to beat the slope's steep angle as he turns right and goes toward the thick growing trees. He feels the softpack of needles under foot, then finds a downed tree and attacks it, levering his body against the branches, breaking some, allowing others to defeat him. He goes back to the den, arms loaded, the fever rising steadily within, and then returns for more. After several trips he is exhausted. He gets a load of dry leaves and makes himself a bed next to the pile of firewood.

Each pant ends in a shiver now. His throat is parched and narrowing so fast he fears his Adam's apple will be trapped between floors. He forces himself up one final time and retraces his evolution up from the water. At the river's edge he gets down on all fours and waters carefully, picking his head up now and then to satisfy himself that there are no enemies. I'm a deer too, he thinks. After drinking his fill, he removes the shreds of shirt still clinging to his chest and arms, and soaks them to sponge with later on. As he moves back up the moraine, he hurts all over as if from some collision. He is slow returning, act disentangling from impulse only after long debate.

Back on the rock, he lies down and allows chills to attack and sweat to break out. Fire, that's what he needs. He searches for some atavism of woodcraft to help him get one started. Might the ancient gods have dropped flint here? He grabs two small flaking stones and strikes them together for long minutes without seeing any sparks.

He selects two dry branches from his pile, two pieces straight and sober as a stave, and rubs them madly above the kindling. He feels the heat of friction and smiles. The exertion drains him, but he thinks he sees a wisp of smoke and pushes past his limit, laughing. *I can do it, Pop, I can do it by myself.* The heat is there but will not convert to fire. *No, I can't, help me.* He lies back exhausted, hurting, the rock freezing his sweaty back, hugging himself against the swiftly alternating hot and cold. He has the dry heaves, retching deep down into his intestines and bringing up only a green froth of bile.

The enterprise of survival is vain and shallow. He reminds himself that he really doesn't care. A coma can cancel hard decisions. Like a samurai, he wraps himself in a robe of fatalism and points his mind toward the sweet haiku of cherry blossoms raining down and gentle death in courtyards. Then he remembers: the watch. He finds it among his scant belongings and in his excitement comes close to knocking it off his rock. The dial is soggy and peeling; the hands float in a half-moon of water at the bottom. He unscrews the crystal and poises it above the kindling, wondering if its magnifying powers will concentrate the heat. His hand shakes so badly that the beam won't focus; he grasps the wrist with the other hand. The sun is about to fall below the trees when a hole finally perforates the amber spine of leaf, growing black within an aureole of red. Don't dare to hope, he counsels himself, for then the disappointment won't be so great at the inevitable failure. He tries to coax it with his breath, but blows too hard and chases the glow away. Once again. After the nurtured glow, a jump of a flame. *We did it, Pop!* He fuels the fire with care, expending the last of his concentration in building a tepee first of twigs and then of coarser wood. He lies back in his nest of leaves, sucking on his rags like a baby.

The fire is now the center of his universe. His side closest is fecund, tropical; the side deprived lapses into arctic despair. Spitted on in-betweenness, he turns constantly to balance the gain and loss of heat, burrowing into his leaves, trying to germinate deep down.

He realizes now his error in standing as a slave-master over his organic nature. *I have sinned against you*: he sends this admission to his body. But it comes too late to save him. The rebellion has already begun. His heart races in machine-gun bursts; the lungs greedily reach for more air than he can give them; the bowels spasm painfully and trickle warm jets of excrement down between his legs. He shakes like a piece of subtly frying meat. The reign of the involuntary muscle has begun. The will, once sovereign, is now the kingdom's poorest serf.

Barriers are being broken down inside him; his opposites are being drawn close together. Time and order slip away, stealing through his clawing fingertips. Day and night are blinks, he understands now, of the same eternal eye. He thinks of all this as he finds himself in a dark channel. It is a reverse birth: he is being sucked up some long passageway, compressed and contracted.

He passes over rapids of hallucination, feels undertows take him down through bright grottoes of dream, allow him to eddy for a time in watchfulness, then seize him again. These are not separate states, but a single continuity, viscid and dense. He swims through it, remembering that he has known what it is to be web-footed and finny. His critical faculty, last and most vain of the illusions, is stretched into odd and uncertain shapes. It breaks.

He lies there and watches his father and great-grandfather playing catch. Joseph and the first and original Cabell Hart together. They laugh as the baseball sails lazily between them, seams rotating slowly as if knuckled, slapping into the left hand, transferred to the right and pitched back. They love that rhythm in which they are mere slaves to the ball's needs. Then the velocity starts to change. Each time the ball is caught, the one receiving takes it a little further behind his back and kicks the left leg higher to get more zip when throwing it back. They begin to hum the ball, putting hot speed on it, catching it with a backswing of their bare hands to cut the sting of impact. They are in deadly earnest, trying to hurt. "What's going on, Pop?" he calls out. "Why are you doing this?" Getting ready to wing the ball in the direction of the impassive man in black broadcloth and hobnailed boots, that notorious ancestor and progenitor of their woe, his father says: "It's time we had a showdown. It's time we got things straightened out. Got to see who's who and what's what."

He is a spectator. This baseball show ends, but he knows it will be replaced by others. He seems phantoms and cannot tell their wisdom from their foolishness.

"What's happenin?"

He doesn't think it strange when he looks up and sees Jim Henry on the other side of the fire, rich brown skin gleaming in the yellow light, eyes shining in the blue jet at the tip of the flame. He is glad to see him, but fears making too much of a demonstration.

"Where the hell have you been?"

"Here and there and everywhere. But mainly around the same place as your bitch." He makes his eyes big and flashes his Mr. Bones smile. "Ooo-wee. She one white devil. I shoulda known better than to put her on you. When one of them come up to a brother and start talkin coalition politics, it time to watch out for sure."

"Who iced you?" Cabell asks. "There was all kinds of weird talk going down. It blew my mind."

"No doubt. Tell you, if I went into the details, it would just confirm your worst fears about the way the world wags.

You'd wind up sitting here on your candy ass until you no more than a mess of skeleton."

"I'm not going anyplace." Cabell flexes his body and finds it encased in heavy mud. "Tell me. I've got to know. I need to know something that's certain."

"Nothin certain, man, you know that."

"Something's got to be."

"Nothin. Not even death and taxes. Look at them Rocke-fellers. They live forever and never pay a dime."

Cabell is silent for a while. Then he says, "There's no way to put things right."

"I hear you."

"Then what's the point?"

"You tell me. I mean I hardly qualify as one of your Faulknerian niggers who *endures*."

"Listen, Jim," he tries to get the words out right. "I can take dying. I can. Death is no stranger now. First you, then Jill. In the last little while I've seen my father die. I've heard how my sister got offed by these rednecks. I've been lying here shitting my pants like a baby. I can take it. Really. But you know what I can't take? Losing my mind. I can't take that."

The other laughs and bends over to slap his thigh. "Man, now that a honky worry for sure. If it was a question of your tool going out of operation, I could dig the panic. Going crazy? Nothing wrong with that. Probably do *you* some good. Look at all that time you *didn't* go crazy and what a damn mess you made of things."

"Fuck off." Cabell closes his eyes wearily.

"You asked what happened to me." The black face raises an ironic brow. "I don't know if you know it or not, but I was doing a little H, a subtle little habit, just chipping really, but requiring a little extracurricular action—not exactly deal-ing, just *facilitating*—on the side. The job I had was righteous cover for that. I burned a couple of dudes and they got me down in Foster City. Gave me a hot shot with battery acid one night and then banged me on the head a few times and launched me in the Bay. That's not to say the comrades wouldn't have gotten around to it sooner or later, of course. They had a little contract out for my political malfeasance."

"I thought it was a political murder."

"You had the right idea. You were just a little premature. It was one of those things that seem to fit so good they *got* to be true."

"Things aren't what they seem," Cabell says.

"No shit." Jim Henry shakes his head knowingly. " 'Bout time you began to see that. What we got here is the famous cosmic onion, a different layer every time you peel. But since you're staging this little business here, you don't ever know if *that* perception has any weight. Maybe it's just to get yourself further anchored down in your disillusion here. Maybe the Panthers *did* do it. Them that knows don't say; them that says don't know."

"What should I do?" Cabell pleads.

"Root, hog, or die. Isn't that one of nature's laws?"

Easy for you to say," he whispers after his friend's departing shade.

He sleeps. Occasionally he rises—or watches a wraith impersonating him rise—and reaches out for a piece of wood to place upon the embers. After a while Jill is there, as he knew she would be, appearing suddenly in the fire, profiled against the rock, one of the shadows dancing on the wall. Her good side toward him, she sits cross-legged, eyes closed, breathing deeply in a yoga of perfection. He studies her, squinting through the swirls of smoke that gust into his tearing eyes, trying to make her out through the heat vapor that rises in the night and makes her shimmer like a mirage of water on the desert. He expects her to speak, to take the initiative as always; but there is no sound except the coughing of the night winds.

"Take up meditating?" he asks, wondering if her spirit will prove more docile than her flesh.

"Maybe. Take up dying?"

"Maybe."

"Don't you care?"

"I do and I don't."

"Now there's a snappy answer. What comes next, a recitation of 'To be or not to be'? There's something I meant to tell you all those years and never got around to. You're not Prince Hamlet nor were meant to be. You're not even an attendant lord. It's getting stupid, this fantasy of yours, although I'm not surprised that you'd be attracted to the rant of a self-indulgent coward trying to figure out a way to accommodate to a fascist state. What did his father ever do to justify all that whining, anyway? Conquer old Fortinbras and annex all his lands: an imperialist pig. Enduring all those fops and fools and spies; killing by what seems accident so he can preserve that elitist sense of his own superiority. Some hero."

"Since when is there a mass line on *Hamlet*?"

"Since now. Shakespeare is not progressive."

"You're a cliché, Jill. You and your wild bunch murder all distinctions. It oppresses me. Go away."

She slowly turns to face him, drawing out the suspense with a methodical movement, amused that he should be mesmerized by the rotation of her head and fear the appearance of the destroyed side.

"You don't think I'd come to you like *that*, do you?" she laughs, revealing herself to be whole again. "Although I must say that if your little death wish here is granted, you'll see a whole lot worse."

"Are you here to get me?" he asks timidly, afraid now.

"To *get* you? Am I the Messenger of Death, do you mean, the Exterminating Angel? Hardly. My current state doesn't lend itself to such self-dramatization. I doubt that George Jackson is strutting around out there calling himself the Black Dragon, or that Willie Wolf continues to go by the name Cujo. But to answer your question: my being here is your idea."

"Let's talk."

"About us?" The irony is gentle.

"I suppose. About us all. There were things I never got a chance to ask. . . ."

"Ah, ultimate questions. Like the ones you asked your

aunt when you were a teenager. *Why*. That's what you want to get into: why. Believe me, that's a slippery slope. There's no answer to the questions you want to ask, at least none that will comfort you. *Why* did you catch me *in flagrante*, as you would put it? Might as well start there. Because I wanted you to. And I mean that literally, not just in a Freudian sense. You were baggage weighing me down, Cabell. I saw that you would never get rid of all the old romantic notions."

"It wasn't fidelity *per se*," he interrupts. "You must know that. It was just that I didn't think we had to live in that world where no tie meant anything; where every emotion, every attachment was only worth what it would bring on the market that day according to the latest radical quotations. I thought we could live in it without being consumed by it."

"Touch pitch and not be defiled. Right? The great American delusion. You wanted us to be the oasis of faith in a desert of faithlessness. But I had seen that revolutionary love and sex are a destruction, a deprogramming, a means of attaining discipline. In New Era there were six of us, three men and three women. We did it for weeks before we undertook any action. I mean *did it*. We did it in every position, in every possible combination: in the beds, on the floors, on tables, in the backyard, even in the car. We fucked our brains out. The object was not ecstasy, but to mark each other with our revolutionary juices, penetrate each other, ream out individual hang-ups, bond the group together, make disparate individuals into one keen weapon. Sex is power, not pleasure. This and other revelations were beyond you, or I would have arranged it so that you stayed. But I had business to take care of. There wasn't time to wait until we could enter the new world hand in hand."

"Getting rid of me"—he shakes his head sarcastically—"became part of the Process: Smash Capitalism, Kill the State, Die for the People."

"The revolutionary's life must be exemplary in its integration." For a moment, she lapses into a tentative silence, then rises as if to go. "But I never loved anyone but you."

Suddenly he sees how she might have suffered beneath her metallic shell, caught between a sense of duty that dicated his sacrifice and a love for him. He is flooded with sadness by this blocked latency, this tragedy of love chewed up in the contradictory motion of large imperatives.

"Cabell, you flake!" Her voice pokes down from above. "You ordered me to say that and you know it! Just like you try to round things off with a piece of rotten sentimentality. You Ryan O'Neal and me Ali McGraw, dying of terminal Marxism-Leninism? Good God! Will you always define yourself according to who loves you at any given moment?"

"Yes, always." His words feebly trail her vanishing essence. He feels as though she has sucked his blood. He wallowed deeper in his nest, victimized by thoughts that are his but don't belong to him.

It is still dark when she comes back, but not dark from the same night. He has watched his shrinking essence rise up once and leave the fire, make the vast journey down to the water's edge, drink quickly and soak the rags to suck on later, then return before it is too late, stopping to try to pick up a piece of driftwood along the way, but having to drop it when the burden threatens to keep him from returning. As it was, he tripped and fell three times. The last time he lay on cold rock for a long time, feeling his blood begin congealing and his extremities tingle and go numb. "It's not worth it," he said to whoever might be listening and closed his eyes. Then something—a fear of Jill being out there to see and ridicule this weakness—made made him rise and force himself up the incline to his granite ledge. He crawled the last few yards, and by the time he fell heavily into his nest, his feet felt badly bruised, his hands were cut so badly that they printed the rock with palms of blood.

"Well, congratulations!" She is waiting by the fire. "You made it. I didn't think you had it in you."

"Thanks for the compliment. I never could have done it without you."

"I came back to find out one thing," she says. "Tell me, didn't you feel bad for bailing out? Seeing us on the bed that day could actually have been interpreted as an invitation to stay—on altered terms."

"No, I was right to leave."

"You turned coat."

"Like my grandfather might have said, I didn't leave the Left, it left me. It went berserk and committed suicide. It freaked out when the war was over."

"The war's not over. It's just had a change of venue. It will come again. And as for the revolution, all revolutions fail except the final one. You know that."

"This one rotted from the inside out. It got to be theology, not politics; theology where we weren't talking about real things, the theology of buzzards. We were corrupted by what we fought against."

"What do you mean, *we*? As I remember, you spent most of your time sneaking off to basketball games. You were there by accident anyway. You didn't belong. You were always a closet Tory. I wanted to raze things to the ground, assassinate the history of this mad country, start again. Anyway, your perspective is narrow. What you think is over is just the completion of the first stages of a long process."

"Please. Spare me. If there's anything I don't need now, it's lecture number eight hundred twenty-three on the dialectical process. It was simple: they had a gang and we had a gang. The only difference between the gangs, the only reason theirs was worse, was that it had more power. The only effective agencies of change history has developed are the auto-da-fé, the secret police, and the Mafia hit man."

"Who's making speeches now? You use Stalin the way the liberals use Munich: the universal analogy. You sound more and more like one of *Commentary*'s rotten little ass-kissers. Your whole thing comes down to fear of being disappointed. You're afraid to believe because you might be wrong. So you sit on your butt and let the fascists do their stuff. All the old talk about 'moral complexity.' How many times have I heard that! It comes down to this. You don't care about anything except the moving spectacle of your righteousness. You'd rather be dead than wrong."

"You should talk." He is surprised that she gives him the opening. "You managed to be both at once."

"We made mistakes." The answer is unhurried and calm. "The military error, the idea of the-heavier-the-better: prematurity. But at least we were wrong for the right reasons. Your thing is to motivation-bait, to sit on the sidelines and complain about the excesses of both sides. You're a soldier of the status quo."

"I'm not a soldier of anything. I deserted."

She pretends not to hear him. "Better to act from an excess of belief than to sit on your ass from an excess of cynicism. Like right now. You'd rather handle this thing by giving up, by just dying, than by taking care of business."

"That's what Jim said."

"He was right."

"What can I do?"

"Blow the motherfuckers up." She is beginning to disappear. "Halcyon is the system. Start there."

"You're wrong." He hurls the words into the dark that closes around her. "There's got to be some ethical basis for action. This abstract violence of yours is crazy. It's like the B-52 pilot who drops those bombs as if he were up there seeding clouds. We've got to get consequence and connection back into our lives."

"You're a jerk." Her words waft back on a breeze of laughter.

For a long time he lies there, the fever compressing him, wringing him out, pushing him deeper down into a sarcophagus of mud. He feels unable to move his limbs. The hours compact into units of time with the texture of cement. They fall on his poor body. He plays dead for fear that there will be more visitors.

There comes a moment when his parts separate. Although anchored down, he is also light, insubstantial, pneumatic. He rises, a wafer floating on air, two-dimensional, riding his way upward in the heat vectors of the fire like an airy piece of ash. Up high above, high as the flames will carry him, he looks down at the recumbent body he left behind. It no longer sweats now, but sleeps with mouth ajar, jaw jutting out, rib cage working freely like the bellows of a child's concertina.

So this is it, he thinks. I'm going now. This floating piece of me, this disembodiment is my immortal soul. It has vacated the casing. Just as well. What next? A certain time in purgatory here?

He tries to float, to navigate this new environment. He has no fear of the unearthly state. He wonders if he can choose an animal to settle this thin piece of soul into and thinks he would like it to be a mountain bluejay. Cheeky robber of others' nests. But some force below is reeling him in, bringing him down again to that weakened form below. Why bother? he wonders. It's just a matter of time. But finally his ectoplasm surrenders and allows itself to be coaxed back into the body.

He opens his eyes, having to strain to crack the dried rheum that binds them. He sees his great-grandfather sitting nearby, grizzled, diffident, staring down into the coals. The fire is about out. He looks up as if to ask Cabell's permission, and then reaches out for a couple of branches to start it up again.

"There, that's better," the old ghost says.

"You can talk."

"I can"—the voice has the sound of prairies in it—"but I usually don't."

"You've never said a word to me before."

"No." The light-gray eyes look into the growing fire and the horny hand scrapes the stubble of beard. "You didn't want to hear me."

"I'm sorry. I do now."

"You won't ask me to tell you what to do, will you? Not me of all people?"

"I won't." Cabell stares at the jumping shadows of the fire playing on that face, old for forty-two, the eyes so starkly pigmented that they seem frozen, the hair recently cut and cowlicked in the back. "I've done you wrong," he says and sees the hunched shoulders shrug. "I've never tried to get it clear, to understand how it must have been. I've always blamed you for being the root of all the things that held me down. Let me try now."

"Begin with Gillette." His ancestor speaks without breaking his stare at the fire.

Gillette—it begins to unfold—Walker Gillette: there at the bar with a glass of smooth-drinking whiskey in one hand and an aromatic cheroot in the other, six feet tall even without the two-inch heels on his hand-tooled boots. A handsome man in men's eyes quite as much as in ladies'. . . .

"Is this the way to go about it?" he asks the first and original Cabell Hart.

"More or less. Go on."

Gillette: the only man in town to buy his suits in Chicago. But he wore them with such grace that the description coming to mind was not dandy, but well turned out. Glistening with pomade and parted as if by calipers, the black hair looked like patent leather. A brush moustache spaced and balanced the dark eyes; when it lifted in laughter now and then, the revelation was of teeth surprisingly white. Smelling of talc from the daily visit to the barber, he absent-mindedly massaged the scar along one right cheek. Such a mark might have made another man shirk the profile, but it had been honorably obtained, or at least so Gillette said—from the saber of a Confederate officer at Vicksburg who had paid for the blow with a bullet above the nose—and it was worn, this cicatrice, with a pride that invited questions about its origin. He chatted easily with the four men standing at the bar beside him.

After the first shift of the Homestake let off, the miners would be in here in the New Era banging elbows reaching for shotglasses of rye, bellying up to wash the itching dust down their throats. But right now there was a lull. Near the sleepy faro game at the back of the room, rouge-cheeked girls in red satin and black feather boas lounged in small groups, a piece of thigh occasionally showing from the indolent posture, mouths agape, eyes fixed on infinity: more sensuous in repose than in action. The piano player was under the cover of his instrument, jerking flaccid wires. The bartender had not yet put his apron on and was laboring over an inventory of the aquamarine bottles like a distillery bursar. Everyone was costumed and ready, but the performance had not begun.

Looking down for a moment, the leading citizen of Deadwood scuffed a shiny place on the plank floor with a sharp toe, distastefully sanding off the oyster of dried mucus some drunk had hawked up the night before. Then he rested the small of his back on the bar with one heel perched on the brass rail and surveyed the room with the confidence of one who knows that his voice will hold listeners with no help from his eyes. The men listening to him faced the other way, subtly admitting inferior caste. Staring down into their beer or scratching at a nit under their hats, they were aware that they drank with the only man in the whole of Dakota territory to travel regularly to New York, enter the railroads' great headquarters there on Broadway, and sit in boardrooms with merchant princes and barons to talk of the time when lines would extend into the heart of the Hills. He brought back calfbound books, stereopticons, exotic household machines. He brought back stories of advances in the arts and sciences and of witnessing the nation's great centennial in a great hall at the capital where the myriad nations of the planet Earth had sent testimonials to the youthful country about to take a position of leadership among them.

This was the sort of a day that made a man conscious of history: June 2, 1882, eight years to the day since the Black Hills opened up; the anniversary of the region's Columbus voyage and Plymouth Rock. Walker Gillette could tell a thing or two about that day in '74—it seemed an eon past, didn't it? —when George Custer had set out on the famous expedition. Nothing like it before or since: the actual opening of a piece of *terra incognito*. There had been some isolated exploration, but nothing like this; no organized expedition for the purpose of claiming it from the distant gods those sacrilegious heathen Sioux called the Thunder People.

A thousand soldiers in all, their double line unwinding like a ribbon for near a mile. There were civilians, too, riding protected between the lines—George Bird Grinnell and his scientists, government mining engineers, newspaper men, and, believe it or not, photographers. Bloody Knife and his Ree scouts were prancing out ahead.

Gillette could tell a thing or two about that day. At thirty-three, he was a topkick in the Seventh, and since five in the morning had been working to mold the sluggish military line into the proper form. Horses farting and rearing up, men half drunk: a chore to shape them up. But yet by eight o'clock, they were all ready to move out, a miracle of management, including even the orderlies responsible for the general's twenty-three bloodhounds, the creatures all baying in unison, their pink tongues lolling over jowls in anticipation of the chase. It would have been a hard heart indeed that hadn't thrilled when the sixteen bandsmen led off on white horses playing the Seventh's own "Gary Owens." Custer lifted his hat to wave at Libby and the ladies of Fort Abe Lincoln standing behind his faithful wife—a casual way of unfurling that famous hair of his, if the truth were known—and snapped commands to Forward ho! They were off.

No white had been in those parts before them and probably few redskins, for the Sioux, who feared nothing else, regarded this as a sacred place. The Black Hills were holy land, they thought, hunting grounds of the Thunder People, supernatural beings whose play and anger the Indians presumed responsible for the terrifying sounds that came crashing down onto their encampments during wild summer storms. The troopers did not believe this bosh, of course, but still, the meanest soul among them knew that he was setting his prints onto the last large piece of virgin ground in America, excepting Seward's Icebox. It was a kind of Eden. Game was scarce down on the plains, but as they progressed up into the Hills, it was sometimes necessary to rein up and wait for a herd of elk to go by. They brushed wild turkey away like eye-gnats. Believe that many a grizzly was quickly transformed into a winter rug. You could be out there killing game all day and not have to move an inch from where you stood. God's country: that's what it was.

But that was no hunting expedition, leastways not for animals. Washington didn't sponsor that sort of thing. They had been after something else and had found it a few hours after getting to the high country. Gold, that was it. Gold and the land that it was buried in. That was why they had gotten the War Department's go-ahead. A few old sourdoughs had been claiming that it was there for years, and people were massing in the camps below. They feared the Indians but wanted to break into the area. The rumors were right. There was gold all over: on the ground and in the water. Gold tangled in the roots of grass and present from there down to the lowest point they dug. Hook-nosed Bill Curtis, the man from the Chicago *Inter-American*, sent the news back by courier to the telegraph station at Bismarck, and from there it went out to the world: *gold!*

Yes, Gillette could tell a thing or two about that trip. It had changed many lives, his among them. Before, he had thought of himself as army through and through. Although descended of a French nobleman beached on the shores of the New World two hundred years earlier, he had been content to have "Boots and Saddle" be the theme song of the rest of his days. But during that expedition, he had been given a vision. Even if there hadn't been a horde of newspapermen exaggerat-

271

ing the already fantastic, there was bound to be a stampede. Wasn't that the point of it all? To get such an irresistable tide of settlement flowing in, that the government would have no choice but break the '68 Laramie Treaty? Where there was gold there would be men—men in towns and settlements. This Eden would settle fast.

When his tour was up early in '75, he mustered out and hightailed it back on up. It was scarcely six months since Custer's column had left the Hills, but already miners were up there pulling the gold out. Hand over fist. They congregated at the rich diggings. The richest was a gully lined with sluice boxes and placer ditches leading down to a gulch all tangled up with deadwood. The name stuck: Deadwood.

He had started off like the rest, scratching away in the mud from first light to last, taking a little hardtack and bacon at day's end and then falling into his bedroll, smelling like a billygoat in rut. He got enough to keep going, but little more than that. No matter. He had been watching what was going on down in what used to be the gulch. They had gotten it cleaned out. A few buildings—well, actually, tent tops over wooden siding—were springing up down there. Deadwood had gotten itself born and booming. Less than two years after Custer broke trail into the Hills, there were three banks, seventy saloons, and nearly two hundred stores. There were two thousand people. The sawmill couldn't cut the timber fast enough. People built green, using planks still juicy wet from milling, wood that would age on the wall, and then shrink down to leave such gaps that folks could talk and eyeball each other between rooms.

It was a whole lot easier to take gold off men than off the mountains. It didn't take any second sight to see that. Gillette started with a dry-goods store, sold it to a newcomer from Boston and parlayed the proceeds into a small hotel; from there he started investing in everything from banks to bathhouses. He got himself made postmaster, arranging the mail every Saturday night when the coach arrived from Bismarck, and then climbing up on the top of a packing crate of a Sunday morning to call out the miners' names, an assistant sitting below with assaying scales weighing out the fifty cents in gold dust each letter fetched. He started a business to contain these diverse interests and called it the National Exposition Company in honor of that great celebration of the nation's hundredth birthday he had seen on his first trip back East.

Those were wild times. Guns went off so regular that people paid them no more mind than they do now these six-eight years later to the noon whistle down at the Homestake. Men died aplenty, too, sometimes two or three a night. It took something of a talent to stay healthy. The race was not so much to the swift or even the strong, but to the careful. This had struck him especially after that famous poker game. Almost blind Bill Hickok was at the time, though few knew it, eyes all soapy-looking from a social disease contracted, of all places, back in New York where he had toured awhile with Cody and Buntline, riling up the Indians in the show by setting off his empty guns so close they got their arms and legs peppered with powder burns. By '76, he was much fallen from the man who'd been a crack scout for the Seventh a few years back. But he was still deadly at fifteen feet or so with those two .36 Navy Colts he wore butt-first in the scarlet sash cinched around his waist. But ever since Custer got his two months earlier, Hickok had had a premonition that his time was also due. Sooner or later, some young rowdy was bound to brace him in the street and that would be that.

Hickok had been in and out of the game four times that afternoon, plagued by a run of bad luck that had been with him since he came over from Cheyenne, and by kidneys so bad shot that he had to take a leak straightaway after every beer. But he couldn't stay away. There are men who can't believe they aren't destined for good fortune. Every time he came back, he'd buy back in and ask somebody to kindly change seats so he could be against the wall. Three times he was obliged. A man that's left forty-two dead behind him, not counting Indians, Mecs, or rebel soldiers, has earned the quirk. The fourth time, they laughed him out of it. Come on, Bill, you're among friends here; don't worry.

Nobody had paid attention to that short cross-eyed devil standing at the bar. But not five minutes later, that bastard, that Jack McCall, rushed over, put a gun behind his ear and hollered, "There, now take that." Already dead, Hickok sat straight in the chair for maybe five seconds, then just slumped over. The ball had passed out of the cheek and lodged in the arm of Charlie Utter, sitting next to Gillette. As for Gillette himself, after recovering from the shock, he looked down to find a thin stippling of blood reaching from the cards to the sleeve of his dark coat. Those little pieces of transparent white, like snot they looked, he realized later on were particles of Wild Bill's brain.

Just eight short years and what a world of difference. The streets were no longer thigh-deep in mud and rutted in animal and human filth every spring. Gunshots had not been banished, to be sure, but there weren't any ten or twelve killings a week anymore. That sort of thing couldn't be tolerated in a growing town. George Hearst had the Homestake going at peak now. Men lured by gold and disappointed in their quest had work to occupy them. At night the ground around old Deadwood Gulch glowed red as the smelter that now employed more than four hundred men poured slag down into the dump below. Proper buildings had been raised since the fire of '79.

No more filthy ginmills poisoning customers with lice as well as red-eye. The New Era (in which Gillette, as everybody knew, was a significant, if silent, partner, holding enough of an interest through the National Exposition Company to drink free with his chums on a day like this one) had helped run them out of business. Not by violence, of course, but by offering a decent establishment, clean and hospitable, and by selling better liquor at a lower price. The American way.

No more two-bit whores with names like Dirty Dolly, Large Bore, and Sluice Box wandering around town like water-headed idiots, ready to do anything anywhere for anybody.

Man's frailties had to be catered to, especially the working man's. But that element had been wildcatters through and through. The girls of the New Era were washed, perfumed, checked over once in a while, good, wholesome girls. Gillette himself had seen to that as a condition for buying in here. When the symptoms got too bad, they had to be discarded like sick sheep. They could go on over to Chinatown after that and lie around sucking on opium pipes and worse.

The Sioux had been whipped back to the Rosebud and other reservations for good. Crazy Horse dead these five years, and with him the fighting spirit. Old Sitting Bull sneaking down from his Canadian hideout to surrender just last year. It's done for them, the glory days. Railroads, telegraph lines: that's the material of history now. Towns springing up all over the Hills—Rapid City, Spearfish, Belle Fourche, Lead. Their own town, needless to say, would be the central diamond in this necklace if Walker Gillette had anything to say about it.

Inscribing small circles in the air in accompaniment to his words, the glowing ash of his cheroot exercised a mesmerizing hold. It was like a magic wand drawing a picture of the good things in store for them. There was reverential silence in honor of how far they had come.

The New Era had begun to fill by the time Gillette finished this anniversary monologue. He now shifted to current events, telling friends and listeners alike of a marvel he had glimpsed on that last trip east: the Pearl Street Electric Power Station. Designed by Thomas Edison and already in operation, supplying enough current to light some four hundred incandescent bulbs in sixty different buildings. A wonderment, it was. To think that Deadwood would have such things itself in time!

"Is that the way it was?" Cabell looked up and asked, aware of the first rumblings of thunder in the dark void outside his lair and the first tapping of rain.

"Close enough," his great-grandfather answered, spreading his palms over the glowing coals.

"Why did you wait outside so long?" Cabell asked.

"I didn't want to be accused of sneaking. I thought it would be better to wait until everyone was there. Best to do these things out in the open if you've got to do them. Revenge is a dish that tastes best cold."

"Oh, yes. That's right. Gillette is easy. I know his kind. You're harder. I'm not sure I can get it straight."

"Go ahead and give it a go. You should know. We're flesh and blood and even more connected than that."

"Okay, I'll try." He isolated his thoughts from the storm that was now crashing down around them. Something hinged on getting this right.

Hart: Cabell Hart stood outside looking through a spit-rubbed porthole on the New Era's dusty window, looking at Gillette and knowing what he said without hearing. What did such men always say? That things were getting better and better, and the machine of civilization was getting greased up and oiled so that it would run like a perfection. That we were not piebald nags at essence, but really the wreckage of beautiful creatures: Rousseau's lie.

His face had lines accentuated by dust from the road he'd walked. There was a five-day growth of beard, dark auburn like his hair. The clothes he wore did not smell good. But the moral reek was even more pronounced than the carnal one. People walked off the plank sidewalk clear into the street to avoid his space.

Once they had looked up to this hungover, down-and-out Cabell Hart, now trying to discipline himself into some odd act. Once he had been as important to the town as Gillette himself. A man of solid stuff. Son of a wagonmaker who'd come over from the Old World in the thirties, he had known from the beginning of his manhood that he wanted to spend his life spreading the good word. He studied at a teacher's college. By the time he was a young man, he had a small flock in Urbana, enough to provide a good living for a young man with

276

a wife and beginnings of a family, but threw it up when he heard of Custer's mission. He wanted to be the first man of God in that virgin land.

It had been a fertile field for his harrowing. He had visited every mining camp, riding from one to another on his old chestnut mare, baptizing men in rain barrels, sluice boxes, and frog ponds when necessary, breaking ice in the winter to get them submerged, taking joy in the heavy going because he was one of those muscular Christians who believed the way to the New Jerusalem must be paved by callused hands.

He settled down in Deadwood because of the need, and called his wife Eliza to come and join him. Between the time when the dust was cleaned out of the bedrock and the coming of the mills to crush quartz, there were a hundred losers for every winner, dispirited men who got ground down by things. Life shouldn't be that way. This Cabell Hart had strived as hard as anyone to bring advancement and stability to the town, to provide succor to those fighting the constant war for survival.

On June 6, 1876, he helped his friend Will Laughlin get out the first issue of the *Black Hills Pioneer*. It was important to make sure that riches didn't outrun civilization too far. Not long after that he and his good supporters raised the first proper church in the Hills. It was a little peak-roofed building on the three-lot parcel he'd claimed when he first arrived—on the outskirts of the settlement then, but now in the center of the growing town. It was an occasion for pride when he rose to the pulpit that first Sunday and spoke to the congregation of thirty men and seven women. The text from Psalm 34:7, "The Angel of the Lord encamps around Those who fear Him," was appropriate, for at that time, Crook's men had just been beaten back after going out to show the Sioux that Custer's defeat meant no general uprising, and Deadwood was at the Indians' mercy.

He settled down to the ministry, trying to build his flock from among the disappointed and downcast. He got good help from Eliza. She was at his side in his work; she and Evan and Sophia too. She started up a little school inside the church and taught there until young Laughlin came along. She donated the first book to what became the town's small library: a copy of Malory's *Death of Arthur* she'd brought all the way from Chicago.

There was plenty to do. But was he doing everything he could? Hadn't he gotten himself a little too well situated? He thought about it awhile, then early in '78 surprised the deacons of his church by saying that he was anxious to go back on his old circuit one last time, back up into the roaring camps and one-month bonanzas still cropping up in remote parts of the Hills. They had tried to talk him out of it, but his mind was set. They could get a substitute from back East. He needed a task fit for a man, and one that would test his God against a fuller range of odds than that you found in a settlement. As company and for a kind of baptism in this work, he'd decided to take his first son, Evan, a sixteen-year-old towhead. Eliza watched them go, waving till they were specks with a handkerchief she wished she'd given as a gage, for she believed in the nature of this quest as much as her husband did.

He came back a little over two months later. Alone, vanquished, shrunk down on the back of that old chestnut, his eyes bearing the look of someone whose soul has been taken out and charred over hot flame, then been put back in. There was no public statement, although everybody knew that the boy's bones had been left to bleach up in the high country. Hart sold his city holdings to this same Gillette he now watched through the spithole in the glass. The family—once so full and happy but now so abbreviated—moved into a small house several miles outside of town at a place called Indian Wells.

Occasionally he would hitch up the team and then Eliza would drive in for provisions, the pretty girl Sophy and little boy Laughlin in the backseat behind. She had lost three children to childbirth and one to her husband, yet remained a proud woman, her head held high, not explaining her Cabell Hart to the people of Deadwood, letting them know in no uncertain terms that whatever had happened up there in the Hills had to do with issues of belief and was now being thrashed out between her husband and his Maker, and no one else need intervene.

One old prospector said he heard how it happened from someone who got there right after. The story he spread around Deadwood had it that the man and boy were going down a narrow defile, the mountain falling away sheer on one side. They were walking the horses down and for some reason the boy's stopped. Young Evan went to check the cinches to see what ailed the creature, but on the wrong side, the side nearest the edge, and before his father could holler, got nudged on over. Down he went, ass over elbow, somersaulting down. The father looked over, calling down for him, probably praying very rapidly inside, for the cliff was so sudden that he couldn't see anything when he stretched over the edge. Down the trail a ways, there was a tree growing out at an angle. He ran down there and climbed out, leaning into the wind and looking down. The boy was about a third of the way down, curled over a fallen log that Providence had placed in the steep decline. Hart praised the Lord that Evan hadn't wound up in a broken pile far down below. It was a miracle. He called out again, and the boy turned frontwise a little. Oh God! The log had caught him all right, but not as a handhold; just at the midsection a stumpy branch stuck up like a dirk that had been thrust into the boy's stomach.

Held there by it, the boy touched hands to shirt and they came away red. The Reverend Hart saw the skin above the wound. A little lower was a dark purple, not just blood, but membrane too with a suspicion of gut poking out. He knew he had to do something, fetch a rope and stub it against the tree and then rappel himself downward to get the boy. But he couldn't. He felt paralyzed. He was afraid of moving, afraid of the height, afraid of touching that body down below. He knew it was a body and not a boy, for he had hung there on the swaying tree and watched the lights fade out from behind the eyes and saw them glaze over like varnish. He was still there when some miners passed him by. Clinging to the tree like a lizard. They pried him off, went down on a rope and got the youth.

They had to bury him then and there because meat didn't travel well at this time of year. After it was done, they put the preacher on his horse and sent him home.

They sold their lots in town and moved to a little place away from everyone. The thoughts that went through this man's head in the next two years! God could tolerate the existence of nasty flies, but not of his poor son. There was no reason for it. It served no end. God's word was not spread by the senseless death of one small boy. If it didn't *mean*, all of it, then it was all a sham.

He spent time alone during those two years. They lived off the voucher they got on the seventh of each month for eighteen dollars from the National Exposition Company to pay off the mortgage on the land they'd sold Gillette. Cabell Hart worked hard to restructure the size of his belief so that it was just large enough to cover those around him. He came to take a little joy in seeing the remaining girl and boy growing up. There was still a spark of life in his loins. He got his wife with child again. It couldn't replace the dead one, nothing could do that. But it could signal a commitment to life on their part, to a life organized not around God, but around themselves. That was the first obligation. The mortgage money was running out; it was time to do something new.

The next thing people in town heard, he'd saddled up his horse and ridden off to the railhead at Bismarck, and caught a train. It was not long after Garfield's death. He took the little stake they had left after two years of nothing and went out to Oregon to look for a piece of ground out there, choosing that place because of pictures a Chicago man had shown him once. The place looked peaceful and good, the sort of place to raise that new baby in, start all over, this time unburdened by high ideals. He put two hundred seventy dollars down on a full section of land fronting on the MacKenzie River.

He figured to get home directly. But winter came early that year and the passes got clogged up bad. He wrote home that he might as well just stay there till the spring and try to raise them a little house and clear some land. When he did get home, he was too late. Money had grown scarce. His wife had sent a note by Laughlin when the eighteen dollars didn't get there on the seventh of December. The clerk at the National Exposition Company had scribbled on the bottom of her note that he was holding out thirty-six dollars, two months' payments, because of repair work they had to do on a well jacketing. She'd gone off to town herself to argue, tried to see Gillette himself but was told he was busy; taken cold in the buckboard ride back home and gone straight to bed. She got sicker and sicker. The half-Indian woman Look they'd taken on to live there had been with her day and night. But she didn't come out of it; the baby died aborning.

Sophy, full grown at sixteen, had looked for a way to take care of herself and brother Laughlin. But the family was star-crossed. Nobody was anxious to hire bad luck. She moved into town and took a room in a boarding house, sending out groceries and a few dollars a week so Look could feed and care for her little brother out at their place. She made a series of missteps and wound up at the New Era: one of Gillette's new-fashioned dance-hall girls.

He had come to fetch her home, straight upon returning. But by that time she was bad sick and fallen low. Rumor, that many-tongued hag, had spread it out that she'd been boarded one night by some drunken fool who'd had a violent fit of passion and bit one pert nipple, near severing it and leaving a suppurating wound above the heart that sometimes scabbed but never really healed. It required a constant dosage of laudanum just to keep her from crying out. They saw her now and then sneaking between the buildings in Chinatown.

He took her back home. He and the Indian woman spent some time nursing her and trying to reassemble things. But she could not recover her health or leave her need for the painkiller which killed more than body pain. She was a changed and different person from the one he left. A dead person had replaced the living one. She was rotting from the inside out. It finally dawned on him that there was no point in continuing to pretend that you could recover what was lost. He took the girl aside one day and told her that she should go to live in Urbana with the boy. He had a sister there. There were doctors in Chicago. He'd be coming to join them as soon as things were wrapped up here. He'd driven them to Bismarck himself, then sold the buckboard and team, and put the money in an envelope to send after them.

He spent some long weeks out there at Indian Wells, drinking heavily, not wanting to do what he was about to. A frontier melodrama—that's what Eliza would have called it if she'd read it in one of those penny dreadfuls shipped from back East. So it was. But it had to have an end. He walked into town on that June afternoon. He stood outside the New Era for an hour or so with the Indian woman, giving Gillette time to finish his praise of history, then he went on in.

He tried to make himself blend with the general flow of patronage, but even among those rough men he was a canker on the rose. He smiled as the solid human line parted to let him through and men grew suddenly absorbed in conversations with neighbors they had previously ignored.

Gillette glanced at his entrance with a kind of contempt, impatient with any man who wore such a kicked-dog look. He knew that the sum of thirty-six dollars would no doubt come up, and in his mind he readied an explanation to cut like a legal brief.

As Hart advanced, something in those frozen eyes made Gillette wish for the comforting weight of the .41 Williamson derringer he'd just recently stopped carrying in his vest pocket after all those years. He moved to intercept the unkempt man, extending a hand. "Well, Cabell, long time no see. How you been? We heard the terrible news about the Missus, and we . . ."

The sentence drifted when Hart pulled a rusty old cap-and-ball pistol from under the filthy waistcoat. Gillette's thoughts whirled like a roulette wheel, perhaps stopping on the irony of the notion that his fate should be contaminated by such a one as this. But there was little time for reflection.

"You have done cheated me!" Bystanders were stunned

by the manly strength of the words. Then the jump of the gun and a magnificent puff of black smoke and a flash that briefly caught Gillette's sleeve afire. He fell backward, hands clutching a spot two inches above his navel, almost exactly the same spot where young Evan had been gored by the tree two years earlier. Hart set the gun down on the floor and turned and walked back out the door.

The people ran to comfort the fallen man who lay on the floor, legs phantom-running, gut-shot, blood gouting through undergarments onto expensive serge. He looked up to the faces circled above him. He seemed to be searching for memorable last words but gave up. "I'm killed, boys, done for by a crazy man."

After he was gone, the crowd worked its way to a fever, ignoring old Sheriff Thompson's feeble pleas. Then it climbed up on horses, onto buckboards and anything else that would travel, and beat it for Indian Wells. Hart was there, waiting along with the woman Look. After he'd gotten back, they'd bathed together. She cut his hair and trimmed his mustache. He brushed her raven tresses. He dressed up in his old black broadcloth reverend's suit, and sat down to write out a piece of wisdom he remembered by heart, and tucking it in the old Bible he hoped someone would send the children. They sat down and ate a good hot meal she'd cooked. Then waited. He in a rocking chair puffing on a pipe; she sitting beside him chanting low and soft.

They had called for him to come out but were just as glad he didn't. They poured gunfire into the house, more than seventy shots. They just stood out there like it was a turkey shoot. The bullets knocked holes in the siding and broke the oil-paper windows. In all, some eighteen shots found the bodies.

"Cheated you?" Cabell searches the downturned face whose poker eyes stare into the fire. "I always thought you meant the money."

"Not hardly."

"It was Sophia, wasn't it?"

"That and more."

"Do you feel you put things right?"

"No." The word bounces up like a hammer on concrete. Cabell feels the tears on his cheeks. Misery is everywhree clogging the record of human relations. Injustice is the building material of history. You never put things right; you just create more injustice, which continues vibrating after you are gone.

He feels himself rising from his bed of leaves, separating from that pungent odor of organic breakdown and reformation. He is a useless thing, hurting and pained, fouling the world by his contact with it.

Getting energy from some unknown source, he begins to climb the wall on which his great-grandfather's shadow played a moment ago. He places his body into the crease between rocks leading to the granite ceiling above, and inches himself up by feet and back. He puts his palms onto the interface behind him, suctioning and then pushing. Finding a desperate strength, he forces himself up higher. At the top he twists and makes his fingers into grappling hooks, then pulls himself up. Unprotected, he can feel the storm's sheer punishment. Wind comes to ripple his body, rain beating down so hard it hurts his tender skin. His feet slip as he is almost on the top. He dangles without a point of balance for a moment before managing to drag his body up into the black night.

He lies there on his stomach, hugging the dome, the thunder crashing down upon him now, the howl and whistle filling his brain and rain blinding him. He raises his head and sees a bolt of lightning hit a nearby treetop and ignite it like a candle. The flame burns for a moment and goes out. With the wind whipping all around him, shrieking as if night terrors had suddenly been unloosed from the cage that kept them, he rises. He is like a daredevil stunting on the wing of a biplane, angling himself into the wind to keep from being carried back. Swaying, he inches forward, sensing where the edge was by that prior experience, getting there according to the

"So that's it," the ghost tugs at an earlobe. "You've seen it now."

"What?" Cabell asks.

"Life's one truth. Whatever happens in the in-between, at the end you've got exactly what you had at the start: yourself, your people."

"It's something I saw too late."

"There's still time," the ghost says. "Things are always arranged that way: in favor of the final try. Don't expect any bronze plaques, though."

"I'm past all that."

"Good." He lays a hand on Cabell's shoulder for a moment. "I'm going now."

Cabell elevates himself on one elbow. "They were wrong," he said. "You were true."

"I am with you always," his great-grandfather calls out as he leaves.

Cabell Hart lies down to perfect sleep, knowing that he will not see the ghost again in this life.

8

He awoke and knew immediately that the fever had gone in the night. There was calm at his center. He moved out on his ledge to catch the sun and lay on his back for a long time watching three hawks circling above the valley, dipping a wing to sail lower or rise high, calling to each other in shrill signals. His fire was out, the cache of wood used up. He tried to establish a chronology for events taking place after he had been lured to the bridge, but couldn't. It was all one experience, something in circles, not linear. He rubbed fingers over his chin, calculating that he had been entombed in the sickness for perhaps three days. He noticed that the storm had washed away the monotony of previous days. This one was charged with newness.

He stood and stretched, then climbed down from the ledge and skied down stone rubble toward the riverbed. He stopped at the jagged rocks where he would have hit if he had managed to take wing last night. He looked up to the platform high above and heard in his imagination the sound of a watermelon breaking. I'm lucky to be alive, he thought.

At the river's edge, he stood for a moment letting the swift rush of water hit his face. Then he got down and drank deeply. He took off the fetid pants and put them on a flat rock, then he waded out into the current. The water was stinging cold, numbing to genitals and underarm. He reached a hand down to the river bed and brought up a palm of sand, then scrubbed himself harshly, scouring off the dead skin and the decadent smell of that other self. When he was pink and new, he returned to the shore and found a piece of stone, volcanic and big-pored, and used it to scrub his pants, beating and rinsing them until they were clean and soft. Allowing the sun to soak into his body, he felt the simple joy, of one who had recovered.

The heat kneaded his body, soothing joints and cartilage bruised by fever. He breathed deep and slow, inflating his lungs all the way. He listened. For the first time since landing here he realized that there was absolutely no opening or shutting, no dull mechanized hum, no screams for help or mercy. He felt like the first one here.

He held his arms out and studied the tremulousness at his fingertips. It was not from fear or worry, but from lack of food. He couldn't remember the last time he ate.

He walked across the hill that led up to his den. The stone rubble gradually gave way to sparse undergrowth and finally to tree cover. The effort tired him. He stopped and rested on a log inside the scrub oak and pine. He looked down near his naked foot and saw a tendril. Following it backward, he saw a plant winding up an aspen's peeling trunk. It was a wild grape vine. He rose and hurriedly stripped the purple fruit, cramming it into his mouth, feeling the sugar enter his system almost immediately, a strong narcotic.

He stood up again, ready to forage, picking his way carefully, entering groves of ponderosa that allowed light only in splashes. He was walking near a thicket of manzanita when an explosion detonated. He dropped to the ground, ready to be hurt, his heart beating wildly from the sound. Then he watched as a covey of quail reared up into the air, flew fifty feet, and then disappeared with wagging cockades into another bramble. He picked up a rock and stalked them, creeping up to their refuge on tiptoe. He waited for a long time and heard them jabber in code within. But they didn't re-emerge. After a long time, he saw it was getting late and turned for home.

On the way back, he picked up some fibrous vines of wild ivy and then collected an armload of deadfall. Back on his stone floor, he felt the cold coming and hurried to trap some rays of the late-afternoon sun in the watch crystal and begin another fire. After it was going, he sat down cross-legged before it, working with the vines to fashion a snare. He tied and knotted, loosened, started again. He knew what was needed— there was a vision in his mind—but he had trouble educating his fingers. After a long time he had a loop that allowed him to enact the drama; a guileless rabbit came along, tripped the triggering knot, and was trapped. But his struggling wrist easily broke the snare. Before sleeping, he discarded the twisted vines and hoped to dream of something else. The question was how fast he could learn.

He was awake before sunrise. He lay curled around his fire watching forms trying to seize a shape from gray. The whole valley was tumescent with anticipation over the arrival of the sun. Then it came: a single diamond beam over the mountain's dip. *Ah!*

He lay there watching the creation of long shadows on the rock. He could tell the extent of the hunger: no longer just a contraction in the gut, but now a sense of self-consumption, cells meant for strength being taken for food. He couldn't die now.

At the river's bank he went down on quavering hams to drink from cupped palms. He sat there for a time, lightheaded, modulating his body movements for conservation. He saw a pillar of white half his size on the opposite shore. What was it doing here among the green and gray? He studied it over the water's rush, watched it for motion. Was it a river god? Another ghost? As the sun rose, it became more distinct, separating from the backdrop of rock. It was a water bird, an egret. It moved two quick steps further into the river then was still again. After a moment, the long head cocked, as if one eye were looking toward the heavens and the other down into the water. It was still as sculpture. Then suddenly, too fast for him to realize if there hadn't been a change afterward, the golden bill flashed down, stabbing the water. A struggling fish was impaled. The head tilted back and poured it down the gullet, bright blood splashing down onto the white breast, a series of peristaltic jerks to get it swallowed. The egret looked over in his direction, preened itself for a moment, and walked back into the shadows whence it had come.

Grateful for the sign, he etched the bird's sharp movements on his memory. With the sun rising up above the treeline and pouring down around him, he walked out into a safe pool up to his waist. He floated outward, fully extended, then kicked down in a surface dive, and grabbed a rock below to keep from being taken by the current. Anchored, he looked up into the river's course, watching the velocity of bubbles that marked its terrifying power. There were fish dancing in and out of the current, letting it carry them backward, then kicking forward with powerful tail. Salmon: advance guard of the spawning run. He rose to the surface for another breath and came back down. He loved watching them, these black and silver lines, and reached to touch them as they passed. Light flashed off their sides as they avoided this stranger in their element, the one moored there obsessed by their transcendental negotiations of the stream.

He came up blowing froth. He stood and looked down at the water's surface and saw that he could discern the fish by occasional sworls they made. There was no trapping them with slow hands. He needed a beak to hunt them. He climbed back up and headed for the forest. It was still cool and dark there, and he dripped water on the pine needles. He walked until he found a limb already partially severed. A test of hand showed it had dried enough to be hard but was not yet brittle. He used his naked knee to force it off the trunk. He stripped the leaves and twigs on his way back home.

He took the pocketknife from its niche of rock. He tested

the blade lightly against his thumb and felt it cut the surface of the callus. Then he began to work the branch down. Hunger was inside him, making his joints loose and his movements too coarse. But the wood must be lathed precisely. He worked at it carefully, sweating in the sun, turning it over and over and sighting down its length for curvatures and imperfections. His feet emerged from a covering of curled shavings as he rose and walked down into the rock field below him, returning with an abrasive stone he used to pumice the stave smooth. After it was balanced, knots and nodules planed down, he turned it around and began carving the end, working with the knife toward him now. He angled one side of the point more severely than the other, notching a barb into it. He then held the finished spear up toward the sun, studying its symmetry, grateful that he had been given the skill to accomplish it.

He waited until the sun had declined from midday high so that he could predict the shadow, then walked back to the water and found a pool near the swift current. Positioning himself so the sun was in front, he waded in up to the navel, ignoring the stinging cold that rushed his thighs like hemlock. He found a foothold and dug below the silt at the bottom until toes gripped rock. He planted himself, raised the spear overhead with both hands, and waited, stone-still.

The sun was burning his shoulders and insects buzzed his eyes. His arms ached. There were dark forms out there. He could not see them because of the reflection off the mirror surface, but he knew they were there. Then a fin broke surface about four feet away. He thought to lunge for it but didn't. He would wait. In his condition, the first strike was the only one.

The sun beat mercilessly on him and sent drops of sweat burning into his eyes and itching down the insides of his arms. One calf cramped intermittently. There were crawling things all over: biting flies, water skippers. He disciplined himself to be still and quiet.

After several minutes, a shadow came his way. He'd seen it move out of the center of the river, slide laterally into his space to rest before continuing on. The lithe form trod water easily, drifting closer to his legs. He wondered if his arms were locked, if they would be able to move when the time came.

The fish was directly beneath the spear point. He could tell that it had almost completed its rest and would soon be heading out again to challenge the river. It turned, presenting a silver side. His arms plunged down. As if in slow motion, he saw the spear enter the lower part of the body, hit firm flesh, penetrate, click against bone, emerge on the other side. A bubble of bright blood rose lazily to the surface of the water and broke like an oil slick. The salmon kicked violently, ripping the spear from his hands, seeking to die in the middle of the river. He lunged after it and managed to grasp the shaft with one hand, but the effort pulled him off his foothold and sent him out of his depth. He was under water, and he remembered that recent journey when his head had scraped the bottom. Then his face found air and he was moving downstream, still holding the end of the spear. Something brushed his leg. A water snake? No, the branch of a submerged log. He grabbed wildly and caught it. He pulled himself backward, gaining his feet, tugging the fish with him back to shore.

He was on the sand, lying there exhausted, the salmon at his elbow. It slipped off the spear, gasping feebly. Blood pulsed out of the wound. He reached over and dipped his fingers into it, then brought them to his mouth and licked the salty clots. As the amber eye filmed in death and the movement stopped, he felt a kind of sadness. "Godspeed you, fish," he said out loud.

He lifted it and estimated the weight at perhaps fifteen pounds. He covered it with wet grass and hid it in a tree where no other predator would easily find it, then climbed up to his den for the knife. Returning, he started to clean the fish at water's edge. The moment he touched the vent, a dribble of eggs fell out, an attempt to procreate after death itself. He opened the stomach carefully, and took out a handful of roe and put them in his mouth; they crunched like grapes and flooded him with thick oil. He scooped out the rest of them and set them on a flat rock while he finished cleaning the fish. Then he placed the eggs in the salmon's jutting jaws and carried it up the hill.

Building the fire back up, he cut off the bottom third of the fish, sawing partway through thick vertebrae with the knife and then snapping it. He set it near the flame. The silver skin crisped and parted from the flesh, revealing a sheet of bruised fat that melted in white curds. He dabbed them from the rock with the shreds of shirt and sucked them while turning the fish from side to side, watching the red meat go pink. As thick lamina cooked and parted, he picked them off and ate them. Nothing had ever tasted like this.

He fought the urge to stuff himself, stopping after a few minutes. He moved the uneaten portion back from the fire where it would finish cooking more slowly. He opened the fish's mouth and poured the rest of the eggs into his hand. While eating them one by one, he looked at the salmon's head. The jaw was elongated, open in a stiff, sawtoothed smile. The eye had its depth preserved by death's lacquer. He looked down into it, trying to penetrate the black epicenter.

"Sorry," he said, not caring that the animism would have sounded foolish to a bystander. "Sorry to have taken you before you did your work, Mrs. Fish. I was starving. I feel you in my stomach. I hope I got your spirit with your meat. I've got to go upstream, too. I'd welcome help."

He picked a piece of charcoal from the fire and drew two crude symbols on his wall: a fish and a long-beaked bird. Then he went down to the river for water. He relieved himself against a tree he considered well within his territory, saturating the rough radius of bark so that any inquiring nose would know: he was there.

For the next days the fish came. They boiled the center of the water with their passion. He walked along the river until he found a flat rock above a falls. He climbed up and lay on his stomach, watching them thrash and fight their way toward him. They gathered in the churning pool below, lolling

in the eddies, then circling slowly and finally catapulting up
out of the froth, trying to fly in air, bashing against rocks,
and falling back in twisting arcs to where they'd begun. Vault,
glide, hit, fall back; he watched them one by one as they came
and rose up huge to try to climb the falls. He heard himself
saying out loud, "Come on, you can do it!" He could feel the
violence of the urge: to find that gravel bed of birth, then
pour out the stored essence before the clock ran out and it was
time to die in the shallows. He shouted hoarsely when a piece
of the arching silver managed to get over the top of the falls
and quickly began cutting through the water on the higher
plateau. "Go!"

He saw a fish that had hurt itself. It was listing on its
side and swimming dumbfounded in concentric rings. He
climbed down and took it from the pool, killing and opening
it up. Marveling at the wondrous pack of guts, he cut the membrane around the pink coil and opened the intestine, studying
the process that made insects into excrement. Then he cleaned
the fish and took it in both hands and carried it back up to his
den, its weight sagging in the middle like a burlap sack. He
filleted the flesh and laid it out on hot rock to begin drying in
the sun. Then he found forked branches from among his supply of wood, put a crosspiece between them, and used the
structure to support a latticework of sticks. He built a smolder-
ing fire beneath and set the strips of salmon there to smoke.
Sitting back, he took one of the large rib bones from the car-
cass. He scraped the clinging shreds of pink from it and
pierced it at the top with the point of his knife. Squinting
through the needle, he thought: *In the land of the blind, the
one-eyed man is king.*

He could tell that time was passing. The moon had been a
slender arc, brand new, shaped like the curved bow of the
hunter. Now it was half full and ruptured at the leading edge
with further growth. The nights were cold. He had to keep the
fire built high so that it reflected down upon his bed of leaves

from his three stone walls. He cut densely needled branches of pine to cover himself.

One day he saw a glint in a calm place in the water. It was a glass soft-drink bottle, floating there in the white scum. He waded out and got it, holding it up high to see if there was some note inside saying that the tyrant had been deposed, pleading to be rescued from the cities, or some other portent from that other world. But there was nothing. He scoured the bottle with sand. While it dried in the sun, he carved a wooden stopper for it.

He filled the bottle with water and stuck it in the sling he'd made from vines. He put on his pants and placed the knife and watch in one pocket, and a chunk of fish in the other. Carrying the spear as he walked, he felt he could become nomadic if he chose. He was ready to explore outside his territory.

He was not looking for a way out. He knew that he need only ford the river and strike out to the east to find a strip of highway. That would come in time; in the fullness of time. Right now he was looking to go deeper into the forest, to find the secrets there.

At first he stayed close to his place, wanting to be able to scramble back up that rock slope and hide in his den if danger came. But gradually he became more confident. Every day he went a little further, turning over old logs and rocks, looking down into burrows, watching spiders spin drop-lines and then throw themselves out into the breeze like parachutists. He set his course parallel to the river and went downstream, not returning until dark.

Sometimes he worried that he would be stumbled onto, apprehended before he was ready. He began to bury his feces and give the mound of earth a natural look by brooming it with branches. As he walked along he cataloged the warning signals of birds and squirrels so they could watch for him. Sometimes he jumped sideways over deadfall, or climbed a tree and jumped to another before swinging back down to ground. *I'll leave no easy trail for them,* he thought.

Once he was walking and found a stand of mammoth redwoods growing in a circle. High above him they seemed to join like cathedral spires. One of the giants had fallen down inside the circle and was hollowed out within, a spongy chamber almost large enough for him to stand upright. It was growing dark and he used the watch to build a tiny fire in the sunshine, then carried it into the shady circle on a slab of redwood bark and set up a round of stones and fed it there.

Kicking through the leaf mold on his camp's perimeter, he uncovered a piece of porous white. He squatted and freed it from the clinging humus, then carried it back to examine it in firelight. His imagination sheathed it in muscle and fur and saw that it had been a mountain lion's skull. He ran his fingertips along the sutures at the top of the frontal lobe, poked them into the gaping nasal passages and the fearsome mouth. This had been liquid graceful death, ruler of the forest; even now the teeth retained their sharp point. He hefted the skull and held it so the yellow flames shone through the empty eye sockets. "Why are you smiling?" he asked. The fire guttered for a moment, causing the eyehole to wink. "What's your message?" he asked. He stuck his wrist into the snarling jaws and let the teeth prick his skin. "Where is thy sting?"

That night he slept inside the chamber of the fallen tree. It was warm, and he allowed the fire to dwindle. He awoke three times. Once it was the sound of claws being sharpened on the rough circumference of the bark outside him. Another time it was the hideous noise of a screech owl out beyond his circle. He began to be afraid, for it sounded like the familiar of dark spirits, but then he took faith and drifted back to sleep.

The third time there was a panting right beside him, a panting and occasional chop-licking of tongue. He could almost see the coyote's yellow eyes and smell its heavy breath. Just half asleep, he allowed the creature to place a dream behind his eyes.

It went like this: his father and sister and the boy were with him here, sitting in a circle around the fire, passing a bowl of food between them, enjoying the rich smoky taste. Drawing in the night above the flames with his hand, his father made a roundness and said, "The circle is the perfect figure. God made it so. In the beginning He gives each family a full bowl. Ours is almost empty but He will soon replenish it."

Then his mother joined them, and Mama Bessie, Aggie and the twins, Laughlin and his dead wife and children, the first and original Cabell Hart and his family. They were all there. The sight of them made him happy. Somewhere in the shadows out beyond the strength of the fire, he thought there might be others. He got up to look and saw Jill and Jim, standing uncertain, scuffing down at the ground. They completed his joy. He grabbed their hands and said, "Come, come join us. You're part of me. I'm grateful for you. I love you all."

He dreamed the dream he was given: that they were all there; all as he remembered them; all happy at the thought of being together, being named by him to be part of this occasion. He posed them all in a group in front of the old-fashioned camera of his dream, children kneeling and adults sitting behind them. His father and Charley were in the center, smiling and whispering to each other. The first and original Cabell Hart was on either side of them, once a young man full of family and then older with the Indian woman at his shoulder. Cabell moved the nine-year-old Laughlin so that he stood in front of Laughlin as a white-haired old man: a nice contrast. Jill was next to Mama Bessie: two doughty women. Jim was with Emma, the grandmother who'd dared to dance with blacks. "Okay, now hold it there," he said and put his head inside the black hood of the camera and saw them upside down on the glass plate. He held the shutter ready to snap them. "No, wait!" he heard his father's voice call out, "You come and get in this, too. Let's make this thing complete!" Laughing, he set the camera for a delayed exposure, started the time device clicking, and ran to get into the picture. Just as he got there between his sister and his father, he heard the shutter trip, and the flash exploded in an antique puff: the family.

After this dream, he heard the coyote move away. As he was settling into sleep the palindrome came to him: God's dog.

Waking in the gray morning, he felt refreshed. He relieved himself outside the circle, then came back in to get his things. He was about to leave when he remembered the mountain lion's skull. He picked it up and pried the largest tooth out of the jaw with his knife. "This for luck," he said. Then he took wood ash from the fire and water from his canteen and used a piece of his ragged shirt to polish the tooth until the filligreed fractures on its surface shone gray within the ivory. He put it in his pocket and started off back toward his territory.

The moon was full, almost overripe. Days were shorter, nights colder. But he saw change most of all in himself. The weight that had hung on him like a restraining hand had melted down. His body was red-brown from the sun, scratches and cuts of recent times showing new and pink beneath the skin. When he lifted things he could see a map of blue vein surge upon his forearm and muscles tense.

Each morning he was awake at first light, fully aware on opening his eyes, hoping that the sun had not yet resurrected on the eastern hills. He sat cross-legged, looking out into the gathering light, breathing deeply, forcing air into the diaphragm, holding it and forcing it further, air that flooded the muscles with strength. As the first beams came over the mountain, his breath erupted from the bottom of him. "Kihaiii!" The sound bounced off the rock overhang above him and pierced the valley below.

His body was coming back to him. He tested it by laying out a course on the steep peak rising a quarter of a mile up the mountain on the other side of his den. He scrambled it twice a day. The first few times his lungs were on fire and his legs felt dead. But after a few runs he could tolerate it. Now he could achieve the top with legs pumping and breath to spare.

He found a place in the river where the current slowed somewhat, a match for his own strength. Edging out into the water and pointing himself upstream, he began to swim this treadmill, stroking and kicking with full power, just trying to hold his own and keep from being ripped away by that vast force. As he felt his arms and shoulders tighten and his legs grow stronger, he ventured further out toward the middle each day. Finally he was challenging the river directly, no longer afraid of it. He swam it to a standstill, pushing himself hard, cupping the water and kicking it. Diving below, he imagined himself a salmon, a member of a family of powerful swimmers, fish whose sense of direction and instinct for return is a mystery to all but those who have known—as he did—that chemical memory is imprinted on the genes and jets through the blood.

At night he sat before his fire, carving on the spear and thinking of what was past and yet to come. When he saw his sister now, it was not as a battered shape, swallowed by the river after being abused and pounded to death. When he thought of his father it was not as a shrunken and pathetic victim of wasting, but as the virile and smiling man who held their hands and bred them up. He took a charred branch from his fire and wrote on the rock wall above him: *Carlotta 1944–74. Joseph 1907–74.* Above the names he wrote *HART* in large letters, and drew a circle around it all.

One morning he rose early and sat cross-legged. His plan was made by the time the sun rose—*Ah! It comes*—focused, encompassed. He took the smoked fish out of its niche. The flesh peeled off in moist symmetry. He held it in his mouth as if it were a eucharist, allowing it to melt, feeling the flavors release. He went to the river and bathed, then lay on a rock while the sun beat down into his skin, making it taut as the water evaporated. *I love being alive,* he thought. *I love every act of living. I could stay here forever.* He felt capable. This was a good day for it. Readiness is all.

He rose and stretched, testing the ligaments in the back of his thighs, extending his shoulder and back muscles. He walked briskly back up the hill to his den, and was still breathing through his nose when he got there. He set the watch on a crevice in the stone, a relic for some future hermit to wonder over. Then he spread out his pants on his cold hearth. He put a handful of red clay dirt in the pocket, along with some charred wood. He placed the knife and polished tooth at the center. He added shoes, canteen, the ragged remnants of his shirt, put the remaining smoked fish there, too, and then rolled it up. He took one last look at this place, seeing it with the eyes of an outsider. A nest of leaves; some wood shavings and fish-bones; a watch that told no time; the charred remnants of fire and strange markings on the wall: what manner of man lived here?

Then he picked up his bundle and trotted down the hill.

He walked a good distance upstream before he found a ford. It was a place where the river widened into a broad channel. He could see the bed of gravel clear and white below and he plunged in, holding the cloth bundle and his spear high above his head. The water never rose above his chest; he gripped the mossy rocks with his toes and angled his body into the current, making it across without capsizing. He reached the other side feeling sadly severed from what he had been. He put his pants and shoes on, the clothing foreign after all this time, and placed the articles in his pockets.

After walking for perhaps two hours, he heard the sound. It was nothing specific at first, just an abstract hum that settled on the silence like fine dust, muting and redefining it. As he went on, he recognized it: the whir of tire on con-crete; the friction of lubricated metal parts against each other. He sat down for a moment below a tree and adjusted himself to it, reacquiring the sense of how things were done, by what schedule and means: the mechanics of it all. Then he was up and walking again. At a moment when he least expected it, he broke through the trees and saw above him the flash of sun reflecting from speeding chrome. The sight jarred him.

He stopped at a large stand of pine and cached the spear and food under a fallen log. Then he began climbing the high slide of rock, granite tailings made when the road was gouged out of the mountain rim. At some point he crossed an invisible line and the river's sound was now subordinate to the noise of machine. The last few yards, when he could only hear, not see, the onrushing cars above him, were terrifying. Although he was going up on all fours, his sense was of descending down to some deep underworld, a world of frozen desire and blighted purpose. It was all he could do to force himself to take the last few steps and stick his head up above the road.

He began walking up the highway, with the traffic. Each time a car approached, he flinched, readying his body to be tossed and torn, squinting his eyes against the fine spray of debris, holding his breath against the nauseating poison of exhaust. Twice horns were blown at him, ungodly noise. Once two young women made odd faces at him out the back window as their car sped on.

He could feel himself being drawn into the town's gravity. There were arteries cutting off the highway and winding up into the mountains: fire and service roads, newly bulldozed; paths with ribbons of red plastic marking planned developments. As he looked up, he saw the glint of pitched tin roofs signaling down from various places in the mountains, and large patches of clear-cut.

There was a gas station with a telephone booth. He remembered it from before. A middle-aged man with a florid face and cap pulled down over his ears was bent over swabbing stains off the pavement between the islands supporting rows of pumps. The attendant did not see or hear him until he stood at his back. Then he stood up in fright, his sudden rancid smell of fear mixing with gasoline vapor.

"Sorry to bother you." Cabell tried to make his voice reassuring. "I need to use the telephone. I have no change, and the calls I'm making are collect. If you could lend me ten cents I'd return it right away."

Looking into the man's eyes, he could see himself: hair tangled and clotted; no shirt; muddy, cracking shoes; pants ripped in spots; a scabbed-over slash that marked his forehead like a lightning strike. He could tell that the man wanted desperately to say no; to tell him to get away and never come back. But he was afraid. Making a face, the attendant propped the mop against one of the pumps, and went to the locked money box. Pulling out a key on a retracting chain, he flipped back the lid.

"We don't have hardly any money here," he said as if to deter any contemplation of future robbery. "Mainly credit cards." Then he took a dime out of the tray and handed it over. "You can have it." Distaste was engraved on the words. "Just keep it. No sweat."

"No sweat." Cabell was surprised he still spoke that language. He saluted with two fingers and walked over to the booth. He shut himself inside the squeaking doors to screen the sound of passing traffic. The claustral feeling made sweat trickle down his armpits. It was all strange, an unfamiliar technology. He got toll-free numbers for the airline and car rental, then called and made reservations for tonight. Then using the same coin he called Aggie collect. There was a sharp intake of breath as he told of Charley and then sobs she tried to mute. Then she reacted to the calm urgency of his voice; not taking time to grieve, just questioning what he asked, double-checking times and places; preparing and placing herself inside the schedule; agreeing to what he said without asking why because he said it had to be that way.

"Are you off the deep end, honey?" She couldn't repress the concern as they were about to hang up.

"Probably," he answered.

"I'll be there to meet you," she said.

He was sweating freely at the end of the conversation, almost suffocating inside the booth for lack of air. The door was recalcitrant in moving and he almost ripped it off the hinges to escape. The station attendant was watching him from behind plate glass, having retreated inside the office. As he approached across the asphalt parking lot, the man became suddenly busy, scrubbing furiously at some imagined malignancy of grease on the metal desk. Looking at him with amusement, Cabell held the dime aloft, pinched between thumb and forefinger, then set it down on the top of the locked money box and walked away. He knew that as soon as he disappeared from view, the man would be out to examine the coin like a curious squirrel.

It was late afternoon when he got back to his cache in the trees. He tipped the glass canteen and wet his old shirt, then wiped himself off and allowed the sun to dry him. He took the smoked salmon and ate slowly, reclining on a rock, tossing out shreds of the pink fish for a crested jay that hopped about in a carnivorous semicircle in front of him. Afterward he put a fine point on the spear and then worked the knife carefully against a flat and porous stone to rectify its edge. He sipped water and lay back, pillowing his head on a fallen log.

The distant grating on the highway evanesced into a vision. He saw himself a stranger, ill-clothed and shabby, in a mechanical world where air was misted with chemical vapors; a world of ceaseless friction—steel on steel, rubber on asphalt, flesh on acrylic: a world of speed and deterioration. The world was his but he hadn't made it. He was walking its interminable road, along the side where people could not see him as they flew by, trapped inside machines that were subtly in charge, machines that stopped and ejected them, then demanded that they return. He went up a rise and then stared down on a vast white city. In large chromium ejaculatoria, sperm was milked and stored for future usage; nearby big-headed fetuses slumbered *in vitrio* like canned pears and a white monkey's head was transplanted onto a brown monkey's body; and in a long white room, a bull's furious charge was changed to mincing walk as white-smocked men activated electrodes. Apart and down from this were tiny rooms where people lived, probing and massaging each other without pleasure; where they conceived and aborted, and consumed chemicals giving cancer and sad hopes; where they lived and died believing they were cowards. Above them all, at the top of this domed metropolis, sat a few men and women in a cockpit working levers, in charge of the laboratories and of the brief lives of those below.

He saw himself running away from this whiteness, into green forests. He was traveling swiftly, swift as a deer, surging over underbrush and fallen trees. He came to a place where a hill was tabled off and jutting out into the night.

"I can't go back there," he called out into the darkness. "There's nothing there for me."

"You must go back one final time," the voice called out. "This forest is no real alternative."

"I know that," he said.

"Are you ready?" the voice asked. "Are you ready to save your people?"

"I am," he said. "Today is a good day to die."

"And what name do you take?"

"I take the name of Cabell Joseph Hart."

9

When he roused himself, it was getting dark. He sat up and drank, then emptied the rest of the water from his bottle onto the handful of dirt he had brought with him from downriver, mixed it until it was a paint of red clay, then daubed it on his right cheek. Then he took the piece of charred wood he had brought from his fire and streaked it on his left cheek. Red for vengeance, black for justice. He stood up, made sure that the knife was in his pocket, then climbed back up to the road with his spear and began dogtrotting toward the town.

Inside its limits, Halcyon was quiet. It now seemed to him to be a collection of people living together only out of fear, each one waiting for the other to make the first mistake.

It was barely nine-thirty, but already shops were closed. On the way into town, people had gawked at him as he passed through the sudden glare of automobile headlight or the harsh fluorescence of service station or other roadside business: a solitary half-naked freak leaning on a stick. When he got onto Halcyon's main street, he merged with shadows.

The police station was still a small bastille in white stucco. The lightbulb above the door cast yellow light onto the sidewalks and left long shadows beneath the eaves.

He slid behind the bushes and looked in the side windows where venetian blinds slivered space. He saw two leather boots crisscrossed on a desk. No other part of the room seemed occupied. He propped the spear in an oleander and opened the pocketknife, laying it flat in the palm of his hand, point at finger, haft up his wrist. He pulled softly at the door to make sure it was unlocked, then opened it and moved swiftly into the room. Boots scraped the desk and hit the floor, and the chair swiveled lazily to face him.

Cabell hit him at the temple with the heel of his hand before Strapp recognized him. Then he was on him, seizing the collar with his left hand and holding the knife's point at the throat with the other. The mouth seemed ready to scream; he pushed the knife a fraction as a warning, causing a drop of blood to appear and roll down the blade and pearl handle onto his fingernail.

"Where do the other two live?" He was repulsed by the smell that came off the man in waves.

"The other two?" Still stunned from the blow, the flat face tried to charm. "You mean Mel and Billy. I'm not opposed to telling you, I'm really not. But I think you ought to take some time to think things over." The face was desperate to stall. "Looks like you had a bad knock up on your head."

Cabell bored the knife into flesh. "Where do they live?"

"Mel, he lives over at Mill Street. One-forty-nine Mill. Just two blocks." A shaking index finger down below the knife pointed north.

"The other? Captain Hook?"

"Billy? He's got a house up at the end of Smith Road. The last house. Nice redwood place right where Smith dead-ends. You can't miss it. It's carved right out of the forest there."

Finding that he could talk without punishment, Strapp

began to blabber, tears of gratitude at the chance for salvation gathering in the corners of his eyes. His smell was nauseating.

"It was Billy. From the word go, honest to God. Melvin and me, we're family men. We never did such a thing in our lives. It was Billy, he's sick that way." He was swelling into the role of the informer. "I didn't even do anything to her. You heard Billy say that down at the river. Remember? Billy's been a little crazy since he got back. Always says he's got to have his meat raw or can't eat. Know what I mean? Hey, I just held the kid. Swear to God."

The bad-smelling one held me tight. I felt his hard spot in my back. He laughed all the time.

The lips continued to move after Cabell had cut and stood back. The hands fluttered to the throat, trying to pinch the wide slash that smiled there like a second mouth. Blood fell down over the khaki shirt like a liquid tongue.

"Where is your laughter now?" Cabell asked as he watched the fingers twitch nervously as if trying to suture the opening, then give up and compose themselves in the lap. The noise was of someone gargling. Then the body tired and collapsed back in the chair. The head rotated, lolling to one side, and the eyes' incandescence dimmed. There was a steady drip on the floor like a leaking faucet.

He could not make a noise, but in his mind the exulting cry was loud, stabbing the silence of the room like an icepick. He wiped the knife on the fabric over one of the sagging shoulders and closed it, then he put a finger in the blood and brought it back close to his eyes. He watched it coagulate under the heat of overhead lights, going from red to rusty brown.

Shutting the door softly behind him, he moved out of the sickly light into the bushes. He stood still for a moment to make sure that nobody was looking, then he went to the place where his spear stood, took it, and set off, heading where the bad-smelling one had pointed. Except for the distant sound of trucks laboring up the grade below the town, the only thing he heard were his steps slapping the sidewalk and his measured breathing. He found Mill Street and turned onto it, stepping out into the gutter to check the black house numbers stenciled there on a silver patch. It was dark and there were no street lights; he had to bend low to make sure.

Number 149 was a white clapboard, sitting back from the street, small and compact with a respectable hedge around the lawn and primroses growing in flowerboxes under casement windows. He moved closer and saw the outlines of a child's wagon and tricycle parked neatly on the front porch. A television sent moving shadows through the curtains. Reluctance tugged at him when he thought of the gap to come in the tidy life within this house, the imbalance that would be created, the irregularity. Then he remembered that evil most often hid beneath order. *And the Cat got down over her head, kneeled there and did something on her face.* He moved down the driveway to the side of the house.

There were garbage cans in the backyard, near a group of young beech trees. He hid himself behind their trunks and rattled the lids of the cans with his spear. Above him, a shade was raised and light poured out briefly. He rattled the lid again. There were muffled voices and soon the back door opened and a dark figure came out. The man came down toward him tentatively, squinting into the darkness, barefoot and with shirttails out. He wore the hat's indentation on the hair above his forehead. His whiskers wiggled inquisitively. He had turned around and was about to return to the house when Cabell moved out of the darkness.

"I'm back," he said softly. The Cat man moved to face him, and Cabell jabbed him in the midsection with the butt of the spear, doubling him over.

"Do you think this will bring her back?" the man sneered in a gasping voice without looking up.

"No," Cabell shook his head. "I'm doing it to make things equal." Then he was on him, grabbing hair to pull the face up and hitting him with an open-hand blow that popped the bridge of the nose. When the man fell, Cabell stood astride him, making a fist and hitting him hard on the jaw. Then he dragged him back deep into the yard and laid him out, stripping down the pants.

He was tired by the effort and stood up, watching the body trying to writhe back into consciousness. With surprising speed it tried to rise. Cabell lunged with his spear, catching him below the breast. He drove down with all his weight, feeling the point slide in easily and grate on the hard-pack of ground below the back. The man was pinned like an insect, looking straight up and issuing a soft repetitive moan. Lights went on in the back of the house. A voice called out, "Mel? Melvin? You out there?"

He worked fast with the knife, feeling for folds of skin. The flesh lurched beneath his cutting touch, legs stiffened and back arched, heels moved softly in the dirt like a cat curling paws in sleep.

"You wanted to be sucked," he hissed, backing off slowly as the convulsing mouth shifted the severed penis from one side to another, like a cigar being chewed. "And now you got your wish." Then there was motion on the back porch. He jumped out of the shadows, ran across the yard, and vaulted the chain-link fence at the back of the lot, crossed another backyard on the run, then another. Trailed by dog barks, he emerged onto another darkened street.

The night air was cold on his sweating back. Trotting up a hill in back of town, he found Smith Road and followed it, watching the space between the houses grow larger, the tree cover more and more dense. At the end was the large redwood house. He was on the porch quietly. He scraped his fingernails on the screen, then knocked. But there was no sound within. He looked down the driveway and saw no car.

He could sit and wait there in the bushes and take the man as he returned. But it might be too long. Aggie would have landed now and would be in the car on her way. He trotted back down the hill.

He was winded by the time he reached the long winding road leading up off the highway, and paused at the overpass, listening to the rush of water down below. It would be nice to be down there, to enter the river and let its current take him back downriver. I must finish this first, he thought.

He moved off at a lope. The gibbous moon was riding high over the treetops. The pavement before him phosphoresced. He looked down and tried not to think of how far it was he had to go and how steep the incline. He thought of the salmon fighting upstream and tried to tighten his motion, getting as far as possible on the least effort. Running, he had that pain in his side that he remembered from his childhood. He wanted to stop but kept going, trying to whip himself into a second wind.

By the time he came to the house, sweat was pouring off his chin and splashing onto his chest. He stopped at the arch of trees along the gravel driveway and crouched down to rest a moment. The house was dark, forbidding. He walked to the carport and drew out his knife, bending low to insert the blade into each of the tires just above the rim, feeling the imprisoned air rush out onto his hands. As he walked away the car lay low, like a ship torpedoed below the waterline. They would not follow.

He mounted the creaking porch and tried the front door. It was locked. He went around to the back of the house. Beyond a field of berry brambles, the ground began to fall away. Through spaces in the trees, he could see all the way down to the bottom of the gorge where the river ran in the moonlight like escaped mercury. He tried the back door and found it locked too.

At the side of the house there were two windows. He judged it was the direction the boy had come that other time. He decided to take a chance. He picked up some pebbles and pitched one up as softly as he could. It thudded against the wood siding with a noise that froze him. The second hit the glass with a loud crack. He saw a shape rise up. The boy looked like he was wearing whiteface. The luminous eyes were wide with wonder and fright, two palms were pressed against the glass. Then as he experienced recognition, the head nodded seriously as if it was something he had expected all along. The head ducked down and Cabell went to the front.

He thought he heard a muffled sound. He waited for the boy to unlatch the door and come sneaking out. But nothing happened. He went back to the side and pitched another pebble at the window; the face did not come up again. He felt time running through his fingers. He saw a large trash barrel, three-quarters full, up in front of the car. He picked it up and dumped the litter, then carried it to the front. With effort he raised it above his head, found a point of balance, then ran it toward the bay window, launching it from three feet away. The window shattered like new ice; the barrel made thunder on the floor inside. Moving fast, he stepped in over the jagged sill, knife ready, looking up to storm the stairs.

"Stop there!" The command came from above him. He looked to see the shotgun pointed at his face from six steps up the staircase. The man's T-shirt hung down over jockey shorts bulging at the crotch. Eyes glittered inside the rash of warts on cheek and forehead. Cabell could sense his excitement over having succeeded in the stalk.

"Just let me take the boy," he said. There was motion on the landing up above. The woman stood with curlers in her hair and a flannel bathrobe flapping open as she struggled with the boy. Her hand was on his mouth imprisoning his noises of struggle and warning. "Just let me take him. That's all I want."

"Like hell." The voice was frightened and triumphant, tempting him to move. "You fucking maniac, it's the last time you'll show up at this house."

The toad man raised the gun unnecessarily to sight. Cabell thought, *I'm sorry, father, I did not go far enough.* He saw a blur, heard a shriek, and then a heavy blast in the entryway that rained drywall down upon his head and shoulders. When he replayed it later, he was able to isolate the elements: the small body had hit the man low in the back, jackknifing him, making the belly go out and the head go backward. The gun flew out and hit butt first on the landing down below, hit and discharged, taking the man's chin off. The woman screamed. The man lay at the bottom of the stairs, his chinless head turned backward at an improbable angle. The woman had sagged down on the top stair, mouth opening and closing, the fingernails scrabbling on the hardwood floor, the robe parting to show legs spread apart like a worker at lunchtime as she tipped backward.

The boy picked himself up and hopped down to the bottom, climbing Cabell's body as if it were a tree. They turned and left. On the porch Cabell hesitated, shifting the frail body up onto his shoulders. Then he was trotting down the driveway to the surer footing of the road, the boy holding handfuls of hair as if to steer him from above.

The boy spoke in a small voice, "I was afraid they'd gotten you. They said you were a goner."

"I should have been here sooner," Cabell said. "I had to get my mind straight. But you: you saved my life."

"We saved each other," the boy said.

For a long time the only sound was the creak and jangle of their movement. After perhaps a mile, when they were halfway down the mountain, Cabell slowed to a walk. The boy had mastered his perch and gripped with legs like a jockey, hugging low to break the wind. Cabell felt the small hands brush his face and stop at the scabbed-over wound at the temple, caressing it like a blind person feeling for character.

"You got hurt," the boy said. "How?"

"Wolves," he answered, conserving breath.

"Oh. Yes, they hurt everybody."

The boy shifted his weight slightly and spoke again. "I thought you wouldn't come back. I didn't think you wanted to."

"Papa Two sent me," he said.

"He's gone, passed on like Mama."

"Yes." Cabell heard the call of an owl in the trees to his left.

"But they're not dead, not dead to me. I see them in my dreams. I speak to them in my mind."

"So do I," Cabell said. He held the boy's foot for a moment, then raised a hand behind his shoulder and patted the thin back.

They reached the bottom of the road, crossed the overpass, and turned onto the highway. Cabell judged it to be after eleven. She would be there now.

"Do you remember your Aunt Aggie?" he asked between gasps for air.

"Yes." The boy's voice was noncommital. "I remember. I used to stay there when I was littler. She has some children living next door on both sides."

"Her grandchildren," Cabell said. "Your cousins. Well, Aggie's going to meet us."

"Now?"

"Yes, up ahead. She's going to take you back to her house. It's a good place. They are a big family. They have three houses in a row. Aggie is Papa Two's sister. She's your Mama's aunt. She's your great-aunt."

"I want to stay with you."

"Another time," Cabell said. He thought he saw the outline of the car up ahead.

"I wish I was a grownup now," the boy said.

"Why?"

"Because I'd kill those bastard wolves. It's not right. They shouldn't be able just to walk around town like regular people."

"Don't worry about them, Joey." Up ahead he could make out the car parked on the soft shoulder where he had instructed her to meet them.

"Don't worry?" Cabell felt the boy's body stiffen.

"They're dead."

"Dead?"

"Dead."

"All of them?"

"Two."

"Which ones?" the boy persisted.

"The bad-smelling one and the Cat."

"Oh." The satisfaction was alloyed. "The hook man was the worst. He hurt Mama the worst."

"I know. He won't get by."

"You sure?"

"I swear to you."

Aggie had jumped out of the car and come running to meet them. She hugged with a strong grip that encircled both Cabell and the back of the boy's legs. Joey reached down and patted her head. The three of them hung onto each other and rocked.

"Good God, Cabe, what has happened?" She smelled of tobacco.

"I'm not sure," he said, swinging the boy down off his shoulders.

"Do we have time to talk?" she asked. "I don't mind the cloak-and-dagger stuff, but there are some gaps that need filling in."

"Joey can tell you," he said. "Joey knows what happened. He's been keeping a good record in his memory for the right person. You should talk to him."

With Aggie above him holding his shoulder, Cabell kneeled down to the boy's level. He picked up the small right hand and sandwiched it between his two.

"You're a brave boy, Joey." He looked into the dark eyes. "Papa Two knew that. He knew you'd try to take care of your Mama, and that you did your best. He was proud of you. He wanted me to tell you that, and he wanted me to give you this." He handed him the pocketknife. "This was once his father's. It was his, and mine for a while. Now it's yours."

He stood up and hugged his aunt again. "Aggie, I knew I could count on you. In the back of my mind I kept thinking, Thank God for Aggie. I think you ought to get a move on now, though. Strange things happen up here."

She was looking at him over the top of her glasses. "Are you all right, Cabe?"

"Sure," he nodded reassuringly.

"No," she grabbed his hand. "I mean *really* all right."

"I'm fine," he said. "My life has been leading me to this moment." *I am the true and perfect revolutionary.* The thought bloomed and filled his mind as he began herding them toward the car. "You'd better get going. Pay attention to what Joey says."

"You come with us." Her voice implored at a level that would not alarm the child.

"No." He smiled. "Not this trip. Joey can tell you why."

He got her into the driver's seat and opened the back door for the boy who suddenly grabbed his leg and hugged it tight. It was not meant to restrain him nor to cling. Cabell bent down and whispered in his ear. "You tell your Aunt Aggie about things up here, Joey. Tell her exactly what happened. I think she'll listen better than I did. Tell her as clearly as you can, and repeat it as much as you have to. Then after a while, start to let it fade into the back of your mind. I don't mean forget: just let go of it. It will find its place. Take care of Aggie. She helped your Mama once when she was in trouble. And one more thing: I never had a son of my own. But if I had, I would have wanted him to be just like you."

He closed the door and leaned forward, gripped Aggie's hand for a moment, then stood back as a signal to go. The car pulled off, and the serious white face popped out of the back window. "I'd be your boy," the high voice pealed. "I'd be your boy any day."

He walked back toward town; no need for running now. He felt his fate all around him, so close that he could hold it in his hands, mold it. *My whole life has led me to this*, he thought. *Everything I've done and everyone I've met has been part of the preparation. I can do it.*

At the point where the real estate signs became thick, he had walked into the trees, wanting to avoid the center of town and drop down on Smith Road from behind. But when he got there the space around the house was silvered with outdoor lights. The lawn and the trees out beyond looked like a winter scene with the cold white light. He hesitated in the shadows for a moment, reaching into his pocket to hold the puma's tooth. Then he ran for it.

He was on the first step leading to the porch when a shadow filled the doorway up above.

"I knew you'd be here." Hunter's words riffed out on whiskey breath. Cabell saw the army-issue .45 belted to the waist with khaki webbing. The good hand hovered above it; the hook was akimbo on the other hip. "The word is out that some goddamned nut is on the loose killing people for no reason. Naturally, I saw the connection between the victims. I figured you'd returned from the dead. Still obsessed with the dicking of the sister. Come to get me now? To abolish evil once and for all?"

"No," Cabell said, "it's a question of balance."

The triangular face rearranged itself in a smile. "Man, you *are* crazy," he said. "You really are. Some of your brain must've oozed out of that hole in your head. What have you been doing out there on the river, listening to the voices?"

"I've been getting ready."

"Well, you've got as far as you're going to get. When I was in Nam, the Devil stopped by and tipped his hat to me. I know for a true fact that your little games of good and evil—call it whatever you want—don't apply in this world. You say it's a question of balance. I say that your sister was a juicy piece."

Cabell watched in fascination, knowing he was being baited, yet feeling sluggish, anesthetized. The man pulled a cigarette out of his breast pocket with the good hand and placed it in his mouth. Then came the packet of matches. He tore one out with the claw fingers, then held it vertical for a moment as if it were a trick of legerdemain, and brought it down in a violent stubby motion. There was fire. He inhaled, and used his human hand to remove the match. Cabell found it hard to hold and return the unaltering stare of those black eyes. The man had the magic of machinery, of something that can operate efficiently without belief.

Cabell felt the man's mere presence on the verge of disarming him; imprisoning him in this white world where one was either the hunter or the meat. With the hand in his pocket, he held the polished tooth tight, thinking of the place downriver. He tried to absorb the tooth's medicine. There was too much space to cover in his spring, yet he tensed his legs to try. As the man's good hand rose to take the cigarette from the arrogant curl of mouth, daring him, he launched himself up the stairs. *You have done cheated me!*

The gun was out as his shoulder hit the retreating knee. The white explosion he saw was tinted blue at the edges. The concussion entered his body like a thorn, but by then they were on the floor, writhing, trying to extricate their essence. As he struck that flesh and steel and felt the other one hurt from his strength, Cabell smiled. His world was pulled together again, balanced at the point of this striving.

The first night I dreamed about Old Coyote. He was laughing and laughing, his mouth open and his head thrown back. He laughed with a man's laugh. Just watching him made me start laughing in the dream. We laughed together. We'd stop awhile and then one of us would giggle and that would set the other one off.

I dream about a lot of things, Papa Two. Aggie says that dreaming must run in the family. Sometimes I dream of the wolves, but not too often. I wake up and touch the walls and think of downriver. My walls are forest green. If I try, I touch them and smell pine.

This house has lots of corners. That was the first thing I noticed about this house. There are books and ashtrays and no TV. This house reminds me of you. It's clean and tidy—like you used to say: shipshape.

At first I slept with Aggie in the big bed. She said, If I start snoring just tap me on the shoulder and tell me. The first night I woke her up three times. I tapped her on the shoulder and said, Aggie, you're snoring.

Now I've got my own room. It's the room where me and

Mama stayed the time we lived here. I barely remember that. One day Aggie said, Come on, Joey, let's paint that old room. We went down to the paint store to look at colors. She handed me the cards and said, It's your room, you decide. I looked all through them and then handed her the one I liked. She said, Oh, forest green, pretty dark but if you like it, it's okay with me. I like it, I said. She said, Green, nature always wears the color of the spirit.

The day after I got here I met the other kids. I like Uncle Wally's family, but the kids are too young for me. So I spend most time at Uncle Tay's house. I like Sheila and Marcie, but Ricky's my best friend. He's only three months older but lots bigger. My head only comes up to his chin. He stutters. He'll be talking along and all of a sudden he'll get stuck and he won't be able to go further until he sort of touches his mouth with his hand. It's like he's trying to wipe the stutter away.

The day after I got here we had a big dinner at Uncle Tay's house. Everybody was there, Uncle Wally and Aunt Ellen, Uncle Tay and Aunt Pat, all the kids. Six kids counting me. Can you believe it? After dinner me and Ricky went out back in Aggie's yard. He said, You walk like a cripple. I said to him, You go ba-dee, ba-dee, ba-dee like Porky Pig. His face got red and he made his hands into fists. I thought, Uh-oh, here comes the fight. I got ready. But then he said, I can ta-ta-ta-talk normal if I'm not th-th-thinking about what I'm going to say or if I'm mad. I said, Well, one of these days my foot will be fixed. He said, You don't talk about my stutter and I won't talk about your foot. I said, Okay by me.

I play with all the other kids, but Ricky is my best friend. One night I stayed at his house. We slept in sleeping bags on the floor of the den and watched TV after everybody else was asleep. It was the late show and it was about gangsters. We watched this show and talked about school. We're going to the same school. There's no bus. You walk by yourself. When we woke up in the morning the TV was still on.

We found out what happened this afternoon. Aggie and me had just got back from buying some school clothes and we were in our living room. She heard a knock and looked out the blinds.

She saw the car with the sticker on the side and said, Joey, honey, why don't you go on upstairs.

I went up and sat on the landing at the top where I could see but nobody could see me. I saw the man. He had a gray suit on. He showed his wallet and said he was trying to fill in the picture of what happened that night. After he sat down, Aggie said she had no idea. I could have told him.

When Uncle Cabell came, I was in bed. I wasn't sleeping. I couldn't sleep. I had decided to go ahead and grow up in that house and act like a regular boy until I got old enough to kill those bastard wolves, but I couldn't get rid of the marchers. They wouldn't leave. I was thinking, Go away! Please! I'm tired and want to sleep! But they wouldn't leave.

Then I heard the clink on the window and I got up. I looked out the window and saw him down there. At first I didn't recognize him. He was half naked and the moonlight bounced off his skin like it was fur. I thought to myself, It's Old Coyote and he's finally come to teach me a trick or two. Then I saw it was Uncle Cabell. He pointed to the front door and then walked around that way like he expected me to meet him. I shook my head and would have yelled to him, No, I'm locked in by the chain on my door, except that I didn't want to wake up the toad man.

I didn't know what to do. Then my door opened and the woman came in. She saw me standing up at the window and said, All right, get down, you're not going anyplace. She was afraid I was going to break the window and try to get out that way. I thought to myself, What's the matter with you, do you think I'm crazy?

Then the toad man was in the hall with his gun. They had heard Uncle Cabell out there. He looked at me and said, Now you just watch it, Mister Man. Then he said to the woman, You stay up here, I'm going to take care of that nut for good.

He was putting long bullets in his gun, taking them out of a box and loading them up one by one. Then he walked down the stairs and waited and the woman held onto me up higher so she could see. She had an arm around my mouth and one around my chest. I thought, Uh-oh, this is very bad.

There was a big crash, and then Uncle Cabell was down there in the living room. The woman bent down to see him and when she did I saw him too. He was different looking from the time before. He was thinner and stronger looking, like he was ready for anything that happened. I saw the toad point the gun down at him and say some nasty stuff and I thought to myself, Oh no. The woman was holding me, pressing me hard against her like the bad-smelling one did down at the river. She had her face right near my head. I just took my head and threw it back so it banged into her nose. I felt her hands let go and then I flew right down the stairs. I dived at the toad and plowed into his back. The gun went off and it felt like the ceiling was snowing. His face was ruined. I jumped for Uncle Cabell.

Then we were out in the fresh air. Free! I was riding his naked shoulders like a horse and he was going right along the way I wanted. Go, horse!

I didn't want to leave him, Papa Two. But I had to. I could see that. He had things to do. Aggie drove all the way down here without stopping except for gas. She had come up on the plane and got the car at the airport, but she didn't even stop there on the way back. She just kept going. I told her what had happened to me and Mama. She couldn't hardly believe it, and she just shook her head that people could be that way. I told her about Uncle Cabell the first time, and about how he was getting them now, how they were dead and dying. She mumbled to herself, Good, I hope to God he gets that last one too. I was sleepy. The next thing I knew here we were in this house with all the corners.

Sitting up at the top of the stairs, I could see the man who came but he couldn't see me. He looked tired and had a rumpled-up gray suit on. He sat down there on the big, soft chair where Aggie listens to the radio—right on the edge of it like he was afraid that if he leaned back, he wouldn't be able to get up. He had some papers on his lap, and a little suitcase with brass buckles next to him on the floor. The thing I noticed most about him was that he had shiny socks, the kind that stick tight to your legs. Right above them you could see some white skin and hair before his pants started.

He was saying that they knew Uncle Cabell did it. That much was clear. But he didn't call him by his name. He kept calling him Your Nephew to Aggie, like whatever he had done was part her fault. He talked slow and regular like a tape recorder. He said the whole town of Halcyon was worried and that they were all carrying guns wherever they went. He kept saying that they were investigating to see how such a crazy thing could have happened, how Your Nephew could have done such a thing, and all that. Aggie just shrugged her shoulders and said nothing. She had her cigarette going and was blowing smoke at him.

He kept talking. He told about the bad-smelling one and the Cat. Uncle Cabell got them good. Then about the toad man and the woman. Her heart gave out. That's no surprise. People like that must have a tiny heart. He said that the strangest was Captain Hook. He said he was down all the way from Eureka mainly because of him. He said that the Hunters had been one of the oldest families in the whole area, and that they had owned all this land and timber. He said he had been a hero in the war. I almost stood up and yelled, He wasn't any hero to me, that bastard wolf!

He said to Aggie, Your Nephew must have snuck up on him, but Hunter managed to put up quite a struggle. Somehow he got to his gun and managed to pull off at least one shot. You know a forty-five, at that range it socks a hole the size of an apple in a man.

He stopped for a moment to see if Aggie wanted to say anything, then went on. He said, Everything in the living room was smashed. People on the street who heard it said that this fight went on for several minutes. There was blood all over the house—on the woodwork, the walls, even the ceiling. It wasn't all Hunter's either, not by a long shot. He must have got the upper hand at least once because the woman next door who was looking out her window saw him come to the doorway, bend down to look for something, maybe for the gun. Then Your Nephew grabbed him from behind and they went to it again, out of view. It was quiet for a while and then there was this ungodly screech. Like a wild man. Your Nephew came out of the doorway and from what

I've been able to determine he was blood all over. Now when the investigators got to the house they couldn't believe it. Hunter was beat up, beat to pieces. The back of his head was staved in like pulpy cantaloupe. No weapon, it had just been pounded on the floor. As if that wasn't enough, Your Nephew had torn off the prosthetic, managed to straighten out the fingers enough so he could stab it down into that poor man's chest. No wonder that when the word got out, people figured there was a maniac on the loose committing ritual murders. It's like those mutilated cows you read about sometimes.

Your Nephew had been hit, though. He left a trail of blood a kid could have followed. It led down to the river. I don't know what crazy reason led him there. But the investigators followed it about a mile and a half out of town, down over a cliff and onto a footbridge. It ended there. We don't believe there's a snowball's chance in hell he could have survived. He was critically wounded. He had to be from all that blood. He must have just taken off and gone where his feet took him. The Fortuna will probably kick the body up one of these days. On the other hand, we've got to touch all the bases. That's why I'm here.

Aggie was looking off at that picture of Ralph Waldo she has on the wall but the man kept talking. We don't expect you to be able to turn the body over or anything like that, but we're hoping you could give some answers about motives. Why did he do it? Why did he go up there to this little town and go berserk and kill five people? What did he do with the boy? We'd like to question the kid. Is he dead too? Is it true that Billy and the boy's mother were sweethearts? I understand Your Nephew was a leftist, is that involved in any way?

Aggie shrugged and blew more smoke at him. She said, Well, you know, I can't help you. I hadn't seen much of Cabell in the last few years. He was a different branch of the family and you know how that is.

After that the man talked some more and shuffled through his papers. I didn't want to listen anymore. I got up and came here to my room. I got out the knife he gave me, your knife and your father's too, and thought about things.

They were right about everything, but not about what happened to him. I think it was different. He was hurt, Papa Two, hurt bad, but not as bad as they think. I can see him in my imagination. He is running—not fast and scared, but steady. He comes down the road heading for the footbridge. He knows the way now. He's all tired out from the fight. His wound is bleeding. He gets down into the water to wash it off. He's smiling, feeling good because things are all taken care of now. He's never felt better. Things are not all right. They can't ever be that. But at least they're equal. He can't go back. He knows they'd never believe him about the wolves. So he just sets out, swimming in the river, getting right to the center, kicking like a fish, letting the water take him downriver. He'll be safe there. He knows that.

I hear Ricky downstairs now, Papa Two. He said he'd come early. We're going to the game tonight and we've got to practice in case any foul balls come our way. A week to go and then the World Series! So I've got to go now. If I don't write you letters in my mind like I used to, it's not because I don't love you, but because I don't have to remember so much now. Uncle Cabell kept his promise. It's over.

Yesterday Ricky and me were playing with two boys from down the street. One of them said to me, Where's your mother? I said, Dead. He said, What about your Dad? I said, I don't know, I think killed in the war. The other boy said, Then you're an orphan. The first one said, Yeah, an orphan, hiya orphan boy, how you doing? Ricky stood up to the bigger one and said, Shut up, fucker, he's no orphan, he's my cousin, you talk like that again and we'll beat the snot out of you. I got up too and said, Yeah, that's right. They were bigger, but they just turned and went on home. Thank goodness. While we were standing there Ricky said, See, when I'm mad I don't st-st-stut-stutter at all.

Love,

Joey